D0953052

COUNTDOWN TO MIDNIGHT

ALSO BY DALE BROWN

COUNTDOWN
TO
MIDNIGHT

A NOVEL

DALE
BROWN

WM
WILLIAM MORROW
An Imprint of HarperCollinsPublishers

COUNTDOWN TO MIDNIGHT. Copyright © 2022 by Creative Arts and Sciences, LLC. All rights reserved. Printed in Canada. No part of this book may be used or reproduced in any manner whatsoever without written permission except in the case of brief quotations embodied in critical articles and reviews. For information, address HarperCollins Publishers, 195 Broadway, New York, NY 10007.

HarperCollins books may be purchased for educational, business, or sales promotional use. For information, please email the Special Markets Department at SPsales@harpercollins.com.

FIRST EDITION

Designed by Kyle O'Brien

Library of Congress Cataloging-in-Publication Data has been applied for.

ISBN 978-0-06-301508-1

22 23 24 25 26   FRI   10 9 8 7 6 5 4 3 2 1

This novel is dedicated to my fellow storytellers, all of whom amaze and inspire me with their imagination and skill. The art of turning a geopolitical "what-if" into a believable and exciting story is a driving force for me. Let's press on and see what more we can create. The possibilities are endless.

The lofty pine is oftenest shaken by the winds; High towers fall with a heavier crash; And the lightning strikes the highest mountain.

—Horace

It is not the roaring thunder that smites, but the silent lightning.

—Ivan Panin, Russian émigré
literary scholar

ACKNOWLEDGMENTS

As always, many thanks to Patrick Larkin for his hard work, expertise, and talent.

CAST OF CHARACTERS

THE QUARTET DIRECTORATE

NICK FLYNN, agent, former U.S. Air Force intelligence officer

LAURA VAN HORN, agent, and a captain in the Alaska Air National Guard

CARLETON FREDERICK FOX, head of the Directorate's American Station, Avalon House

GWEN PARK, chief of security, American Station, Avalon House

GIDEON AYISH, head of the Directorate's Israeli Station

TADEUSZ KOSSAK, agent, former officer in Poland's Special Forces

SHANNON COOKE, agent, former member of the U.S. Army's ultra-secret Mission Support Activity

ALAIN RICARD, agent, former officer in France's elite Marine Commandos

SARA McCULLOCH, Predator drone operator, former staff sergeant in the U.S. Air Force

MARK STADLER, security officer, Avalon House, former member of U.S Marine Corps Force Reconnaissance

TONY McGILL, agent, former sergeant in the British Special Air Service (SAS)

COLE HYNES, agent, former enlisted man, U.S. Army

WADE VUCOVICH, agent, former enlisted man, U.S. Army

JACK "RIPPER" INGALLS, LM-100J pilot, major in the Alaska Air National Guard

THE RAVEN SYNDICATE

PAVEL VORONIN, owner and chief executive officer

VIKTOR SKOBLIN, team leader, former major, Russian Spetsnaz special forces

VASILY KONDAKOV, Voronin's top deputy, a former colonel in the GRU (Russia's military intelligence agency)

YURI LINNIK, operative, former Spetsnaz officer

KIRILL ZAITSEV, operative, former Spetsnaz officer

DIMITRI FADEYEV, operative, former member of GRU assassination force, Unit 29155

YVGENY KVYAT, drone operator, former officer in the GRU

KONSTANTIN DANILEVSKY, team leader aboard SSBN-64 *Podmoskovye*, former colonel in the Russian Spetsnaz special forces

CENTRAL INTELLIGENCE AGENCY

CHARLES HORNE, director of Central Intelligence

MIRANDA REYNOLDS, head of the Directorate of Operations

PHILIP DEMOPOULOS, head of the Directorate of Analysis

RUSSIANS

PIOTR ZHDANOV, president of the Russian Federation

COLONEL MIKHAIL KRYLOV, 12th Main Directorate, Russian Ministry of Defense

MAJOR ANATOLY YAKEMENKO, 12th Main Directorate, Russian Ministry of Defense

CAPTAIN LEONID KAZMIN, 12th Main Directorate, Russian Ministry of Defense

ADMIRAL BORIS PLESHAKOV, commander, Northern Fleet

CAPTAIN FIRST RANK MIKHAIL NAKHIMOV, Russian Navy, commander, SSBN-64 *Podmoskovye*

SENIOR LIEUTENANT IVAN POKROVSKY, Russian Navy, navigating officer, SSBN-64 *Podmoskovye*

CAPTAIN SECOND RANK MAXIM ARSHAVIN, Russian Navy, executive officer, SSBN-64 *Podmoskovye*

LIEUTENANT LEONID VOLKOV, Russian Navy, radio officer, SSBN-64 *Podmoskovye*

GENNADY KOKORIN, Minister of Defense

ADMIRAL NIKOLAI GOLITSYN, commander, Russian Navy

LIEUTENANT GENERAL YVGENY ROGOZIN, commander, Russian Air Force

KONSTANTIN YUMASHEV, head of the Federal Security Service, the FSB

SERGEI VESELOVSKY, head of the Foreign Intelligence Service, the SVR

ALEKSANDR IVASHIN, head of the General Staff's military intelligence agency, the GRU

MAJOR GENERAL KONSTANTIN REZANOV, commander 42nd Rocket Division, Strategic Rocket Forces

SENIOR LIEUTENANT ANATOLY YALINSKY, Russian Navy, diving officer, SSBN-64 *Podmoskovye*

IRANIANS

MOHSEN SHIRAZI, commander, Revolutionary Guard Aerospace Force

ARIF KHAVARI, high-ranking official in Iran's state-owned shipping company

DR. HOSSEIN MAJIDI, chief missile engineer, Shahrud Missile Test Facility

NAVID DANESHVAR, naval architect employed by the Shahid Darvishi Shipyards, Bandar Abbas

LIEUTENANT HASSAN NOORIAN, member of Revolutionary Guard escort force for MIDNIGHT truck convoy

CAPTAIN REZA HEIDARI, Revolutionary Guard Corps naval officer, commander of the *Gulf Venture*

TOURAJ DABIR, Revolutionary Guard Corps naval officer, second-in-command aboard the *Gulf Venture*

ISRAELIS

LIEUTENANT COLONEL DOV TAMIR, military attaché to Austria, also a member of the IDF's Secret Liaison Unit

RIVKA AMAR, Mossad officer, chief of security, Israeli embassy to Austria

MIRIAM WEISS, chief of the consular section, Israeli embassy to Austria

AVI ELAZAR, high-ranking official in the Israeli government

COMMANDER RAFAEL ALON, head of Shayatet 13, Israel's naval commando force

AFGHAN

MASOUD BOKHARAI, government official, Nimroz Province, Afghanistan

COUNTDOWN TO MIDNIGHT

PROLOGUE

ABOARD IRIS *DAMAVAND*, IN THE SOUTHERN CASPIAN SEA

JULY

Off the northern Iranian coast, a sleek, 1,500-ton missile frigate lay at anchor, riding gently up and down as low waves rolled across the vast inland sea. On the open ocean, the *Damavand* would have been dwarfed by larger destroyers, cruisers, and aircraft carriers in the service of the world's major naval powers. On the waters of the landlocked Caspian, however, the gray-painted Iranian war vessel, armed with anti-ship cruise missiles, a 76mm gun, and torpedoes, was the local equivalent of a mighty WWII-era battleship. The navies of most of Iran's neighbors, Azerbaijan, Turkmenistan, and Kazakhstan, were little more than collections of even smaller and more antiquated missile boats and other patrol craft. Even Russia's Caspian Flotilla, based at Astrakhan, more than a thousand kilometers north across the sea, had no warships larger than the *Damavand* ready for duty.

For all of that, Pavel Voronin knew, this frigate, the pride of Iran's Northern Fleet, was far more useful as an observation platform for today's test than it would be in any real modern war. Naval guns and short-range cruise missiles were mere toys in any all-out struggle waged between nations armed with rockets capable of striking targets half a world away. And despite their stern religious fervor, many of Iran's theocratic rulers understood this reality better than most. Which was why video monitors and computer consoles manned by white-coated technicians and scientists were currently crammed into almost every available square meter of deck space aboard the small warship.

Smiling inwardly, the trim, fit Russian moved to the windows lining one side of *Damavand*'s bridge, followed by his Iranian hosts—a group of bearded Revolutionary Guard officers. Voronin's elegantly tailored Savile Row suit and handmade Italian shoes stood out plainly among their dark green uniform tunics, rank-emblazoned shoulder boards, and wide-brimmed caps. Surrounded by these hard-faced men whose brutal tactics kept Iran's radical Islamic regime in power and spread terror around the globe, he appeared to be nothing more than a cultured and prosperous businessman. He found that a useful facade, one that concealed his true nature—ruthless, predatory, and utterly self-interested.

"The countdown is proceeding normally," one of the technicians stationed on the bridge behind them reported in Persian. His words were echoed in Russian by a translator assigned to Voronin. "The test vehicle is completing its transition to a vertical launch position."

Voronin raised a pair of binoculars to his pale gray eyes and peered out through the windows. There, several kilometers away, a large barge motored across the sea. A gleaming white rocket topped by a black nose cone swung slowly upright from its deck, hoisted into position by a powerful hydraulic crane. Moments later, it locked into place, towering more than twenty-five meters above the barge.

He nodded appreciatively at the smooth completion of this delicate operation. While not large compared to the enormous heavy-lift rockets developed by the United States, Russia, and the People's Republic of China, the Zuljanah space launch vehicle still massed more than fifty-two tons. And the solid-fuel engines in its first two stages and its liquid-propellant upper-stage motor could send a good-sized payload into space up to five hundred kilometers above the Earth's surface.

"The launch pad's stabilizers and motion compensators are engaged," the technician said calmly, parroting reports radioed to *Damavand* by the flight crew controlling operations from inside an armored trailer bolted to the barge's aft section. "Go for launch in sixty seconds."

Still focused on the distant rocket, Voronin nodded again to himself, this time pleased by the demonstrated efficiency of his Iranian hosts. Tehran had carefully scheduled this test for a relatively short window when there were no American or Chinese spy satellites in position to observe the launch. Their infrared early-warning satellites in geosynchronous orbit would certainly detect the Zuljanah's rocket plume as it roared aloft and provide tracking data on its trajectory. But the absence of visual and radar imagery would still conceal certain key elements of this planned test flight from both Washington and Beijing.

The last remaining seconds sped past in a monotone blur of engine status and other system readiness reports relayed from the flight crew. All around him, Voronin sensed a sudden spike of tension as the critical moment approached. Finally, the technician called out, "Five . . . four . . . three . . . two . . . one . . . ignition!"

Across the sea, the barge disappeared suddenly, hidden by a billowing cloud of gray smoke—a cloud lit from within by a bright orange glow. Moments later, the bright white rocket appeared above the cloud, riding a scintillating pillar of fire and trailing a plume of exhaust as it soared skyward and arced toward the northeast. It was accompanied by a loud, crackling roar as the first sounds of liftoff finally reached the Iranian frigate.

Voronin tracked the missile as it rode higher and higher, smiling openly now. He knew that launching the Zuljanah to the northwest instead of the northeast would have better simulated an operational flight. But it would also have sent the rocket's payload arcing high over Ukraine and Poland, apparently on a course toward Berlin or London. And there was no point in alarming those in the West. Not yet, at least.

Once the rocket disappeared from sight, he turned his attention to a monitor set up at the back of the warship's bridge. Its screen showed flickering images of the Zuljanah captured by long-range tracking cameras as it arrowed onward through the upper reaches of the atmosphere. Puffs of white vapor blossomed abruptly around the midsection of the rapidly accelerating vehicle. Suddenly, the bottom third separated and fell away, tumbling end over end back toward the earth.

"Staging nominal," the technician reported. And, as a new plume of flame appeared at the base of the now-truncated rocket, "Second-stage ignition." Moments later, the process repeated as the Zuljanah's second-stage engine finished its planned burn and detached—leaving the much smaller third stage's motor to propel its payload the rest of the way into space.

Voronin saw the wavering, blurry pictures on the monitor vanish, replaced by a digital map with a bright green arrow depicting the spacecraft as it flew high above the central wastes of Kazakhstan. The speeding rocket had passed well beyond the range of Iran's earthbound tracking cameras. From now on, the crew monitoring its flight would be dependent on telemetry from the spacecraft itself. "Payload deployment confirmed," he heard the technician say. "The vehicle is now more than twenty-three hundred kilometers down range, and rapidly approaching the planned apogee of this suborbital test flight."

Based on an earlier mission planning briefing by his Revolutionary Guard hosts, Voronin knew what to expect next. So he wasn't surprised by the next flurry of reports.

"Telemetry indicates trouble aboard the spacecraft," the technician said suddenly, still sounding calm. "Key flight control systems show signs of cascading hardware and software failure."

Voronin noticed sly smiles appearing around him. The telemetry data currently being broadcast by the Iranian satellite was completely false. It was intended to deceive Iran's enemies who must, by now, be closely monitoring every signal from this unannounced rocket test flight.

Mohsen Shirazi, the senior officer aboard, stepped forward. As commander of the Revolutionary Guard's Aerospace Force, the gray-bearded brigadier general had shepherded this missile project from its earliest days—approving every detail of its design, construction, and flight testing. He stabbed a finger at the waiting technician. "Initiate autodestruct," he ordered.

Seconds later, Voronin saw the telemetry feed abruptly cut off. To outward appearances, the "dying" Iranian spacecraft had been destroyed by conventional explosive charges as a safety precaution, so that its scattered debris would burn up harmlessly on reentry. In reality, this final detonation had been carefully planned. The payload's precisely timed explosive destruction was one of the crucial elements of this entire experimental flight.

Shirazi turned toward him. "Well, Mr. Voronin?" he asked.

"Most impressive," Voronin replied honestly, with a thin smile. "Your Zuljanah rocket is all that you promised . . . and more. I will recommend to Moscow that we proceed as agreed with *POLNOCH'*, MIDNIGHT."

Shirazi and his comrades nodded in grave satisfaction. Though he kept a low profile, they knew Voronin was a wealthy Russian entrepreneur, a private citizen whose shadowy company—Sindikat Vorona, the Raven Syndicate—provided military and intelligence expertise, services, and equipment to the highest bidders in trouble spots around the globe. His close ties to the Kremlin and especially to Russia's autocratic president, Piotr Zhdanov, were less widely known, but they made him the ideal go-between for this high-risk, high-stakes secret operation.

Russia and Iran might not share a common ideology, but both governments knew only too well that they had a common enemy in the United States and its global network of allies. And in the murky, amoral world of Realpolitik, the old adage "the enemy of my enemy is my friend" pointed the way forward for Moscow and Tehran. The two countries were also painfully aware that time was not on their side. Though outwardly militarily strong, confident, and aggressive, each faced growing internal challenges and weaknesses—troubles that might topple even the most repressive regime if left unchecked. Their growing fear of the future, Voronin knew, was what had made his masters in

Moscow, along with Tehran's theocrats, so eager to find some way, any way, however dangerous and however deadly, to overturn the world's existing balance of power.

Cold amusement flickered in Pavel Voronin's pale eyes. President Zhdanov, Shirazi, and all the others involved in this plan were convinced that MIDNIGHT was the answer to their prayers. And so it was. Left unsaid was the reality that it would also pave his personal path to even greater wealth and power.

ONE

JANUARY

Shadows cast by the setting sun stretched across a long, winding ski trail bordered by snow-dusted pines. Down in the narrow valley at the foot of the mountain, the Kitzbüheler Horn, lights were beginning to glow—outlining the streets and buildings of one of Austria's most popular and charming Alpine villages. The forested heights of another peak, the Hahnenkamm, the Rooster's Comb, climbed skyward on the other side of the town. Curving white trails crisscrossed the slopes of that mountain as well. Kitzbühel was the center of one of the largest ski areas in the Tyrolean Alps, attracting crowds of competitive skiers and the world's jet-setters during the winter months.

Nicholas Flynn came gliding around a curve in the trail and turned to a quick stop off to one side. His skis sent a little curl of loose powder pattering downhill. He raised his goggles briefly, squinting down the slope ahead. This late in the day, the light was going flat, making it difficult to spot any bumps or dips along the surface. Fortunately, this was a trail designed for intermediate skiers, and not one of the steep, rugged runs favored by experts or amateurs with lots of medical insurance and a death wish.

He looked across at the Hahnenkamm. One of the sheer twisting and turning trails he could see was known as the Streif, the Streak.

Since 1937, it had been the site of the World Cup's most challenging race. Skiers plunging down the run's two-mile length routinely topped more than sixty miles an hour—with nothing between them and a catastrophic crash but their own skill, agility, and experience.

Flynn felt a wry grin tug at the side of his mouth. Fighting hand to hand against Russian Spetsnaz commandos and parachuting into winter storms was one thing, but there was no way in hell he'd ever be crazy enough to believe he could handle a race on something like the Streif. "After all, a man's gotta know his own limitations," he murmured. As a kid growing up in mostly snowless Central Texas, family winter vacations to Colorado and Utah had taught him enough to make it downhill without face-planting . . . and to realize that any thoughts of hurtling straight down the local equivalent of a double black diamond slope were purely delusions of grandeur.

Fortunately, he wasn't here to show off. Far from it, in fact.

About a hundred yards farther along, Flynn spotted another skier pulled off on the same side of the trail, apparently taking pictures of the spectacular views with his cell phone. The other man's white parka, dark green ski pants, and red knit cap signaled that he was Flynn's contact for this clandestine rendezvous. Arif Khavari was a high-ranking official in Iran's state-owned shipping company. He'd come to Austria as part of an Iranian delegation to an OPEC meeting in Vienna. A short ski excursion had given Khavari a chance to escape the constant scrutiny of his compatriots and their official security detail.

Flynn glanced back the way he'd come. There were no other people in sight. The lifts would close at four o'clock, and with the light fading and temperatures falling fast, most skiers were already headed off the mountain to get ready for a busy evening of après-ski drinking, dining, and dancing in Kitzbühel and the even smaller neighboring villages. Satisfied for the moment that they were as alone as it was possible to be in a public place, he swung around and skied down to join the Iranian. He stopped again a few feet below Khavari—not far from the edge of the woods lining the trail.

The other man, shorter by a few inches and dark-eyed, looked nervous.

Flynn donned a friendly smile. "Excuse me?" he asked, in plainly American-accented English. "Can you tell me the time?" He nodded over his shoulder. "I've got a business call at five, but I'd still like to make one more run down the mountain if I can."

Khavari made a show of checking his phone screen. "The Hornbahn gondola stops running in minutes," he said hurriedly, rushing through the agreed-upon recognition phrase selected for this rendezvous. "I do not believe you could reach it soon enough to ride back up."

"Too bad, but I guess those are the breaks," Flynn answered with a shrug, finishing the protocol. He allowed his easy smile to tighten just a bit. "Okay, Mr. Khavari, now that we've confirmed our respective bona fides, maybe you can clue me in on just why you needed to see someone in person instead of communicating through the usual secure channels. We can't take a lot of time here." In the shadowy world of espionage and counterespionage, any face-to-face contact was highly risky, no matter how many precautions those involved took. It was something that should be done only when absolutely necessary. And keeping any meeting as short and to the point as possible was one way to minimize those inevitable hazards.

The Iranian swallowed hard. "You represent your decision-makers in Washington?" he asked quietly.

Flynn nodded, opting for discretion over the absolute truth. If Khavari was under the mistaken impression that he was in touch with an official U.S. government intelligence agency, so much the better for operational security. What the Iranian didn't know couldn't be forced out of him if the Revolutionary Guard's goons ever figured out that he'd turned against the regime.

Besides, Flynn thought dryly, up to about a year ago, he *had* been working for the government—as a captain assigned to U.S. Air Force intelligence activities. Unfortunately, acting boldly to salvage things when the CIA's own people screwed up not just one but two of the agency's sketchy covert operations in a row turned out to be a really bad career move. The bureaucrats at Langley needed a scapegoat to blame for their own blunders. And Nick Flynn, a junior military officer without a drop of influence in D.C.'s political circles, must have seemed perfect for the part.

So he'd been laid up under guard in a military hospital, recuperating from his last brush with one of the CIA's "brilliant" plans, when the mysterious Mr. Fox arrived to recruit him to join what the older man had modestly described as a "little private intelligence outfit." Months later, after intensive courses to further hone his language, espionage tradecraft, and weapons skills, Flynn had come to understand that the Quartet Directorate—commonly referred to as Four by those in the loop—was actually something considerably larger and more important. This mountainside rendezvous with Arif Khavari was his first solo operational assignment for his new employer.

"I have a friend; a good friend," the Iranian said, lowering his voice even further. "Like me, he secretly despises the corrupt men who are ruining our country." He hesitated briefly before going on. "First, you should know that we both love our nation and our people. We are *not* traitors. The insane mullahs in Tehran and their evil servants are the real traitors."

Flynn nodded his understanding. No one except the utterly mercenary or sociopathic could find it easy to break faith with his or her own native land, no matter how vile its current government might be. He fought down an urge to hurry the other man along again. Spooking Khavari or unintentionally insulting him now would do more harm than good.

"My friend is a naval architect," the Iranian went on. "He works at our state-owned shipyards west of Bandar Abbas. Recently, he approached with me strange news about one of their current projects. Strange and disturbing news."

Flynn hid his surprise. Iran's seemingly perpetual quest for nuclear weapons was the hot topic in Western intelligence circles, not its ship-construction plans. "Go on," he prompted.

Quickly, Khavari explained. According to his friend, Navid Daneshvar, major modifications had been ordered to a large oil tanker named *Gulf Venture* now under repair at the Shahid Darvishi shipyards—modifications which made no sense for any vessel genuinely intended to carry petroleum products to ports around the world. No commercial oil tanker needed concealed compartments, hydraulic cranes, special ship stabilizers, and additional high-speed pumps.

Equally troubling were strict new security measures that seemed intended to shroud this project in absolute secrecy. Among other things, Tehran had ordained the construction of a huge temporary roof over the yard's largest dry dock in order to block any satellite imagery of the work in progress. And all shipyard personnel assigned to the project were being kept under close watch in special housing, forbidden to communicate with their families or anyone on the outside, except under very limited circumstances. The only exceptions to this policy were a handful of senior staff believed to be absolutely loyal to the regime, like his friend Daneshvar. Finally, large numbers of special commandos from the Revolutionary Guard's Quds Force had been deployed as guards around the Darvishi complex—backed up by foreign "mercenaries," probably Russians.

"Russians?" Flynn said, unable to hide his surprise at the thought of Iran's notoriously xenophobic rulers allowing armed foreigners of any stripe to operate inside their jealously guarded territory.

Khavari nodded darkly. "So Daneshvar says. Either Russians or maybe Eastern Europeans. Slavs of some kind, for sure."

Flynn thought for a moment and then asked, "Can you get your hands on blueprints that show the specific alterations being made to this ship? That'd give our analysts a much better shot at figuring out what your government is planning."

Sorrowfully, Khavari shook his head. "It's proved impossible to smuggle out any documentation from the shipyard complex. Everyone is thoroughly searched on entry and departure. And it's strictly forbidden to take anything, whether on paper or a USB drive, beyond the gates. Or to bring any data storage devices inside. Even the main computer systems are 'air-gapped'—cut off from any physical or wireless connection to the internet. So far, Daneshvar has been forced to relay every scrap of information to me solely by word of mouth. And even that is incredibly dangerous."

"Yeah," Flynn frowned. If only half of the security measures the Iranian described were actually in place, Tehran was taking no chances. Besides a defense against espionage, blocking both physical and internet access to the shipyard's computers would also prevent cyberattacks like those periodically used by the Israelis and other hostile countries to sabotage Iran's nuclear and missile development facilities. Thinking hard, he dug one of his ski poles a little deeper into the snow. "Look, what's the time frame on this project? When are the modifications to this tanker supposed to be complete?"

"Not long," Khavari told him gravely. "Perhaps only a matter of weeks. Two months at the outside. The yard is working around the clock to finish its work on the *Gulf Venture*. No delays are tolerated."

Flynn's jaw tightened. "A couple of months? That's not much time to—" He stopped abruptly, aware that his subconscious had just sent up a warning flare. Something was off, somewhere. He stared over the Iranian's shoulder, peering at the slope higher up the trail. Was that movement in the trees over on the other side? Maybe around a couple of hundred yards off?

Suddenly, Khavari's chest exploded high up, right over his heart—spraying bright red blood and bits of pulverized bone across the white surface of the snow. He'd been shot in the back.

Shit, shit, shit, Flynn thought furiously. He threw himself prone, just as another bullet ripped past his own head and smacked into a tree farther downslope. A third round slammed into the Iranian, who was already dead. His corpse toppled sideways and fell in a heap just uphill.

Flynn reacted without hesitation. Khavari's body wasn't good cover. Not for long, anyway. It wouldn't take whoever'd just bushwhacked them more than a few seconds to find a new vantage point, one with a clear angle on him. So it was move and move fast. Or die right here.

He punched the tip of one of his poles into the binding release levers on his skis—popping them free. Then he curled around, grabbed both skis, and tossed them sideways into the woods lining this side of the run. Frantically, he rolled after them across the slope. Ice crystals spurted up near his face from another near miss.

Swearing under his breath, Flynn reached the wood line and scrambled behind the trunk of a pine tree, whose heavy, snow-covered lower branches almost brushed the ground. "Son of a bitch," he muttered through clenched teeth. Being shot at sure got old fast. Especially since he wasn't armed himself right now. Austrian gun laws were more relaxed than those of many other European countries, but he'd still figured the local authorities would pretty seriously frown on a foreign "business consultant" carrying a concealed pistol if he was caught. Well, mark that decision down as a triumph of excessive caution over common sense, he thought bitterly.

Then again, he realized, the assassin who'd just killed Khavari and tried to blow his own brains out had to be using a scoped rifle. And one with a hellaciously effective suppressor at that. Even through the crystal-clear Alpine air, the sound of the shots had been remarkably muffled, more like the mechanical *snap* of a bolt cycling than the sharp-edged *crack* usually made by a high-powered round exploding outward from a rifle barrel. So even if he had a sidearm right now, charging back up the mountain through the snow to go mano a mano with a trained sniper would be a terminally stupid plan. The enemy would nail him the instant he broke cover and came out into the open.

No, Flynn decided. There were situations where attacking into an ambush was the least bad option. But this was most definitely *not* one of those situations. Instead, much as he hated it, the smart play now was to bail out and get clear.

Swiftly, he scooted downhill to where his skis had slid, careful to keep the trees between him and that unseen, distant gunman. It took only moments to brush away the caked snow from his boots and bindings and snap back into his skis. He paused for another few seconds to get his bearings. He'd ducked into the woods on the northwestern edge of the trail. And according to the trail maps he'd studied before meeting Khavari, there was another run just on the other side of this thin strip of forest, one that would get him off the mountain.

Flynn's mouth twisted in a self-conscious grin. So much for his earlier plan of taking the easier way down the Kitzbüheler Horn. His chosen alternate route was marked as a more advanced slope, a lot steeper and more rugged than he ordinarily found comfortable. Still, he was okay with taking the risk of sprawling flat on his ass in front of more experienced skiers if it meant staying out of the rifle sights of an assassin. Moving carefully through the softer, deeper snow under the trees, he glided away at an angle, heading for the neighboring run.

He stopped again just before coming back out into the open. Both native caution and his training dictated that he make a few rapid changes to his appearance. For one thing, the bright blue outer shell of his ski jacket was spattered with Khavari's blood. That was bound to draw unwanted attention, whether from the ski area's security personnel, the general public, or, just conceivably, other members of the hit team who might already be looking for him near the lower lifts.

Quickly, Flynn unzipped the shell from its insulating layer and then reversed it to show the black inner lining instead. Next, he pulled off his goggles and stuffed them out of sight in a pocket. This late in the day, they were more hindrance than help anyway. Finally, he tugged a ski hat down over his bare head. Taken separately, none of these tiny alterations were exactly major measures of disguise. But together, he hoped they would alter his visual profile just enough to confuse anyone hunting for the man who'd been seen talking to Khavari right before he was shot.

Satisfied that he'd done all he could for now, Nick Flynn squared his shoulders and skied out from the tree line.

———

Several hundred meters higher up the Kitzbüheler Horn, Viktor Skoblin finished disassembling the VSS Vintorez sniper rifle he'd used to eliminate the Iranian traitor. The separate components of the silenced weapon, originally designed for use by Russia's Spetsnaz units, fit easily into an inconspicuous backpack of the type carried by many skiers. He zipped the backpack closed and slid it across his broad shoulders.

Then he glanced over at his spotter, another former Spetsnaz officer like him. "Any sign of movement?"

The other man, slimmer and shorter than the bullnecked Skoblin, lowered his binoculars. "None. Our second bird has flown. There's no way we can hope to catch up to him now."

Skoblin scowled. Their orders from Pavel Voronin were explicit: the security leak represented by Arif Khavari must be permanently sealed shut, by any means necessary. Dead men, the Raven Syndicate's head had reminded them tartly, could tell no further tales. That made this failed attempt to kill the Iranian government official's unknown foreign contact deeply worrying. Voronin was not known for forgiving those who disappointed him.

Still, the Russian reminded himself uneasily, there were only so many ways out of Kitzbühel. Sooner rather than later, they would get another shot at their second, more elusive target. And in the meantime, he and his spotter still had one more task to complete here on the mountain. He stomped back into his skis. Then, together with the other Raven Syndicate operative, Skoblin moved off down the slope toward the red-stained patch of snow marking the location of Khavari's bullet-riddled body.

TWO

KITZBÜHEL, AUSTRIA

A SHORT TIME LATER

With a friendly wave goodbye to the staff, Nick Flynn stepped out of the shop where he'd just returned his rental skis, poles, and boots. His breath steamed in the cold evening air, a brief puff of fog visible in the warm, golden light from streetlamps and windows. Softly falling snowflakes swirled down out of the sky, deadening sounds.

After a quick glance both ways to make sure he wasn't being observed, he joined the other tourists sauntering along the little town's narrow streets. Brightly lit buildings painted in pale blues, yellows, greens, and other colors created a festive atmosphere. From the snatches of different conversations he overheard in multiple languages, most of those who were out and about were headed for dinner or drinks at one or another of the local restaurants and bars. There were a few couples strolling hand in hand, but the majority were clumped in larger groups, abuzz with laughter and good cheer after an enjoyable, active day on the ski slopes.

Conscious that someone obviously on his own in the middle of this convivial scene might draw unwelcome attention, Flynn tucked himself in behind a gaggle of casually dressed men and women around his own age. Casually, he ambled along the sidewalk a few feet from them— close enough to make it seem like he was one of the group to anyone watching, but just far enough away that none of them felt crowded by a stranger. And whenever they stopped to check out shop windows or read one of the menus posted outside different restaurants, he followed their example.

From what he could make out, these people all worked for the different regional offices of a larger multinational enterprise—some of them British, others French or German or Swiss—who'd been invited to Kitzbühel for a corporate "team-building" exercise . . . which really translated as a lavish ski weekend with lots of late-night partying. One hell of a nice boondoggle if you could wangle it, he decided with a touch of cynical amusement. Maybe he should pitch a similar idea to the sharp-eyed Mr. Fox, his Quartet Directorate boss. But at the thought of his new employer's likely reaction, one side of Flynn's mouth quirked upward. Considering the questionable results of his first assignment so far—a dead senior Iranian government informant and at least one unknown assassin on the loose—it might be wiser if he held off on making smart-ass suggestions for the time being.

While he was pretending to be interested in a display of new ski jackets and other winter apparel in a store window, his cell phone vibrated once. It did the same thing again a moment later. Those back-to-back aborted calls were a signal confirming that the brief mission status report he'd sent to Four had been received. Structured as a routine business communication, his text had read: *Client meeting productive but no firm agreement reached. Unfortunately, competition reacted fast and beat our price.* That was it. Short, simple, and completely dull. But while there were no hidden layers of encryption buried in the message, the ordinary-sounding phrases he'd chosen were sufficient to let Fox know that his rendezvous with Arif Khavari had yielded intriguing intelligence, but no hard evidence . . . and that the Iranian had been killed before he could say more.

At least the elderly Englishman who'd tutored him in the Quartet Directorate's covert communications protocols would have applauded his technique, Flynn hoped—though perhaps not the results he was reporting. "Tell me, in your view, what is the very best sort of code?" the other man had asked in a dry, Oxbridge-tinged voice at the very beginning of their lessons.

"One that doesn't look anything like a code at all," Flynn had shot back.

"Full marks, Mr. Flynn," the Englishman had said with a slight smile. The world's major intelligence agencies, like his old employers in the UK's premier signals intelligence organization, the Government Communications Headquarters (GCHQ), routinely sifted all phone calls, texts, and emails—using powerful supercomputers to scan for anomalies, key phrases and words, and indications of unusually strong encryption. "Which is why those of us in Four, when we communicate amongst ourselves, are very careful to avoid any such nonsense. Plain language messages, innocuous-seeming, thoroughly uninteresting, and perfectly appropriate to your current cover story, are the surest means of flying under the radar of unsympathetic people like my former colleagues at Cheltenham, those in your own country's NSA, and others working for Russia's SVR and GRU or China's Ministry of State Security."

Flynn winced inside at the painful memory of what had come next. Like most things involving the Quartet Directorate, what had seemed simple at first was actually fiendishly complex. Making this "hidden in plain sight" communications method work in the field required the rote memorization of hundreds and hundreds of seemingly ordinary phrases and words in different languages, each of which had specific secret meanings depending on how they were used in any given sentence. Thanks to a good ear and a near-perfect memory, he'd managed the arduous task over the course of a couple of weeks of intensive practice, but only at the cost of grade-A migraines and dry, bloodshot eyes.

He looked up, suddenly aware that the international group of late-twentysomethings he was tagging along behind had finally de-cided on a place to eat. Smiling and laughing, they all began filing into a little Asian restaurant next door. Which meant he'd just lost his primary source of camouflage.

Unhurriedly, Flynn glanced around, discreetly scanning his surroundings again. The dinner-and-drinks crowd was definitely starting to thin out, but there still seemed to be a few people headed toward Kitzbühel's train station—which was his destination. He checked his phone. The last train that would get him to Vienna tonight was due to arrive in a half hour. And he planned to be aboard when it pulled out.

He slid his phone back out of sight and started off, trailing after an older couple towing rolling suitcases. Mentally, he crossed his fingers. So far, this entire supposedly low-key operation had seemed jinxed from start to finish. Now, if ever, would sure be a good time for some of the luck his Irish immigrant grandfather so often swore by.

Five minutes later, Flynn figured out he was not going to be that lucky. From a shadowed vantage point across the street from the train station, he'd spotted trouble waiting for him on its brightly lit platform. He could make out two hard-faced men trying to blend in with the other passengers already gathered there. Although they were dressed in ski apparel pretty much like that worn by everybody else, their behavior was different. And it was clear to him that they were covertly surveilling the small crowd . . . looking for someone.

Looking for him, he was sure.

He dismissed the possibility that these guys were just plainclothes Austrian federal police keeping travelers safe from pickpockets and other petty criminals. They didn't have the right demeanor. If he had to bet his life on it, and he did, he was confident those two men were part of the opposition team that had taken out Khavari so effectively and permanently. But neither of them looked Iranian or even Arab. Instead, something about their facial structure and mannerisms practically screamed "made in Moscow" to his twitchy subconscious. Which strongly suggested they might be more of the foreign mercenaries Khavari had warned about.

Flynn frowned. In his considered judgement, he had just two chances of slipping past those watchers to board the train without being detected—slim and none. And he sure as hell didn't want to give them another shot at him sometime during the four-hour-plus nighttime rail trip to the Austrian capital, especially since he'd have to change trains en route. He might be able to take one of those guys in a fight. Maybe. On a good day. But going up against two of them in the close, confined quarters of a railway coach or at some semideserted transfer stop? *No sale*, he thought grimly. If he wanted to commit suicide, he'd pick a much less messy and far less public option.

Unfortunately, that still left the problem of how he was going to get out of Kitzbühel in one piece. If the bad guys had a surveillance team keeping tabs on the train station, they probably had someone watching the bus depot and even the car rental agencies in this little town—all two of them.

Suddenly, he felt a woman's warm arm slide through his. At the same time, her cheerful, friendly voice said loudly, *"Da bist du, Max! Ich fragte mich, wohin du gegangen warst.* There you are, Max! I wondered where you'd gone." Her German was perfect, with just the slight vowel and consonant changes that would mark her as Austrian to any trained linguist eavesdropping on them.

Startled, Flynn looked down and saw Laura Van Horn looking back up at him with a mischievous expression on her attractive face. When he'd first met her, she'd been the copilot of a crippled Air National Guard C-130J that had made an emergency landing at his last duty station, a lonely radar outpost on Alaska's frozen northern coast. Later, he'd learned that her primary job was as one of Four's top special agents. And it was her recommendation that had prompted a final decision to recruit him into the Quartet Directorate.

Which left the question of just what on earth she was doing here in Kitzbühel now? This was supposed to be a one-man operation, with Flynn as that one man. But this wasn't the right moment to ask awkward questions, he knew, at least not while they were out in the open and under probable observation. Instead, it was time to put on a show for anyone paying close attention to them. Adapting fast, he matched her phony conversational gambit on the fly using the same idiomatic Austrian German. "Oh, I thought I'd check to see if Karl and Clarissa had gotten here yet. In case we needed to change our dinner reservations, I mean."

Van Horn laughed softly, playing along. "Those two? You must be joking. They wouldn't be caught dead on a train. I bet they'll drive in later tonight. So, for now, I have you all to myself." Tightening her grip on his arm slightly, she turned him around until they were headed directly away from the train station.

A block farther on, Flynn glanced down at her. "Okay, Laura, what's the deal here?" he asked quietly. "And no bullshit."

"Bullshit? Who, me?" she said with exaggerated innocence. Seeing his pained expression, she shrugged. "I tagged along on this op purely as a precaution, sort of an emergency backup," she said. "Br'er Fox wanted someone flying distant cover for you, just in case the shit hit the fan." She looked him up and down. "And based on those goons I saw parked at the train station, I guess it has."

Somberly, Flynn nodded. Quickly, he filled her in on the sniper ambush during his meeting with Arif Khavari.

Van Horn's eyes narrowed. "So what's your estimate of the opposition strength?"

"No way to tell," he admitted. "Those two men at the train station, for sure."

"Make that three-plus," she told him. "I spotted another one keeping an eye on the station parking lot. Whoever these guys are, they want you bad."

"I've always been a popular fellow," Flynn said virtuously.

Van Horn snorted softly. "*Popular* isn't really the word I'd have chosen, Nick."

"So now what?" he wondered.

She grinned impishly. "Simple. We blow this cow town and leave the bad guys standing around in the cold wondering where you went. My ride's parked not far away, outside a really cute little *Gasthaus*."

Flynn stared down at her. "You got a *car*? *And* a hotel room?" He shook his head in disbelief. "All Four gave *me* was a second-class train ticket."

"Senior operative status, remember, Nick?" Van Horn murmured in amusement. "There are some perks, you know—along with the occasional inconvenience of being tasked with rounding up a newbie gone astray."

For just a moment, Flynn felt himself bristle. Finding out how far he'd been kept in the dark on this assignment pissed him off. But then he forced himself to relax. In the circumstances, Fox's decision to position Van Horn as discreet support if things went wrong had proved to be a very sensible safety measure. With an inward sigh, he decided to bow to the inevitable and let himself be rescued. "*Moo*," he lowed in agreement, mimicking a lost steer she'd just roped.

H alf an hour later, they drove out of Kitzbühel in the four-door Mercedes Van Horn had rented when she flew into Vienna. Her usual preference in cars was something flashier, in bright red, but she'd opted for a more discreet dark blue sedan for this assignment. "Just another of the cruel sacrifices I make for undercover work," she'd told Flynn with theatrical sigh and self-mocking smile when they got in. "They never stop."

At her insistence, he drove, following her directions to take a two-lane highway heading northeast, toward Salzburg and Vienna. Outside of town, the snow-covered fields and small clumps of trees lining the road were in darkness. Clusters of bright lights—ski chalets and on-mountain restaurants—dotted the steep slopes rising on either side of the valley. It was still snowing lightly, and the falling flakes caught in their headlights glittered briefly as they flew past.

Apart from the tiny red taillights of a car briefly visible far ahead before vanishing around a curve, they seemed to have the road all to themselves. Much as Flynn wanted to put distance between himself and their unknown enemy's kill team, he fought the temptation to floor it. The snow wasn't accumulating fast enough to make driving dangerous, but there was no point in making themselves unnecessarily conspicuous by speeding.

Despite his careful driving, they were just a couple of miles north of Kitzbühel when Flynn saw a pair of blue flashing lights appear suddenly in his rearview mirror and turn out onto the highway behind them. It was a lone rider on a motorcycle. And he was closing the gap between them fast.

"We've got company," he muttered to Van Horn.

She craned her head around to peer back through the sedan's rear window. "Yeah. How truly nice."

"Is that a cop?" Flynn asked.

She turned back around with a frown. "Maybe. And maybe not." Her right hand slid inside her jacket. "But somehow I don't think Br'er Fox will be very happy if we end up in an Austrian slammer after a high-speed chase through the Alps."

Nodding tightly, Flynn eased his foot off the accelerator, moved over onto the narrow verge of the road, and then braked to a stop. He tapped a control to roll down the driver's side window. A blast of cold air whistled in, along with a few snowflakes that spun and swirled around the interior before melting.

In his rearview mirror, he saw the rider pull in behind them and dismount from his motorcycle. The blue lights on the bike strobed rhythmically, eerily illuminating the night around them. The cyclist pulled off his white plastic helmet and hung it on the handlebars. Then he strode forward confidently, with one hand on the pistol holstered at his hip.

Flynn's eyes narrowed in concentration. Was the other man wearing a police uniform? Or just a mix of dark-colored civilian clothing? In the weird, oscillating blend of light and shadow created by those flashing lights, it was almost impossible to be sure one way or the other.

The motorcycle rider reached the window and bent down to peer inside.

"What's the problem, Officer?" Flynn asked politely in German.

The other man shrugged. "*Nur eine Routineprüfung. Ihr Führerschein, bitte?* Just a routine check. Your driver's license, please?"

Flynn's hackles rose. He'd caught the faint hint of an accent—the *wrong* accent—in the man's voice. He felt a rush of adrenaline flood his system, ice-cold even in the already frigid winter air. Time seemed to slow. One part of his brain noticed the man's right hand darting fast toward the weapon at his hip. *Oh, hell.*

"Lean back, Nick," Laura Van Horn said conversationally. Then she fired twice with her own pistol, the sound of the shots deafeningly loud inside the car.

Hit dead center by both rounds, the motorcyclist staggered back from the window. His mouth opened wide in shock. Reddening stains spread outward from the holes punched through his black leather jacket. He fumbled again at his holster. Without hesitating, Van Horn leaned even farther around Flynn and squeezed the trigger two more times. Her third shot slammed into the man's chest. Her fourth caught him in the face and exploded out the back of his skull.

He collapsed onto the road and lay still.

Flynn didn't wait to see more. He put the Mercedes in gear and pulled away. He glanced at Van Horn.

"*Not a cop*," she mouthed. Both their ears were still ringing from the sharp crack of four shots fired in rapid succession.

He nodded grimly. Whoever these guys were, they'd launched a full-court press to find and kill him—with lookouts apparently posted at all the exits from Kitzbühel. He sped up. The more miles they put between themselves and the dead man lying twisted on the highway, the better.

A little farther up the road, Van Horn had him swing left at a junction—turning onto a highway that would take them west to

Innsbruck, then south to the Brenner Pass, and from there into Italy. "Change of plans," she told him, reading the text she'd just received from Fox. He wanted Flynn back in the States ASAP, and it had just become blazingly obvious that Austria was too damned hot for both of them. With Arif Khavari dead and their still-unidentified opposition out in force and looking for blood, returning to Vienna would be a sucker's move.

THREE

THE NEXT DAY

Pavel Voronin stood perfectly at ease, looking out the east-facing, floor-to-ceiling windows that formed one whole wall of his spacious private office. From here, forty-four stories up the Mercury Tower, one of six ultramodern skyscrapers that made up the city's International Business Center, he could see all the way across the frozen Moskva River to the Kremlin's redbrick walls and spires and beyond. A cloudless blue sky overhead signaled the arrival of a massive wave of high pressure from Siberia, sending temperatures in the Russian capital plunging to well below zero. In the bright sunlight, the Mercury Tower's bronze-tinted reflective glass glowed like a soaring pillar of fire on Moscow's skyline.

It was an ostentatious display that mirrored the self-proclaimed status of the building's prosperous tenants—five-star restaurants, luxury-apartment owners, high-end retail stores, and the business offices of some of Russia's most successful enterprises.

Including his own Sindikat Vorona, the Raven Syndicate, which now occupied three full floors of the gleaming skyscraper.

Idly, with a thin, cold smile that never reached his pale gray eyes, Voronin gazed down across Moscow's icy streets, so full of tiny-seeming cars and trucks and scurrying, antlike pedestrians. It was a view he relished—especially since this office had once belonged to Dmitri Grishin, one of Russia's most powerful and wealthiest oligarchs, the man who had been his mentor for more than a decade.

Grishin had prized both Voronin's outward polish—the product of the best preparatory schools and universities in the United Kingdom and the United States—and his utter ruthlessness. And he had used the younger man to run his most illegal ventures, culminating in a daring scheme to secretly orchestrate the theft of Russia's most advanced stealth bomber and then sell it to the highest bidder. In the end, they'd obtained huge sums of ransom money from *both* Moscow and Washington, D.C.—only to have the aircraft unexpectedly crash and explode deep in Alaska's uncharted wilderness, making it impossible to return the technological marvel to their own country as promised.

But in this seeming setback, Voronin had immediately seen the opportunity he'd long craved, a chance to permanently end his apprenticeship to Grishin. He'd callously betrayed the oligarch to Russia's state security services and to the lethal vengeance of the nation's authoritarian ruler, President Piotr Zhdanov. Then, posing as a patriot appalled by the older man's "crimes," he'd helped the Kremlin also retrieve the hundreds of billions of rubles it had paid into some of Grishin's secret accounts. Of course, now secure in Zhdanov's good graces, he'd kept for himself the three billion dollars so unwisely paid into other hidden accounts by the American CIA—using it to fund the creation of the Raven Syndicate, his own private military and intelligence "consulting" firm.

His smile widened slightly at the memory of watching Dmitri Grishin's bullet-shattered corpse drift out to sea. That one small, perfect act of treachery had freed him to pursue his deepest ambitions . . . and simultaneously provided the wealth he required. In little more than a year, he'd built up a deadly and efficient organization—luring many of Russia's best-trained special forces soldiers and intelligence specialists away from its vaunted Spetsnaz commando groups, its foreign intelligence agency, the SVR, and its military intelligence unit, the GRU, and into his own service. Poaching so many of their best people hadn't won him any friends in Russia's Ministry of Defense or its official intelligence organizations. But he didn't really give a damn.

After all, thanks to MIDNIGHT, the audacious covert operation he'd first conceived, and to the irreversible strategic changes it promised to unleash on an unsuspecting world, Pavel Voronin had become, as he planned all along, President Zhdanov's indispensable man.

He turned at a discreet knock on his office door. A specific tone chimed, indicating the visitor waiting outside was his top deputy, Vasily Kondakov, a former colonel in the GRU. He tapped a small icon on his smartwatch, disengaging the door's security lock. It buzzed open and Kondakov hurried in carrying a manila folder. Nearly as tall as Voronin, the ex-intelligence officer was balding and wore a pair of horn-rimmed spectacles.

"Well?" Voronin snapped.

"Our courier from the team in Vienna just arrived," the other man told him. He held up the folder. "With Skoblin's full report on the Khavari . . . affair."

Voronin hid his amusement. In more than a decade of service with the GRU's notorious Unit 29155, agents under Kondakov's direct command had been responsible for the deaths of a number of dissidents, defectors, and even foreign nationals deemed dangerous to Russia's national security. Despite that, he was still oddly squeamish, preferring vague euphemisms like "affair" to blunter, more accurate terms like "hit" or "murder."

He sat down behind his desk and gestured Kondakov into the lone chair on the other side. "And?"

The other man frowned. "As ordered, Skoblin and his people took Khavari off the board. Quite permanently."

Voronin nodded. The Iranian shipping official had been under suspicion and surveillance for some weeks. His sudden attempt to arrange what was clearly a covert rendezvous while part of a delegation to an OPEC conference in Austria had triggered the quick decision to kill him. With the final preparations for MIDNIGHT so close to completion, it was imperative to seal any potential security breach. "So what's the problem, Vasily?"

"Khavari managed to make contact with an enemy agent before they were able to silence him," Kondakov answered.

Voronin's lips thinned in irritation. He leaned forward. "Then I assume this agent is dead, too?"

"Unfortunately not," Kondakov said grimly. "Somehow, he evaded the team's best efforts to eliminate him. He even took out one of our own people, one Skoblin had posted to guard the northern exit from Kitzbühel."

"Took out how?" Voronin demanded.

"Skoblin's team found our agent dead on the road," Kondakov replied. "He'd been shot four times, at point-blank range."

Voronin sat back. His jaw tightened. "And has this mysterious paragon of mayhem been identified?"

"Not yet," the other man admitted. He opened the manila folder and slid several photographs across the desk. Taken through the scope of Skoblin's sniper rifle and his spotter's binoculars, they showed only part of the unknown agent's face. Making identification even more difficult, dark-tinted ski goggles hid the man's eyes and part of his forehead. "Thanks to your authorization from the president, we can run these pictures through the SVR and GRU databases without giving them the whole story. But I do not expect definitive results."

Voronin took one of the photos and studied it briefly. He saw Kondakov's point. It would be almost impossible to match these partial images with that of any known enemy operative. From what little they had to go on, Khavari's contact could be working for any one of half a dozen Western intelligence agencies. He said as much aloud.

Slowly, Kondakov nodded. He tapped the best photo of the bunch, one that captured more of the man's profile. "He might be American," he said hesitantly. "There's something about that jawline—"

"Working for the CIA?" Voronin said with a snort. "Or one of their other intelligence groups?" He shook his head dismissively. "Not likely,

Vasily. I doubt any of their people could have acted so swiftly and ruth-lessly against Skoblin's watcher. The American spy agencies are too risk averse. They frown on the use of unplanned violence by their officers, do they not?"

Again, the other man nodded. The fictional depictions in so many films and thrillers of CIA officers singlehandedly taking out enemy spies and terrorists were a source of private amusement to those in Moscow, who knew how tightly their rivals' hands were so often tied.

Voronin looked more intently at the photo Kondakov had singled out. "The Israelis, on the other hand, aren't such old women. They are not at all afraid to act decisively when necessary," he mused softly. He glanced up. "And Israel is already locked in its own long-standing covert war with Iran. That gives them a strong motivation to cultivate a traitor like Khavari."

"You think this man could be Mossad?" Kondakov asked.

"The Mossad. Or a member of the Sayeret Matkal," Voronin said, re-ferring to the special forces unit controlled by AMAN, Israel's military intelligence service. He leaned back in his chair. "Taking everything into consideration, it's the most likely possibility."

"So what now?"

"Tell Skoblin's team to institute tight surveillance on the Israeli em-bassy in Vienna," Voronin ordered. "I don't want those people able to make a move without us knowing about it. That's essential in case they try to penetrate MIDNIGHT's security again—by going after another of Khavari's government colleagues, for example. We can't risk further security breaches. Not this late in the game."

Kondakov looked worried. "It might be better if we turn that task over to the SVR or GRU," he suggested. "Close surveillance operations are manpower-intensive. And if any of their people are spotted and identified, we might be able to pass it off as just a routine intelligence-gathering effort."

"Absolutely not," Voronin said coldly. "Calling in your old comrades or those clowns in the SVR would mean briefing them on the potential gap in our operational security. Right now, President Zhdanov trusts us completely. Which is why we've been given a completely free hand to carry out MIDNIGHT as we see fit. Naturally, there are many small-minded men in our government who are jealous of our growing power and influence. They would jump at the chance to discredit me and the Syndicate. So I have no intention of affording them any such opportunity." His eyes hardened. "Is that clear, Vasily?" Hurriedly, Kondakov nodded.

"Then you tell Skoblin that I want this matter handled entirely in-house," Voronin directed. "With our own people and our own resources."

"And if they spot the agent Khavari spoke to?" Kondakov asked.

"I want him terminated," Voronin said harshly. "Without hesitation. Without delay. And without any more mistakes."

FOUR

A FEW HOURS LATER

Nick Flynn turned off a quiet residential street and drove up a long, private drive shaded by rows of tall palm trees. Through more trees ahead, he caught the dazzle of sunlight reflecting off the placid waters of a small, almost circular lake. He followed the driveway around through a half loop and parked in front of a two-story mansion over-looking the lake. Complete with red roof tiles imported from Barcelona, muted yellow stucco walls, dark wood trim, tall, arched windows, and a wrought-iron entry gate leading to the main door, it would have looked perfectly at home in Spain.

Built in the early 1920s as the Florida winter retreat for a wealthy New York banking family, Avalon House now had different tenants. Weathered bronze plaques mounted near the main entrance told visitors the building currently housed the Concannon Language Institute, the Sobieski Charitable Foundation, and Sykes-Fairbairn Strategic Investments. Their faded, old-fashioned lettering conveyed the impression of stolid respectability appropriate to organizations founded in the late 1940s.

Flynn suppressed a smile. In truth, of course, none of the three were really respectable at all . . . at least not in the sense that most people would use the term. They were actually front organizations for the Quartet Directorate—some of the many different groups created to conceal its clandestine recruiting, training, and operational activities. Avalon House had been deeded over to Four by one of its founding members, an heir to that same prominent New York banking family. He'd served in World War II as a member of Office of Strategic Services, the OSS—the precursor to the CIA. At his recommendation, the mansion had been converted into the headquarters of Four's American station.

At first, Flynn had thought it was odd that the Quartet Directorate had decided to locate one of its major operational centers so close to Orlando. Once known for orange groves and as a refuge from harsh northern winters, the area was now a tourist mecca more famous worldwide for Disney World, Universal Studios, other big theme parks, and sprawling vacation resorts. A private intelligence organization seemed completely out of place in such a setting. But gradually, he'd figured out the shrewd reasoning involved.

Even seventy-plus years ago, Washington, D.C., and its environs had been crawling with U.S. intelligence and law enforcement agencies, foreign operatives, prying journalists, and political busybodies. The situation had only grown worse in the intervening decades. Amid D.C.'s toxic maelstrom of intrigue, spies, and counterspies, it would be virtually impossible for the Quartet Directorate to operate undetected. In contrast, Orlando—especially with its recent emphasis on global tourism and business and travel—was an ideal location for a covert group that wanted to avoid drawing inconvenient official attention. The region's bustling international airport also offered good connections to and from virtually anywhere in the world, like the flights that had brought him back from Milan via London's Heathrow the night before.

Finally, from Flynn's personal perspective, Florida's warmer and sunnier climate was a huge plus. Between duty in Alaska's far north and his aborted mission to Austria's Tyrolean Alps, he figured he'd already seen enough snow and ice to last a lifetime.

He pressed the buzzer firmly and looked up into the surveillance camera mounted overhead, allowing its biometric sensors to scan the contours of his face and confirm his identity. After a moment, the door swung open, revealing a brown-tiled foyer with a large reception desk. More doors on either side led deeper into the building. At the far end of the foyer, a wide curving staircase swept up to the mansion's second floor.

A petite Korean American woman sat primly behind the reception desk. In her stylish red blazer and cream-colored silk blouse, she appeared completely unthreatening, but Flynn knew that was only an illusion. Though strands of gray streaked her dark hair, she was still trim and remarkably fit-looking. More to the point, however, Gwen Park had spent years running intelligence and counterterrorist operations in some of the most dangerous parts of Southeast Asia's drug-infested Golden Triangle before taking over as the chief of Avalon House's small security detail. Among other hidden talents, she had a reputation as a crack shot and was said to be death in high heels in hand-to-hand combat.

"Welcome back, Mr. Flynn," she said briskly when he came inside. The front door closed automatically behind him. "How was your trip?"

"Somewhat more eventful than I would have liked," he admitted.

Her eyes flickered in barely concealed amusement at the wild understatement. "So I heard." She nodded toward the nearest interior door on the right. "Mr. Fox is expecting you."

"Do I get a blindfold? Or just a cigarette?" Flynn asked wryly, pausing with his hand on the doorknob.

A tiny smile danced at the edges of her mouth. "Neither, I suspect," she told him with mock severity. "Please keep in mind that our limited operating budget doesn't allow room for frivolous luxuries."

Flynn shot her a grin and strode through the doorway and down a short hallway. There was another closed door at the end, this one marked: SYKES-FAIRBAIRN STRATEGIC INVESTMENTS, CARLETON FREDERICK FOX, MANAGING DIRECTOR. Pulling his shoulders back straight, he rapped once and went straight in.

The office beyond was small and furnished very simply, with just a desk, a couple of comfortable chairs, and an inexpensive-looking desktop computer. Its most prominent feature was a large window that opened onto a lush tropical garden full of bright-colored flowers. Fox, a thin, middle-aged man with graying hair, turned away from the window. Bright eyes gleamed knowingly from behind a thick pair of wire-rimmed glasses. Except for those eyes, anyone meeting him for the first time would have assumed he was just the boring money manager or anonymous midlevel government bureaucrat he so often pretended to be.

"Take a seat, Nick," the older man said quietly as he crossed the room and sat down behind his desk.

Flynn obeyed. Despite his plan to be oh so cool and casual, he caught himself sitting almost at attention.

Fox smiled. "Expecting a reprimand? Or something worse?"

"Well, yeah," Flynn admitted. "After all, I can't exactly claim to have covered myself with glory on this assignment."

Fox snorted softly. "*Glory* isn't something we care much about in Four," he said mildly. "We're far more interested in people who can obtain the intelligence we need . . . and get out alive, if that is at all possible." He peered at Flynn over his glasses. "Based on the fact that you appear to be breathing, I'll take that as a significant mark in your favor."

"I may be breathing, but Arif Khavari sure isn't," Flynn pointed out tightly.

"True," the older man agreed. He shrugged his narrow shoulders. "Then again, since the enemy—whoever they may prove to be—clearly mounted a maximum effort to eliminate our Iranian friend, that is scarcely surprising. In the circumstances, I consider the fact that you got off the mountain alive, and then escaped the larger trap set for you, to be something of a miracle."

"Maybe," Flynn said. "But if so, it was a miracle with Laura Van Horn's name written all over it."

A half smile sleeted across Fox's face and then vanished as quickly as it had come. "Laura can be something of a force of nature in a tight corner," he concurred. He leaned back. "Judging by the fact that the Austrian authorities haven't reported finding any more dead bodies littering their scenic slopes and highways, I think we can safely assume the motorcyclist she killed was, in fact, a member of the opposition hit team . . . and not some unfortunate local police officer in the wrong place at just the wrong time."

Somberly, Flynn nodded. Sure as he had been that Laura's split-second decision to shoot the man who'd pulled them over was justified, it was still a relief to have that confirmed. Unlike the CIA, the UK's MI6, France's DGSE, and other government-run spy services, the Quartet Directorate's agents had no safety net, no mythical "license to kill," to protect them from imprisonment or even execution if they overreacted on a mission.

"What about Khavari?" he asked.

"His body was discovered earlier this morning, Kitzbühel time," Fox said. "By members of the ski patrol checking the slopes before they opened. Apparently, it had been dragged into the woods to delay any premature discovery."

Flynn nodded grimly. The men who'd killed the Iranian would not have wanted to trigger a police inquiry, not while they were still hunting him. "Has there been any official word on his death yet?"

"Tehran is blaming the Israeli Mossad for what it calls 'the cold-blooded murder of a patriotic Iranian government official,'" Fox replied. "The Austrians aren't saying anything at all, except that the matter is under investigation. And that they remain confident of eventually making an arrest in the case."

Flynn heard the skepticism in the older man's voice. "Which you think is bullshit?"

Fox nodded again. "Quite probably." The corners of his mouth turned down. "Even if the Austrian government suspects the truth—that Khavari was killed because he had turned against the regime—it won't want to risk provoking a diplomatic firestorm by interfering in what could be considered Iran's own domestic affairs . . . however messy they might be. It might be a different matter if any of its own citizens had been hurt or killed, but, as it is—" His shoulders rose and fell expressively.

"Khavari's murder will be swept under the rug for the sake of political convenience," Flynn finished bitterly.

Fox eyed him closely. "Yes." He cleared his throat gently. "Which leaves us with the challenge of making sure his death has meaning. Something in those fragments of intelligence he was able to pass to you before being shot must explain why Tehran or its allies were so desperate to silence him. Otherwise, if they simply believed he had turned his coat, why not wait to arrest and interrogate him once he flew back to Iran?"

"Makes sense," Flynn acknowledged. He took a moment to organize his thoughts, and then gave the other man a precise account of the strange story Arif Khavari had relayed. Nothing about it seemed to yield an obvious explanation. Why was Tehran so determined to make so many extensive and odd-sounding modifications to a single oil tanker? And why cloak the project in such tight secrecy and over-the-top security?

When Flynn finished, Fox sat back with his eyes half-closed, obviously thinking through what he'd just been told. "Is it possible the Iranians plan to use this ship, the *Gulf Venture*, for large-scale smuggling operations?" he speculated after a moment, leaning forward again. "As it is, the Revolutionary Guards already run huge quantities of weapons, missiles, and other contraband to various terrorist groups and their other allies, like Syria and Venezuela. But the addition of a hundred-thousand-ton vessel would enormously expand their capabilities. You could cram a lot of lethal cargo aboard a ship that size, enough to supply any number of bad actors around the world with up to a year's worth of munitions, explosives, and arms in a single smuggling voyage."

Flynn considered that. Looked at one way, the older man's theory was plausible. But, at the same time, something about it just didn't ring true to him. Finally, he shook his head. "That oil tanker the Iranians are fixing up is damned big all right," he said. "But that's exactly the problem I see with using her simply to run guns."

"The *Gulf Venture* would be too conspicuous, you mean?" Fox suggested quietly.

Flynn nodded. "Yep." Before reporting to Avalon House, he'd done some quick internet research. "Between its own merchant marine and ships operating under false flags, Iran's got dozens, maybe hundreds, of other cargo vessels and tramp freighters at its disposal. Sure, they're all significantly smaller, but by the same token, they're also a hell of a lot less likely to draw attention than would an eight-hundred-foot-long tanker. Maybe the *Gulf Venture* could slip past the various navies still enforcing some sanctions on Iran, but why take the risk? It's a bad option."

"Because it would involve putting too many eggs into just one basket," Fox realized.

"Bingo," Flynn agreed. "I can't see the Iranians being dumb enough to risk shipping so much valuable contraband in a single hull. Smuggling ops work best using multiple ships. Sure, our Navy guys or the Israelis can stop and board a dhow here and a tramp freighter there, but there's no way they can possibly catch them all. Trusting to luck to sneak a single huge oil tanker through a blockade without being intercepted? That's amateur hour stuff . . . and those murderous sons of bitches in Tehran don't strike me as amateurs."

"Our lives would be much easier if they were," Fox said dryly. "Anything else?"

Flynn nodded again. "Yeah. For example, some of the changes they're making to the *Gulf Venture* don't square at all with the idea of using her for smuggling runs. Concealed centerline compartments and extra hydraulic cranes? I get why you'd need those on a ship converted to carry contraband. But then why retrofit those special stabilizer fins and extra high-speed oil pumps Khavari's naval architect friend made such a big deal out of?"

The older man looked closely at him. "Why indeed?"

"I don't have a doggone clue," Flynn told him wryly. "I was an English major in college, remember? The closest I ever came to taking an engineering class was first-year calculus. That's sort of like comparing flying a kite to launching a Saturn V rocket to the moon."

"Point taken, Nick," Fox said with the faint hint of a smile of his own. "I'll pass the problem on to those with more in-depth knowledge of ship design and construction. Though very discreetly, of course."

"Which raises another point," Flynn continued. "Why put all these extreme security measures in place around the Bandar Abbas shipyard in the first place? Units of special Quds Force commandos? Locking down the whole workforce? Even bringing in armed foreigners as additional guards? For what? Just to hide the fact that Iran wants to smuggle even more weapons to bad guys around the globe? Hell, that's not exactly a secret to anyone who reads the news. And it sure doesn't explain why someone sent in a whole assassination squad just to shut Khavari's mouth." He frowned. "No, whatever these guys are planning, it's got to be something much bigger and nastier."

"No doubt," Fox said. He tapped at his chin reflectively. "You're confident the men you spotted watching the Kitzbühel train station were Russians?"

"Pretty sure, yes. And while the biker Laura shot spoke reasonably fluent German, I still picked up a faint Russian accent."

Fox's mouth tightened. "That certainly fits. The tactics you've described match those used by Spetsnaz assassination squads in the past."

"You think the Kremlin ordered the hit on Khavari?" Flynn asked curiously. "Not the mullahs in Tehran?"

Fox sighed. "It's certainly a disquieting possibility we need to consider. The obvious alternative is that the killers are somehow connected to those so-called foreign mercenaries working inside Iran." His frown deepened. "All of which suggests that either the Russian government is working hand-in-glove with Tehran on this mysterious oil tanker project . . . or that Iran's leaders see whatever they're planning as so important that they're even willing to rely on outsiders to handle crucial elements." He pinched his nose, looking suddenly tired. "One thing's absolutely clear: learning more about their real intentions is now our highest-priority task."

"That may mean putting an agent, or even a small team of agents, on the ground inside Iran," Flynn said carefully. He never slept very well on planes, so he'd spent a number of hours over the darkened Atlantic last night exploring different ways to bypass the information roadblock created by Khavari's murder.

Fox looked skeptical. "Just getting into Iran safely is a highly risky endeavor. The whole country is the very definition of a hostile environment. But even assuming that proves possible, what are our people supposed to do next? Sneak inside the Bandar Abbas shipyard and take a closer look at the *Gulf Venture*?"

Flynn grinned at him. "Oh, hell, no. I may be loco, but I'm not a complete lunatic. Based on what Khavari told me, it would take an armored battalion with full-on air support to penetrate the security cordon around that tanker. Which doesn't really seem like the subtle approach Four ordinarily prefers."

"To put it mildly," Fox said, matching his ironic tone. "And, of course, that's setting aside the minor problem of finding a force of spare tanks and fighter planes just lying around for us to borrow." He turned serious. "So what do you have in mind?"

"Right now, the only real loose thread we have left to pull on is that friend of Khavari's, Daneshvar—the guy who first clued him into all the weird shit going down at that shipyard," Flynn explained. "If we can make contact with him directly, we might pick up some of the answers we need."

Fox frowned. "There are quite a number of 'if's lurking there, Nick."

"Yes, sir, I realize that," Flynn agreed evenly. "I just don't see any other way forward right now."

Slowly, the older man nodded. "Very well, start working up a proposed infiltration plan and any necessary cover stories. But I'll need to consult closely with my colleagues at the other stations before authorizing this mission."

Flynn wasn't surprised by his superior's reluctance to act without approval from the other members of Four's upper echelon. From its very beginnings in the earliest days of the developing Cold War, the Quartet Directorate had used a collegial approach to leadership. The reality that power corrupts and absolute power corrupts absolutely was abundantly clear to those who'd already risked their lives fighting Nazi Germany— only to see the growing threat posed by the Soviet Union in World War II's chaotic aftermath.

Four's first recruits were all veterans of the American OSS, Britain's SOE (the Special Operations Executive), and the Resistance movements of France, Norway, Poland, and several other Allied countries. Deeply troubled and even angered by what they viewed as the growing politicization, penetration by Soviet moles, and increasing risk aversion of the West's official government intelligence agencies, these men and women banded together to create an organization that could act swiftly, secretly, and decisively against serious threats to the free world. Aware, however, of the inherent dangers involved in creating a private intelligence group expressly intended to operate outside strictly lawful channels, Four followed one inflexible rule: The Quartet Directorate *never* involved itself in the domestic politics of any friendly nation. As a safeguard, if time allowed, large-scale or unusually dangerous operations required explicit approval from the separate national stations scattered around the world.

"And in the meantime," Fox went on, "I'll pass the key elements of what we've learned to a couple of my contacts in the CIA."

Like most of Four's senior executives, the older man maintained discreet, arms-length relationships with people in the regular military and intelligence services—though only after they'd been meticulously vetted. And he was always careful to conceal the true nature of the Quartet Directorate's structure, aims, and capabilities from these contacts.

"Do you think that'll do any good?" Flynn asked skeptically. His own bad experiences with some of the CIA's "best and brightest" had soured him on both its basic competence and its real interest in anything except its own narrow parochial concerns.

"Probably not," Fox conceded. "I don't have all that much faith in Langley's ability to separate the wheat from the chaff." He shrugged. "But who knows? There could always be a first time."

FIVE

THE NEXT DAY

The conference room on the top floor was crowded. A dozen people, all of them high-ranking executives in the Central Intelligence Agency, sat around a large rectangular table. Their coffee cups, tablet computers, and notepads littered the table's surface. More men and women, senior staffers for those around the table, occupied the chairs lining three sides of the dark-paneled room. The fourth wall held a large digital screen currently showing the CIA's seal, an eagle above a shield embossed with a compass rose.

A heavyset, florid-faced man sat alone at the head of the table. Charles Horne was the recently appointed DCI, the director of Central Intelligence. His thick lips pursed as he jotted down a quick a note to himself. Finally, with a satisfied nod, he looked back up. "Very good. That last report from Science and Technology takes care of all of our priority agenda items." He ran his heavy-lidded gaze around the table. "Now, does anyone have anything else we should discuss this morning?"

Miranda Reynolds, head of the CIA's highly secret Directorate of Operations, hid a grimace. In the weeks since he'd taken over the reins at Langley, Horne had definitely put his own personal stamp on the way things ran. Unlike many of his predecessors, he'd spent most of his government service in the State Department—where talk was more valued than action—and it showed.

Focused one-on-one meetings between the director and his senior subordinates were now rare, replaced instead by seeming endless daily conferences like this one. Not only did these talkathons waste time, something that was always in short supply for those at the top of the CIA's food chain like her, they were also an added security risk. Bringing so many people into the loop on matters they had absolutely no need to know anything about was just asking for trouble. Unauthorized leaks to the press and to Congress were already a serious problem for the agency. In Reynolds's cynical view, all these gabfests really accomplished was to expand the list of suspects for any internal security investigation.

She fought the temptation to check her watch. With luck, her colleagues would keep their mouths shut so they could go ahead and adjourn. Important messages from CIA stations around the world were piling up in her email inbox. It wasn't as though America's adversaries took a timeout while Horne made his senior people and their top aides suffer through these interminable, unproductive meetings.

Reynolds snarled inwardly when she saw Philip Demopoulos lean forward to catch the DCI's attention. Demopoulos, a wiry man with wavy gray hair and a stylish goatee, was her counterpart in charge of the Directorate of Analysis. In general, his analysts were supposed to evaluate the raw data gathered by her officers and agents—together with snippets of intelligence accumulated from other sources—and produce coherent, accurate intelligence reports on trouble spots around the world. Sometimes it worked the other way round, when his analysts needed her people to confirm wild rumors or stories they'd picked up elsewhere. All too often, those were nothing but dead ends, a waste of precious manhours and scarce resources.

"It looks as though the Iranians are working on a very unusual project in one of their shipyards near Bandar Abbas," Demopoulos said. "At least that's what we're hearing through previously reliable sources."

Reynolds frowned. That wasn't anything her people had dug up, which meant this was another case where the Analysis Directorate was freelancing. Wonderful. She listened intently while he rattled off an impressive-sounding recitation of Tehran's plans to heavily modify one of their AFRAMAX-sized oil tankers for some unknown purpose.

To cap off his short presentation, Demopoulos pulled up a satellite photo of the shipyard in question. "This image was taken earlier today," he explained. "During a pass by one of our KH-11 recon birds." He highlighted the enormous ship occupying the yard's large drydock. An odd, tentlike structure obscured all but the forward sections of its bow. "As you can see, this image confirms part of what we were told by our sources. The Iranians are definitely taking extraordinary precautions to keep us from seeing the kind of work they're doing on this tanker."

The DCI stared at the satellite image in silence for several moments. Then he turned back to Demopoulos. "Does this story of yours come from the Israelis, Phil?" he asked. His tone was skeptical.

"No, sir," the analysis chief said. "At least not directly. This information was relayed to us through a small private security firm with corporate contacts in the Middle East."

"Relayed from who, exactly?" Horne asked sharply.

"We're not quite sure," Demopoulos admitted. "But our best guess is that what we're hearing probably originated with one or more of the various Iranian dissident groups. There's also a possible connection to that Iranian official found murdered in Austria a couple of days ago. He worked for their state shipping company."

Horne's lips thinned in irritation. "The man the Iranians claim was assassinated by the Mossad, you mean?"

"Jerusalem has unequivocally denied any involvement in his death," Demopoulos said carefully.

Horne snorted. A scowl settled on his jowly face. He looked down the table at Reynolds. "Can you confirm any of this material, Miranda?"

She saw the way the wind was blowing. Horne might be a career diplomat by training, but he was a political animal by inclination. He'd climbed the ladder steadily over the years by attaching himself to rising stars on the political side of the State Department—appointees who moved up in successive administrations to more and more powerful positions. Whenever these men or women looked around for a trustworthy subordinate, they always found Charles Horne waiting, eager and willing to do their bidding and happy to toe the chosen party line.

At this moment, the president and his advisers were orchestrating a major diplomatic push to lure Iran "back into the community of nations." They faulted previous administrations for treating the Islamic Republic as a pariah state. Tehran's isolated rulers, they argued, would respond more positively to carrots—trade deals, relaxed sanctions, and renewed arms limitation negotiations—than to insults and threats. So the last thing the new DCI wanted to do now was go to the White House with worrying new intelligence about Iran's possible plans and intentions.

Miranda Reynolds thought very quickly. Two recent blown covert operations in a row—one in Libya, the other in Alaska—had painted a target on her back. So far, she'd kept control of the Operations Directorate by pulling political strings herself . . . and by not so subtly reminding those above her that she was one of the few women in the CIA's top echelon. For the moment, no one wanted to endure the media frenzy that could result from firing one of Langley's pioneers for women's equality. But making an enemy of Horne now by siding with Phil Demopoulos might easily tip the balance against her.

No, she decided, she had nothing to gain here. Especially since the reports passed to the Analysis Directorate seemed so vague and open to different interpretations. Certainly, nothing about them suggested any level of threat to the United States or its interests that might make this situation a hill worth dying on.

"Confirm these fragmentary reports? No, sir. I can't," Reynolds said firmly, ignoring the surprised look on Demopoulos's face. "None of our own sources inside the Iranian government have reported anything about this mysterious oil tanker project. Not a peep."

Left carefully unstated was the inconvenient and rather embarrassing fact that the CIA only had a few agents inside Iran. Or that none of them were based anywhere near Bandar Abbas. Left equally unstated were her growing suspicions that a significant number of the Iranian nationals her officers had recruited as sources were actually double agents for Iran's own Ministry of Intelligence.

"I see." Horne looked satisfied. He turned back to Demopoulos. "I don't think this tanker business is worth pursuing further, Phil." He shrugged. "More likely than not, it's just a wild rumor planted by Israeli or Arab hardliners. Or by Iranian no-hopers feverishly imagining we can be tricked into supporting some lunatic effort to overthrow the government in Tehran."

"But—"

The DCI rode roughshod over Demopoulos's half-hearted attempt to object. "Whatever sort of changes the Iranians are actually making to this ship, one thing's sure: it can't stay hidden forever. And if this converted tanker really does pose a genuine threat to our national security, I'm quite confident that we can stop it cold when the time comes." He shook his head. "I won't condone jumping at shadows on my watch. And there's certainly no justification here to jeopardize one of the president's top foreign policy initiatives by going off half-cocked." He stared hard at Demopoulos. "Is that understood?"

Reluctantly, the analysis chief nodded. "Yes, sir. Completely understood."

Watching the uncomfortable byplay through narrowed eyes, Miranda Reynolds made a mental note to have one of her staff discreetly dig into who was really feeding Demopoulos these juicy morsels of intelligence out of Iran. She didn't buy the obvious fairy tale he'd spun for Horne. Material like that coming over the transom via some unnamed self-styled private security firm with connections in the Middle East? Not in a million years. No, she thought coldly, someone else was pulling the strings here. Someone who was poaching on her turf.

SIX

A DAY LATER

Lieutenant Colonel Dov Tamir handed over his phone to the stern-faced guard posted at the entrance to the embassy's secure intelligence room. Personal electronic devices of any kind were strictly forbidden inside. By definition, any information shared in the small, windowless room was classified at the very highest level.

He joined the handful of others who'd already arrived. Besides the ambassador himself and his chief of staff, they included the section heads responsible for consular affairs and trade. Together with Tamir, they formed the executive core of Israel's diplomatic mission in Vienna.

Tamir nodded politely to the ambassador and the others and took his seat. On paper, the square-jawed former paratrooper served as Israel's military attaché to Austria. But he wore another hat, one with far more significance at this urgent security briefing. Within the Israeli Defense Forces, the IDF, he was also a member of the Secret Liaison Unit—a group responsible for coordinating special operations with the Mossad and allied foreign intelligence outfits.

Rivka Amar was the last one to arrive. Lean and wiry, with short, curly dark hair, she was the Mossad officer attached to the embassy. She operated covertly under diplomatic cover, masquerading as a junior consular official. Once she was inside the room, she signaled the security guard to close and lock the door behind her. It latched shut with an audible click.

The ambassador waited until she took her place and then asked, "Well, Rivka, what's the situation?" He looked understandably worried. Requests from the Mossad for emergency, top-secret meetings never involved pleasant news.

"Over the past forty-eight hours, we've detected signs of an around-the-clock, close surveillance operation being mounted against this embassy," Amar said crisply. She touched a control on the keyboard in front of her. A monitor lit up. "Cameras we've covertly placed to cover every avenue of approach have confirmed our initial suspicions. Every person entering or leaving here is being monitored by unknown operatives using a variety of means—mostly by direct observation on foot or from vehicles, but also by at least one miniaturized aerial drone."

As she spoke, different pictures appeared on the large screen. Some were of cars and vans parked on neighboring streets. Others showed individuals dressed either as workmen or ordinary pedestrians loitering in front of different nearby buildings. Three were views of rooftops. Enhanced versions of these images showed what appeared to be the same tiny, rotor-driven drone perched inconspicuously near chimneys and dormers. A few of the photographs were grainy, obviously taken in poorly lit conditions at night, but most were exceptionally clear.

Tamir frowned at the monitor. Lately, he'd strongly suspected they were being watched closely by someone. But he hadn't realized the full scope of the operation until now. He swung back toward the Mossad officer. "What's your assessment of this effort?"

"It involves a significant commitment of resources," Amar told him. "We've identified at least six separate individuals among the watchers. And counted close to ten separate vehicles being used at different times. The use of remote-controlled drones is another significant indicator."

"Of what?" the ambassador asked quietly.

"That this is a highly professional operation, one organized either by a state actor or by a sophisticated terrorist group with significant capabilities," Amar answered somberly.

Miriam Weiss, the chief of the embassy's consular section, frowned. "Could this be something organized by our *friends* over at Jaurègasse?" she asked, referring to the location of the Iranian embassy in Vienna. "Maybe as a response to the recent murder of their government official? The one who was found dead at Kitzbühel?"

Amar nodded. "That is a strong possibility. What little evidence we possess suggests this man Khavari was eliminated because he was trying to contact a foreign intelligence service . . . and it would be logical for Tehran to assume he was reaching out to us, their most determined enemy."

"And are they right?" the ambassador prompted gently. "Were we trying to recruit him?"

She shook her head. "No, sir." Then she turned toward Tamir. "Unless your people in military intelligence had their eyes on Khavari?"

"Sadly not," he said. "I checked with colleagues in Jerusalem. This was not our baby."

The ambassador sighed. "So this net thrown around our doors could be blowback for some other country's espionage efforts?"

"It's likely," Tamir agreed. Besides checking with the IDF's military intelligence command, he'd also privately reached out to contacts in the CIA—to see if the mess at Kitzbühel was one of their ops gone wrong. So far, though, he wasn't getting any answers from the Americans. The current administration in Washington wasn't especially friendly to Israel, and it was increasingly obvious that the CIA and other American intelligence agencies were playing it safe.

"Wonderful," Weiss said dryly. "Here we sit in the crosshairs of those fanatics in Tehran, and this time it's not even our fault."

"Maybe," Tamir said slowly. "And maybe not."

Amar looked at him questioningly. "Meaning what, Dov?"

He nodded at the monitor, which was still showing the pictures taken by the Mossad officer's concealed cameras. "Those guys don't look at all Middle Eastern to me. More northern European or Slavic, I think. Sure, they could be disguised, but there's a limit to what you can do with wigs or hair dye, cheek pads and the rest." His fingers drummed lightly on the table as he studied the images closely. "If anything, I'd bet on them being Russian, or at least in Russian pay. They could be black ops specials brought in off the books by the GRU or the SVR."

"Perhaps carrion birds of a kind are flocking together," the ambassador suggested wryly.

"Perhaps so," Tamir agreed. Moscow was known to be extremely interested in strengthening its already close ties to the radical regime in Tehran. Ironically, Russia's embassy in Vienna was located just around the block from that of Iran, an accident of diplomatic geography that made potential cooperation between the two countries here in Austria even easier to organize and harder to detect. "It would not be the first time we've had enemies unite against us."

The ambassador nodded unhappily. "Well, then, as I see it, our immediate problem is to decide what we should do about these men who are spying on our every move."

"The situation is dangerous, sir," Rivka Amar pointed out. "And the danger will only grow with every passing day."

"How so?"

The Mossad officer gestured toward the monitor. "This hostile surveillance team is gathering an enormous amount of data about our operations here—not just our faces and those of the other embassy staff and employees, but also our vehicle registration plates, and even our regular patterns of movement." She frowned. "This could be the precursor to something even worse—like a terrorist attack either aimed directly at the embassy or at some of our people whenever they travel out into the city at large."

The ambassador nodded gravely. Terrorism was an ever-present concern for any Israeli, whether an ordinary civilian or a member of the government or military. "What is your recommendation, Rivka?"

"We should act against these watchers," she replied fiercely. "I can have a team snatch one of them off the street. A short, sharp interrogation ought to tell us who they are . . . and who they're working for."

The professional diplomats in the room—the ambassador, his chief of staff, and the two section chiefs—looked alarmed by her bold proposal. None of them were cowards, but the idea of initiating a physical confrontation on the streets of a neutral foreign capital was far outside their comfort zone. Tough action in the diplomatic world meant issuing a strongly worded protest note, not forcing a hostile agent into the back of a car and hauling him off for questioning. If anything went wrong, the embassy could easily find itself entangled in an embarrassing no-win confrontation with its host country, Austria.

Dov Tamir tamped down a grin. Amar reminded him of himself as a young soldier—fearless, aggressive, and focused on achieving victory, whatever the cost. Unfortunately, he had enough experience now to see the likely outcome here. The odds were very much against the embassy's senior paper pushers approving Amar's plan. Caution was the virtue drummed into members of the foreign service, not daring.

Warily, the ambassador turned to Tamir. "Dov?"

"Rivka's idea involves a significant amount of risk," Tamir conceded. He shrugged his shoulders. "But it's equally true that doing nothing carries its own set of hazards. So I think we should do what she suggests. Personally, I would rather be damned by the Austrians for acting on our own, than get caught with our pants down later by a terror attack we could have preempted."

There was silence in the room for a few moments. But then, slowly, almost regretfully, the ambassador shook his head. "Aggressive action seems . . . premature," he said at last. "I'm not yet persuaded the situation warrants extreme measures." Miriam Weiss and the others looked relieved.

Seeing Amar open her mouth to object, Tamir caught his Mossad colleague's eye and shook his own head slightly, almost imperceptibly. There were times when it was necessary to fight against overwhelming odds. This was not one of them. The ambassador and his senior counselors had plainly made up their minds, and it would do no good now to alienate them. She sat back in her chair, looking frustrated.

"We could file a confidential complaint with the Austrian authorities," Weiss suggested. "Surely, the local police are better equipped to handle this matter."

"That would be a mistake," Tamir warned.

"Why?" the consular chief asked, puzzled.

"Because whatever we tell them is bound to leak," he explained patiently. "Especially if the Russians are involved. We're not the only ones with contacts inside the government here. And if these people learn that we're onto their game, they'll just pull back a bit and set up a new surveillance perimeter outside our easy reach. At least now, we can watch *them* while they watch us."

The ambassador nodded in agreement. "Dov makes a good point, Miriam. For the time being, it's best if we simply watch and wait." He looked at Amar. "Please keep your eyes open, Rivka. And let me know at once if there any further developments." Unhurriedly, he rose and left the secure room, followed by Weiss and the others.

Rivka Amar waited until they were gone and then shook her head in disbelief. "So that's it?" she said indignantly. "We just sit here on our asses under virtual siege . . . and do *nothing*?"

"Welcome to the wonderful world of high-level international relations," Tamir said with a thin, dry smile.

She glared at him. "If you're trying to comfort me here, Dov, it's not working."

"No comfort intended," he told her. "Just a reality check." He shrugged. "But that doesn't mean I plan to do nothing."

"Oh?"

"I've got one card left to play," Tamir said. "An old friend and former colleague in Jerusalem named Gideon Ayish. He's a research fellow at an international think tank now. They monitor terrorist groups and terrorist-supporting governments, like Iran. In the past, I've found sharing insights and information with him to be extremely useful."

"A think tank?" Amar said pointedly. "What is it you hope this Ayish will do for us? Craft an impeccably researched position paper that will somehow persuade the ambassador to stop screwing around?"

"Not quite," Tamir said cryptically. "Gideon has a very wide range of rather unusual friends and contacts. And some of them, I suspect, do a lot more than just write research papers."

GLOBAL INSTITUTE FOR THE STUDY OF
TERRORISM, JERUSALEM, ISRAEL

LATER THAT EVENING

Gideon Ayish finished reading Dov Tamir's email and sat back with
a frown. His high forehead wrinkled in thought. His longtime friend
had used a simple personal code they'd arranged between themselves
years ago. To an outsider, it would have seemed like nothing more than
a breezy summary of Tamir's recent life in Vienna—where the usual
grind of boring government business was broken only by rare interludes
of pleasure at coffeehouses and concert halls.

The real message it conveyed was significantly more worrying.

He swiveled around in his chair to look out the windows of his
office. From here, high up the slopes of Mount Scopus, he had a view
of the Old City and the Mount of Olives. The golden-topped Dome
of the Rock gleamed, lit by the last rays of the sun setting beyond the
western hills.

Ayish steepled his fingers for a few moments, considering his options.
Then he checked his watch. At this time of day, it wouldn't take him
more than an hour to get to Ben Gurion Airport. One of the benefits of
living in a small country, he thought—though that was a cold comfort
when missiles started flying. He swung back to his desk and picked up
the phone.

His personal assistant answered it on the first ring. "Yes, Professor
Ayish?"

"I want you to book me on the next available flight to the United States," he said.

"To Washington, D.C.? Or New York?" she asked, not fazed by this sudden request. Ayish's work for the Institute often involved a great deal of overseas travel.

"Whichever will get me there the soonest," he told her. "But then I'll need a connecting flight. To Orlando."

Now he heard the surprise in her voice. "Orlando, Professor? In Florida?"

Ayish smiled ruefully. "Relax, Sarah," he reassured her. "I may be older than I would like, but I'm not slipping into my second childhood. This is a work trip, not a vacation excursion to Disney World."

SEVEN

OUTSIDE MOSCOW

THE NEXT MORNING

Built to Pavel Voronin's exacting specifications, his country home was a far cry from the usual ramshackle rustic Russian dacha. Set on a hill ninety kilometers southeast of Moscow, it was surrounded by an extensive pine forest that belonged exclusively to him. The sprawling two-story steel-and-glass villa had wall-length windows offering unimpeded views of snow-shrouded woods and the frozen Moskva River, a wide silver-gray ribbon of ice. At the touch of a button, these windows could be darkened for privacy or energy efficiency, thanks to enormously expensive experimental electrochromic technology. Modernist furniture from the most fashionable designers filled every room, along with original paintings by Kandinsky, Rothko, and other renowned abstract artists. A spacious, glass-roofed atrium held a heated swimming pool and sauna.

To avoid spoiling the image of carefree luxury, the compound's extensive security measures were kept discreetly out of sight of the main house. But anyone approaching uninvited would run head-on into defenses that included infrared cameras, motion sensors, razor wire–topped perimeter fences, armed Raven Syndicate sentries, and roving guard dog patrols. In a very real sense, Voronin's opulent weekend retreat was also a heavily guarded fortress.

Clad in an impeccably cut tweed jacket, Voronin himself waited at the dacha's front portico to greet the visitors he'd invited for this morning's secret meeting. Behind him, a pair of solid bronze doors opened into the dacha's central hall. Although it was well below freezing outside, powerful space heaters discreetly built into the portico's spiraling steel columns kept him perfectly comfortable.

Precisely on schedule, the large black Aurus Senat L700 limousine he'd dispatched to bring his guests from Moscow appeared over the crest of the hill. All-weather tires crunched softly across compacted snow as it rolled smoothly up the long, open drive and pulled in under the shelter of the portico. Powered by a Porsche-developed, twin-turbocharged 4.4 liter V8 engine, the Senat L700 model was the Russian-made equivalent of a Rolls-Royce Ghost or a top-of-the-line Cadillac. These luxury cars were ordinarily reserved for very high-ranking political leaders. Owning one as a private citizen was a mark of extraordinary power and prestige.

At Voronin's nod, two of his bodyguards stepped forward and opened the limousine's doors. Somewhat hesitantly, four middle-aged men climbed out of the luxuriously appointed passenger compartment. For a moment, they clumped together at the foot of the steps leading up into the villa, plainly unsure of what they should do next.

"Gentlemen, my name is Voronin and I'm your host. Welcome to Raven's Nest," he greeted them politely. "I'd like to thank you for so promptly responding to my invitation." Left hanging in the air was the fact that his "invitation" had been accompanied by direct orders from Russia's president, Piotr Zhdanov. With a genial smile, he waved them on ahead of him through the main doors.

Immediately, a small army of servants bustled up to relieve them of their gloves, overcoats and fur hats. More staff led them deeper into the dacha's interior and into a large, high-ceilinged living room. There, the four men stopped dead, plainly staggered by their first look at the pieces of expensive furniture and priceless art carefully arrayed around the room.

Voronin watched with carefully hidden amusement. He noted the quick glances each darted at these extravagant surroundings—glances that mingled curiosity with poorly concealed awe. He also observed that they all seemed distinctly uneasy in civilian business suits and ties instead of their more familiar and comfortable military uniforms.

He nodded to himself in satisfaction.

These men were quite obviously out of their depth, which was exactly what he had intended. Centuries of tradition inclined officers in Russia's armed forces to see themselves as a superior caste—as sacred guardians of the State set high above the grubby, inconsequential world of commerce and private enterprise. It was a fable, of course, he knew, but one that held a powerful grip on every Russian military man's mind. Breaking this myth was essential to his plans.

Voronin motioned to a set of leather high-backed chairs arranged in a conversational semicircle around a mirrored glass coffee table. "Please sit down, gentlemen."

Warily, they obeyed, though clearly uncertain of the proper etiquette involved here. Everything about this unusual situation indicated that their "host"—civilian or not—stood far above them in wealth and position and power. In the circumstances, his extravagant politeness seemed somehow ominous.

Voronin himself casually strolled around the room while another group of his servants served drinks—vodka, whiskey, or brandy to each guest's preference. There was a moment of worried silence as each man suddenly realized he'd been offered only his personal favorite brand. The implication was clear and chilling: Their formidable host undoubtedly knew a great deal about them. Far more than he should.

Once the four men had their drinks, the servants withdrew. As the doors closed behind them, grim-faced bodyguards took up their posts at every entrance. Slight bulges marked the weapons concealed under their suit coats.

Voronin moved out to the middle of the room. For a long moment, he studied his guests without speaking. Under his silent, pale-eyed gaze, they fidgeted slightly in their chairs, adjusting ties or shirt cuffs or quietly clearing their throats—all telltale signs of anxiety.

At last, he broke the increasingly uncomfortable silence. "I know that you must be wondering why you're here."

After glancing at his colleagues, the oldest man among them, a colonel in the Ministry of Defense's 12th Main Directorate named Krylov, nodded carefully. "Yes, sir."

Voronin smiled broadly. "It's quite simple, Mikhail Sergeyevich. You've all been temporarily assigned to my firm, the Raven Syndicate, for a very special project—a project of enormous importance to the Motherland . . . and to President Zhdanov personally."

His guests exchanged puzzled glances. There were occasions when officers in the ground forces or even air force pilots might find themselves posted to private industrial firms—to provide professional advice on the development of new armored fighting vehicles or combat aircraft, for example. But that was never the case for soldiers from their particular, highly specialized, and tightly controlled branches of the armed forces. Like Krylov, two of them served in the 12th Main Directorate, which was directly responsible for the security of Russia's nuclear weapons stockpiles. The fourth man was a weapons specialist in the Strategic Rocket Forces, which controlled its ICBMs.

Krylov put his drink down untasted. "I don't quite understand what it is you expect us to be able to do for this Raven Syndicate of yours, Mr. Voronin. For one thing, our respective security clearances strictly forbid the disclosure of any information—"

"Your clearances forbid the *unauthorized* disclosure of information," Voronin interrupted. He shrugged. "But as it happens, I've been granted the necessary authority by the president himself. You now work for me. And for me alone."

He smiled again, this time at the shock on their faces. "Relax, gentlemen. I'm aware that this situation is unprecedented, but I think you'll find the terms entirely acceptable."

"How so?" Krylov asked bluntly.

"From this moment forward, your pay will be ten times that of your regular military salaries," Voronin said. "And you will earn substantial bonuses upon the successful completion of this special project. Bonuses on the order of two hundred million rubles each."

One of the younger officers whistled involuntarily. Two hundred million rubles was the equivalent of roughly 250,000 American dollars. Like everyone responsible for Russia's nuclear weapons and strategic missiles, they were better paid than those serving in conventional branches of the armed forces—but a promised bonus of that size still represented nearly ten years' pay.

Krylov frowned. "Your offer is generous indeed. But what exactly do you want in return?"

"You'll be thoroughly briefed," Voronin assured him. He snapped his fingers once. An aide hurried over from the far end of the living room with a briefcase. Opening it, the young man handed out copies of a single page document and pens. "But first, I must ask each of you to sign these agreements." His voice hardened slightly. "You'll find them perfectly clear and quite easy to understand, without any of the usual legal gibberish."

The four officers turned pale when they saw what he meant. In the plainest possible terms, they were being sworn to absolute secrecy for life. Any breach of security involving the operation code-named MIDNIGHT, however small, however unintentional, would result in death.

Voronin nodded coolly to them. "Let me assure you that I mean what I say. If you betray me or my secrets, there will be no appeal to any higher authority. There will be absolutely no recourse or reprieve. And should it prove necessary, I will personally act as your only judge, jury, and executioner."

AVALON HOUSE, WINTER PARK, FLORIDA

A DAY LATER

Nick Flynn took the steps of the mansion's wide, curving staircase two at a time. Besides several suites set aside for Quartet Directorate agents who needed rest and recuperation between field assignments, the upper floor held several other rooms used on relatively rare occasions—including a private study that had once belonged to the prominent New York banker who'd first had Avalon House built. As the decades passed, the room's leather chairs had grown rather worn and shabby, though they were still comfortable. Four allocated its funds to operations, not fashionable décor.

Two other men were waiting for him in the study. One was Fox. The other was a short, older man with a high forehead and wispy tufts of bright white hair. They rose to greet him.

"Nick, this is Professor Gideon Ayish," Fox said quietly. "He's just flown in from Jerusalem."

"Oh?" Flynn asked, shaking hands with the newcomer. He hid a moment's surprise. For an academic type, Ayish had one hell of a grip.

Somehow, the other man read his mind. "I may not be in the first flush of youth, Mr. Flynn," he said good-naturedly. "But perhaps that doesn't mean as much as it seems, eh?"

"I'll let you know when I get the circulation back in my fingers, Professor," Flynn told him with a quick grin of his own.

They all sat down. "Gideon is Four's head of station in Israel," Fox explained. "But before joining us, he had a very active career in the

IDF—serving with some of its most lethal and effective special operations units."

Flynn nodded his understanding. The Quartet Directorate drew its personnel from a variety of sources. Some were disenchanted veterans of various official intelligence agencies. Others, like him and apparently this guy Ayish, too, were ex-military, usually with a set of very specialized skills. A small number were recruited directly from civilian life by Four's talent scouts.

He looked from one man to the other. "So does this little get-together have anything to do with my plan to put people on the ground inside Iran?" he asked.

"Not directly," Fox answered. He took off his glasses, polished them briefly, and then put them back on. "I'm afraid your proposal is still under debate, Nick. You've got Gideon's vote, but there are a couple of others who aren't yet convinced such a risky operation is worth it, especially since we can't guarantee a payoff in actionable intelligence."

Flynn frowned. One of the things that had drawn him to Four in the first place was Fox's guarantee that he would be allowed room for independent action, without being continually held back or second-guessed by superiors. Coming as it did after he'd been railroaded by both the CIA and the Air Force brass for making them look bad that had been a mighty attractive prospect. He'd hate to find out it was all bullshit, like so many of the bogus promises made by armed forces recruiters through the ages in order to get their prospects to sign on the dotted line.

"If there's such a thing as a sure bet in the intelligence business, I've never seen it," he pointed out stiffly.

"True," Ayish agreed. "Which is why I'm confident you'll be given the green light before too long." He shrugged. "Remember, there are few enough of us in Four as it is. Sometimes that makes it difficult for those of us held out of the field by age or injury to easily sign off on sending younger men and women into such grave danger. But the worriers will get there in the end. Just give them a little more time to wrestle their consciences into submission. Eventually, necessity will triumph over caution."

Flynn sighed. "And in the meantime, I just sit here and twiddle my thumbs?"

"Not quite," Fox assured him. "Thanks to new intelligence supplied by Gideon here, we might have a good chance to learn more about the Russians who seem to be working so closely with Tehran on this mysterious tanker project."

"Really?"

"Really, Mr. Flynn," Ayish said. Calmly, he outlined what he'd been told about the sophisticated surveillance operation now being run against Israel's embassy in Vienna.

Flynn looked back at Fox. "And you think these mysterious watchers are some of the same guys I ran into?"

"The ones who killed Arif Khavari and almost blew your head off?" Fox nodded. "Yes, I do. The timing's too coincidental for me to think anything else. These people must believe Khavari was working for the Israelis. Why else would anyone mount such an elaborate surveillance effort against their embassy within twenty-four hours of his death?"

Flynn nodded. "Yeah, I see how that fits." His eyes narrowed. "So, what's your plan?"

"Well, as a first step, we would need you to return to Austria," Ayish said. "Once you're on the ground there, the operation I have in mind becomes feasible."

Flynn stared at him. "And exactly what kind of operation are we talking about here?" he demanded.

"A fishing expedition of sorts," the professor replied evenly.

"With me as the bait," Flynn realized.

"Yes," Ayish admitted.

Flynn shot him a lopsided grin. "Oh, swell." He shook his head in disbelief. "Just so you know, I did a lot of fishing with my grandfather when I was a kid. And I don't remember ever seeing a worm that was worth spit when we were done."

EIGHT

NEAR THE ISRAELI EMBASSY, VIENNA

TWO DAYS LATER

The district around Israel's embassy was a mix of mostly nineteenth- and twentieth-century structures. Some were elegant homes in brick or stucco or stone, now usually broken up into separate flats and business offices. Others were plainer, slab-sided concrete apartment blocks, though even these were often lined by open-air balconies whose window boxes, in the summer months, would be awash in bright flowers. Most of these buildings backed onto yards full of trees and gardens—currently bare-limbed and dormant under gray winter skies.

Several streets over from the embassy, a four-story-high Art Nouveau building was under extensive renovation. Scaffolding and debris netting obscured its ornate exterior. The original owners had run out of money halfway through the project, leaving the partially gutted structure to fester for several months as an eyesore in the neighborhood. Spray-painted graffiti—a mix of art and obscenity—covered a wood fence erected around its ground floor. Then, about a week ago, new owners had bought the building, apparently with the intention of finishing the long-delayed renovation effort. So far, however, the only sign of any new work was a dusty blue electrician's van parked along the curb just outside the construction fence.

Inside the back of the windowless van, Viktor Skoblin rubbed at his bleary eyes. Then he took another long drag of his cigarette. Irritably, he stubbed it out on a workbench that ran the length of the compartment, adding another scorch mark to the dozens already scattered across its rough surface. Maintaining around-the-clock surveillance on the Israelis with his team's limited manpower meant twelve-hour shifts for everyone.

He scowled. At least the men he'd assigned as outside watchers were able to move around. In fact, it was vital. Periodic changes of clothing, position, and even vehicles were necessary to make it harder for those in the embassy to figure out they were being spied on. Unfortunately, the same relative freedom didn't apply to him. As the Raven Syndicate's senior operative in Vienna, it was his task to coordinate the whole operation. And only the radios and computer gear crammed into the back of the van made that possible.

With a grunt, Skoblin squirmed around in his chair, making yet another futile effort to make himself more comfortable in the cheap folding seat. For a man of his large build and overall size, being forced to spend hours locked inside this cramped vehicle felt like some new form of torture.

Abruptly, the voice of one of his watchers crackled through his headset. "*Roter Kurier zum Versand. Red Courier to Dispatch.*"

Skoblin keyed his mike. "Dispatch here. Go ahead, Red Courier." Although their transmissions were automatically encrypted and sent over little-used frequencies, they stuck to German. There was no point in risking anyone overhearing a barrage of Russian-language radio calls over the airwaves of Austria's capital city.

"*I've got a new delivery just arriving,*" the watcher reported. "*It could be a hot item. Do you want the specifications?*"

The big man tapped a key on his laptop, bringing up a street map on the screen. Icons showed the assigned positions of every Raven Syndicate agent currently on surveillance duty around the Israeli embassy. And right now, the former GRU captain tagged as Red Courier for this shift should have an excellent view along the street out in front of the embassy building. "Copy that, Red Courier," he radioed.

"*On the way*," the other man replied tersely.

A new window opened on Skoblin's laptop. Immediately, the zoomed-in cellphone video uploaded by his underling started playing. Though slightly jerky, it was still clear enough to make out details. He watched closely as a sky-blue sedan, a Skoda Octavia, drove up and parked directly across from the embassy's front door. That was a spot reserved for important and expected visitors.

He tugged at his chin. By itself, the car make meant nothing. The Czech-manufactured Octavia was one of the bestselling automobiles in Austria, with thousands on Vienna's crowded streets at any one time. On the other hand, he thought, it was just the sort of unobtrusive vehicle he'd have chosen himself if he wanted to avoid drawing unwelcome attention. In contrast, the genuine diplomats assigned to the embassy seemed to favor more expensive, more conspicuous BMWs, Audis, and Mercedes.

On the screen, a fit-looking man emerged from the car and walked across the street to the embassy. He flashed an ID to the guard on duty there and went straight in.

Skoblin froze the thirty-second video, ran it backward, and then watched it intently a second time. Somehow, this new visitor didn't strike him as being just an ordinary diplomat or a businessman, and he was definitely not a tourist. His movements were too careful, too precise . . . too *controlled*—as though he were completely aware of his surroundings at all times. In the Russian's experience that was the mark of a soldier, especially one with experience operating deep in hostile territory.

No, he thought darkly, something about this man rang a very loud bell in his subconscious. An alarm bell.

Quickly, Skoblin copied individual frames from the cellphone video into a separate folder—selecting only images that clearly showed the newcomer's face. Once that was done, he fed them into a special facial recognition program supplied by the Raven Syndicate's computer specialists. Several seconds passed while this program compared his chosen images pixel by pixel with the photographs he'd snapped just before shooting Arif Khavari.

They matched.

A cruel, satisfied smile settled on the ex–Spetsnaz officer's wide face. "Finally," he growled. His thick fingers pounded across the laptop's keyboard as he rapidly composed a short, coded alert message to Moscow: *PRIMARY TARGET SPOTTED. WILL ENGAGE AND DESTROY AT FIRST AVAILABLE OPPORTUNITY.*

THAT SAME TIME

Nick Flynn sat down across from Lieutenant Colonel Dov Tamir. Although he wore civilian clothes at the moment, the blunt-featured IDF officer's past service in Israel's elite parachute unit was readily apparent. The walls of his small, but well furnished office were covered with photographs showing Tamir and others in the maroon berets, red-brown boots, and winged snake shoulder flashes of the Paratroopers Brigade.

The Israeli looked up from the passport and other documents Flynn had offered to confirm his identity. They named him as Jonathan Schmidt, an international business consultant. That was the same legend, or cover, he'd used during the aborted rendezvous with Khavari.

"These are nice work, Mr. . . . *Schmidt*," Tamir said dryly, sliding the papers back across his desk. "Very convincing. Your document specialists in Washington are quite skilled."

"Thanks," Flynn acknowledged with a wry smile of his own. He slid the false passport and other materials back into his jacket. He knew that Gideon Ayish had told his old friend that he was actually an operative for an unnamed "friendly outfit." Plainly, Tamir assumed that meant he was working either for the CIA or one of the Pentagon's own intelligence organizations, like the Defense Intelligence Agency. But he also knew the Israeli lieutenant colonel wouldn't push any harder on the subject, since Ayish's message introducing Flynn had emphasized the need for absolute discretion.

"So, then. I understand from our mutual friend that you have a story to tell me?" Tamir said quietly.

Flynn nodded. "Yep, that I do." He lowered his own voice slightly. "Now, while we haven't been able to pin down more details yet, we still learned something from Arif Khavari that we think your country needs to know. And pronto."

"Go on," Tamir said tightly. The fact that he didn't ask who Khavari was spoke volumes. Clearly, the Israelis had already connected the surveillance op against their embassy to the Iranian's death.

Clearly and coherently, Flynn walked through exactly what he'd been told by Khavari—leaving out only the fact that he'd been the one with the Iranian when he'd been murdered. If this sparked action by Jerusalem to probe Tehran's mysterious tanker project too, so much the better. One of the strengths of the Quartet Directorate was that it didn't play institutional power games. Four didn't care who got credit for stopping threats against the West and its allies . . . only that they *were* stopped and stopped cold.

When he finished, Tamir sat silent for a few moments with his head bowed in thought, obviously mulling over what he'd just learned. Then he shook his head and looked up at Flynn. "Worrying indeed," he commented. "And very strange also."

"Then we're on the same page," Flynn agreed.

"Naturally, I'm grateful that you've shared this information," Tamir said carefully. "But at the same time, I can't help being puzzled by this sudden burst of candor now." His mouth twisted slightly. "Especially since my earlier attempts to reach out unofficially to my best contacts in Washington were met with such absolute and profound silence. To be honest, I'd started wondering if I should put on a leper's rags and have a bell rung before me in warning when dealing with your country."

Flynn bit down on a piece of choice profanity. Knowing that the CIA's paper-pushing ass-kissers had decided to do diddly-squat with the intelligence Fox had surreptitiously passed to them was bad enough. Learning now that Langley's bureaucrats had also apparently decided to conceal this information from America's most important ally in the Middle East was even more infuriating.

Tamir studied his face. "You seem surprised, Mr. . . . . Schmidt."

With an effort, Flynn managed to shrug and smile slightly. "A little. But I guess this is just one of those occasional screwups where the right hand doesn't know shit about what the left hand is actually doing."

From the Israeli officer's pained nod, he knew he'd scored a point. If anything, the other man probably saw this as further confirmation that Flynn worked for some part of America's labyrinthine intelligence community—which was infamous around the world for its occasional inefficiency and costly duplication of effort.

"Still, you have my thanks for this," Tamir assured him when he got up to go. "And if there is anything I can do for you in return, just ask."

"As a matter of fact, there is," Flynn said calmly.

"Oh?"

Flynn looked squarely at him. "Well, I'd sure appreciate it if you could walk me out of the building and to my car to say goodbye."

Tamir stared at him, unable to hide his surprise. "I'm quite certain that Gideon told you that we were being kept under extremely close watch here," he said slowly.

"Yeah, he did," Flynn assured him matter-of-factly.

"Then you must know that being seen with me will be a clear signal that you're anything but a routine visitor to this embassy," the other man pointed out. "You might as well put up a billboard advertising your connection to secret intelligence."

Flynn nodded. "Yep. That's kind of the whole point." He let a little of his native Texas drawl emerge. "Because while it's been nice meeting you, Colonel, this ain't *just* a social call. From here on out, I've got my own set of orders to obey."

Dov Tamir shook his head with unconcealed astonishment. From the look on his face, he was obviously convinced that his American guest—and those who'd given him his orders—might very well be completely crazy.

Privately, Flynn wasn't so sure he was wrong.

NINE

THAT SAME TIME

Skoblin watched the man he'd failed to kill at Kitzbühel come out of the embassy. The stranger had company with him this time, the Israeli military attaché. His eyes narrowed. Tamir was known to be a high-ranking IDF spy as a well as a soldier. Monitoring his activities had been one of the surveillance team's highest priorities.

He thought fast. Voronin's current orders left no room for discretion. He and his men were expected to immediately eliminate the enemy agent who'd met with Khavari. Until now, accomplishing this task had seemed relatively straightforward, if not entirely risk-free.

Skoblin had planned to carry out the hit using a "box group"—one motorcycle rider and a pair of Syndicate operatives in a separate car. The technique was time-tested and uncomplicated: wait until the intended target's vehicle was stuck behind traffic at a red light, and then pin him in from behind with the Syndicate-driven car. Once that was done, their motorcyclist would simply pull up beside the stopped car and open fire with a concealed Steyr 9mm machine pistol at point-blank range. A messy and very public method of assassination to be sure, but one that was also very certain. And in all the ensuing confusion and chaos, the gunman should easily be able to evade any immediate pursuit, ditch his motorcycle, and get clear. All of the vehicles Skoblin and his men were using had been thoroughly "sanitized," stripped of any serial numbers that would identify their real owners. None could be traced back to the Raven Syndicate.

But now they had clear confirmation that Khavari's contact was an IDF military intelligence agent run by Dov Tamir. So, Skoblin wondered, wouldn't it be wiser to first try to find out how deeply the Israelis had already penetrated MIDNIGHT's security? And perhaps even learn more about Jerusalem's next planned moves? True, making a snatch off Vienna's streets would be more complicated than a quick hit, but it could be done. Anyway, he thought coldly, he could always put a bullet in the back of the Israeli spy's head once they'd squeezed him dry. Considering the inconvenience the bastard had already caused them, that would be a pleasure.

"*The package is on the move,*" one of his watchers radioed. "*Heading west on Anton-Frank-Gasse.*"

Skoblin grimaced. He needed time to persuade the Syndicate's Moscow headquarters to approve an attempt to kidnap this man, rather than simply gunning him down. For now, he decided to set his chosen hit team in motion, but to hold off on giving them the kill order until he heard back from Voronin.

Quickly, he studied the detailed city map open on his laptop. Fortunately, the streets around Israel's embassy were all one-way, which made it much easier to discreetly vector his men onto the enemy agent's tail. He keyed his mike. "Dispatch to Uber One-Five. Pick up your next customer near Sternwarterstrasse."

"*Understood, Dispatch,*" Yuri Linnik, the driver of the "box" car he'd designated, replied immediately. Like Skoblin, Linnik and his partner Zaitsev were ex-Spetsnaz officers who'd been recruited into the Raven Syndicate. They were using a silver BMW with a phony Uber windshield sticker. With Zaitsev posing as a passenger, this was an excellent cover. Uber cars were a common sight in Vienna.

"Flower Delivery, this is Dispatch," Skoblin continued, calling the Syndicate motorcycle rider waiting along a nearby side street. "Tag Uber One. Your customer wants *uncut* roses."

"*Copy that*," the rider said curtly, acknowledging the coded directive to join Linnik and Zaitsev in following the enemy agent, but to wait for further orders before carrying out the planned attack. Dmitri Fadeyev was a veteran of the GRU's special assassination force, Unit 29155, with several high-profile kills to his credit. "*I have Uber One-Five and the customer in sight. Joining the parade now.*"

Skoblin checked the digital map on his laptop. The icons representing his box group's car and motorcycle were in motion—falling in behind the target's sky-blue Skoda sedan as it turned right onto another narrow street two blocks north of Israel's embassy. That suggested Tamir's man might be headed east, toward Vienna's Innere Stadt, the old city.

Thinking hard, he lit another cigarette. Linnik, Zaitsev, and Fadeyev shouldn't have much trouble keeping the enemy agent in sight on those more congested streets . . . but why take chances? He decided to add one more element to the force he'd assembled. Swiftly, he issued new instructions to an operative posted on a rooftop about a kilometer away. In moments, another icon began moving on his map. This one marked the position of the surveillance team's miniature aerial drone.

Skoblin nodded to himself in satisfaction. Boxed in from above and behind, the man they were after was as good as dead or captured. Now it was just a matter of waiting for Voronin to make up his mind about which of those two fates it was to be.

IN THE WÄHRING DISTRICT, VIENNA

THAT SAME TIME

Nick Flynn glanced up at his rearview mirror. Both the BMW and the motorcycle he'd spotted earlier were still behind him, lagging back a little to keep a couple of other cars or trucks between them. The guys tailing him were good. If he hadn't known beforehand what to expect, he might have missed them completely.

Carefully, he turned left onto another one-way street heading east. In this part of Vienna, most roads ran in only one direction—a direction that usually reversed at the beginning of each new block. It was effectively impossible to drive in a straight line for very long. Getting anywhere meant zig-zagging through the district, turning right and then left and then right and left again just to make any progress at all.

Flynn smiled ruefully. This street layout might have been tailor-made to make it difficult for anyone to speed . . . or to shake off an unwanted tail. Maybe that was just as well, he thought. It definitely made it easier for him to play the role he'd been assigned in today's little drama, wriggling like a fat, dumb worm. At least for a little while longer.

Elevated train tracks crossed the road ahead. Carried on arches of stone and brick, they ran north and south right through the heart of Austria's capital city. And beyond the tracks, he could see the twin stone towers of a neo-Gothic-style church soaring nearly three hundred feet above the ground.

Unhurriedly, Flynn made another turn, this time onto a broad avenue. Six lanes divided by a tree-lined median carried traffic in both directions. This was a belt road which marked the border between the Währing District and the rest of the city. He tapped the Skoda's turn signal and moved over to the leftmost lane. Behind him, the BMW and motorcycle did the same.

A light ahead turned red.

Flynn slowed to a stop behind a large white Volkswagen cargo van. He kept his eyes fixed on the Skoda's rearview mirror. If these guys were going to jump him, this was exactly the kind of setup they'd be looking for. If either the BMW or that motorcycle made a move to come up alongside him, he figured he'd only have a couple of seconds at most to decide how to react. With his left hand, he gripped the steering wheel a little tighter. His right hand slid inside his unzipped jacket and touched the butt of the compact Glock 19 he was carrying in a shoulder holster.

The light turned green.

Flynn breathed out again. He turned left to cross under the elevated railway line and drive southeast on Währinger Strasse. A single lane of traffic ran in each direction, separated by two sets of rails set in the pavement down the center of the street. Hundreds of electrified trams were a major component of Vienna's public transportation system, and one of the city's nearly thirty tram lines ran along this road.

He saw the BMW appear again a couple of car lengths behind him, followed a second or two later by the motorcycle. So far, so good. But the timing from here on out was going to be tight. Really tight.

Flynn passed a large white building that housed the Vienna Volksoper, the People's Opera, with high arched windows above a street-side portico. Several hundred yards behind him now, he caught sight of a red-and-white tram as it turned onto Währinger Strasse. Right on schedule, he thought with satisfaction.

He passed a small park on the right with its trees standing bare and forlorn under the gray cloud-covered sky. Off to the left, another big structure loomed—part of the University of Vienna. He deliberately slowed down just a little to let the trailing BMW and motorcycle close up a bit. For the moment, it was vital that they stay on his tail.

Just past the university building, Flynn took a sharp left, curving around onto a one-way street that led almost straight back in the direction he'd just come. He tapped the gas pedal, speeding up again. A slight smile crossed his face when he caught sight of both of his persistent followers hurrying around the bend after him. Right now, he'd bet they were starting to sweat. This narrow road ran straight to the American embassy. And whatever unpleasantness they had planned for him would be a complete nonstarter if he pulled in and parked under the watchful gaze of the embassy's U.S. Marine guards.

But instead of continuing on toward the embassy, he made another left turn to drive back toward Währinger Strasse on a side street that paralleled the northern side of the massive university building. It was exactly the sort of precautionary circling maneuver anyone checking to see if he were being tailed would make. Both the BMW and the motorcycle reacted by slowing down a little and dropping back a few yards.

Flynn headed on down the little road. Dozens of cars, most belonging to faculty members, were parked in angled spots on the left. At this time of day, every place was taken. *Here we go*, he realized, feeling his pulse accelerate. He flashed his headlights once.

In response to his signal, a dark green Audi four-door sedan backed out of its parking place near the end of the block and drove away. It turned the corner at the intersection and disappeared.

Without hesitating, Flynn pulled straight into the now-empty spot, killed the Skoda's engine, and hopped out. He didn't bother wasting time locking the car. Nothing inside would tie it to him or to the Quartet Directorate. Instead, he ran to the intersection. There, taking advantage of a momentary break in the traffic, he darted south across Währinger Strasse. Horns blared in sharp protest, but he ignored them.

About fifty yards away, the tram he'd seen earlier was just arriving at its next scheduled stop. Brakes squealed shrilly as it slowed and then came to rest. Doors *whooshed* open. He gritted his teeth, lowered his head and ran even faster.

With a final burst of speed, Flynn jumped aboard the last car just as the doors closed. Frantically, he grabbed a railing next to the door to keep from colliding with the elderly woman who'd gotten on just ahead of him. She glared at him in outrage. *"Entschuldigen Sie, gnädige Frau. Ich bin in Eile,"* he apologized. "Excuse me, ma'am. I'm in a hurry."

"So viel liegt auf der Hand, junger Mann!" she said tartly. "That much is rather obvious, young man!" With a dismissive sniff, she turned away and moved down the aisle toward an empty seat.

Great, Flynn thought wryly. This was one more chapter to add to his planned magnum opus, *How Not to Win Friends and Influence People in Foreign Countries.* He glanced back through the tram's rear window as it pulled away. The silver BMW that had been following him had braked to a halt at the intersection he'd just sprinted across— apparently unwilling to make an illegal left-hand turn in front of so many witnesses, especially with a police patrol car parked near the tram stop. As he watched, it turned right instead and accelerated away up the street.

He smiled to himself. By the time that BMW managed to make a U-turn in this traffic, it would be stuck blocks behind the moving tram.

The motorcycle rider tailing him was bolder. Risking a traffic ticket, he revved his engine and sped across the street to slot in behind the tram. He got lucky. Either the cops weren't looking in his direction, or they'd simply decided the biker's illegal turn wasn't worth making a fuss over.

Flynn shrugged. One down. And another to go.

THAT SAME TIME

Watching the situation unfold both on his digital map and in real time video from the drone flying overhead, Skoblin snarled a litany of obscenities. Linnik and Zaitsev were out of the picture for now.

A new message from Voronin popped up on the side of his laptop's screen: CAPTURE REQUEST DENIED. EXECUTE YOUR ORIGINAL ORDERS.

Skoblin stared at the decrypted message in disbelief. Moscow's timing was impeccably bad. A minute ago, it would have been relatively easy to carry out a simple assassination. Now, with two members of his kill team completely out of position and still headed in the wrong direction, it would be much harder. Furiously, he clicked his mike. "Fadeyev! Do you have a shot at the target?" he demanded.

"*Maybe*," the other man's voice said over the purring roar of his motorcycle engine. "*But it wouldn't be clean. I'd hit a lot of other people on the tram.*"

"*Der'mo.* Shit," Skoblin muttered. The ex-GRU assassin's assessment was undoubtedly correct. Firing a long burst of 9mm rounds into the back of the tram would be certain to kill or wound many of its passengers—turning what was supposed to be a carefully targeted hit into a major terrorist incident. And though Voronin wouldn't shed any tears over the deaths of innocents, he'd be furious if Skoblin and his team triggered a high-profile international counterterrorist investigation that could threaten the Raven Syndicate's operations. "Hold off for now," he ordered. "But stick with that tram. The line ends at the Schottentor, so this bastard will have to get off there."

"He could be making for the U-bahn," Fadeyev warned. *"There's an entrance to the U2 line at the station."*

Mother of God, Skoblin thought. The other man was right. He'd counted on their drone to keep the enemy agent in sight even if he managed to evade all his other tails. That wouldn't be possible if the man switched to Vienna's subway system. They would lose him completely. He felt cold. Voronin would never overlook a failure of that magnitude. He leaned forward. "Listen closely, Dmitri. If he makes a break for the U-bahn, you dump that goddamned motorcycle and stick with him."

"Got it." There was a brief pause. *"And then?"*

Skoblin gritted his teeth. "He can't ride the fucking subway forever. So the moment, he's back out in the open, you take your first clear shot and put him down. Is that understood?"

"Understood," Fadeyev acknowledged calmly.

Skoblin sat back, glowering at the drone's eye view of the red-and-white tram as it squealed and rattled toward the end of Währinger Strasse. This situation was quickly spinning out of his control.

TEN

THAT SAME TIME

Nick Flynn edged his way toward the front of the crowded tram car as it swung onto tracks that ran around an elongated oval at the intersection of several major streets. Schottentor, the Scottish Gate, was once a part of Vienna's massive medieval walls. But those fortifications had all been pulled down in the mid-nineteenth century. They had been replaced by the Ringstrasse, the Ring Road, a wide and beautiful boulevard that encircled the core of the old city—with its ornate palaces, public buildings, museums, and churches.

The tram shuddered to a stop.

Flynn let several of the other passengers get off first before making his move. Instead, he stood aside until people waiting to board were starting to swarm around the door. Schottentor was the terminus for ten separate lines, so trams were constantly arriving and departing. Satisfied that he had enough cover, he stepped out onto the platform and, as politely as possible, pushed right in among the milling crowds. There was no sense giving the motorcycle rider still on his tail an easy shot.

A quick glance over his shoulder showed his pursuer halted indecisively along a narrow curb between the street and the tram tracks. Although a helmet with a tinted face shield hid the man's expression, Flynn could read frustration and anger in the rigid set of his shoulders. *Sucks to be you, amigo,* he thought coolly, before turning back and striding on faster toward the other side of the station.

He dodged around a couple of lost-looking British tourists consulting a Vienna transit map and came out on the far edge of the platform. Moments later, a southbound tram glided in along tracks that paralleled the broad Ringstrasse. He nodded in satisfaction. There came his next ride . . . exactly as planned.

As soon as the flood of debarking passengers ebbed, Flynn made his way onboard and took a window seat. His last glimpse of the motorcyclist who'd been dogging his heels for so long was of the man slamming his fist down repeatedly on his handlebars in exasperation.

Flynn smiled. Along this stretch of the grand boulevard, cars, trucks, and motorcycles were only allowed to travel northbound. There was no way his pursuer could follow him now. "One more down," he said quietly to himself.

RAVEN SURVEILLANCE VAN

THAT SAME TIME

Skoblin watched the new tram pull away down the Ringstrasse in disbelief. He had the sudden, uneasy feeling that he'd just seen his death warrant being signed. "Keep after him," he radioed the drone operator.

"*That's no problem,*" the other man assured him. "*My little bird has plenty of battery power left. I'll keep this guy in sight until you can vector the others back onto him.*"

Skoblin grimaced. So far, they'd been tricked at every turn by this man. He'd managed to shake off every ground-based tail with what appeared to be consummate ease.

Sweating now, he followed the tram as it trundled onward around the Ringstrasse. There had to be something more he could do, he thought desperately. But what?

"*Dispatch, this is Raven Eye,*" he heard the drone operator report suddenly. "*The target has left the tram. He's back on foot again.*"

Skoblin gritted his teeth. As he watched, the drone operator toggled his onboard camera, zooming in to give him a closer look. Yes, that was definitely the same self-assured prick he'd identified outside the Israeli embassy. And now here he was strolling confidently across the Ringstrasse between cars stalled in heavy traffic as though he didn't have a worry in the world. "What the hell is this *etot skol'zkiy ublyudok*, this slippery bastard, up to now?" he growled softly.

Tracked silently by the tiny drone flying unobtrusively a couple of hundred feet above him, the man headed directly toward a set of arched gateways set in one long wing of the Hofburg Palace. Beyond those arches, Skoblin knew, was a vast inner courtyard, and then, through more gates, the other side of the enormous palace complex. It was a common and scenic shortcut from the Ringstrasse into the very heart of the inner city.

He swore luridly again. Vienna's medieval core was laced with narrow winding streets, many of them set aside solely for foot traffic. Dozens of shops and stores, coffeehouses, and restaurants were nestled among its historic churches and museums. It was the perfect place for someone being followed to disappear, especially someone only under aerial surveillance. A quick duck into a shop or café with a restroom, a few hasty changes of clothing, and, hey presto, out would come a brand-new man. Human watchers would still have a shot at spotting someone they'd been tailing for a while, because it was difficult to disguise a distinctive gait or even the set of one's shoulders. But a camera, especially one mounted on a distant, moving platform, might easily be fooled.

Skoblin reacted quickly to this horrifying realization. He snapped out a series of new instructions to the several observers still deployed around the Israeli embassy. They were to leave their current posts immediately and drive straight to the Innere Stadt. By dispersing in a rough perimeter around the old city, there was at least a small chance that one of his team might be fortunate enough to spot, follow, and then kill this enemy agent who'd already caused them so much trouble. He licked his lips nervously. He'd better damned well get lucky. Because if this man escaped, Voronin would show him no mercy.

A SHORT TIME LATER

The spire-topped clock tower of St. Michael's Church climbed nearly eighty meters into the air. Its windows overlooked a wide cobblestoned plaza. The Hofburg Palace's famous Spanish Riding School and its St. Michael's Wing formed the expanse's western arc. Slightly less ornate, but equally imposing, buildings separated by four narrow streets enclosed the remainder of the Michaelerplatz. St. Michael's itself was one of the most ancient churches in the city. Portions of the structure went back to the thirteenth century. And though the clock tower was a somewhat later addition, its lower levels were still around seven hundred years old.

Two-thirds of the way up the tower, Tadeusz Kossak gently eased one of the narrow, high-arched windows partway open. For safety, it had long been painted and puttied closed, but a few minutes' work with a sharp knife had stripped those layers away. When the window was open far enough, he knelt down and picked up a scoped, magazine-fed rifle. It had a black polymer handgrip and handguard, and a gray metal barrel and receiver.

Kossak checked his watch. *It should be very soon*, he thought, if even half of this complicated plan played out as expected. He tucked the rifle's butt stock firmly against his shoulder and sighted through the scope. Its crosshairs settled on the centermost arch of the palace gates across the square. As he watched, a lean, dark-haired man walked out through the gate and into the open.

A pleased smile crossed his weather-beaten face. The American was right on time. Which, in turn, should mean—

Kossak raised his aiming point, scanning the sky above the Michael-erplatz. There. A tiny drone hovered noiselessly in the air, held aloft by four rotors. He zeroed in, breathed out, and gently squeezed the trigger of his Sig Sauer PCP air rifle. *Pop.* Then, rapidly, he fired two more times. *Pop-pop.*

Hit three times by .22-caliber hollow-point hunting pellets moving at seven hundred feet per second, the drone staggered in midair. Shards of shattered plastic flew away from each impact point. One after another, three of the four rotors stopped. Tumbling out of control, the dying drone spun around and around all the way down to the ground and smacked hard into the cobblestones.

Kossak nodded to himself in satisfaction. Scratch one robotic spy. He lowered his air rifle and closed the window. Taking out a target at sixty meters was not an especially difficult task for a sniper who'd spent years in Poland's elite special forces before joining the Quartet Directorate. Still, he always enjoyed the chance to exercise his shooting skills . . . even using a weapon better suited to killing squirrels than to actual combat. Action of any kind was better than the dull routine of ordinary civilian life. It kept him sharp and focused.

F lynn saw the smashed drone clatter to the ground. People around him turned in surprise and moved to inspect the wreckage. He grinned. No one seemed to have heard the air rifle's whisper-quiet shots. Just as Tadeusz had promised. He turned and walked away toward a car parked on a side street at the north end of the plaza. He already had the keys in his pocket.

Unhurriedly, he pulled out his phone and made a call. "I'm clear. You are go for roundup," he said simply and then disconnected.

RAVEN SURVEILLANCE VAN

THAT SAME TIME

Skoblin stared blankly at the black square on his laptop. The live video feed from their drone had gone haywire only seconds ago—breaking apart into a chaotic, dizzying swirl of distorted images before it went completely dark. His hands clenched. "Raven Eye, what just happened?" he barked.

The drone operator's voice was strained. "*I don't know, Viktor. Everything just suddenly dropped offline.*"

"Oh, really? Well, nice work, Yvgeny. I'm so glad I've got an expert like you around to confirm that for me," he ground out sarcastically. "Look, is there any chance you can get the signal back?"

"*Negative,*" the other man admitted after a moment. "*I think the drone must have crashed.*"

Skoblin felt cold. So now their sole remaining means of tracking their target had died, leaving them completely blind? He felt sure this was not just an unfortunate accident. It had to be hostile action.

A sharp rap on the back of the van startled him. Reflexively, he grabbed for the Walther P99 9mm pistol lying on the workbench next to his laptop. Holding it ready, he reached out and cautiously peeled back the sacking he'd used to block the rear windows. He peered out. Through the dusty, tinted glass, he saw a female police officer in a peaked cap standing next to the van. Thoroughly bundled up in a heavy uniform jacket against the cold, she looked hugely irritated.

"Now what?" Skoblin muttered. Quickly, he tucked the Walther back out of sight in a toolbox and closed the lid. Then he got up, unlocked the van's rear doors, and stepped awkwardly outside. After the thick fug of mingled sweat and cigarette smoke he'd been breathing for hours, the crisp, icy air was like a tonic.

"Is this your vehicle?" the police officer demanded, looking him dubiously up and down. Her nose wrinkled slightly at the smell.

Skoblin nodded.

She folded her arms. "Look, we've been getting a lot of complaints about this van of yours being parked out here day and night. The residents say it's an eyesore. And they don't see why you can't at least move it somewhere out of sight once you've finished work for the day."

With an effort, he hid a scowl. This was all he needed after this shitstorm of an afternoon . . . complaints from the local busybodies. Donning a look of regret, he shrugged his shoulders. "I'm sorry about that, Officer. But this is a big job, you see. And our client wants it finished fast. So we've got crews working around the clock."

She glanced up at the conspicuously deserted building beside them and then turned back at him with an eloquently raised eyebrow. "Around the clock?"

Skoblin forced a twisted smile. "They're on break just now. Union rules, you know."

"I see," the policewoman said dryly. Her voice hardened. "Do you have a permit for this restoration work?"

"Of course," he assured her. He jerked a thumb over his shoulder. "It's in the glovebox."

"Show me," she ordered.

Officious bitch, Skoblin thought furiously. She was toying with him. But with an obsequious nod, he turned away to retrieve the genuine permit the Raven Syndicate had paid through the nose to acquire.

Abruptly, the world around him flared bright white as though a bomb had just gone off. Involuntarily, he stumbled forward and collided with one of the van's open rear doors. Slack-jawed, unable to speak, the

Raven Syndicate agent slowly slumped over and collapsed facedown on the ground—completely incapable of controlling his twitching arms and legs.

aura Van Horn calmly holstered the Taser she'd just used to stun the phony electrician. Then she turned around and whistled sharply.

Another van, this one white with sliding side doors, came barreling around the corner. It braked sharply and stopped at an angle right behind them, preventing anyone on the street from getting a good look at what was going on. The moment it stopped moving, two of her men jumped out. Quickly and with practiced efficiency, they bound the tased man's hands and ankles using plastic flexicuffs. Then they blindfolded and gagged him for good measure. Once he was secured, the two men unceremoniously bundled him into their own vehicle—sliding him between two rows of seats. A tarp hid his body from view.

While they were doing that, Van Horn busied herself inside the blue electrician's van. Working swiftly, she collected their semiconscious prisoner's laptop, toolbox, and every piece of radio gear in sight. She didn't bother going through the glove box. Whoever these people eventually proved to be, she could already tell they were definitely professionals. They'd never be stupid enough to leave a paper trail for her to find.

Once she was finished, she scrambled into the front passenger seat of their own van and nodded sharply to her driver. He put the vehicle in gear, pulled back out onto the road, and drove away. Gleefully, she grinned over her shoulder at the rest of her team. From start to finish, their work had taken less than a minute . . . and not one of them had needed to utter a single word.

A SHORT TIME LATER

Nick Flynn closed the door to a maintenance room on the deserted lower level of a public parking garage outside the city center. "Our friend inside is still tied up tight," he said quietly. "He won't be going anywhere until we're long gone." Laura van Horn and the rest of the action team nodded in satisfaction. Like him, they all now wore clothes suitable for travel—jeans and khakis, button-down shirts and sweaters, and light-weight blazers or jackets.

One of them, a short, compact, and forceful man named Shannon Cooke, shoved Van Horn's discarded police uniform into a trash bag for later disposal. Cooke was a veteran of the Joint Special Operations Command who'd been recruited into Four several years ago. Before joining the Army, he'd actually started law school, only to decide that if he was going to hurt people, he'd rather do it honestly using guns and knives instead of just bankrupting them with overpriced billing. While on active duty, he'd served in the Army's ultra-secret Task Force Orange, otherwise known as the Mission Support Activity. Its highly trained and independent-minded operatives often deployed into hostile territory first to gather the vital intelligence needed for high-risk U.S. special forces missions. Now he did similar work for the Quartet Directorate.

Flynn checked the time. Except for Tadeusz Kossak and Cooke, who would also see to their weapons and other specialized equipment, they were all booked out on various flights from Vienna's International

Airport over the next several hours. He turned to another member of the team, Alain Ricard, and indicated the pair of CCTV cameras rigged to scan this floor of the parking structure. "Are we still good on those? Plus the camera covering the garage entrance?"

Ricard clapped him on the shoulder. "No sweat, Nick. You can relax." The tall Frenchman, a former officer in his nation's elite Marine Commandos, was proud of his grasp of American slang. "They will turn back on at staggered intervals, starting ten minutes from now."

Flynn nodded. There'd been a slim chance that temporarily disabling those surveillance cameras would be noticed. But he'd judged it a risk worth taking to conceal their brief activity here. After all, there were dozens of public multistory garages dotted across Vienna's metropolitan area. Which meant, in turn, that the municipal employees overseeing all those parking structures had to monitor hundreds of separate CCTV feeds at any given time. So no one would be especially surprised or worried if two or three cameras went offline for a few minutes here and there.

Van Horn handed him a rolling bag. "You've got the laptop." She patted her jacket pocket. "And I've got the cellphone. Br'er Fox's technical boys and girls should have a field day combing through them." She smiled. "Not a bad haul for a harebrained operation cobbled together in just a couple of days. Good thing our lords and masters decided to use the first string for this one, right?"

He grinned back at her. "If you do say yourself?"

She shrugged. "Who? Little me? Never. Remember, modesty is one of my many virtues."

Flynn laughed. "I'll bear that in mind." He looked at the other members of their team. "Everybody set?"

Heads nodded.

"Then let's move out," he said quietly. "We've got what we came for. But stay sharp all the way out of Austria and back to your respective stations. Let's not give the other side any opportunities to even the score."

In ones and twos, the Quartet Directorate team climbed into their various cars and the white van and drove away.

ELEVEN

THE NEXT DAY

Disheveled and dirty after an overnight flight from Austria crammed into the back of a chartered air cargo plane, Skoblin was marched into Pavel Voronin's private office on the second floor. Two stern-faced bodyguards gripped his arms. Without a word, they pushed him into a chair and stepped back.

Voronin turned away from the window and stared at him in silence for a few moments.

Skoblin looked down at his feet, unable to meet the other man's icy gaze. This discussion could have only one end, he knew miserably. Rumors within the Raven Syndicate spoke of unmarked graves already scattered through the forest surrounding Voronin's country estate.

At last, Voronin broke his increasingly ominous silence. "This is an unfortunate turn of events, Viktor," he said almost casually. "Your mission was to identify and eliminate Arif Khavari's contact, the foreign spy you initially failed to kill. Instead, your mistakes have exposed this organization to our enemies. Worse yet, you have also managed to rip an even wider hole in MIDNIGHT's operational security." The younger man watched Skoblin's face turn gray. "You are right to be afraid," he said. "You have been well compensated in my service—extraordinarily so, in fact. But I pay men for success, not for failure."

Nervously, Skoblin tried to moisten lips that were cracked and bone-dry. "Sir, I—" he said, fumbling for words, any words, of explanation that might somehow help stave off the inevitable end of this meeting. He knew, however, this was futile. For all practical purposes, his fate had been decided the moment his second rifle shot missed the enemy agent who'd been talking to Khavari. Painfully, he forced himself to look up. "I have no excuse," he said at last, almost too softly to be heard.

Voronin smiled, but it was an expression that never reached his pale, unwavering eyes. He reached out and gently patted Skoblin's shoulder, pointedly ignoring the way the other man flinched. "That's true, Viktor. There are no acceptable excuses for your unforced errors and obvious incompetence. Or at least none that I'm interested in hearing. But despite that, you're in luck all the same. Because I find myself in an oddly generous mood today."

Scarcely daring to hope, Skoblin stared up at him.

Voronin nodded. "I'm going to give you another chance—though not at the same sort of work, of course. Intricate, subtle operations are quite evidently not your strong suit." He shook his head. "No, I'll find you a task that is much simpler and more direct. One that requires guts and brawn more than brains."

"Thank you, sir . . . I . . . I swear that I won't let you down again," Skoblin stuttered hurriedly. "I will do anything you ask of me."

Voronin nodded coldly. "Yes, you will." He inclined his head toward the door of his office. "You can go now, Skoblin. You'll be briefed later on your new assignment." Deliberately, he turned back to the window, ignoring the other man as he was led away.

When the door closed, his deputy, Vasily Kondakov, shook his head in wonder. "You let him off surprisingly easily."

Voronin glanced at him with a sly, crooked smile. "You think so?"

"Ah," said Kondakov in sudden realization. "What do you have in mind for Skoblin, then?"

Voronin shrugged. "We'll put him and his team aboard the *Gulf Venture* when it sails. He can act as our security liaison with the Iranian captain and his crew."

Kondakov, aware of their full plans for the converted oil tanker, nodded approvingly. "An elegant solution," he said.

"It is, isn't it?" Voronin agreed. "After all, if I'm forced to use someone like our error-prone friend Skoblin, I might as well use him up."

AVALON HOUSE, WINTER PARK, FLORIDA

SEVERAL DAYS LATER

A tiled veranda ran along the entire length of the lake side of the Spanish-style mansion. A number of battered rattan chairs and settees provided seating, most of them angled to take full advantage of the pleasant view. Ceiling fans mounted under a wood-beamed roof kept the air moving.

Nick Flynn held the door to the veranda open for Laura Van Horn.

A tiny smile twitched at one corner of her generous mouth. "Ever the gentleman," she murmured.

"Blame it on my childhood training, ma'am," he replied, allowing his native Texas twang full rein for once. "My mother was very particular on the subject."

Van Horn's smile broadened. "I'll be sure to thank her," she said demurely. "Should we ever be introduced."

Fox was seated by himself at a small round glass table set near the far end of the veranda, staring out across the sparkling waters of the small lake. He had a manila folder in front of him. When they reached him, Four's chief of the American station greeted them with a surprisingly genial nod. "Nick. Laura. Welcome back to Avalon House."

They took the chairs he indicated around the table.

"First, congratulations on the success of your Vienna operation," Fox said quietly. "You achieved all of our hoped-for objectives, and did so cleanly—with near-surgical perfection. It's a rare plan that even survives contact with the enemy, let alone one that unfolds so neatly and so precisely."

Flynn shrugged. "A lot of credit for that goes to Professor Ayish," he admitted. "He anticipated almost every move the opposition would make."

"And to Tadeusz, Alain, Shannon, and the rest of the action team," Van Horn added. "They executed their parts in the overall op flawlessly."

Flynn nodded in agreement. "Yeah, they're all really good. Probably the best I've ever worked with."

Fox smiled dryly. "Points taken." His voice took on a sharper, more focused tone. "But now, if we've reached the end of this little session of mutual praise, perhaps we can move on to other, more pressing matters?"

Flynn and Van Horn exchanged amused glances. Although he occasionally allowed himself a human moment or two, the older man's all-business, all-the-time nature was never lurking far below the surface.

"While many of the files were encrypted at very high level, our technical experts have still managed to retrieve significant information from the laptop computer and smartphone you obtained so efficiently," Fox told them. "Among other things, we were able to clearly identify the man you briefly took prisoner, the one who headed up the surveillance operation against Israel's Vienna embassy." He flipped open the manila folder at his place and took out a color photograph, obviously a digitally downloaded copy of a formal portrait.

Flynn studied it closely. It showed a bullnecked man in Russian military uniform with the twin red stripes and gold star of a major. The unit badge on his shoulder showed a winged golden crossbow on a black background, the emblem of Russia's special operations forces. He frowned. That was the so-called electrician all right. He looked up at Fox. "So this guy's Spetsnaz?"

"He *was* Spetsnaz," the older man corrected. "His name is Viktor Pavlovich Skoblin."

"So who's he working for now?" Van Horn asked carefully.

Fox sighed. "That's where the story gets somewhat murkier," he admitted. "In a curious bit of symmetry, it appears that this man and the others you encountered in Vienna, all of whom have similar backgrounds in Russia's various covert services, are currently employed by a brand-new private military and intelligence firm headquartered in Moscow." His mouth tightened. "Apparently, they call themselves the Raven Syndicate."

"Catchy name," Van Horn said with a sniff. "If these guys are our new competitors, maybe Four should start calling itself the Falcon Group to get more up to date."

Flynn smiled across the little table at her. "Or how about something along the lines of Eagle, Inc. Patriotic *and* catchy, right?"

Fox studiously ignored their byplay. "What matters," he said patiently, "is that from what little we know about this Syndicate, it appears to have acquired the services of a substantial number of highly trained members of the SVR, GRU, and various other Russian black ops organizations."

"Acquired how, exactly?" Flynn wondered. "Last time I checked, Moscow doesn't exactly encourage people with those kinds of cloak-and-dagger skill sets to set up shop in the private sector."

"Money, apparently," Fox said bluntly. "And a great deal of it."

"How much money exactly?" Van Horn asked.

Fox frowned. "It's difficult to say. Corporate finance records in the Russian Federation aren't at all transparent or reliable. But the best estimate by analysts I trust is that this Raven Syndicate has access to resources totaling in the hundreds of millions of dollars—and perhaps more."

Flynn whistled softly. "And this group supposedly just popped into existence? Out of nowhere?"

"Like the dragon's teeth sown by Cadmus and Jason in the Greek myths," Fox said with a grim nod. "Which then sprouted into deadly warriors."

"Maybe they're being funded by the Kremlin on the sly," Flynn said speculatively. "Zhdanov could be building himself another deniable special operations force, like the Wagner Group—only with a heavier emphasis on covert intelligence missions this time." The Wagner Group, purportedly a private military company, was known to have extremely close ties to Russia's Ministry of Defense and the GRU. Its "contractors" had fought in civil wars and low-level conflicts around the world, everywhere from the Ukraine to Syria, Libya, Venezuela, and half a dozen other countries. Not so mysteriously, their lethal work always tended to advance Russia's national interests.

Fox nodded. "That's a reasonable theory." He frowned. "But there is another, even more troubling, possibility we need to consider." He drew out another photo and placed it in front of them. This one was black and white and blurred, as though it had been taken surreptitiously by a concealed camera. "This is the only contemporary image we have of the man who heads the Raven Syndicate, Pavel Voronin."

Van Horn leaned in closer. "He looks pretty damned young to be heading a business of that size, whether it's a front group for Zhdanov or not."

"Voronin is young," Fox agreed. "Still in his early thirties. But he's been very expensively educated." He pulled out three more photos, these in color. Formal school portraits, they showed a much younger Voronin at different ages. He tapped the first. "This was taken during his time at Phillips Exeter."

Flynn frowned. Located in New Hampshire, Phillips Exeter Academy was one of America's oldest and most selective prep schools—with a long list of prominent and influential alumni. He nodded at the second picture, showing a somewhat older Voronin. "And this one?"

"As an undergraduate at Oxford." Fox pointed to the last photo. "And that was taken while he was getting his MBA from Harvard Business School."

"'Expensively educated' was an understatement," Flynn said, shaking his head in amazement. "You're looking at close to a million dollars on the hoof, minimum." He looked across the table. "Who's his father? Some bigshot industrialist? Or a high-ranking politico in the Kremlin?"

"Neither," Fox said quietly. "His father was only a colonel in the KGB. And when the Soviet Union collapsed, he ended up holding the same rank in the SVR."

"He's the son of a spook?" Van Horn said with a toss of her head. "Not much mystery there, then. Odds are the Russian intelligence services were grooming this guy Voronin for years, planning to use him as a deep-cover agent."

Fox nodded. "That is the most logical assumption, Laura. But if so, their plans miscarried." He tossed a final photograph onto the desk. This one showed a much older, larger-boned man with a full head of thick white hair. "Instead, our best information is that Voronin went to work for this man, Dmitri Grishin—one of Russia's richest and most influential oligarchs."

"As what?" Flynn asked.

"On paper? As a personal assistant," the older man told him. "In reality? We suspect he worked as Grishin's top corporate troubleshooter, his personal hatchet man."

Flynn shook his head. "I can't imagine his father, the old-school KGB colonel, was real happy about that career choice."

"I don't imagine he would have been," Fox said flatly. "But both of Voronin's parents died soon after he returned to Russia."

Something about the older man's matter-of-fact tone sent a chill down Flynn's spine. "Died how?"

"They burned to death in an apartment fire," Fox said.

Van Horn's mouth tightened. "An accidental fire?"

"If it wasn't, the Moscow police arson investigators were never able to prove otherwise," Fox told her coolly. "Hard as they tried."

"Swell," Van Horn said. She pulled out the grainy, black-and-white image that was their most recent photo of Voronin. "So you're telling us that the son of a bitch in charge of this Raven Syndicate is a stone-cold psychopath."

"Almost certainly," Fox acknowledged.

Flynn sat back in his chair with a grimace. Learning more about Voronin was a lot like turning over a rock and seeing all sorts of creepy, crawling things wriggling away out from underneath. "What happened to his old boss, Dmitri Grishin? Nothing pleasant, I assume."

"Grishin was assassinated a little over a year ago, quite probably on President Zhdanov's direct orders," the older man answered.

Flynn stared at him. "Assassinated? Why?"

"Because Zhdanov discovered that he was responsible for arranging the theft and attempted ransom of Russia's stealth bomber prototype," Fox said.

"That would be the high-tech plane you crashed in the ass-end of northern Alaska, Nick," Van Horn reminded him with a cheerful grin. "The one the CIA thought they were buying."

He snorted. "Yeah, thanks. I sort of figured that out on my own." He turned back to Fox. "So the fact that this Voronin character is alive and definitely prospering in Moscow, after his boss was killed for treason, strongly suggests —"

"That he betrayed Grishin to the authorities and cut a deal to go free?" Fox finished for him. "Yes, it does."

Flynn shook his head in disgust. "Nice. Real nice." He looked closely at the older man. "Okay, then why don't you believe the funding for Voronin's Raven Syndicate is coming out of the Kremlin's secret accounts? Where else would he get that kind of money?"

"From our own government," Fox said simply.

"Very funny," Flynn shot back.

Fox shrugged. "I only wish it were." He looked off toward the lake. "My sources inside the CIA admit—very reluctantly, I might add—that Langley transferred a substantial sum to secret accounts they now believe were controlled by Dmitri Grishin. And this money has never been recovered." He turned back to Flynn and Van Horn. "I suspect Voronin now controls those same secret accounts . . . and that they were a motivation for betraying his employer to Zhdanov."

"Wonderful," Van Horn muttered caustically. "Basically, then, we're up against a bunch of highly trained Russian spies and special ops soldiers who're using our own taxpayer dollars against us?"

Fox nodded. His face was impassive.

Flynn eyed him. "But that's not the worst of it, right?" he challenged.

"Perceptive as ever, Nick," Fox said with the faintest ghost of a smile. He shook his head. "No, what troubles me more is that we now know this Raven Syndicate is run by someone who is both supremely ruthless and a consummate survivor. A man, moreover, who seems drawn to daring, large-scale schemes."

"And now we have clear confirmation that Voronin and his agents are working hand-in-glove with Iran's radical regime," Flynn pointed out quietly.

Fox nodded again. "Yes, and very clearly with explicit authorization from President Zhdanov himself," he added.

"Which brings us right back around to square one," Flynn realized.

"True," Fox said. "Knowing the identity and quality of our opposition is useful indeed, but I admit that it doesn't bring us any closer to under-standing the top-secret project Arif Khavari gave his life to warn us about. We still don't know how the Iranians—and their Russian backers and allies—actually plan to use this heavily retrofitted oil tanker, the *Gulf Venture*. All we have right now is the code name they've given to this operation: MIDNIGHT."

"MIDNIGHT?" Van Horn repeated. She frowned. "That's it? Just the code name? Nothing else?"

"Nothing," Fox confirmed. "From what we can tell, the full opera-tional details are tightly restricted to a very small group. Bit players like Skoblin and his men are only given the bare minimum of information they need to carry out their assignments."

Flynn sat quiet for a moment, thinking things through. There was only one place left they might be able to find the answers they needed—inside Iran itself. And acquiring and repositioning the equipment and personnel required would take time, some weeks at a minimum . . .

which meant they were already right up against the clock. Further delay could be fatal. He looked straight across the table at Fox. "You know we don't have any easy options left," he said deliberately. "Except, I guess, maybe just sitting back on our hindquarters and hoping that someone else, somewhere else, will take care of this problem for us."

Slowly, and with evident reluctance, the older man's mouth twitched in a tiny, almost imperceptible, smile. "Sadly, Nick, sitting idly by is not a real option. Not for those of us in Four—as you're well aware. In this particular case, we are the only 'someone else' available." He shrugged his narrow shoulders. "As my colleagues at the other Quartet Directorate stations now also admit."

"Does that mean I'm authorized to go into Iran?" Flynn pressed.

Fox nodded. "You are."

For a moment, Flynn felt a wave of satisfaction. And then he realized the magnitude of the task he'd just set himself. Successfully infiltrating Iranian territory was one thing—and a damned difficult thing at that. Surviving undetected long enough to penetrate the veil of secrecy the Revolutionary Guards and Voronin's Raven Syndicate had thrown up around the *Gulf Venture* was quite another. *I must be out of my fricking mind*, he thought with a touch of dismay.

"Oh, man, I am such an idiot," he muttered under his breath.

Laura Van Horn patted his shoulder. "No, you're not, Nick," she said consolingly.

"I'm not?"

She grinned at him. "An idiot? No. Suicidal? Oh, hell, yes."

Almost unwillingly, Flynn laughed. "Fair enough." Crazy or not, he was committed now. Which meant he didn't have any real choice left but to buckle down and make sure that his complicated plan, which looked workable enough on paper, would actually pan out in practice.

He rose to his feet with a fleeting smile. "What's that British commando watchword? 'Who Dares Wins,' right? Well, I guess I'm about to find out if that's true."

TWELVE

A FEW WEEKS LATER

A twin-engine An-72AT cargo plane sat on the airfield's long concrete apron. Painted in the subdued white and gray colors of the Russian Air Force, it was dwarfed by the dozen or so much larger Tu-160M2 swing-wing supersonic bombers lined up nearby. Dubbed the "Cheburashka" after a famous Soviet-era children's cartoon animal with huge eyes and huge ears, the An-72AT had two enormous jet nacelles mounted above its wings and very close to the fuselage. The extra lift provided by engine exhaust blowing over its wings made it a short-takeoff-and-landing aircraft able to operate from rough, improvised airstrips.

Cradling AK-12 combat rifles, security troops in body armor formed a perimeter around the plane. No one without express written authorization from the base commander could approach within a hundred meters of the An-72AT's open rear ramp and forward fuselage door. The officer in charge, a major, walked slowly around the ring of soldiers, making sure they were alert and prepared for anything.

Abruptly, his phone beeped. He answered it impatiently. "Yes? Mishnev here."

"This is Captain Storchak at the main gate, sir. The convoy from the Saratov-Sixty-Three Weapons Storage Complex has cleared our position and is heading your way."

"Understood, Storchak. We're ready." The major ended the call and stuffed his phone back into a pouch clipped to his battle dress. Briskly, he rubbed his gloved hands together trying to work some warmth into his fingers. Spring was still a few weeks away and it was bitterly cold.

"Here they come," one of his men called out. The major peered toward the airfield's southwestern edge. There, about a kilometer away, he saw the weapons convoy turn off an approach road and drive onto the apron's wide, concrete surface. A column of several heavy-duty Ural-5323 cargo trucks lumbered along behind a single, olive-drab GAZ Hunter four-wheel drive out in front. They were closely escorted by lethal-looking, low-slung BTR-82 wheeled armored fighting vehicles.

The jeep-sized Hunter accelerated ahead of the rest of the slower-moving convoy and pulled up in front of the major. He stiffened to attention and saluted as two officers, a colonel and a lieutenant colonel, swung down out of the vehicle. Their shoulder flashes bore the badge of Russia's 12th Main Directorate—a red shield topped by a silver mace inside a stylized atom symbol.

The senior officer returned his salute rather causally. "These are your troops, Major?"

"Yes, sir."

The older man nodded abruptly. "Right, then. I need you to widen your security perimeter. Nobody gets within two hundred meters of my trucks or that aircraft. Not your regimental commander. Not the general in charge of this base. Not even the Archangel Michael himself. Is that clear?"

The major nodded. "It is, sir." He hid his irritation. The 12th Main Directorate's specialists—directly responsible to the Minister of Defense for Russia's strategic and tactical nuclear weapons stockpiles—had a widely known habit of throwing their weight around when dealing with line officers. But there was nothing to be gained from pushing back.

Their expertise and the overwhelming importance of their mission made them effectively untouchable by anyone outside their direct chain of command. Instead, he snapped another parade-ground-quality salute and spun around to shout new orders to his men.

Obeying immediately, they spread out across the airfield apron—adopting wider intervals as they moved farther away from the An-72 cargo plane.

olonel Mikhail Krylov concealed his satisfaction as the Engels-2 security troops dispersed to their new stations. Even from a hundred meters, there hadn't been much danger that the major, his junior officers, or any of their enlisted men would notice anything amiss. But why take unnecessary chances?

He turned to watch the rest of his truck convoy arrive. The big 8x8 cargo carriers pulled in and parked close to the An-72's tail section. Their armored BTR-82 escorts rolled into position to ring the aircraft, well inside the loose perimeter formed by the ground troops. Their turret-mounted autocannons swiveled outward, covering every possible approach to this section of the airfield. If any of the base security soldiers noticed they were also covered by the arcs of fire from those 30mm cannons, they kept their mouths shut. When it came to protecting the powerful weapons in their charge, the 12th Main Directorate's personnel trusted no one.

The rumbling noise made by the Ural truck motors died away as their drivers switched off. For a long moment, absolute silence reigned, without any sign of movement among the parked vehicles.

Krylov turned to his ranking subordinate, Lieutenant Colonel Potkin. "Note the time carefully, Andrei."

"I'm ready, Colonel," the other man assured him. He held an old-fashioned stopwatch in one hand.

Nodding, Krylov pulled a whistle out of his breast pocket and blew three shrill blasts. In response, the officers and men waiting aboard his trucks instantly swung into action—clambering down out of cabs and over back tailboards. Within minutes, they had lowered a pair of forklifts out of one of the trucks and were using them to unload sealed metal crates from the others. Every green-painted crate bore radiological warning labels indicating it contained a live nuclear warhead or bomb. Each also had a unique serial number to identify the precise weapon stored inside.

Krylov watched closely while one of the forklifts carefully hoisted the first of the unloaded weapons containers. Slowly, it trundled up the An-72's rear ramp and into the cargo compartment. A group of his officers and senior enlisted men shepherded the forklift at every step. As far as the air base command staff and most of his own subordinates knew, this was a strategic readiness exercise designed to test the Saratov-63 depot's ability to rapidly transfer its stored weapons in the event of a major international crisis. If events appeared to be sliding toward all-out war, large numbers of those nuclear missile warheads and air-dropped bombs were supposed to be flown to the different airfields and missile complexes dispersed across Russia's vast territory.

Today's drill was expected to evaluate how well the 12th Main Directorate's procedures and personnel performed under pressure. That was true as far as it went, Krylov knew. But the real purpose of this exercise was actually a carefully hidden secret, one known only to a small, tight-knit group . . . starting at the very top, with Russia's President Zhdanov, and working down from there to Krylov and two of his junior officers.

Inside the An-72's spacious cargo compartment, Major Anatoly Yakemenko supervised the crews tasked with stowing the heavy crates and securing them to the aircraft's deck. They were following a carefully drawn up loading plan. Each container was assigned its own precisely calculated place inside the plane. Too much weight stowed either forward or aft of the cargo jet's center of gravity could lead to a crash—an unthinkable prospect for an aircraft that would be carrying megatons of fission and fusion weapons if this exercise were the real thing.

"That's the last of them, Major," a young lieutenant reported, pointing to where a group of senior NCOs were methodically tightening the restraints used to latch a crate into position on the An-72's deck.

Yakemenko nodded. Under his careful eye, the crew checked its work and then stepped back. He tugged hard at one of the straps, making sure there wasn't any excess give. Satisfied, he spoke into his handheld radio, "Colonel, this is Yakemenko. The loading phase is complete."

"Roger that, Anatoly. Your crews have worked hard and done very well," Krylov responded. *"As a reward, we'll give everyone a thirty-minute rest break before concluding the exercise."*

The colonel's whistle shrilled again, this time ordering his men back outside the cargo aircraft. Yakemenko stayed right where he was. Instead, he watched through narrowed eyes while all of the others trotted down the An-72's ramp. They were in a hurry to get back to the relative warmth of their trucks.

When the last man was off the ramp and out of sight, he moved to the cargo compartment's forward bulkhead and rapped twice on a locked door that sealed off the An-72's crew area and cockpit. It opened at his signal, revealing a group of four solidly built men in Air Force flight suits. The uniforms were a cover, since he knew these men actually worked for the Raven Syndicate.

"All clear?" one of them asked.

Yakemenko nodded. "You've got twenty-nine minutes," he warned. He stepped aside to clear the way.

Without bothering to reply, the four Raven Syndicate operatives bent over and picked up what looked exactly like another weapons crate from inside the An-72's crew area. Straining under its weight, they muscled it awkwardly through the door and into the cargo compartment. Carefully, gingerly, they lowered the heavy container to the deck. Any loud noises now would be disastrous.

Captain Leonid Kazmin, the youngest of the select group of 12th Main Directorate officers now secretly in Pavel Voronin's pay, followed them out. He flashed Yakemenko a jumpy, nervous half smile. "Is my special package ready, Anatoly?"

Yakemenko pointed to one of the first warhead crates that had been loaded aboard the An-72. It was tied down not far from the cargo compartment's forward bulkhead. "Right over there, Leonid. And it's all yours."

With a tight nod, Kazmin signaled his work crew. As quickly and quietly as possible, they loosened the straps holding the real crate to the deck. Once the container was free, they lugged it across the compartment, faces purpling with effort, and set it down next to the duplicate they'd just brought out from concealment.

Kazmin knelt beside the two crates, making one last check. First, he compared the placement and appearance of their respective radiological warning labels. They matched perfectly. So did the serial numbers prominently displayed on each container. Just as promised and planned. He breathed out in relief.

Scrambling back to his feet, he gestured for his men to replace the real weapons container with its phony twin. Sweating, they moved the fake crate into position and refastened all the straps and tiedowns.

Impatiently, Yakemenko watched Kazmin and the others finish up by manhandling the genuine container back through the door into the cargo jet's crew area. When it closed and latched shut behind them, he quickly ran his eyes over the rows of crates secured to the An-72's deck. Nothing seemed out of place. Mentally, he crossed his fingers. Now it was time to find out if all their careful planning would pay off. Presidential authorization or not, Voronin had made his expectations of absolute secrecy in this carefully contrived shell game abundantly clear.

An hour later, with the truck convoy safely on its return trip to the Saratov-63 Nuclear Weapons Storage Complex, Pavel Voronin watched the An-72 taxi onto the rightmost of the airfield's two long runways. It held in place there for a few moments, waiting for permission to take off.

"*Freight Seven-Two, Engels Tower. Winds light at zero-one-five, cleared for takeoff on runway zero-four right. Safe flight,*" he heard the controller radio.

"*Thank you, Tower. Freight Seven-Two, cleared for takeoff, zero four right,*" the cargo jet's pilot acknowledged.

The An-72 ran its twin turbofan engines up to full power, released its brakes and rolled down the runway—picking up speed until at last it lumbered heavily into the air. Slowly, it climbed higher and banked to the south, turning onto a flight path that would carry it high above the vast open steppes east of the Volga River.

With a gratified smile, Voronin lowered his binoculars and glanced at the Air Force general standing at his side in the Engels-2 Control Tower. "That was a most impressive exercise, General Turgenev," he said politely. "I very much appreciate being allowed to observe it."

Turgenev, the commander of this vital strategic bomber base, seemed unsure of the best tone to take with his unusual guest. Only a direct order from President Zhdanov himself had persuaded him to allow a mere civilian to witness this classified nuclear weapons drill. He cleared his throat. "You're very welcome . . . Mr. Voronin," he grunted at last, opting for a measure of courtesy he would ordinarily have reserved only for high-ranking political dignitaries. Highly irregular as this visit was, the president's intervention strongly suggested this man Voronin was much too powerful to risk offending.

Voronin ignored the interplay of emotions crossing the general's craggy face. Instead, he raised his binoculars again, refocusing on the now-tiny dot of the An-72 as it flew onward—bound for the Shahrud Missile Test Facility in northeastern Iran.

After months of careful preparation, MIDNIGHT was moving into high gear.

THIRTEEN

ZARANJ AIRPORT, NIMROZ PROVINCE, SOUTHWESTERN AFGHANISTAN

A COUPLE OF DAYS LATER

The city of Zaranj lay right on Afghanistan's border with Iran. Built mostly of traditional mud-brick buildings, it was home to around fifty thousand inhabitants, with another hundred thousand or so in outlying towns and villages. Most of them were members of the minority Baloch ethnic group—a people split between Pakistan, Iran, and Afghanistan. The city, whose roots went back more than two thousand years, was also the capital of the thinly populated Nimroz Province.

Largely ignored by whatever passed for a central government in Afghanistan at any given time, the citizens of Zaranj and its surroundings traditionally relied on a mix of both contraband and legal trade goods for any modest prosperity they enjoyed. Water in this parched land was particularly scarce, so agriculture rarely supplied more than a fraction of the local population's needs. Instead, for centuries the region had survived thanks to its location on one of the major land trade routes between the Middle East and Asia. In recent decades that meant a steady flow of heroin, illicit weapons, and black market gasoline.

Zaranj's airport had one runway, a rough 7,400-foot-long gravel strip. Apart from occasional civilian passenger flights from Herat and

Kandahar, it saw rare visits by military aircraft belonging either to the distant Kabul government or to the various regional warlords. Even more rarely, the poorly maintained runway was used by commercial charters.

Now one of those charter aircraft—a large four-engine Il-76 cargo jet in the colors of a Ukraine-based air freight company—was parked just off the runway. Two large, open-sided canvas tents had been erected close to its open rear ramp. A number of men in coveralls could be seen working in each tent to assemble two smaller aircraft whose crated components had been flown in aboard the larger Russian-built plane.

The smaller of the two flying machines was a kit-built two-seater BushCat propeller-driven aircraft conceived by SkyReach, a South African company. Constructed around a tubular aluminum frame and covered with a Dacron-Trilam composite fabric in desert camouflage colors, the high-wing, light sport plane weighed less than fourteen hundred pounds when fully loaded. Originally designed for service in Africa's vast bush country, the BushCat could take off and land on almost any grass or dirt field—and in incredibly short distances, usually around the length of an American football field. The second aircraft was a pusher type, with its propeller mounted in the tail. It was a General Atomics MQ-1 Predator UAV, unmanned aerial vehicle—complete with a bulbous, windowless domed nose, long, thin fuselage, wide, narrow wings, and three down-angled tail fins. Among other less visible modifications, its landing gear and aft engine section had been upgraded to allow it to operate safely on Zaranj's rough-surfaced runway.

Several men in camouflaged fatigues, baseball caps, and body armor were posted as guards around the tents and the parked Il-76 cargo plane. They were armed with military-grade HK417 7.62mm carbines.

Not far away, a wire fence surrounded several white, flat-roofed buildings that contained offices and other facilities for the airport's small staff and local government workers. Inside one of those offices, Nick Flynn sat comfortably across a low table from the representative of the ruling local warlord who'd come to meet him.

Squarely built, hawk-nosed, and about the same height as Flynn, Masoud Bokharai was clean-shaven, with a thick shock of curly, dark hair. At the moment, he wore traditional Afghan men's clothing, a knee-length, open-collared tunic with long sleeves, baggy trousers, and an open waistcoat. Flynn had a sneaking suspicion the other man would be just as comfortable in an expensive Western-style business suit and silk tie.

On official tables of organization, Bokharai was listed as the deputy assistant provincial administrator for development and trade. But the Quartet Directorate intelligence brief on this part of Afghanistan indicated that he wielded a great deal more power and influence than his relatively low rank would suggest. Foreigners interested in doing business in Zaranj and the rest of Nimroz were well-advised to keep on his good side—especially if their enterprises weren't likely to withstand careful legal scrutiny.

Bokharai finished leafing through the full-color brochure Flynn had brought to their meeting. He looked up with a narrow smile. "A most intriguing concept, Señor Duarte. I confess the idea of Nimroz Province as a potential market for village-centered solar power installations had never occurred to me." His English was excellent and the irony in his tone was palpable.

Probably because you're not an idiot, Flynn thought coolly, pretending to wait while the interpreter he'd brought from Kabul translated the Afghan official's comments into Spanish. The passport he was currently using identified him as Simón Bolivar Duarte, a citizen of the socialist republic of Venezuela. Before flying into Afghanistan, Flynn had darkened his hair even more and let his beard grow out to a rough stubble. Brown-tinted contact lenses concealed his light blue eyes. His Spanish was flawless, and that, plus the Tejano ancestors on his mother's side of the family, allowed him to pose convincingly as a native of South America.

"It is certainly a revolutionary idea, Administrator," he acknowledged in Spanish when the interpreter finished. "But my principals see

these smaller, locally based power facilities as a natural fit for your region."
He shrugged his shoulders apologetically, as though regretting the need
to bring up an unpleasant subject. "That is especially true considering
the unfortunate . . . problems, let us say . . . that large-scale infrastructure
projects tend to encounter here."

Flynn watched the other man's eyes closely and saw the quickly
hidden irritation he'd been expecting. Bokharai knew only too well
that the Taliban, who controlled most of the surrounding countryside,
routinely sabotaged power transmission lines, roads, medical clinics,
schools, bridges, and other major public works. Even before the recent
effective collapse of central authority in Afghanistan, tens of millions of
dollars' worth of international aid to this isolated corner of the country
had been reduced to heaps of blackened rubble.

The other man spread his hands. "A perceptive analysis," he admitted.
His expression, if anything, become even blander. "I am somewhat
curious about something else, however, Señor."

"Indeed?"

"Those light aircraft your men are putting together outside,"
Bokharai said carefully. "What role are they intended to play in this
solar power marketing *scheme* of yours?"

Flynn heard the edged emphasis in the other man's words. He concealed a grin. Now they were getting down to the core of what the
Afghan official was really interested in. He clearly didn't believe a word
of all the bullshit he'd just read and heard about small-scale solar facilities. "We plan to use that little two-seater passenger plane, the SkyReach
BushCat, for maintaining customer contact in remote rural areas," he
explained mildly. "Since it can land and take off again from almost anywhere, we'll be able to ferry company sales representatives and service
technicians out to even the most isolated villages."

"I see." Bokharai studied his fingertips for a moment before looking
back up with a slightly harder expression. "And the Predator drone you
are also assembling? What real commercial purpose can *that* possibly

serve?" He met Flynn's eyes. "We Afghans have seen much of those unmanned aerial vehicles over the years—and the air-to-ground Hellfire missiles they carried."

Flynn nodded. The other man's scarcely hidden suspicions were reasonable. Until they were retired from combat service in 2018, both the U.S. Air Force and the CIA had employed General Atomics MQ-1 Predator drones for reconnaissance and attack missions in Afghanistan and in many other conflict zones around the world. He leaned forward. "Our drone has absolutely no military capability," he assured Bokharai earnestly. "My principals discreetly acquired it from the U.S. Customs and Border Patrol—as they were phasing out their Predator surveillance fleet. Before we took possession, all equipment of warlike utility was removed."

"Which still doesn't explain how you plan to use this vehicle," the Afghan said bluntly.

Flynn smiled genially. "We see two significant uses. First, the Predator makes it possible for us to conduct unmanned aerial surveys of likely sites for our small solar plants, avoiding the risk of losing lives should your local bandits react aggressively to our plans. And second, our technicians have equipped this particular Predator to carry cargo. So we'll be able to deliver up to a hundred kilos of machinery and spare parts to job sites in remote villages as needed . . . at a considerable savings in man-hours and transportation and labor costs."

"Of course," Bokharai said dryly. "I can see the advantages."

Oh, I just bet you do, Flynn thought with the same measure of cynical amusement he could hear in the other man's voice. In reality, he could tell that the Afghan official strongly suspected "Duarte" and his associates of being smugglers—of drugs or black market weapons or both. In which case, their real plans would involve using the BushCat light plane for covert meetings with suppliers and prospective buyers well away from prying official eyes. As for the Predator drone, its role as a trafficking tool was even more obvious. Being able to covertly transport a couple of hundred pounds of heroin or guns and explosives over long distances, avoiding every government checkpoint on the way, was a criminal's dream.

This guy Bokharai knows that I'm lying, Flynn thought, fighting down a grin. *And I know that he knows I'm lying. And he knows that I know that he knows I'm lying. But he doesn't know exactly what I'm lying about.* Which was good enough.

More relaxed now, the Afghan official folded his hands over his stomach. "You present a persuasive case, Señor Duarte," he allowed. "I have only one more concern. Do you intend to confine your firm's efforts solely to Nimroz Province? Or are there plans to expand your reach over time, perhaps to international markets?"

"Naturally, we hope to grow our business," Flynn said. He smiled. "My principals are ambitious men."

Bokharai's eyes narrowed slightly. "And do their ambitious plans include operations in Iran?" he asked pointedly.

"Iran? Not at all," Flynn said with equal bluntness. "We might find the business climate there . . . too challenging." He drew a finger across his throat. "Profits are useless to dead men."

"So they are," Bokharai agreed. Tehran's revolutionary regime trafficked heavily in illegal drugs, but it did so for its own foreign policy purposes and for hard currency. And it dealt harshly with foreigners who tried to horn in on its smuggling business or who sold narcotics to its own citizens. "So then? You are thinking about Pakistan?"

Flynn nodded once. "We believe conditions there are promising. Very promising."

The Afghan nodded sagely. Like Iran and his own country, Pakistan was a major transshipment point for heroin and other illicit substances. But unlike Iran, the central government had considerably less real control over many of its outlying territories and even some cities. That made it a much safer place for international criminal gangs to set up shop. "Well, then, Señor," he said at last. "It seems your organization has thought out its plans to the last detail. Naturally," he continued delicately, "there are certain regulatory and legal formalities that must be observed. Paper-work and other bureaucratic requirements that govern the conduct of business here. A burden, I admit, but still—" He left the rest hanging unsaid.

And there's my cue, Flynn realized. He'd been wondering how long it would take Bokharai to get to the real purpose of this visit. "Of course," he said with conviction. "We understand fully that every government has its own set of rules. And my organization would never dream of cut-ting corners or of subverting local laws." With a visible effort, Bokharai tried to hide his displeasure. "Still, we also understand the importance of custom in ensuring that these procedures operate smoothly," Flynn went on. "And with a minimum of red tape."

The Afghan official suddenly looked more hopeful, and the Kabul-based interpreter appeared to be secretly amused. No doubt he'd seen this same ritual dance enacted a dozen times over in as many different parts of the country. Fluent in at least five languages, his services were much in demand whenever foreign businessmen came calling.

Flynn lifted the leather briefcase he'd brought with him and put it between them on the low table. "It's extremely important to my prin-cipals that we establish good relationships with our local partners," he said. "So I hope you'll accept this *first*, small token of our appreciation . . . and ensure that it is distributed to some worthy charity." He slid it across the table.

Almost hungrily, Bokharai flipped the catches open and raised the lid partway. His eyes widened slightly, seeing stacks of U.S. dollars. He must have known that he was looking at a sum in excess of one hundred thousand dollars. Forcing himself to adopt a studied air of carelessness, he closed the case again. "You can be sure of that, Señor Duarte," he said. His teeth gleamed. "Your gift will bring great happiness to orphans across the province."

Only if both your parents are dead, you sleazy bastard, Flynn thought cynically. At least Bokharai had a reputation as an honest crook, one who would stay bought. That was what Four's intelligence analysts claimed anyway. He sure hoped they were right, both for his own sake and for that of the others involved in this high-stakes operation he'd set in motion. Because if the Afghan decided to sell them out to his Iranian counterparts just across border, Flynn and his team were up shit's creek. And without a paddle to be found anywhere within ten thousand miles.

Resolutely, he pushed his worries aside. There was no going back now. It was time to focus, not to fret over things outside his control.

Forcing himself to smile, Flynn parted from Masoud Bokharai with the flurry of insincere final courtesies common between men who trusted each other only as far as their shared interests would carry them. He walked the provincial official out to his car, a spotless black Mercedes sedan, and waved farewell as the other man drove away.

Then he turned to the interpreter and slipped him an envelope containing a substantial sum of cash, along with an airline ticket for the next flight to Kabul through Herat. "You have my thanks for your services, Ahmad," he said in Spanish. "I've made a reservation for you tonight at the Tamadon Hotel. It's the best available. Your flight leaves tomorrow morning, and I'll have one of my men pick you up in time."

The interpreter stuffed the envelope into his jacket with a nod of thanks. He raised an eyebrow in unabashed curiosity. "You will no longer need my assistance, Señor Duarte?"

"My immediate business is done here, so I'll be leaving very soon," Flynn explained. He shrugged. "The associates I'm leaving in charge speak enough English to get by."

"Ah," the interpreter said knowingly. "And, after all, *this*," he tapped the bulge in his jacket where the envelope of cash rested, "is a form of universal language."

"That, too," Flynn agreed. He waited until the interpreter left and then walked back to the parked Il-76. Two of the men on sentry duty moved to join him at the foot of the aircraft's lowered ramp.

"Any problems?" Tadeusz Kossak asked quietly.

"None." Flynn said. "Our crooked Afghan friend seems to have bought our cover story hook, line, and sinker." He grinned. "The implicit one about us running drugs and guns, I mean. Not the upfront solar power scam I pretended to sell him."

The Polish sniper shook his head with a mock sorrowful expression on his face. "My faith in the evil effects of original sin remains intact."

Shannon Cooke clapped his taller friend on the shoulder. "Cheer up, Tad," the American ex-Special Forces operator said with a hint of laughter in his voice. "Sooner or later, we're bound to run into an honest government official on one of these secret missions."

"Yes," Kossak agreed. "And that will be a very bad day for us," he said mournfully. "Which proves my point, I think."

Flynn choked back a laugh of his own. He nodded up at the jet cargo plane towering above them. "Speaking of bad days, how's Laura doing?"

Cooke pushed his baseball cap up slightly to scratch his forehead. "Well, Nick, the last time I saw her, she told me she wanted to see you as soon as you were finished out here. Discretion being the better part of valor, if she said anything else, I was too busy backpedaling away to catch it."

"That good, huh?" Flynn said with a wince.

Cooke nodded gravely.

Flynn sighed. "Okay, guys. If I'm not back out in time for supper, tell my mother I love her . . . and to please feed the dog."

Nerving himself up, he walked up the ramp and into the Il-76's wide aft section. A curtain had been rigged across the forward quarter of the cargo deck to stop overly curious observers from seeing what was going on in that part of the aircraft interior. Straightening, Flynn cautiously rapped a couple of times on the side of the fuselage. "Y'all decent in there?" he called.

"Oh, real funny, Flynn," Laura Van Horn said crossly from behind the curtain. "Like I could be anything else while I'm stuck in this stupid gunny sack." She yanked the curtain aside far enough to let him pass. Clad from head to foot in a shapeless black chador, she looked uncomfortable and mad enough to hit somebody—or maybe just shoot them. Since the presence of a Western-looking woman as part of a gang of supposed drug smugglers might arouse suspicion, she'd been forced to stay out of sight when possible, and to wear the traditional garb of most women in Zaranj.

She ran a skeptical eye over his own appearance. "So, were you trying project a suave, Antonio Banderas–type image, Nick?" she asked with a raised eyebrow. Then she shook her head dismissively. "I sure hope not. Because if that was your plan, I gotta say you missed it by about a mile."

Flynn adopted a hurt tone. "A mile? Really? That much?"

"That much," she confirmed with a short nod. Then she shrugged. "But I guess it doesn't matter now, since I'm assuming this stunt you've got planned is a go after all."

"Yes, it is. Just as soon as it gets dark." He turned toward the other person with them behind the curtain. "Can you have your gear ready by then, Sara?"

Sara McCulloch, a staff sergeant in the U.S. Air Force before she joined the Quartet Directorate, swiveled around in her chair. Unlike Van Horn, the petite redhead wore a flight suit. She'd be staying aboard the Il-76 for the entire duration of this mission—leaving it only virtually, through the cameras and other sensors fitted to the MQ-1 Predator she would be remote-piloting. Confidently, she waved a hand at her console, indicating the large display screen, keyboard, and pair of flight controllers. "No sweat, sir. Once the guys finish bolting my bird together, all we need to do is set up my satellite communications dish outside and connect. Everything else is good to go now."

Van Horn breathed out. "Glad to hear it. Because the sooner I can get into the pilot's seat of that BushCat myself, the happier I'll be."

"This flight's going to be risky as hell," Flynn warned. "Both out and back."

"Tell me about it," she said with a half smile. "I'm the one who wrote up the flight plan, remember?" She tugged at the tight neck of the chador. "But as far as I'm concerned, any amount of risk is worth it to ditch this damned thing."

"That bad?" Flynn asked sympathetically.

She nodded. "You have no idea." She shook her head. "If I'd been smarter, I'd have just cut my hair off and come in disguised as one of you guys."

For a split-second, Flynn tried to imagine the curvy, attractive Laura Van Horn successfully passing herself off as a man. His imagination failed him. He grinned down at her. "That might have worked, I guess," he conceded. "Assuming, of course, that everyone here in Zaranj was blind."

Her eyes gleamed. "Flattery, Nick?" She leaned closer. "Well, who knows? It may get you somewhere. Someday."

"But today is not that day?" he guessed.

"Nope," she said simply. She winked at him. "We're going to be kind of busy flying tonight, remember?"

"Plus, *not* crashing into mountains? Or being shot down?" Flynn suggested.

"Yeah, those, too," Van Horn agreed evenly.

FOURTEEN

THAT NIGHT

The sun had set a little over an hour before, plunging Zaranj and its surrounding villages into almost total darkness. On the ground, a few points of light scattered across the blacked-out city showed where the influential and well-connected few lived. Most of those buildings were clustered in the blocks around the local warlord's fortified compound.

A few more lights were on at the airport, the majority around the Quartet Directorate team's chartered Il-76 cargo aircraft and its large canvas-roofed tents. The long gravel runway itself was unlit, largely invisible in the darkness. Since there was no moon tonight, only the faint glow of starlight offered any natural illumination.

Flynn stepped out of one of the tents. He shivered slightly in the cooler air outside. Once the sun went down, the temperature had dropped fast into the midfifties. He paused briefly to zip his light windbreaker all the way up.

Tadeusz Kossak followed him outside. The Polish sniper slung his HK417 carbine over one shoulder and tugged a plastic bottle out of one of his equipment pouches. He offered it to Flynn. "One last drink before you go? For luck?"

"For some strange reason, I'm guessing that's not water," Flynn said with a smile.

"Water?" Kossak sounded aggrieved. "What do you take me for? A savage?" He unscrewed the cap. "No, this the very best Polish-made vodka. One hundred proof."

Flynn shook his head regretfully. "I'd better not." He shrugged. "They're not real big on alcohol around here as it is. But my next stop takes that kind of fundamentalism to a whole new level."

The Pole shook his head in disgust. "Heathens," he muttered. "However, I see your point." His teeth gleamed in the darkness. "Then I will drink for you, Nick. *Na zdrowie*! Your health!" With a flourish, he took a quick swig and then decisively recapped the bottle before stowing it away. He made a show of looking out into the darkness around them before taking the short-barreled rifle off his shoulder. His voice turned more serious. "Come, I will escort you to your plane, as would any decent bodyguard of a very evil drug lord."

"You think we're being watched?"

"I *know* that we're being watched," Kossak countered gravely. "Certainly by at least one of that man Bokharai's spies. And also quite likely by an agent for the local Taliban."

Flynn nodded. Cover story or not, the presence of armed foreigners and a small squadron of different types of aircraft in this isolated corner of Afghanistan was bound to attract a lot of unwanted attention. But as long as both Bokharai and the Taliban anticipated making a profit from their activities here, neither side would want to cause trouble. In all probability, they would only watch and wait for several days to see what was really happening before they took any action. And that ought to give his Quartet Directorate team the opportunity it needed to carry out this mission—and then to vanish before the rival Afghan factions realized they had been duped. "Think you and Cooke and the others can hold down the fort here while I'm gone?" he asked.

"It will not be a problem," the Pole assured him. "And if, as I expect, our friends in the Taliban come around soon demanding their own protection money, we will act like good little criminals and meekly pay what they ask." His teeth showed again. "Admittedly, it would be cheaper and more satisfying to shoot them, but life is never perfect."

Flynn nodded. This operation was expensive and getting more expensive by the minute. Between chartering the large Il-76 cargo jet, upgrading the BushCat and Predator as needed, and the bribes required to pay off potential troublemakers here in Afghanistan, the costs were already north of two million dollars. And unlike a government, the Quartet Directorate could not simply print more money. Thanks to shrewd investments made decades ago by its wealthier founding members, Four had deep pockets . . . but its resources were not limitless.

He shook himself mentally. That was another good reason to kick this mission into higher gear as planned. Besides, nothing about it would get easier or safer with the passage of time. With a curt, imperious gesture to the Pole for the benefit of any hidden observers, he headed straight for the BushCat, which was parked at the edge of the runway. Kossak trailed close behind him, still playing the role of a dutiful bodyguard protecting his dangerous employer.

The small fabric-skinned plane already had its propeller turning. Flynn came around behind the tail and ducked under its high overhead wing. There, safely out of sight of any watchers, he turned back to Kossak and thrust out his hand. "Okay, Tadeusz. Stay safe."

"And you as well, Nick," the Pole said solemnly as they clasped hands. "Good hunting."

With a nod of thanks, Flynn swung away and climbed up into the cabin's right-hand seat. He buckled in and put on a radio headset. Then he pulled the soft-sided door closed and latched it.

Laura Van Horn, looking far more comfortable now in jeans, a khaki shirt, and her own light jacket, was in the pilot's seat on his left. Her eyes flicked from left to right across her instrument panel, studying the readings it showed. "Oil pressure and engine temperature are both in the green," she confirmed aloud, evidently running through the last items of a preflight checklist. She reached out and tapped an icon on the large multifunction display Quartet Directorate technicians had installed in place of some of the original controls. A small bar turned from green to red. "Our transponder is off."

She glanced sideways at him with a quick grin. "There's no point in telling everyone where we are, right?"

Flynn nodded emphatically. Aircraft transponders were a critical part of air safety and traffic control. When interrogated by radar, a transponder automatically sent back a code identifying the plane and reported its current altitude. That gave radar operators a good picture of where all the aircraft flying in their sector were, greatly reducing the odds of midair collisions. But having a simpleminded radio transponder ever ready to blurt out your identity and precise location was the very last thing you wanted when you were attempting a covert, low-level penetration of hostile airspace.

Van Horn reached back into the tiny cargo area just aft of the Bush-Cat's cabin. Flynn's small suitcase was already stowed there, behind his own seat. She turned back around holding two pairs of night vision goggles. She handed one to him and donned the other herself, adjusting it to fit over her radio headset.

He followed her lead and switched the goggles on. The darkness around him brightened immediately, turning their surroundings almost as clear as day, though without any real distinct color. Everything was in shades of black, white, and gray. The unlit gravel runway, largely invisible before, now stretched out plainly to both sides of the small plane. "Let there be light," he said with satisfaction.

"And a darned good thing, too," Van Horn replied with a husky laugh. "Because otherwise I'd basically be flying blind." She pushed another control, tuning the BushCat's radio to a low-powered tactical channel. "Tomcat, this is Tiger Cat. We're ready for takeoff," she said into her headset mike. "Report your status."

"*Tomcat is in position, Tiger Cat,*" Sara McCulloch replied from her remote piloting station inside the Il-76. "*Ready when you are.*"

"Copy that," Van Horn said. "Rolling now." She released the brakes and ran up her throttle a little more. The aircraft's one-hundred horse-power Rotax 912ULS four-stroke engine responded smoothly. Slowly, the BushCat trundled forward onto the runway and, guided by her feet on the rudder pedals, swung into position. She braked to a stop. Then she reached up to the flaps control handle over her head, pulled it down a notch, and locked it in. "Flaps set at seventeen degrees." She leaned forward and pushed another icon on her main display. "Fuel pump is on for takeoff."

"*Tomcat is standing by at your six,*" McCulloch radioed. "*I have your aft IR beacon in sight.*"

Flynn checked one of the little mirrors the ground crew had attached just forward of the doors. There, back behind them near the north edge of the runway, he could see the Predator UAV. The praying mantis shape of the drone now looked pregnant. A streamlined cargo container had been slung below its long, thin fuselage. Fully loaded now, the Predator needed at least five thousand feet of runway to get into the air, a far cry from the few hundred feet required by the BushCat. Dust kicked up by the drone's rear-mounted propeller eddied away downwind, appearing as a bright white plume in his night vision goggles.

"Tomcat, this is Tiger Cat," Van Horn said calmly. "Departing runway one-six."

She revved up again and started her takeoff roll. The little plane gathered speed fast and lifted off smoothly, climbing fast into the night sky. At five hundred feet, she pushed the flaps control handle back up and leveled off. They flew on low over Zaranj, continuing south by southeast at eighty-two knots to maintain the deception that they were headed for Pakistan.

Flynn checked the mirror again. The Predator was still on their tail, trailing them by several hundred yards. He turned back around in time to see the last clusters of mud-brick houses on the southern fringe of

Zaranj sliding past beneath their wings. Ahead, beyond the BushCat's whirring propeller, a desolate landscape stretched in all directions—an empty, lifeless country marked only by the snakelike ripples of bone-dry watercourses and low mounds of heaped earth and rock.

Twenty minutes later, Van Horn tweaked her centerline control stick to the right and forward a little, initiating a gentle, descending turn to the southwest. "Tomcat," she radioed. "Starting my run for the border."

"*Copy that, Tiger Cat*," the drone's remote pilot acknowledged. "*Following you around*." A sensitive receiver aboard the Predator had picked up the BushCat's short-range radio transmission and relayed it back to Zaranj via satellite link.

Concentrating hard, Van Horn leveled off again—this time at just a hundred feet. They were low enough now to make out individual boulders, lone dwarf trees, and clumps of withered thornbushes through the windshield. She continued making small adjustments to their altitude, climbing a few dozen feet to clear low rises and then descending back down into the shallow valleys beyond. "Next stop, Indian country," she said conversationally. She shot Flynn a quick, slashing grin. "Having fun yet, Nick?"

"Oh, more than I can say, ma'am," he drawled, working hard to sound unfazed. "But I'd sure appreciate it if you kept your eyes on the road." He'd never much liked flying so close to the ground. And right now, he couldn't help visualizing the little aircraft's fixed landing gear smacking into a big rock or snagging in the branches of a tree—sending them cartwheeling to destruction. Then he shook his head at his own foolishness. All things considered, it was probably a bit late to start regretting his career choices.

Van Horn's smile grew a little bigger. "Relax, cowboy. This is still the easy part of the trip. It only really gets hard when we hit the mountains."

Flynn winced. "You know," he said tightly. "*Hit* isn't exactly the word I'd have chosen right there."

She laughed. "I was speaking figuratively, not literally." She shrugged. "Besides, if you'd been a professional aviator when you were in the Air

Force, instead of an intelligence puke, you'd know that we call the process of interacting with the ground in an uncontrolled manner a *crash*."

Realizing he was in an unwinnable fight, Flynn held up his hands in surrender.

Little more than a shadow gliding through darkness, the BushCat flew on just above the desert floor, arrowing southwest toward the border with Iran. The Predator tagged along behind it. They were still more than three hundred nautical miles and almost four hours flying time from their destination.

FIFTEEN

DEEP IN THE JEBEL BAREZ MOUNTAIN RANGE,
OVER CENTRAL IRAN

LATER THAT NIGHT

The BushCat swooped low over a jagged, sawtooth saddle between two higher peaks and plunged down the other side. Hit by a powerful updraft boiling up those steep slopes, its fabric-covered wings flexed and rippled. "Hold together, baby," Laura Van Horn said quietly, almost as a prayer. She throttled back slightly and raised the nose a couple of degrees to shed some velocity. Though solidly built for a light aircraft, the BushCat's rated VNE, the speed it was never supposed to exceed, was only 108 knots. Going any faster risked having the plane's aluminum frame fold up under the stress—instantly turning what had been a flyable machine into a tangled mess of torn fabric and crumpled metal spinning uncontrollably down out of the sky.

Nick Flynn gripped the strut over his head as she banked hard away from another soaring spire of rock. The lightweight aluminum bar was one of the structural members that formed the basic shell of their BushCat's tiny cabin. Otherwise, the only thing between him and a couple of thousand feet of empty space was a thin layer of zippered Dacron-Trilam cloth.

Mountains rose on all sides, some more than ten thousand feet high. Their towering black masses blotted out whole swathes of stars in the night sky. Formed tens of millions of years ago by volcanic eruption and upthrust, the Jebel Barez ran like a spine of hardened lava through the central Iranian highlands—separating their more fertile plains from the vast, waterless deserts in the east.

Trying to navigate safely through this maze of razor-edged heights, sheer cliffs, and narrow, boulder-strewn clefts would have been tough enough in an aircraft equipped with terrain-following radar and sophisticated navigation systems tied into a full-spectrum heads-up display. It was an order of magnitude more difficult in a tiny plane fitted with only the bare minimum of electronics to save weight and electrical power. A GPS-linked digital map open on the BushCat's sole multifunction display provided some idea of where they were . . . but for the most part, their survival depended on Van Horn's skill as a pilot, her situational awareness, and her uncanny ability to anticipate danger and react in time.

Insane as this harrowing nighttime flight through mountains seemed, Flynn knew it was their only real chance to slip through Iran's air defenses unnoticed. There were relatively few air surveillance radars and surface-to-air missile batteries sited to cover the sparsely populated eastern third of the country. That was not the case farther to the west and along the coast of the Persian Gulf, where a thickening web of interlocking radars, missile units, antiaircraft guns, and interceptor bases lay in wait for any intruder.

He swallowed hard as Van Horn pulled back sharply on the stick, climbing steeply to clear another ridge. Their airspeed bled off fast, dropping below fifty knots. Just before the BushCat stalled out, she lowered its nose again and dove—rolling to follow the trace of a slender gap between two much higher summits.

"You still with me, Tomcat?" she radioed.

"*Roger that, Tiger Cat,*" the Predator's remote pilot replied tersely. "*Still hanging on your six.*"

Flynn could hear the tension in Sara McCulloch's voice. Because her flight control inputs had to be relayed through a satellite link, there was always a tiny delay before the Predator responded to her commands. It wasn't much, usually considerably less than a second. But even flying at only eighty knots, the UAV would travel more than a hundred feet in that short interval. And in this rugged country that was often the difference between survival and slamming head-on into a wall of rock. Trying to thread a remote-piloted drone through the middle of these mountains on its own would have been completely impossible. Only by closely following the IR beacon fixed to the BushCat's tail could McCulloch maneuver her ungainly Predator away from obstacles in time . . . and then often only by the narrowest of margins.

His jaw clenched. If they lost the drone on the way in, this whole operation was a bust—and he and Laura Van Horn would find themselves trapped deep inside Iran, without any real hope of rescue. Right now, they had no room at all for error or accident. His college ROTC instructors would have failed him outright for coming up with a bone-headed scheme like this. And they probably would have been right, he knew. Friction—the combination of random and unforeseen events which could not be predicted—was the only real constant in war.

The BushCat climbed again, cresting over another narrow ridge with less than a hundred feet to spare. Ahead, the ground fell away sharply, spreading out into an open plain. A band of fields and orchards stretched north and south. Flanked by two rivers, the volcanic soil here was immensely fertile. A small sea of yellow lights off to their right marked the location of Jiroft, a city of nearly one hundred thousand people. Other faint specks of light here and there pinpointed several of the tiny farming villages which dotted the broad valley.

Van Horn took them down onto the deck, jogging first right and then back left to keep as much distance as possible between them and any settled places. The Predator tagged along behind. This far inside Iran, the passage of low-flying aircraft wasn't likely to raise an alarm—but there also wasn't any point in giving the fates extra opportunities to screw them over.

"That was some seriously badass flying," Flynn told her quietly.

She nodded tightly. "Just don't jinx us," she warned. They still had two more stretches of rough country to pass through, both of them offshoots of the larger Jebel Barez chain. "What's my current ETA to the landing zone?" she asked.

Flynn studied the terrain map on their multifunction display. He traced their planned flight path. On a straight line course, they were about eighty nautical miles from the LZ he'd picked out using a combination of satellite photos and topographical charts. Of course, there was no way they could fly anything like a direct approach across those mountains and escarpments, not if they wanted to stay low enough to avoid detection by Iranian radars. Dodging and weaving through meandering passes and valleys would add miles and miles to their journey. He did some quick mental math. "Sixty minutes, plus or minus ten either way," he said.

Van Horn's mouth turned down a bit. She reached out and touched the display, switching it to show their engine and other status readouts. "Given our current fuel state, that's really pushing the envelope," she commented coolly.

"Pushing the envelope so far that we run out of gas and fall out of the sky?" Flynn asked.

She sniffed. "Have a little faith, Nick. We'll make it." Then she turned her head and gave him a shit-eating grin. "Even if I have to make you get out and push."

"You know, remind me to lecture you on basic physics sometime," he shot back.

"I thought you ducked out on the hard sciences in school?" Van Horn reminded him.

"Sure, but I figured out gravity the one time I jumped off our garage roof to see if I could fly with a couple of cardboard wings strapped to my arms. Busted a leg and dislocated a shoulder finding out that I couldn't."

Van Horn looked sympathetic. "Tough break the week before your senior prom, I guess."

"I was only six," he said with wounded dignity.

Another wall of steep hills lined the horizon ahead of them. Higher peaks lofted beyond. Thankfully, they weren't quite as daunting as the main range of the Jebel Barez—rising around two to three thousand feet above the valley floor. Van Horn pulled back on her stick a bit, beginning a shallow climb that would take them over the first rise ahead. She contacted the Predator. "We're coming up to the next rollercoaster ride, Tomcat. Stick tight and stay sharp."

"*I'll be on you like glue, Tiger Cat*," McCulloch assured her.

The BushCat zoomed low over a sharp-edged ridgeline devoid of any vegetation. These heights were completely barren, a sea of bare, blackened rock, wind-blasted boulders, and fans of loose gravel scree that would have looked at home on Mars. The little plane banked to avoid a slab-sided knob that spiked several hundred feet higher and then turned back to continue southwest.

"*My bird is picking up intermittent radar pulses at our eleven o'clock*," the Predator's remote pilot suddenly reported. "*Signal strength is pretty low, but my computer evaluates the likely source as a Meraj-Four S-band phased array radar.*" One of the modifications Quartet Directorate technicians had made to the drone for this operation was to install a radar warning system similar to those suggested for its far more capable successor, the MQ-9 Reaper. Without this capability, their two aircraft would have been forced to fly largely blind through Iran's air defense network. Plotting a course that would evade fixed radar sites was relatively easy. But many of the advanced radars associated with Iran's long-range surface-to-air missiles, like the Russian-built S-300s and its own Bavar-373 missiles, were road-mobile—making it very difficult to pin down their operating locations at any particular moment.

Flynn leaned forward and pulled up their map on the multifunction display. He studied the territory shown ahead of them, thinking fast. The Meraj-4 radar system was an expensive piece of hardware. Deploying one anywhere except to watch over high-priority targets like nuclear installations, airfields, and naval bases wouldn't make much military sense. "My bet is that radar is positioned to cover the approaches to Bandar Abbas," he told Van Horn.

Her mouth tightened. "Which puts us what? About a hundred and ten nautical miles away?"

"About that," he agreed. "And getting closer all the time."

Van Horn nodded. "No point in fooling around, then," she said. "We need to really get down in the dirt."

Flynn stared at her. "Our altitude's only a hundred feet right now. That's not down in the dirt?"

"Nope." She pushed the stick forward and the BushCat dove again—dropping until its undercarriage almost seemed to be brushing against the earth. A little cloud of dust and sand kicked up by their propeller and the wind of their passage swirled away behind them. When a massive boulder loomed up through the windshield, she pulled back just far enough to skim a few feet above its cracked and pitted surface before lowering the aircraft's nose again.

"Holy crap," Flynn blurted out before he could stop himself. Instinctively, he grabbed again for the cabin strut over his head.

"Now *this* is flying in the dirt," Van Horn said with satisfaction.

"*No radar pulses detected*," the Predator's remote pilot reported from her post at the Zaranj airport. "*We're masked by the terrain*."

"See?" She said with a rictus grin. "Piece of cake."

Flynn kept his mouth shut. The sweat streaking her face told a different story.

A lmost an hour later, they emerged from the last band of mountains on their flight path. A large barren plain opened up to the west, bordered on three sides by more rugged hills and ridges. A few scattered lights in the darkness pinpointed small villages, most of them built along a north-south, two-lane highway at the mouth of this basin. A patchwork of small fields and orchards surrounded these little clusters of flat-roofed buildings.

With the Predator right on its tail, the BushCat turned due west and flew on, still almost hugging the ground. They crossed the empty, unlit highway in the middle of a mile-wide gap between two of the towns.

Van Horn glanced to her left. The ground there rose in folds and ridges, climbing several hundred feet above the basin floor. Those hills would block any impulses from the Iranian air defense radars deployed south of them, near Bandar Abbas. She raised the BushCat's nose and gained some altitude.

Flynn breathed out in relief.

"I was starting to wonder just how long you could hold your breath," Van Horn observed wryly.

Even a couple of hundred feet gave them a much better look at the terrain they were flying over. Clumps of small shrubs and bare rock dotted the sprawling plain, but its most distinctive features were several alluvial fans that spread northward from the higher ground along its southern edge. These were the accumulations of sand and gravel which had been washed down off the hills over centuries and millennia and then deposited in triangle-shaped patterns across the basin.

Van Horn banked back north and flew low along one of these formations, closely studying the lay of the land through her goggles. The Predator peeled away from behind her and started slowly circling over the valley. At last she nodded. "Okay, this spot looks doable." She glanced at Flynn. "But this could be a little rough," she warned.

"I am in your hands, O great pilot," he said solemnly.

She laughed. "Yeah, don't you wish . . ."

Aware that he'd gone red, Flynn was suddenly very glad that their night vision gear only showed shades of light and dark.

All business now, Van Horn circled back the way they'd come and lined up with a shallow wadi at the heart of the alluvial fan. She reached up and pulled a control handle. The BushCat's wing flaps came down, offering more lift, as she simultaneously throttled back.

Smoothly, they slanted down out of the sky and touched down on the sand surface with a jolt and a little bounce. The little plane shook and rattled, jarred slightly from side to side as it rolled down the dry streambed, with bigger rocks and clumps of brush blurring past on both sides. Plumes of dust and blown sand kicked up by its landing gear trailed behind the tail. Carefully, Van Horn throttled all the way back and applied her brakes gently. The BushCat came to rest a little under four hundred feet from its touchdown point. Its propeller slowed and stopped turning.

With a sense of relief at being back on solid ground, even if it was deep inside hostile territory, Flynn unbuckled his safety harness and un-latched the aircraft's soft-sided door. He dropped lightly out onto the wadi's sand-and-gravel floor and drew his pistol. Then, ducking back under the wing, he moved up the side of the dry stream. At the top, he went down on one knee—checking their surroundings through his night vision goggles. There was no sign of movement. And no new lights showed in any of the villages several miles to the east. From the looks of it, none of the locals—most of whom should be soundly asleep anyway—had noticed their landing.

Turning, he gave Van Horn a thumbs-up signal.

She nodded and radioed the Predator circling overhead. "Tomcat, this is Tiger Cat. We're clear. The winds on the ground are very light, just occasional gusts from the west at less than five knots. Make your drop when ready."

"*Right that, Tiger Cat*," McCulloch answered from her remote station back at Zaranj. "*Stand by.*" The Predator broke out of its orbit and flew a short distance to the west, climbing to around five hundred feet. "*Dropping now.*"

Abruptly, the streamlined cargo container slung under the drone's long fuselage detached. It plunged toward the ground. A moment later, a parachute blossomed above the falling container, dramatically slowing its descent. It slid downwind and thumped to the ground in a puff of dust about fifty yards from the BushCat. The parachute canopy immediately collapsed, fluttering only a little in the light winds.

Flynn sprinted over to the grounded container. It was about eight feet long, four feet wide, and four feet high. He knelt beside it and reeled in the parachute, compressing it into a compact, easily handled bundle at the same time.

Van Horn joined him just as he finished undoing the straps that held the cargo container shut. She helped him pull it open. Mesh netting and more restraints secured five, five-gallon fuel cans at one end. They took up about a quarter of the interior. "Well, gee, I guess I get to fly out of here after all," she remarked with a note of quiet relief. The nearly four hundred nautical mile trip here had almost completely drained the BushCat's relatively small gas tank. Refueling with supplies flown in by the Predator had been their only hope of allowing the light aircraft to make it back to Afghanistan.

Flynn nodded. "And my next ride's intact, too." He patted the small motorcycle fitted tightly into the rest of the cargo container. It was a battered-looking Austrian-made KTM 250 XC-F dirt bike. Motorbikes were a common mode of transportation in Iran's cities and countryside, so this one shouldn't draw undesirable attention.

The next hour passed in a flurry of hard work—carting fuel cans back to the BushCat and emptying them into its gas tank, and then hastily camouflaging the empty cargo crate with dried brush and dirt. With that done, Flynn wheeled the motorbike over to the grounded plane.

Van Horn handed him his small suitcase. She watched while he strapped it precariously onto the back of the dirt bike. "Well, Señor Duarte," she said quietly. "I guess this is where we say goodbye."

He nodded soberly. His Persian wasn't fluent enough for him to masquerade as a native Iranian, so he'd opted to stick with his cover as a Venezuelan, although this time with a passport and travel documents that identified him as a minor official in the South American nation's Ministry of Petroleum. Caracas's revolutionary government was a close ally of Tehran's dictatorial regime, so travel between the two countries was reasonably common.

His forged documents, produced by the Quartet Directorate's top experts, were excellent. They were so good, in fact, that in almost any other country, he could have simply flown in aboard a regular commercial flight, trusting that his false identity papers would pass inspection. Unfortunately, Iran's Islamic government now required every foreign traveler to obtain a special computer-generated visa authorization code before arriving. This new process gave its security officials plenty of time to break anything but the most elaborate and detailed cover story— something that Four had no time to develop for him. Without a genuine code, Flynn would have been arrested the moment his phony papers were scanned at an airport or other point of entry. As it was, he'd have to be extremely careful not to attract close scrutiny from any Iranian authorities. One simple computer check would doom him.

This mission was a high-wire act from beginning to end. Over the equivalent of a pool of molten lava. And all without a net, he realized uneasily. Once the BushCat took off, he would be completely on his own.

Van Horn must have read his gloomy thoughts. She grabbed the back of his neck and pulled him down for a deep, fierce kiss. "You take care, Nick," she said sternly, stepping back. "Do *not* piss me off by getting yourself killed."

Taken completely by surprise, Flynn grinned almost unwillingly. "I'll do my best to avoid that," he promised. "On my honor." He held up his right hand, palm out, with the middle three fingers vertical and his thumb holding the little finger down.

She raised an eyebrow at the gesture. "You were a Boy Scout?"

He shrugged. "Sure."

"Somehow that just figures," Van Horn said with a headshake. "Okay, then, I'll hold you to your pledge." After one final searching look at him, she climbed back into the light plane and started it up.

Five minutes later, Flynn sat astride the dirt bike, watching as the BushCat lumbered down the wadi, steadily gathering speed in a cloud of prop-blown sand. At last, seeming almost reluctant to break contact with the earth, the small aircraft lifted off. Slowly, it climbed away, already banking around to head east. He raised an arm in farewell and saw its wings rock back and forth once in response.

Within moments, the BushCat, again trailed by the Predator UAV, was only visible as a tiny dot in the night sky. And then, quite suddenly, it was gone.

SIXTEEN

SHAHRUD MISSILE TEST FACILITY,
NORTHEASTERN IRAN

THE NEXT DAY

One hundred and forty kilometers southeast of the Caspian Sea, the Shahrud Missile Test Facility sat in a desolate wasteland. A steep, rocky ridge rose above the complex of blue-roofed rocket assembly buildings, concrete blockhouses, and solid-fuel storage facilities. They were surrounded by protective earthen berms and office and headquarters facilities. From the air, it didn't look like much, scarcely a dozen individual buildings set in a square grid pattern that was little more than seven hundred meters on a side. The rocket launch site itself—a large concrete pad, gantry, and flame trench—was located five kilometers away.

Appearances, though, as with so much else in Iran, were deceiving.

Like an iceberg, nine-tenths of the Shahrud Test Facility was hidden from sight—concealed in vast, bombproof tunnels dug into the adjoining ridge. Two green-roofed sheds hid the main entrances to these tunnels from satellite and air observation.

Captain Leonid Kazmin stood in the shade provided by one of these sheds. He felt uncomfortable in the baggy drab green fatigues his Iranian Revolutionary Guard "hosts" had provided to replace his immaculately tailored Russian uniform with its distinctive 12th Main Directorate atom-and-mace unit badge. A frown creased his pale, narrow-nosed face. How long was he going to have stand here, waiting around like an ill-dressed buffoon?

Irritated, he swung toward his two minders. One of them was a slim, almost dandyish major in the Revolutionary Guards. The other, burly and wide-shouldered, was one of Voronin's Raven Syndicate "specialists." Which was really nothing more than a polite euphemism for a hired killer, Kazmin thought with contempt. His mind immediately danced away from the awkward realization that the same epithet could just as easily be applied to him—with the sole difference being that while the other Russian's violent acts might be calculated in terms of small-caliber pistol and rifle rounds fired, his own would be measured in hundreds of kilotons of explosive power. "Well?" he demanded waspishly. "What's the delay now?" He checked his watch. "We have less than three hours until the next American reconnaissance pass."

"Patience, Captain," the Iranian major said soothingly. "Everything is still on schedule." He smiled. "My superiors are well aware of our adversaries' spy satellite orbits. And we are quite used to working around them."

As if in answer, klaxons blared suddenly.

Startled, Kazmin spun back toward the huge entrance dug into the ridge. A massive steel outer door swung ponderously open, revealing a brightly lit tunnel leading deep underground. Almost before the door stopped moving, a long convoy of vehicles rumbled slowly out of the enormous passage.

The first out were seven four-wheel-drive, Iranian-built Raksh armored personnel carriers. Three were equipped with 12.7mm heavy machine guns. Two more carried 30mm autocannons. And the remaining pair were armed with 23mm antiaircraft guns already pointed skyward. All of the APCs were crowded with well-armed soldiers, a mix of Revolutionary Guards and Voronin's former Spetsnaz troops. All of these wheeled fighting vehicles fanned out around the mouth of the tunnel in a protective arc.

A flock of smaller Safir utility trucks, modeled on America's famous World War II–era Willys Jeeps, emerged next. Some carried stern-faced Iranian officers and more soldiers. Others were filled with missile technicians from the Shahrud facility.

Last out of the tunnel were four very large trucks. Three of them towed heavily loaded flatbed trailers. Thick canvas tarpaulins shrouded the long cylindrical shapes tied down aboard these trailers. The fourth big rig hauled a freight container whose doors were tightly sealed and padlocked. It braked to a stop right beside Kazmin and his two minders.

The Iranian major stepped forward and opened the cab's passenger side door with a flourish. "Please get in quickly, Captain," he said politely. He smiled thinly. "As you rightly point out, our schedule is very tight. We have no time to waste."

Kazmin fought down an urge to protest the other man's obvious insolence. For all the fanatical dreams and desires of Iran's theocratic rulers, the sophisticated rockets built at their orders were still only longer-ranged versions of the Nazi V2s that had pummeled London, Antwerp, Paris, and other Allied cities during the Second World War. Deadly as Hitler's vengeance weapons had been on a small scale, they could not change the course of history. Nor could any of Iran's ballistic missiles. Without the combination of his expertise and the special device aboard this truck, the Iranians might as well plan on throwing rocks at their greatest enemy.

Awkwardly, he pulled himself up into the truck cab. Too late, he recognized the other passenger already seated next to their driver. Short, stocky, and white-bearded Dr. Hossein Majidi was the chief missile engineer for Tehran's unconventional weapons programs. And Kazmin had been doing his best to dodge the other man's probing questions ever since arriving at Shahrud. His orders from Voronin required him to cooperate with the Iranians, but only to the extent necessary to make sure MIDNIGHT succeeded. He had not planned to instruct them on the complete details of one of Russia's most carefully guarded nuclear weapons technologies. But now he was trapped.

Still smiling smugly, the Revolutionary Guard major slammed the door shut and stepped back. Then he raised a clenched fist in a signal and brought it down fast. From near the front of the convoy, the deep, echoing *blaaat* of a truck air horn replied. Fitfully at first, with quick stops and starts, the long line of trucks and smaller vehicles lurched into motion. Three of the Raksh armored personnel carriers moved out to take the lead. The rest fell in behind the larger vehicles.

Twin rotors whirling, two armed Agusta Bell 212 helicopters, export versions of the U.S. military's UH-1N Twin Huey, clattered low overhead. They flew onward across the empty desert, scouting out in advance of the slower-moving vehicles. Minutes later, they circled back to orbit slowly over the convoy, watching over its flanks and rear. One by one, the trucks and other vehicles turned onto an access road that would take them south to connect with a wider highway.

Kazmin slumped back against the bench seat. This was only the beginning of an arduous trek south to the Shahid Darvishi shipyards outside Bandar Abbas. Completing the 1,200-kilometer-long journey would take them at least two full days—especially with the need to hide their trucks in tunnels or under special shelters erected along the way whenever foreign reconnaissance satellites were overhead.

Beside him, Dr. Majidi pulled out a notebook and a pen. With a genial smile, the white-bearded scientist leaned closer. "Since we now we have a considerable amount of time on our hands, Captain," he said politely, "I wonder if you could brief me more thoroughly on how to set parameters for the various environmental sensors inside the warhead—so that it will detonate precisely as planned? After all, when the great moment arrives, this will be one of my most important tasks."

Kazmin sighed. Judging how much to reveal and how much to withhold was going to be a nightmare, he thought gloomily. Grimly, he settled in for what he was suddenly sure would be the longest trip of his life.

SEVENTEEN

BANDAR ABBAS

LATER THAT DAY

Long shadows slanted eastward across the bustling port city, home to half a million people. On taller buildings, upper-story windows blazed orange-red, reflecting back the light of the setting sun. Below, the streets were filling up again after a late afternoon lull. Those with jobs were slowly making their way home, some by car or bus and others on foot. Those without work rarely bothered to look up as their more fortunate fellows passed by. Instead, they continued chatting with their equally unemployed cronies or concentrated on the endless games of cards, chess, and backgammon that helped pass so many idle hours.

Partway down a residential street in one of Bandar Abbas's westside neighborhoods, Nick Flynn crouched beside his motorbike. He was apparently engaged in making minor, but time-consuming, repairs. A few simple tools and what looked like a miscellaneous assortment of small spare parts were spread out on an oily rag at his feet. Periodically, he'd switch out a screwdriver or a wrench and pretend to laboriously adjust some engine fitting or other mechanical component.

Most people passed by without paying him any real attention. Do-it-yourself motor vehicle repair work was a common sight in these hard economic times. To better conceal his features, he wore a dirty white baseball cap. Earlier, a few curious younger boys had gathered to observe his seemingly unsuccessful efforts to fix the motorbike, but he'd resolutely ignored their presence and they'd long since drifted away in boredom.

Flynn really had his eyes on a small house about halfway down the block. It belonged to Navid Daneshvar. He hadn't seen any signs of life there during the entire time he'd been keeping watch. An oil-stained patch of concrete near the front door showed where the Iranian naval architect ordinarily parked. There was no car there now.

He discreetly checked his watch. How long would it take Daneshvar to drive here from his job at the shipyards? Half an hour? An hour? He was painfully aware of another unnerving possibility. What if the other man never showed up at all? When he'd talked to Khavari several weeks earlier, trusted senior employees were still allowed to return home after their shifts ended, unlike the lower-level workers who were being housed on-site for the duration of the oil tanker retrofit. What if that policy had changed in the meantime—as an added security measure? If so, this whole high-stakes covert operation into Iran would turn out to be a colossal waste of the Quartet Directorate's time and limited resources.

Flynn gritted his teeth. Admittedly, he'd been eager to make a name for himself inside Four, but becoming known as the greenhorn agent responsible for a record-breaking foul-up wasn't exactly what he'd had in mind. *Stop figuring on the worst and stay focused*, he told himself sternly. While patience wasn't even remotely one of his virtues, there was no reason to anticipate failure. Not yet, anyway. He'd give this stakeout a while longer. But he figured he only had another hour at most until people around here started wondering if he was either the world's crappiest motorbike mechanic . . . or up to no good. He'd have to scoot before then.

He settled himself back down to carry on watching.

About twenty minutes before his self-imposed deadline expired, Flynn saw a badly dented old white Peugeot hatchback turn onto the street. It drove slowly past him and parked right out in front of Daneshvar's house.

Stiffly, a middle-aged Iranian man in a wrinkled business suit climbed out of the car and locked it. He was balding, with a short gray beard.

Plainly weary after what had been a very long day, the driver turned away from the street, fumbled a set of keys out of his pocket, unlocked the house's front door, and went inside. After a moment, lights came on behind the window blinds.

That pretty much settled it, Flynn decided. Although without a photo for comparison he couldn't be absolutely sure, that was almost certainly Daneshvar himself. And apparently he lived alone, which should make dealing with him much easier.

He started to get to his feet. Time was running here, so a direct approach might be best. But then, warned by some instinct, almost a prickling sensation at the back of his neck, he crouched back down by the motorbike . . . just as another vehicle came around the corner. This one was a shiny black Lexus luxury SUV with tinted windows. It pulled off to the side of the street several houses away. No one got out and it was impossible to make out anything through those dark windows.

Seems like this little party of mine is getting mighty crowded all of sudden, Flynn thought uncomfortably. Apparently, trusted servant of the regime or not, Daneshvar was being kept under close observation whenever he wasn't at the shipyards. He could think of a couple of reasons for that offhand, neither of them good. Either the Iranian was currently under suspicion because he'd been a friend of Arif Khavari, or he security precautions surrounding the *Gulf Venture* tanker refit were just as thorough and as paranoid as Khavari had claimed.

He frowned. Either way, the presence of these watchers was going to make contacting Daneshvar much harder . . . and far more dangerous. Originally, he'd hoped his cover story as a junior official in Venezuela's oil ministry would let him talk to the other man for a while before revealing his real reasons for coming to Bandar Abbas. That would have given him the chance to sound the Iranian out first. Clearly, however, that wasn't going to fly now—not with Daneshvar under tight surveillance. Nor would any of the half dozen other fanciful schemes that flitted through his mind while he faked tightening a nut on the motor-bike's front fork.

He wouldn't get very far disguising himself as a take-out delivery guy, a salesman, some kind of municipal worker, or even an appliance repair-man, Flynn knew. Yeah, he might be able to get in to see Daneshvar, but the goons in that black Lexus or someone just like them would be on his ass the moment he left. And they'd start asking some very pointed ques-tions that he would not be able to answer. *Which would be bad*, he thought ruefully. Bad as in "prolonged torture and then a bullet to the back of the head" bad.

Methodically, Flynn started picking up his tools and the little assortment of nuts and bolts and other bits he'd used as window dress-ing. Basically, if he wanted to talk to Daneshvar, he was down to one remaining option. And it was one that required him to take huge risks without adequate information, and without any safe means of retreat if the meeting turned sour. There was a chance, after all, that it was Daneshvar who'd betrayed Khavari in the first place . . . or that he'd been "turned"—induced to cooperate—later by Iran security officials investigating the original leak to the Quartet Directorate. If so, knock-ing on his front door wouldn't be a whole lot safer than riding past the local police headquarters waving an American flag.

Thinking hard, Nick rolled up the oily rag and stuffed it in his back jeans pocket. Risky as that last option was, he'd have to try it. But not today.

Down the street, one of the Lexus SUV's windows rolled down. A hand pitched a cigarette out onto the road. The window stayed down. Evidently, Daneshvar's watchers wanted some fresh air.

Flynn swung his leg over the motorbike and hit the ignition. Its single cylinder, four-stroke engine coughed to life, running a little rough for a few seconds until it smoothed out. He pulled out onto the road and puttered slowly past the parked SUV. His peripheral vision caught sight of two hard-faced men sitting in the vehicle. One of them was blond. The other had light brown hair. They were definitely Europeans, not members of Iran's Revolutionary Guard Corps. Most likely Russians, he judged. Which strongly implied that Pavel Voronin and his Raven Syndicate carried a lot more weight and authority inside this part of Iran than any of them had realized.

His mouth turned down. Nothing about that struck him as good. It was starting to look like wherever he turned, Voronin and his hired guns were already there ahead of him.

POLYARNY SUBMARINE BASE,
NORTHERN RUSSIA

THAT SAME TIME

Icy winds ruffled the waters of the Polyarny inlet and sent white wisps of snow swirling across the hills above the heavily guarded naval base. Spring was only a distant dream this far north on the frozen Kola Peninsula.

Russia's president, Piotr Zhdanov, shivered as a sudden gust stabbed at him. Irritably, he pulled the fur-lined hood of his parka tighter around his face. When he was younger, he would have shrugged off this bitter cold without a thought. But now, much as it pained him to admit it, he was no longer really the powerful model of strength and vitality still portrayed by his nation's lapdog government-controlled media. Below a fringe of thinning gray hair, his round face was pale and bloated. And there were deep, dark shadows under his hard brown eyes. His doctors assured him that he was still healthy enough to govern Russia for decades more. Privately, he no longer believed them.

"Here come the leading elements of our fleet now, Mr. President," the naval officer on his right said with proprietorial pride. Admiral Boris Pleshakov was the commander of Russia's powerful Northern Fleet. He pointed east toward where the narrow waters of the Polyarny inlet joined Kola Bay.

More than a dozen gray-painted warships, each bristling with antennas, radar domes, and missile launchers, steamed slowly past the opening. They ranged in size from the mighty 28,000-ton *Kirov*-class battlecruiser *Piotr Velikiy* down to smaller, but still well-armed, guided missile destroyers, frigates, and corvettes. Signal lamps flashed from ship to ship, relaying orders and instructions as they moved north toward the open waters of the Barents Sea.

Polyarny itself was a hive of activity. Several of the nuclear-powered submarines currently based here were also preparing to cast off. More submarines were doing the same at other anchorages up and down the Murmansk Fjord. Together with most of the Northern Fleet's thirty-odd active-duty surface warships, they were slated to take part in one of Russia's largest-ever naval readiness and training exercises.

Zhdanov turned his attention to the nearest of these enormous submarines. Nearly one hundred and seventy meters long, the humpbacked BS-64 *Podmoskovye* had originally entered service as a *Delfin*-class ballistic missile submarine. Several years ago, however, her missile tubes had been removed. Instead, she'd been converted to serve as a special operations craft, one capable of carrying Spetsnaz commandos and unmanned autonomous minisubmarines.

Now a group of twenty fit, tough-looking men were going on board *Podmoskovye*. They headed carefully up the big submarine's gangplank, bowed down under the weight of their gear and weapons. All twenty wore the black berets and camouflage-pattern battledress of Russia's naval infantry forces. That was a fiction, Zhdanov knew. His jaw tightened slightly. Every single one of those men actually belonged to Pavel Voronin's Raven Syndicate.

Voronin himself stood close to the president and Admiral Pleshakov. Although bareheaded, he appeared unaffected by the near-zero temperatures. His pale gray eyes were as cold as the frigid waters off Polyarny. He had said almost nothing so far, apparently content to let the naval officer assume he was only one of Zhdanov's junior political aides.

Zhdanov understood the younger man's reasons. Neither Pleshakov nor any of his senior staff had been briefed on MIDNIGHT. Nor did they know the troops boarding *Podmoskovye* were not actually part of Russia's official armed forces. Learning that their president's new closest adviser was a phenomenally wealthy oligarch—especially one who seemed to have come out of nowhere with his own private army and intelligence operation—would only raise uncomfortable questions in their minds. It was better by far to let them go on believing their world ran according to its old familiar patterns—where government leaders and private businessmen operated largely in their own separate spheres.

He swung back to Pleshakov, who looked pleased as he watched the fighting vessels of his fleet sail past in long columns. Moving a combined force of more than fifty warships and submarines to sea was a spectacular demonstration of force. And while they had been careful to adhere to every arms control treaty by announcing these naval maneuvers in advance, this massive show of Russian military might was bound to create consternation in Washington, D.C., and the other NATO capitals.

"Do you anticipate any significant trouble from our American friends, Admiral?" Zhdanov asked.

Pleshakov shook his head firmly. "No, sir," he said. "We know the American navy maintains a standing undersea patrol off this coast—using its own attack submarines, either those of the *Los Angeles* class or the *Virginia* class." He shrugged his shoulders. "But their patrols will be completely overwhelmed by the task of keeping track of so many of our own ships and submarines. In all the confusion and overlapping underwater noise, as our vessels engage in anti-submarine warfare drills and other high-speed maneuvers, the *Podmoskovye* should easily be able to slip away undetected and carry out this special mission you've assigned to her."

Zhdanov nodded his understanding, pleased by the other man's show of confidence. Naturally, the admiral had not been given any of the details of *Podmoskovye*'s real role in upcoming events. Although technically one of the units of the Northern Fleet, the converted missile submarine's role in intelligence-gathering and special operations often meant it operated under direct orders from Moscow. In this case, even the submarine's experienced captain, Mikhail Nakhimov, would be starting his voyage largely in the dark. Once Nakhimov broke off from the main fleet maneuvers, his instructions were to sail secretly to a set of coordinates in the mid-Atlantic, well off the coast of France. Not until then was he allowed to open his sealed orders and learn the part *Podmoskovye* would play in MIDNIGHT.

"Thank you, Pleshakov," he said. "I appreciate your professional expertise. And the efficiency you've shown in organizing this remarkable demonstration of Russia's military power. It will make our enemies tremble." With a dry smile, he nodded toward the continuing parade of warships steaming toward the open sea. "Still, with the exercise now fully underway, I imagine you have more important things to do than babysit me here, eh?"

"There are certain critical matters I should attend to back at my headquarters," the other man admitted carefully. No one in their right mind would dream of contradicting Piotr Zhdanov, even when he seemed to be in a good mood . . . at least not more than once. "With your permission?"

Zhdanov nodded graciously. "Of course, Admiral. You may go."

Relieved, Pleshakov threw him a sharp salute and strode rapidly away toward his waiting helicopter, accompanied by the gaggle of staff officers he'd brought to this dockside meeting with Russia's leader.

Zhdanov watched him leave with a calm expression. When the admiral and his officers were out of earshot, he turned back to Voronin. The last of the younger man's Raven Syndicate heavily armed specialists was just disappearing through the *Podmoskovye*'s stern deck hatch. He shook his head dubiously, suddenly feeling less confident about entrusting so much responsibility and power to men working for pay rather than patriotism. "Perhaps it isn't wise to use your mercenaries this way, Pavel," he suggested slowly. "After all, our naval Spetsnaz forces could have been ordered to carry out the same tasks. And with considerably less risk of disrupting the regular chain of command aboard the submarine."

Voronin raised an eyebrow. "It's a little late for second thoughts, Mr. President," he pointed out carefully. He shrugged. "Besides, some elements of our plan require a certain moral and mental . . . *flexibility*, shall we say. That's not a common attribute among soldiers who are more used to obeying precise orders and acting under rigid hierarchical command." He smiled. "On the other hand, the men I've put aboard the *Podmoskovye* are all hardened combat veterans—and they've each demonstrated the sort of dedication and ruthlessness we will need during the final stages of MIDNIGHT."

He paused delicately before going on. "Sadly, the same thing cannot always be said of our Motherland's more conventional military men, even those in our vaunted special forces." His smile grew distinctly colder. "As we all saw last year in Alaska."

Zhdanov frowned. Though perhaps overly blunt for his taste, Voronin's reminder of Russia's most recent military setback was fair. A daring Spetsnaz operation to recapture their country's stolen PAK-DA stealth bomber had ended in ignominious failure—forcing him to go crawling to Washington to secure the return of several prisoners. The stakes involved in MIDNIGHT were far too high to take even the slightest chance of something similar happening again. If this operation failed, the consequences could be catastrophic—both for his own continued hold on power and for Russia as a whole.

He saw the *Podmoskovye*'s stern hatch swing shut and lock. Officers leaned over the coaming of its high sail and shouted orders to the sailors standing ready fore and aft. They sprang into action, detaching the mooring lines holding the converted SSBN to the quay. She was heading out to sea. His shoulders stiffened. Voronin was right, he decided. For better or worse, they were committed now.

EIGHTEEN

BANDAR ABBAS

EARLY THE NEXT AFTERNOON

Flynn wheeled his motorbike into a narrow alley that ran behind Navid Daneshvar's house and the others along his street. Piles of garbage sacks, worn-out tires, and broken pieces of furniture showed that it was used more as a dumping ground than anything else. Flies and other winged insects buzzed lazily in the still, fetid air.

Counting off houses under his breath, he stopped in the rear of the one belonging to Daneshvar. Two small windows showed high up on a mudbrick wall. Both were barred. And just like all of the other buildings backing onto this alley, the small house lacked a rear entrance. In this part of Bandar Abbas, security against potential thieves apparently mattered more than convenience or fire safety.

Nose wrinkling against the horrible smell, Flynn squeezed his bike in between two nearly head-high mounds of trash. It wasn't exactly hidden, but it still couldn't be seen by anyone more than a few feet away. With a bit of luck the parked motorbike should pass unnoticed, especially once it got dark. As a further deterrent against possible theft, he'd thought seriously about removing its spark plugs. In the end, though, he'd decided against doing anything so drastic. After all, if he needed the bike, he was probably going to need it in a tearing hurry—without any time to blow replacing parts.

Flynn left the alley without looking backward. The fastest way to draw unwanted attention was to act nervous. As he'd planned, the street out front was deserted. At this time of day, the local men were away at work or somewhere else hanging out with their friends. The older children were in school. The younger ones were napping. And all of the neighborhood women were either busy indoors with chores or off doing the day's shopping.

Acting as though he had every right to be there, he strode right up to Daneshvar's front door. He'd noticed the previous day that the house didn't have an electronic security system. Now he could see the keyhole of what appeared to be a simple pin tumbler lock set above the knob. That wasn't surprising, since pin tumbler types were some of the most common keyed locks in the world. But it was still a lucky break, because they were also among the easiest locks to pick.

Working quickly, Flynn slid one thin, L-shaped metal tool, the kind locksmiths called a tension wrench, into the base of the keyhole. He put a little pressure on it, not much, just a pound or two, to start turning the lock clockwise. Then he worked a rake pick in at the top of the keyhole, going all the way to the back. He exhaled slightly, carefully tapping at the tumblers inside with the pick until he felt them move up one by one. *Just . . . about . . . there*, he thought, concentrating entirely on the tiny vibrations relayed through his two small tools. Still completely centered on the feelings from his fingers, he slightly increased his pressure on the tension wrench. He was so focused that when the lock suddenly spun smoothly all the way around and clicked open, it took him by surprise.

A lopsided grin creased his face. Nick Flynn, Junior Burglar, had a nice ring to it, he decided. Maybe if Four ever let him go, he could explore other career options—like busting into kids' piggy banks. More complicated locks would probably defeat his limited skills and land him in the slammer.

He pushed the door open and stepped inside Daneshvar's darkened house, quietly closing the door behind him. He found himself in a front room with a sofa, a couple of armchairs, a low coffee table, and several bookcases. Patterned Persian rugs covered a tiled floor. The blinds were tightly drawn against the sun. An arch at one end of the room opened into what looked like a tiny kitchen. Another at the opposite end led into a narrow hallway that ran the length of the house, presumably leading to bedrooms and a bathroom.

Carefully, Flynn slid the lockpicks back into his pocket and drew his pistol. He stood poised for several moments—listening intently for any sounds that might signal the presence of someone else in this small home. Apart from the faint, metronome-like ticking of an old-fashioned clock mounted on the far wall, there was only silence.

Keeping his pistol out for now, he moved deeper into the house. Over the next hour, he systematically searched every single room—first to look for any concealed listening devices or cameras, and second, to get a better sense of Daneshvar as a person. Apart from his name, occupation, and apparent age, he knew almost nothing about the Iranian. By any sensible standard, this near-total ignorance about a potential source was a violation of all the hard-learned rules of the intelligence game, Flynn knew. In the espionage business, ideally you wanted to know as much as possible about a contact's background, motivations, and real intentions before you went anywhere near them. But here he was, nevertheless, reduced to poking through the other man's clothing, personal possessions, and photos in an effort to scope out even the simplest and most basic facts. If nothing else, he thought wryly, while rummaging through a set of drawers, this situation was a pointed reminder that the real world of spying wasn't much like that depicted in the movies—where the fictional hero could always count on receiving an incredibly detailed background briefing before jetting off into danger.

One thing was clear right away. Daneshvar was a widower. And, judging by the mourning band still draped across the photo of a pleasant-faced woman with graying hair, his wife had died relatively recently, certainly no more than a few years ago. There were also framed portraits of three adult children, two boys and a girl. One of the young men wore the uniform of an officer in Iran's Revolutionary Guards. That, at least, strongly suggested that the older man had been able to keep his opposition to Tehran's radical regime a closely guarded secret, even from his own family. If so, there was some reason to hope that he'd also been discreet and clever enough to escape detection in the internal security frenzy that would have followed his friend Khavari's exposure as a traitor and subsequent murder.

The entire house was also neatly kept and extremely tidy, which added to the image of a careful, precise man who paid close attention to every detail. Nor were there any listening devices or hidden cameras that Flynn could find. And that, in turn, greatly reduced the odds that Daneshvar was still free only because he was being dangled as bait for Western intelligence agents probing the mysteries of the Bandar Abbas shipyards.

Satisfied that he'd learned all there was to learn for now, Flynn moved back to the front room. After a moment's thought, he sat down to wait in one of the armchairs. As a vantage point, it was almost perfect, positioned just far enough off to the side of the little room to be out of the line of sight of anyone coming through the door. Calmly, he fitted a suppressor to the threaded muzzle of his Glock 19 and then forced himself to relax. Judging by the events of yesterday evening, it would be some hours yet before he could reasonably expect Daneshvar to return home.

N ear sundown, the sound of a car pulling up outside brought Flynn to full alertness. He leaned forward slightly in the chair, with his pistol at the ready. A key turned in the front door and it opened, sending a shaft of orange-red sunlight slanting across the darkened room. Still cloaked in shadow off to the side, he sat motionless, waiting.

Navid Daneshvar came inside and shut the door behind him. With a heavy, tired-sounding sigh, he reached toward the light switch.

Flynn cleared his throat quietly. "Please, don't do that," he said in carefully pronounced Persian.

Startled, the Iranian swung toward him and froze. His face paled at the sight of a stranger sitting comfortably in one of his own chairs . . . and aiming a pistol straight at him.

Flynn twitched the muzzle of the Glock slightly, indicating the sofa. "I'd appreciate it if you'd take a seat over there, sir," he said politely. "But slowly. Very slowly, if you don't mind."

Swallowing hard, Daneshvar obeyed. He kept his hands open and in full view as he edged over to the sofa and sat down. "Who are you?" he asked nervously. "Do you plan to kill me?"

Flynn shook his head with a wry smile. "On the contrary, Mr. Daneshvar, I've come a long way just to talk to you." He nodded at the pistol in his hand. "This weapon is just a precaution against un-welcome intruders."

"What sort of . . . intruders?" the older man said, with a note of caution plain in his voice.

"Oh, thugs from your Revolutionary Guards. Or maybe some of those Russian hired guns, like the pair in that black SUV keeping an eye on you from down the street," Flynn said with a grin, deliberately dropping into English. "Folks who, I think, neither of us would be especially happy to see crash through that door."

Daneshvar kept a tight rein on his expression. "And you claim that you are not one of them?" he asked in the same language.

"I do," Flynn agreed.

"Then who are you exactly, Mr.—?" the Iranian prodded.

Flynn shrugged. "You can call me Duarte. As to who I work for, which is far more important, I'm a member of the organization your friend Arif Khavari contacted some weeks ago."

Daneshvar frowned. "And if I said I have no idea of what you're talking about, Mr. Duarte?"

"You'd be wasting valuable time," Flynn said flatly. He shrugged his shoulders. "The proof of who I am comes in two parts. First, if I'm not who I say I am, what do I have to gain by coming here like this? If I'm only lying, and I really work for your government or its Russian allies, why wouldn't I just have you arrested? It would sure as shit be a whole lot faster and easier to haul you off for questioning elsewhere—in far less pleasant surroundings."

The older man nodded slightly. His eyes were still wary. "And the second part of your proof?"

"It's this," Flynn said quietly. He carefully removed the magazine from his Glock and dropped it off to the side of the chair. Then he locked the pistol's slide to the rear, ejecting the remaining live 9mm round from its chamber. Finally, he leaned forward and put the empty weapon down on the rug at his feet. He sat back and looked straight across at Daneshvar. "Now, if you still don't trust me, all you have to do is bolt straight out that door over there. I can't stop you. Not before you can call for help from those Russians parked outside your house, anyway."

The Iranian smiled dryly. "You're taking a rather significant risk, Mr. Duarte," he pointed out. "Since turning you in would certainly prove my loyalty to the regime."

"Maybe so," Flynn acknowledged. "But based on what Arif Khavari told us before he was killed, I don't have time to play it safe."

Daneshvar nodded slowly. He sat back against the sofa. His face sagged in grief. "Poor Arif," he said softly. "The information I sent led him to his death. I am at fault."

Impatiently, Flynn shook his head. "You've got that wrong," he said.

"How so?" the older man asked.

"The regime in Tehran and its foreign allies are the ones who murdered your friend, not you," Flynn said bluntly. "And why did they kill him? Simply because he was a man of honor who wanted to warn the world that something very dangerous was happening here."

Daneshvar sat without speaking for a few moments. Finally, he sighed. "What you say is true." He lifted his chin. "Which, I suppose, now leaves that same task to me." He met the American's gaze. "What more do you need to know about the *Gulf Venture*?"

"Pretty much everything," Flynn confessed frankly. "Khavari was shot before he could give us more than a brief outline of the work being done on this tanker. He wasn't able to pass on enough information for us to figure out what your government and the Russians really plan to do with the ship once her retrofit is complete."

"It is complete now," Daneshvar told him quietly. "Our yards finished the remaining modifications three days ago."

"Hell and damnation," Flynn muttered under his breath. Whatever it turned out to be, Operation MIDNIGHT was even closer to kicking off than he'd thought.

The Iranian nodded. "An apt choice of words, Mr. Duarte." His expression darkened. "Unfortunately, I cannot tell you precisely what the evil men in Tehran and Moscow intend. But I now believe it may well be far worse than anything I could have imagined."

Flynn felt his jaw tighten. "Worse how?"

"Today I learned that the secret cargo intended for *Gulf Venture* is on its way," Daneshvar said. "Trucks carrying its key components are expected to arrive at our shipyards late tomorrow evening. Once those components are fully assembled by specialist crews coming with this same truck convoy, our own workers will stow it aboard the tanker." He looked worried. "When that is done and *Gulf Venture* fills its remaining tanks with crude oil, it could sail at a moment's notice."

"So what is this cargo?" Flynn demanded.

The Iranian sighed. "I don't know for sure," he confessed. "But judging by the fact that it is being trucked in from Shahrud, I am very afraid." His mouth tightened. "My government has long been in the grip of madmen. Now I fear that their madness may be reaching its peak . . . and that it could easily consume us all."

Flynn felt cold. Shahrud was the site of Iran's most advanced ballistic missile facility. Whatever MIDNIGHT involved, it sure as hell wasn't anything straightforward like smuggling small arms, explosives, or drugs to some terrorist group. Not even close. Suddenly unable to sit still any longer, he jumped up from the chair and started to prowl around the small room—feeling a lot like a tiger caged in a zoo . . . and just as helpless.

The Iranian watched him for a few moments before asking, "So what will you do now, Mr. Duarte?"

Flynn grimaced. "I'm damned if I know just yet," he grudgingly admitted. The one downside of his oh-so-clever plan to contact Daneshvar covertly was that it had meant effectively putting himself in a box. With that Raven Syndicate surveillance team parked just outside the house, he was stuck here until the Iranian went back to work the next morning—dragging his watchers with him.

He frowned. Sure, once the older man left, he'd regain his freedom of movement. But to what end? Everything he'd learned to this point was still just hearsay, the unsupported word of a single Iranian dissident. To have any hope of triggering real action by the U.S. or by some other friendly government, the Quartet Directorate needed solid evidence. Which still left the job of digging up that proof solidly planted on his shoulders.

The Shahid Darvishi shipyards themselves were definitely a no-go area. Especially now that MIDNIGHT was so close to its start date, security would be tighter than ever, with every vehicle that entered the security zone undoubtedly searched from top to bottom. Even if Daneshvar was willing to risk his own neck, it would be impossible for him to smuggle Flynn in for a closer look at the *Gulf Venture* and its secret cargo.

So what alternative was left?

He turned to Daneshvar. "Do you know which route this truck convoy is taking from the Shahrud missile site?"

The older man frowned. "For certain? No." He stroked his beard reflectively for a moment. "But given the tonnages involved, there are only so many roads which can safely handle loads of such magnitude. And once the convoy gets closer to Bandar Abbas, there is really only one highway it can use." He turned to one of his bookcases in growing excitement and pulled out a thin paperbound volume. "I have a road atlas here."

"Show me," Flynn said tersely. He followed Daneshvar's finger as he traced a route along the network of roads connecting northeastern Iran with the Persian Gulf coast. The other man was right, he realized, seeing the single major highway connecting Bandar Abbas with that part of Iran's interior.

The rough contours of a plan began to take shape in his mind. His eyes narrowed while he calculated the distances involved and tried to get some sense of the terrain he might encounter. He shook his head as the difficulty of what he'd have to do became clearer. What he had in mind could work, he decided, but pulling it off without getting killed was going to take both luck and a willingness to improvise on the fly when his "plan" fell apart—as it inevitably would.

Given the odds against success, Flynn realized, he'd better report first to Fox in Florida and to Laura Van Horn and the rest of the ops team waiting anxiously in Afghanistan. He sat down again, took out his cell phone, and started composing the message needed to fill them in on what he'd learned so far—and what he planned to do next.

His report, written in Spanish, was camouflaged as a chatty personal note about his travels in Iran. Sent to an email address registered in Venezuela, it would be automatically forwarded from there. "*Querida madre y padre, he llegado a la encantadora ciudad de Bandar Abbas y he recibido una cálida bienvenida de mi anfitrión*," he typed slowly, silently cursing the phone's tiny virtual keyboard. "Dear Mother and Father, I have arrived here in the delightful city of Bandar Abbas and received a warm welcome from my host—"

Once Flynn finished, he sat back, placing bets with himself on how long it would take to hear back from anyone. Not long, as it turned out. His phone pinged once just a few minutes later, signaling the arrival of

a text message, also in Spanish, from Fox. Translated, it strongly rec-
ommended against his planned course of action, arguing that it was far
too dangerous and unlikely to yield usable data. But the message ended,
as he'd known it would, with Fox's grudging permission to go ahead if
he still thought it best. Much as he probably would have liked to do so,
the Quartet Directorate's American head of station knew better than to
second-guess an agent in the field.

Van Horn's reply showed up just after he finished confirming his
intent to Fox. It was short and to the point: "*Solo dime dónde y cuándo.*"
"Just tell me where and when." Flynn grinned. She was a woman after
his own heart.

NINETEEN

NEAR THE VILLAGE OF GOHREH,
NORTH OF BANDAR ABBAS

THE NEXT AFTERNOON

Route 71 was a divided highway that ran from Bandar Abbas on the Persian Gulf coast all the way north through the holy city of Qom and on to Tehran, nearly eight hundred road miles inland. Just a little over forty miles north of Bandar Abbas, it passed through a small valley occupied by the tiny village of Gohreh. Small fields and groves of fruit and nut trees lined the highway for a few hundred yards. The little cluster of sand-colored buildings that made up Gohreh occupied the higher, less fertile ground east of the road. Craggy, boulder-strewn heights rose on all sides, separated by heavily eroded defiles. Formed millions of years ago by the collision of two massive tectonic plates, these steep ridges were an extension of the southern Zagros Mountains. They ran east and west like waves frozen in a tempest-tossed sea of stone.

Half a mile north of the village itself, Nick Flynn lay in wait on the forward slope of a gentle rise, an offshoot of the much higher ground climbing to the east. This hill overlooked Route 71. A few clumps of shrubs and dwarf trees paralleled the highway and climbed a little way up its barren slopes. He was prone in a shallow trench he'd scraped out by hand in the softer soil under the low-hanging branches of one of those dwarf trees. To help screen his hiding place from the road, he'd arranged tufts of dried brush along the lip of the trench, with gaps just big enough to see through.

His Austrian-made motorbike was laid carefully on its side close to his hide. He'd covered it over with a tan bedsheet bought for an exorbitant price in Bandar Abbas. Rocks held down the four corners of this cotton cloth, and he'd heaped dirt and more bits of brush across it as added camouflage.

Flynn raised his head above the edge of his shallow trench and peered down the slope. Ahead, in the west, the sun was sinking fast behind a sheer-sided ridge that climbed nearly three thousand feet above the valley floor. It would be dark in less than an hour. The heights behind him were already fading into shadow—still fully touched by light only at their very highest points. He'd finished digging himself into concealment a little over an hour ago, working in fits and starts to avoid being spotted by any of the occasional vehicles driving by along the highway. Since then, not a single car or truck had come north or south—which probably meant the Iranians had started blocking traffic to clear the way for their convoy from Shahrud.

To make sure he was ready, he powered on his phone and checked its battery level and camera settings. Everything still looked good. He settled back down again. Now to see if he and Daneshvar had guessed right.

Suddenly, a helicopter painted in desert camouflage clattered south down the valley. It flew low down the other side of the road and swirls of dust kicked up by its rotors drifted away downwind. The gunner manning its door-mounted machine gun swiveled his weapon from side to side, scanning the ground below. Flynn ducked his head and froze in place. Well, that answered his question. That helicopter scouting ahead indicated the truck convoy was on its way. Its presence also showed the Iranians weren't taking any chances with their security, he realized coldly.

Not long after the helicopter disappeared behind a fold of higher ground, the first vehicles came into view—rumbling down the highway at a steady twenty-five miles per hour. Several wheeled armored personnel carriers were in the lead. They were followed by a group of smaller, open-topped vehicles with passengers filling every seat, some of them soldiers, the others obviously civilians. Three large flatbed trucks and a big rig hauling a freight container came next.

Flynn held his phone up just over the edge of his scraped-out hole and started snapping pictures of the tarpaulin-shrouded cargo carried by those flatbed trailers. Even under canvas covers, the fin-studded shapes of three separate rocket stages—two larger and perfectly cylindrical, and a third that was smaller, with a rounded nose—were unmistakable.

His shoulders tightened. Daneshvar had been right to be afraid. The Iranians were moving a missile of some kind to the Bandar Abbas shipyards—one they obviously intended to conceal aboard the *Gulf Venture*. Judging by the size of those stages, he guessed the rocket would stand at least eighty feet tall when it was fully assembled. While that might seem small compared to something like SpaceX's Falcon 9 launch vehicle, Flynn knew it was still significantly bigger than America's Minuteman III ICBMs. And you could throw a good-sized payload one hell of a long way with a missile of that size, he thought grimly.

He lowered his phone as the last truck rolled past and disappeared around a bend in the road. A few more armored vehicles followed closely behind, bringing up the rear of the convoy. When they also vanished around the same curve, he let out a small sigh of relief. None of the convoy escorts had spotted his concealed position. Quickly, he turned off the phone and stowed it safely away in his jacket pocket. Now all he had to do, Flynn hoped, was to wait patiently for full darkness and then make his way to the extraction point.

And then another helicopter clattered into view from the north, skimming low across the valley.

"Oh, crap," Flynn muttered in dismay. The Iranians had a second aerial scout flying cover behind their convoy. And this one was headed straight down his side of the highway. He buried his face in the dirt just as the twin-engine helicopter roared right over his hiding place. Sand

and dust and bits of brush were kicked up by the powerful downdraft from its spinning rotors. He closed his eyes tight against the stinging debris.

Beside him, the rotor wash whipped at the tan sheet concealing his motorbike. One end tore free from the rocks holding it down. It flapped crazily, caught in the grip of nearly hurricane-force winds.

Aboard the Agusta Bell 212 helicopter, Revolutionary Guard Lieutenant Hassan Noorian held on to an overhead strap and leaned out through its open left side door. He stared back along their line of flight. What had he just seen, he wondered? Was that bit of cloth fluttering so wildly a camouflage cover of some kind? Or just a bit of trash littering the side of the road?

Reacting swiftly, he whirled around and tapped the pilot on his shoulder. "Come around for another slow pass next to the highway," he ordered, motioning back behind them.

Obeying, the pilot yanked his cyclic stick to the left. The helicopter banked sharply, swinging through a 180-degee turn.

As they swooped low, heading north only a few meters above the slope, Noorian leaned out through the helicopter's side door again, searching the ground flashing by below their landing skids. This time when they thundered overhead, the brown cloth sheet he'd first noticed ripped free and went tumbling away across the hillside. His eyes widened. The sheet had concealed a small motorcycle lying on its side . . . right where no vehicle of any kind should be.

That wasn't simply a broken-down piece of junk, he realized excitedly. No villager would abandon so valuable a vehicle in the middle of nowhere. Not while a single spare part or tire could be scavenged. No, he thought, it was far more likely that hidden motorbike belonged to someone who shouldn't be there—someone who'd been spying on their truck convoy and its vital cargo. Almost stammering in his hurry, he yelled into his headset mike. "Command, this is High Guard Two.

Contact. Repeat, contact. We've just overflown a probable snooper north of Gohreh."

"*Copy that, High Guard*," the IRGC colonel commanding the convoy escort radioed back, sounding surprised. Until now, their 1,200-kilometer-long trek had been entirely uneventful. "*Investigate immediately and report back.*"

The helicopter's door gunner patted his 7.62mm PKT machine gun. "I could hose that whole area down if we make another pass, sir," he suggested.

Noorian shook his head. "No, Sergeant, hold your fire," he snapped. "If it's at all possible, we want to take this spy alive. Remember, a dead man can't answer our questions." He leaned forward to shout at the pilot again. "Take us back around one more time," he commanded.

With a curt nod, the pilot banked his helicopter into another tight turn.

The young Revolutionary Guard lieutenant crouched lower, studying the terrain ahead of them through the Bell 212's dust-streaked windshield. The place where he'd spotted this spy's concealed motorbike was on the forward slope of a little hill overlooking the highway. No more than sixty meters high, this elevation was almost the perfect vantage point, he realized. But there were others in this valley and it was already growing dark. If the enemy agent they were now hunting had been clever enough to conceal himself somewhere farther away, landing at the base of the little hill might give him just enough of a lead to vanish into the gathering gloom. That was especially true since Noorian only had a half squad of four enlisted men aboard the helicopter with him. Until reinforcements from the truck convoy escort could double back, his small force was the only one available to make a search.

He grimaced. "When in doubt, take the high ground," was a mantra that had been drummed into him by his tactics instructors as an officer cadet. It was sound advice, he decided. Possession of the hill would give his handful of men excellent fields of fire if the spy made a break for it.

It would also help block his most likely escape route, a dirt track heading east from the highway toward several other small villages in an adjoining valley. He pointed toward the summit of the gentle rise. "Set us down there," he told the pilot urgently. "Right on top of the hill."

The helicopter climbed slightly to clear the crest, came to a hover over a patch of level ground at the summit, and then settled slowly onto its skids with its rotors still turning. Noorian jumped out the moment they touched down, with the rest of his troops right on his heels. His urgent hand signals spread them out in a skirmish line across the slope, with roughly ten meters between each man.

With their Russian-made AK-103 combat rifles held ready, the Guard soldiers began moving downhill toward small clumps of trees and high brush that bordered the highway. Hassan Noorian followed them with his own Browning Hi-Power pistol out and cocked. His eyes darted back and forth across the hillside ahead, probing for the slightest signs of any movement.

Flynn had wriggled around to face the back end of his shallow hole. He peered uphill. Those Iranian troops tromping cautiously down the wide-open slope were headed right for him. So much for the subtle, thoroughly discreet scouting operation he'd originally planned. Br'er Fox would be justifiably pissed . . . assuming, of course, that he lived long enough to report what had gone wrong. Basically, he had just two choices left: fight or skedaddle. And shooting it out with several rifle-armed Revolutionary Guard soldiers from this little ditch only struck him as a way to reenact the Alamo on a one-man scale. He snorted. Proud Texan though he was, he figured some things were still better left to the history books.

His eyes narrowed to slits. With the light going flat, it was increasingly difficult to judge distances accurately, but doing so was crucial. This was a delicate equation, he knew. The farther those enemy soldiers were from their helicopter at the top of the hill when he made his break, the better his chances of getting clear. But if he let them get too close, they'd riddle him with bullets before he'd gone more than a few yards. Almost unconsciously, his mouth twisted upward in a crooked grin. Maybe, just maybe, he mused, it had been a big mistake to join the Quartet Directorate. Because at the moment, the whole concept of lone wolf, high-risk missions behind enemy lines was starting to look pretty doggone dumb to him. "Kinda late to figure that out," he muttered to himself, still watching the enemy draw nearer.

Flynn tensed. The Iranian troops were less than two hundred yards away, about halfway down the hill. It was now or never, he decided.

Still staying flat on his stomach, he scooted sideways out of his shallow hiding place over to where he'd laid the motorbike. He heard a startled shout from up the slope. He'd been spotted.

"Damn," Flynn growled. Rearing up, he heaved at the motorbike's handlebars, straining to lever the machine off the ground. Small though it was, the KTM still weighed more than two hundred pounds. For a moment, it fought him and he had a split-second, nightmarish vision of the handlebars ripping loose from his grip and crashing back down to the dirt. *Not going to happen*, he told himself. He heaved again. This time, the motorbike came up, slowly at first and then faster. It rolled vertical and thumped back down onto its front and rear tires.

There were more yells from the enemy soldiers.

Flynn threw himself astride the bike and hit the ignition. The engine sputtered to life. From farther up the slope, he heard the pistol-armed Guard officer shout a command, "You there! Halt! Halt, or we'll shoot!"

For about a millisecond, he thought seriously about flipping the Iranian off—but then decided that was just the sort of pointless bravado that would only get him killed . . . and make him look pretty damned stupid in the process. Instead, he bent low over the handlebars, put the motorbike in gear, and sped off north across the slope. Still accelerating, he leaned hard left and then back to the right, veering around trees and stands of brush.

The Iranians opened fire.

7.62mm rounds tore the air around him and shredded trees—sending bits of leaves, shattered bark, and broken branches pinwheeling away. Other near misses gouged the slope behind him, hurling dirt and shards of pulverized rock skyward. One bullet ricocheted up off the ground and smacked hard into the motorbike's engine mount less than an inch from his right leg. Spent, it tumbled away in a shower of sparks. Flynn gritted his teeth and leaned over to the right to keep his balance. The sudden powerful impact had almost tipped him over.

He sped between more trees and clumps of chest-high brush and came out onto a narrow path running northeast, around the curve of the hill. Slewing hard in a spray of sand and gravel, he swung sharply onto the rough dirt track and took it at high speed. Abruptly, the ear-splitting *crack-crack-crack* of rapid rifle fire died away behind him.

Flynn risked a quick glance over his shoulder. The Iranian troops were out of sight, hidden from view by the slope and vegetation. He nodded tightly to himself and sped up. Now this was a race.

Lieutenant Hassan Noorian lowered his pistol in dismay. Around him, his men did the same with their own weapons. Hitting a crossing target moving at high speed required both skill and luck—and unfortunately all of their shots seemed to have missed. Only a faint haze of dust hanging in the air still marked the spy's path. Apparently, he was headed around the hill, speeding toward the trail which ran east into the next valley.

There was still time to block his escape, the lieutenant realized suddenly. On foot, he and his troops couldn't hope to catch that motorcycle. But by the same token, their fleeing foe couldn't possibly outrun a helicopter. He shoved his Browning pistol back into his holster, and shouted an order. "Let's go! Follow me!"

With his soldiers close behind him, Noorian turned and sprinted back toward the top of the hill.

TWENTY

ON THE FAR SIDE OF THE HILL

THAT SAME TIME

Flynn came out of the narrow band of trees and tall brush and slowed down, rising higher off his seat to see the ground ahead. The little path he'd been following joined with a wider trail here—one that ran along the base of this hill before disappearing east into a smaller valley. It stretched before him, open and empty and inviting.

Like the jaws of a trap, he thought coolly.

Instead, Flynn swung the bike into a hard right turn that left its nose pointed straight up the hill. He opened the throttle wide and accelerated. Dirt and rocks sprayed out from under his rear tire as he veered from side to side to avoid boulders half-buried in the slope and stretches of loose gravel.

Seconds later, he roared over the crest and onto the almost flat summit. And there, only a few dozen yards away, he saw the twin-engine Iranian helicopter sitting on its skids. Its rotors were still spinning slowly. The skyline on the other side of the hill was still empty. A quick, predatory grin flashed across his lean face. He'd won the race.

Still moving fast, Flynn sped through a tight curve to come in from behind the grounded helicopter. In a cloud of dust, he skidded to a hard stop right beside its open side doors. The crewman crouched there behind his door-mounted machine gun looked up in surprise. His mouth fell open. Frantically, he fumbled for the grips of his weapon—desperately trying to haul it around to bear.

Too late, pal, Flynn thought evenly. He drew his pistol, brought it on target with the same, smooth motion, and fired twice at point-blank range. Hit squarely in the chest by both rounds, the Iranian folded over his machine gun.

Then, still mounted on his motorbike, Flynn leaned in through the helicopter's open door and aimed his pistol toward the cockpit. Startled, both pilots swung toward him. Their eyes widened in horror. Before they could react, he opened fire—squeezing off multiple 9mm rounds just about as fast as he could pull the trigger. Blood spattered across the cockpit canopy. Sparks flew wherever his shots punched through flesh and bone and tore into instrument panels. Hit several times each, the helicopter pilots slumped forward against their harnesses, already dead or dying.

Grimly satisfied, Flynn slid the Glock back into his shoulder holster. Scratch one Iranian helicopter, he thought coldly. Without its flight crew, this bird wasn't going anywhere.

He looked up just in time to see the group of Revolutionary Guard troops charging over the far crest of the hill. He opened his throttle again and peeled out, slewing around to head back the way he'd come. More rifle rounds slashed past him at supersonic speeds. But then he was on the downslope and out of their line of fire.

Focused now on not crashing, Flynn sped downhill and came back out onto the trail heading east. Heedless of noise, he accelerated again and raced ahead, leaving a growing plume of dust in his wake. There was no longer any point in trying to hide. He'd knocked out one Iranian scout helicopter, but the other would be on his tail soon enough. Speed had quite literally become life at this stage of his mission.

He roared past another small village. Not far beyond it, the trail crossed a dry riverbed and petered out. He kept going east, bouncing and jolting along the rough, rock-strewn surface of the wadi itself. He resisted the urge to look back. If the Iranians reacted even faster than he'd feared, he was a dead man anyway.

A mile or so east along the wadi, Flynn spotted a shallower place along the mounded bank it had carved through this alluvial floodplain. He gunned the dirt bike up that easier slope, with loose sand flying out behind him, and climbed out onto more open ground. And there, not more than a couple of hundred yards away, he saw the high-winged shape of the BushCat light aircraft lined up for takeoff with its prop already turning.

His face creased in a huge, relieved grin. Just as promised, Laura Van Horn was in the exactly right place and bang on time.

Flynn slid to a stop next to the BushCat and jumped off, letting it topple sideways with the motor still running. Time was too short to waste wrecking the bike so that it wouldn't fall into enemy hands. Off to the west, he heard the faint clatter of rotors. The surviving Iranian scout helicopter was on its way.

He darted across to the aircraft and scrambled up into its cabin. It smelled strongly of gasoline. On this trip out, without the weight of a passenger, Van Horn had been able to carry the extra fuel she needed for a return flight aboard her BushCat instead of relying on the Predator drone's jury-rigged cargo capability.

From the pilot's seat, she shot him a dry smile. "Hey there, stranger. Need a lift?"

"Why, yes. I surely do," Flynn said, matching her tone. He took the headset she offered and plugged in. "It seems like the locals are mighty pissed off at me right now."

Van Horn shook her head in mock disapproval. "This is becoming a really bad habit, Nick. Stacking up dead bodies behind you is no way to go through life, you know."

"I take your point, ma'am," he said with an apologetic shrug. "But I didn't exactly have any choice this time . . . not if I wanted to go on living, anyway."

She laughed. "Well, I guess it's okay, as long as you're really, *really* sorry."

Still smiling to herself, Van Horn ran the BushCat's throttle up to full power, released its brakes, and started her takeoff roll. Responding instantly, the little plane bounded forward, bouncing and swaying across the bumpy ground while it steadily picked up speed. They'd only covered a few hundred feet when she pulled back on her control stick. Eagerly, the BushCat broke free of the earth and climbed away. She leveled off just a couple of hundred feet above the ground. They were flying east at around ninety knots, the light aircraft's preferred cruising speed.

Flynn checked the mirror mounted on his side of the plane. There, several miles away to the west, he spotted a quick flash of red-tinged sunlight glinting off a clear canopy. He squinted against the glare, just making out the distant shape of a helicopter as it turned toward them. "Well, that sucks," he said somberly. He looked across the cabin. "We've got company."

Van Horn nodded calmly. "Figured so." She glanced back at him. "Fixed wing or whirlybird?" she asked.

"A helicopter," Flynn replied. "Probably an Agusta Bell 212, from what I saw earlier."

"A Bell 212? That's a nice flying machine," she said thoughtfully. She craned her head to check the mirror on her side. "Coming on fast, too. It's probably got an edge of about forty knots on us."

Flynn frowned. "Just swell." For lack of anything better to do, he drew his Glock, hit the release button to drop out the spent magazine, and then inserted a fresh one from his jacket pocket.

"Whoa there, Top Gun Flynn," Van Horn said with a thin smile. "That 9mm peashooter of yours won't be much use in a dogfight if it comes down to that." She raised an eyebrow. "And I'm betting that helicopter's packing serious firepower, right?"

"It's got a door-mounted machine gun," he admitted. "Most likely a 7.62mm Russian PKT-type." The idea of trying to take on a faster, more heavily armed rotorcraft with his pistol did seem pretty crazy, put that way. Then again, what other options did they have? He looked at her. "Can this crate of yours even dogfight anyway?"

She laughed. "Oh hell, no. Aerobatics are strictly forbidden. Remember, this little beauty is made out of fabric and thin aluminum. If I pull too tight a turn, I'm liable to rip our wings right off."

"This just gets better and better," Flynn said flatly. Then he noted her relaxed profile. He sighed. "Okay, Miss Van Horn, what's your plan?"

"What makes you think I have a plan?" she asked innocently.

He snorted. "Because I don't think you even go into the ladies' room without a plan."

Van Horn flashed him a winning smile. "Insulting, I guess, but basically accurate." She spoke into her headset mike. "Tiger Cat to Tomcat. You see the situation?"

Through his headset, Flynn heard the voice of Sara McCulloch, the Predator's remote pilot, responding from her station hundreds of miles away in southwestern Afghanistan. "*I see it, Tiger Cat. Come right to one-three-five and climb to five hundred feet.*"

Obeying, Van Horn banked the BushCat to the right, altering her course slightly until they were heading southeast. She pulled back a little on the stick. The aircraft's nose came up and they gained some altitude. They were now flying straight toward a nearby ridge that rose a couple of thousand feet higher still above the valley floor.

Off to the west, the Iranian helicopter—rapidly closing the gap between them—matched her maneuvers. Suddenly, several miles behind them both, two bright, split-second flashes lit the darkening sky.

"*Fox Two,*" McCulloch called succinctly.

Trailing smoke and fire, two tiny shapes slashed toward the Revolutionary Guard helicopter at Mach 2.2—more than seventeen hundred miles per hour. Eight seconds later, both missiles detonated within yards of their target. Dozens of fragments sleeted through the Agusta Bell 212. Wreathed in flames, the shattered helicopter spiraled down and smashed into the ground. A pillar of oily black smoke curled high into the air from the impact point.

Flynn gazed back at the crash site in silence for several seconds. Then he breathed out. He glanced across the cabin at Van Horn. "Unbelievable. You really brought that Predator drone along carrying air-to-air missiles?"

She nodded in satisfaction. "AIM-92 Stingers, to be precise. It seemed like a sensible precaution."

Flynn stared at her. AIM-92s were the air-launched variants of the U.S. military's shoulder-launched Stinger missiles. "Should I ask where you got them?"

Van Horn shrugged. "I think they fell off the back of a truck at some point. Maybe back in Alaska when I was up there doing one of my stints in the Air National Guard."

He felt his eyebrows go up. "And you don't think anyone's going to notice that a couple of Stinger missiles have gone missing?"

She shook her head complacently. "Nope. Both were marked off as expended in training." Her teeth flashed white in the darkened cabin. "Okay, so maybe that was a little premature." Then she jerked a thumb over her shoulder at the smoke rising skyward behind them. "But it's true now. The expended part, I mean."

Flynn looked back at the burning wreckage of Iranian helicopter. No one could have survived that crash. He shook his head. "And what was that lecture I got earlier? About my bad habit of stacking up bodies behind us?"

Van Horn smiled serenely. "It must be the bad company I'm keeping." She banked the BushCat back to the east—starting the long, arduous night flight through Iran's mountains and across its vast deserts that would take them back to Afghanistan.

SOUTHERN IRAN

THE NEXT DAY

Sourly, Pavel Voronin prodded a twisted and blackened piece of debris protruding from the sand with the toe of one of his handmade boots. He turned to the gray-bearded Iranian brigadier general standing next to him. Mohsen Shirazi commanded the Revolutionary Guard's Aerospace Force. That put him in charge of all of Iran's military missile and space efforts—most important of all now, those committed to MIDNIGHT. "So now we know for sure that an enemy has uncovered some of our most prized secrets," he commented coldly.

Shirazi frowned. "Some, perhaps," he admitted. "But not all of them."

"Thanks to your traitor Khavari, they know about the *Gulf Venture*," Voronin retorted. "And now their agents have seen your Zuljanah rocket in transit. Which means they were tipped off to the convoy from Shahrud by someone." He scowled. "All things considered, Jerusalem has already learned far more about our business together than I find comfortable."

Shirazi looked narrowly at the dapper, well-dressed Russian. "You're still convinced this was an Israeli operation?"

"It's the logical assumption," Voronin pointed out. The ambush carried out against Viktor Skoblin in Vienna had been straight out of the Mossad playbook. And so was this. Who else but the Israelis would have the courage, skill, and, indeed, the sheer ruthlessness to carry out such a daring covert operation so far inside Iran? Certainly not the Americans or even the British, he concluded dismissively. Judging by what he read, their intelligence agencies were much too focused on playing domestic political games right now to willingly risk trained agents and equipment in a high-stakes gamble like the one they'd just witnessed.

Moodily, he kicked at the burnt-out remains of the helicopter again. "If we can be grateful for anything," he said harshly, "it ought to be that the Israelis had only a small reconnaissance unit deployed near the highway, and *not* a more well-equipped commando force. Judging by the results here, a full-fledged attack on your convoy might well have reduced all our hopes for MIDNIGHT to smoldering wreckage."

Slowly, Shirazi nodded in bleak acknowledgement. "If the Israelis have been alerted by what they've learned here—and elsewhere—we can expect them to react even more violently going forward," he warned.

"I am aware of that," Voronin snapped. He fought to regain his composure. He had too much riding on this enterprise to see it end in failure. Zhdanov had given him a blank check so far. But Russia's president would never forgive him if MIDNIGHT resulted in yet another humiliating defeat. If his nation's autocratic ruler had one defining characteristic, it was his readiness to sacrifice anyone he believed had failed him.

"Perhaps we should provide an armed naval escort for *Gulf Venture* when it sails," Shirazi suggested. "To protect the tanker against air attack or a commando raid."

"You think so?" Voronin said acidly. He snorted in derision. "Why not just publish all our detailed plans for this secret operation in the *New York Times* or the *Washington Post*? It would certainly be simpler and cheaper than surrounding what is supposed to be an innocent civilian merchant ship with a flotilla of your fast-attack speedboats and other warships."

The Iranian's mouth thinned in anger. He folded his arms. "Then what do *you* propose we do?"

Voronin told him.

Shirazi frowned. "Your concept has merit," he conceded at last. "But implementing your ideas will add several days and significant costs to the tanker's fitting out process. My superiors in Tehran will not be pleased."

"Better a minor delay now, than complete disaster later," Voronin reminded the other man bluntly. "Especially since neither of us is likely to survive for long if this operation fails."

"A persuasive argument," Shirazi agreed at length. He nodded. "Very well, it shall be done."

TWENTY-ONE

CIA HEADQUARTERS, LANGLEY, VIRGINIA

SOME DAYS LATER

Miranda Reynolds, the head of the CIA's Directorate of Operations, wondered if she ought to mark this down as a red-letter day in the imaginary diary she'd didn't actually keep. High-ranking officials in the Agency had learned the hard way that even the most personal of records might be subject to subpoena by busybody Congressional investigators determined to cause trouble. In the circumstances, it was safer to rely entirely on your own memory, she thought cynically—unless, of course, you needed to jot down a pro forma protest of some questionable, or even outright illegal, order from a superior . . . at least as a measure of limited protection against possible future prosecution.

Nevertheless, she probably should find some permanent way to memorialize this meeting. Since his appointment, Charles Horne, the new director of Central Intelligence, had made it clear that he preferred working with his senior subordinates through a web of toadies and underlings. And yet here she was, summoned to his private office for an emergency intel briefing from Philip Demopoulos, who ran the Agency's Directorate of Analysis. Whatever else was going on, she guessed that was a sign the DCI didn't want any other potential leakers—or witnesses, maybe—to hear what they were going to discuss.

For now, she sat quietly in one of the two chairs placed in front of Horne's desk. Demopoulos, wavy-haired with a trim, graying goatee, occupied the other. She thought he seemed on edge, which probably meant he suspected his news would not be welcomed.

Slowly and methodically, Horne sorted through the sheaf of photographs he'd been handed by Demopoulos shortly after they all sat down. Although he said nothing at first, his thick lips compressed in obvious annoyance as he fanned them out across his desk. They showed what appeared to be a convoy of military trucks and other vehicles on a road somewhere. Canvas-shrouded shapes of some sort were tied down on some of the flatbed trailers shown. His fleshy face reddened slightly while he studied them.

At last, he looked up at Demopoulos. "What's all this supposed to be, Phil?" he demanded, indicating the photos.

"We believe those are the separate stages of a large missile or space rocket," the other man said carefully. "One the Iranians shipped by road to the Bandar Abbas area several days ago."

Horne frowned. "How do you know that?" He tapped one of the pictures. Beyond the line of trucks, it showed a barren, rocky wasteland with sharp-edged mountains rising in the background. "For God's sake, these images could have been taken almost anywhere in Iran. The whole damned country's almost nothing but desert or arid, mountainous wilderness."

"The digital file containing those pictures was sent to us by a well-informed source we've always found reliable," Demopoulos explained. "And we've confirmed the geolocation data provided with every photo. There's absolutely no question that these images were, in fact, taken along a stretch of highway not far north of Bandar Abbas."

Horne's frown deepened. "Ah, yes, your mysterious 'reliable' source," he said heavily. "The same one, I recall, who tried to sell us the bullshit story about that oil tanker Tehran was supposedly retrofitting for some nefarious purpose a while back."

Demopoulos let that pass.

Reynolds grimaced. She'd assigned a small team to discreetly uncover where Demopoulos really obtained his gems of raw intelligence from inside Iran. So far, to her intense irritation, they'd come up mostly empty-handed. All anyone in the Analysis Directorate could tell them was that their chief's eyes-only source was code-named GLASS ISLE. One of her more literary-minded subordinates had rather hesitantly suggested this could be a veiled reference to the Isle of Avalon in Arthurian legend, the place where King Arthur's sword, Excalibur, was forged and where the gravely wounded king was said to have vanished into legend—but where the hell was that type of mythological gobbledygook supposed to lead her?

As it was, her efforts to dig into Demopoulos's activities were already sliding dangerously close to what her colleagues in the Agency would consider spying on another directorate. And that was strictly taboo. In-house investigations were supposed to be the sole purview of the CIA's Office of Security. Power struggles occurred, but they were ordinarily waged within strict bureaucratic limits. No one wanted to risk a messy, knives-out fight inside Langley. Not one that might leak to the press and Congress and make the CIA as a whole look bad, anyway.

"Okay, so those photos were taken near Bandar Abbas," Horne said finally. "But why is that supposed to be significant? The Iranians have hundreds of short- and medium-range ballistic missiles in their arsenal, don't they? So the fact that they're moving one of them around by road is hardly an earthshaking development, is it?"

"Scale analysis indicates this missile or rocket is significantly larger than most of those in Iran's arsenal," Demopoulos said patiently. "Although we can't be sure without getting a close look at the actual weapon itself, my experts tell me that it's most probably a newly completed Zuljanah three-stage rocket—or a comparably sized missile of a brand-new type. One we've never seen before."

Horne looked momentarily blank.

"Either way, this can't be a routine redeployment," Demopoulos told him calmly. "So far, the Iranians have only flown their Zuljanah rocket twice that we know of. Once in early 2021. And one more time last summer—from somewhere in the southern Caspian Sea. Probably off one of their fixed oil platforms converted into a launch site."

"So?"

"There aren't any Iranian missile flight test centers in the Bandar Abbas region," Demopoulos said. "Which indicates this transfer isn't related to a regular research and development program." He leaned forward in his chair. "And there's one more piece of evidence which suggests the Iranians have bigger plans for this rocket. We believe it was shipped to Bandar Abbas from the Shahrud Test Site, hundreds of miles away. But we don't have a single image from any satellite pass over the past two weeks that shows this truck convoy on the road. Not one. That alone tells me Tehran has gone to extraordinary lengths to try to keep this movement secret."

Horne frowned. "And I suppose you've got a theory about why that might be?"

Reynolds saw Demopoulos tense up. *Interesting*, she thought. *Now we're getting to the part of this briefing he's sure won't make the DCI very happy.*

"The most reasonable conclusion is that they intend to smuggle this rocket out of Iran aboard the tanker they've been refitting for the past few months," he said. "We got a good picture of the *Gulf Venture* on this morning's KH-11 pass. The ship has moved out of the repair yard and is currently moored alongside a nearby pier loading crude oil into its remaining storage tanks." He laid another photograph on Horne's desk.

Reynolds studied it. The Iranian tanker was much larger than she'd expected, more than eight hundred feet long and over a hundred feet wide. The damned thing was as big as a battleship, she realized. A maze of piping, other mechanical structures, and what looked like several groups of chained-down, forty-foot-long freight containers covered its enormous deck.

Horne scowled. "Even assuming that this wild-assed guess of yours is correct," he ground out, "what exactly are we supposed to do about it, Phil?" He shook his head. "The UN arms embargo on Iran expired years ago. Technically, Tehran is allowed to sell weapons to any legal government. The methods the Iranians use to ship those arms doesn't alter the ultimate legalities involved."

"Our best intelligence is that Iran's missile programs are controlled by the Revolutionary Guards," Demopoulos pointed out carefully. "Which makes smuggling a long-range rocket out of Iran a clear violation of our country's independent sanctions against the IRGC. And that, in turn, makes the *Gulf Venture* a legitimate target for covert action, either to disable the tanker in port . . . or to seize the ship outright when it's at sea. Plus, the chance to examine one of its most advanced missiles up close would open a goldmine of technical intelligence about Iran's real military capabilities."

There was a long, awkward moment of silence while Horne's face reddened even further. Inwardly, Reynolds started a mental countdown to the explosion she saw coming.

"Have you lost your mind?" the DCI finally barked. "Do you seriously expect me to approve provocative action of that sort? Purely on the basis of what can only charitably be described as rumor and lunatic speculation? And at a time when this whole administration is doing its goddamn best to improve our diplomatic relations with the Iranians? I'm supposed to wreck a major foreign policy initiative being pushed by the president of the United States himself? And to do what, for Christ's sake? Stop Tehran from sending some piss-ass country somewhere one lousy rocket?"

Obviously opting to try to save his career rather than take up the offer to argue openly with Horne, Demopoulos stayed quiet. A muscle twitched slightly at the corner of his mouth, though—revealing his inner fury at being lectured like a schoolboy by a man whose sole qualifications for the DCI job were his political connections.

The DCI's heavy-lidded gaze slid to Reynolds. "What's your view on this, Miranda?" he asked, with deceptive calm.

She shot a quick glance at Demopoulos. She could almost read the appeal for support in his eyes. Oh, hell no, she thought coolly, there was no way she was joining him at the chopping block. Not with Horne already starting to sharpen his axe. Besides, she was confident that the Analysis Directorate chief had let himself be played by whoever was really feeding him all this material about missiles and oil tankers and all the rest.

If she had to place bets, her guess now was that his private GLASS ISLE material had its ultimate origins in Israel. The Israelis were already locked in an undeclared war with Iran. Their small navy and commando units periodically carried out attacks against Tehran's shipping, especially targeting its oil tankers and weapons shipments. To date, they'd been successful more often than not, but the logistical strain of carrying out a prolonged campaign so far beyond Israel's borders had to be immense. Luring the U.S., with its much larger and more powerful Persian Gulf naval task force, into joining in against Iran would be pure profit for her counterparts in the Mossad. Well, she decided, going down in flames to help the Israelis out of a jam was definitely *not* part of her career game plan at Langley.

Firmly, Reynolds shook her head. "Even assuming there really is a missile hidden aboard that tanker, so what?" she asked caustically. "The interagency consensus—one shared by all of our closest allies—is that Iran's nuclear program hasn't been able to produce a working fission bomb yet, right?"

Reluctantly, Demopoulos nodded.

"So what's the real threat here?" Reynolds continued remorselessly. "Does anyone here seriously believe that a single rocket, armed, at most, with a conventional high-explosive warhead—no matter how large— really poses some type of an existential threat to the U.S.? Or to any of our allies, for that matter?"

Gamely, Demopoulos tried to recover lost ground. "Conventional weapon or not, it'd be a hell of a black eye for the administration and for the Agency if the Iranians or one of their terrorist group surrogates managed to lob a warhead into New York or Washington or Houston," he warned. "The kinetic impact alone could knock down a skyscraper and kill a lot of people."

"Maybe so . . . if everything went right for them and wrong for us," Reynolds allowed with an unconcerned shrug of her shoulders. "But how many times did you say the Iranians have tested their Zuljanah rocket?"

His mouth tightened. Plainly, he saw where she was headed. "Twice, so far," Demopoulos said quietly.

She smiled sweetly back at him and then went ahead and stuck her metaphorical shiv right between his ribs. "And what happened on that second launch, Phil?"

"We think the payload vehicle malfunctioned on its way to orbit," he conceded tightly. "Which apparently forced the Iranian launch crew to order it to self-destruct."

Reynolds turned back to Horne, who wore an expectant expression on his florid face. "There you have it, Charles," she said calmly. "I don't believe this is a threat worth getting all worked up over." Her shoulders lifted again. "Anyway, we have excellent coverage of the entire Western Hemisphere. If Tehran does ship this missile somewhere within range of the U.S., we'll spot it soon enough. And, if necessary, we can always blow it up on the launch pad then—without unnecessarily upsetting our masters in the White House."

From the pleased look Horne gave her, she knew she'd made her point. She almost felt sorry for Philip Demopoulos. He should have known better than to hope she'd back him up on this. Besides, if he'd bothered to share that private source of raw intelligence material with her first, she could have warned him off before it was too late. No, she thought coldly, this was all his own fault.

The head of the Analysis Directorate had played games to make himself look good . . . and instead all he'd managed to do was guarantee that the CIA's risk-averse director would turn a blind eye to whatever the Iranians were planning. If she'd honestly believed this missile they were smuggling posed a real threat, that would have bothered her. As it was, Miranda Reynolds was just grateful she'd been given the opportunity to bolster her own standing inside Langley at Demopoulos's expense.

TWENTY-TWO

SEVERAL HOURS LATER

Sixty-eight stories high, the shining steel-and-glass Almas Tower soared nearly twelve hundred feet into the air. Even then, it was only the eighth tallest of the more than two hundred high-rises that crowded Dubai's skyline. *Almas* was the Arabic word for "diamond" and, seen from above, the tower's shape resembled an enormous cut gemstone. It had been purpose-built to house firms linked to the UAE's prosperous diamond, precious gemstones, and pearl trade—including Dubai's Diamond Exchange. As a result, security was extremely tight. That factor alone had attracted the Quartet Directorate's favorable attention back when the office tower opened. Now one of Four's front organizations, Sykes-Fairbairn Strategic Investments, maintained a small office on one of the highest floors. Most of the time it was empty, serving only as a useful accommodation address that helped maintain the illusion that Sykes-Fairbairn was a legitimate investment firm with worldwide connections. Tonight, however, it provided a convenient place for a secure meeting only a hundred and sixty air miles from Bandar Abbas.

Nick Flynn stood at one of the office's large windows, looking out across a sea of dazzling light. Dubai's highways, skyscrapers, and extravagant, palm-shaped artificial islands were all brightly illuminated—

turning night into near-day for miles along the coast. Life in this oasis of commerce and luxury ran around the clock.

Stifling a yawn, he rubbed hard at his tired eyes. Sleep had been scarce over the past seventy-two hours. He'd spent most of those hours arranging the safe departure of his Quartet Directorate ops team from Afghanistan—along with their gear, including the BushCat light plane and the Predator. Once that was done, and everything was on its way to storage in various warehouses Four owned in the United States, Middle East, and Europe, he'd flown directly here to confer with Fox and Gideon Ayish about possible next moves.

Just at the moment, however, they were all waiting to hear back from Fox's contact inside the CIA. At a muttered "damn" from Fox, Flynn turned away from the windows in time to see the other man put his smartphone down with a frustrated expression on his thin face. "No joy from Langley?" he guessed.

Fox shook his head. "None."

"As we expected," Ayish reminded him with a shrug.

"Low expectations are one thing," Fox said wryly. "Having them met in reality is another." He tapped the phone. "I did pick up one piece of fresh information from my source, but it's not good news either. The *Gulf Venture* has moved from the shipyards to a berth at the Bandar Abbas oil terminal."

Flynn frowned. "So whatever the Iranians and their Raven Syndicate allies are planning must be about to kick off."

"That is the most logical assumption," Ayish agreed.

"And even knowing that, the CIA is really just going to sit by on its high and mighty ass and do damn-all?" Flynn asked.

"Langley won't step on White House toes," Fox explained quietly. "Not when the threat seems so low."

"Low?" Flynn retorted. "That rocket I saw on the move is bigger than some of our ICBMs. You can pack a helluva lot of explosives on something that size."

The older American nodded patiently. "True, Nick. But one missile with a conventional warhead still only adds up to the modern equivalent of a WWII-era V2 rocket. A weapon like that might take out a block and do a lot of damage, but it's not a city-killer. And Iran doesn't have nukes. Not yet, anyway."

And then, in the blink of an eye, Flynn saw the piece of this puzzle they'd all been missing from the very beginning. Son of a bitch, he thought, feeling suddenly afraid. As hard as they'd worked this problem, he and the others in Four had still been acting as though it was just the usual spies and counterspies variant of a low-stakes poker game—one where move met countermove and deaths could be counted on one or two hands. But now it turned out that the bastards sitting across the table were actually going all in—and this game was really being played for the life and death of hundreds of thousands, maybe even millions.

"Iran may not have nukes," he said tightly. "But Russia sure as hell does."

Ayish furrowed his brow. "What reason do we have to believe Moscow would ever provide the Iranians with such weapons?"

In answer, Flynn leaned over the table and flipped open the folder Fox had brought with him. It contained all the photos they'd been accumulating from the beginning, those retrieved from Skoblin's computer and other sources, and now the images he'd taken outside Bandar Abbas. He pulled out their single blurry black-and-white contemporary picture of Pavel Voronin and slid it across to the two older men.

"This guy Voronin is my reason," he said flatly. "Why else would Tehran need the Raven Syndicate? That rocket they've stowed aboard the *Gulf Venture* is Iranian-made from top to bottom. So's the oil tanker itself, for that matter. And the Revolutionary Guard Corps doesn't ex-actly have a shortage of trained killers in its own ranks. So the Iranians have zero real need to rely on Voronin's ex-Spetsnaz mercenaries as muscle for this MIDNIGHT operation of theirs." He shook his head.

"All of which indicates the Raven Syndicate must have brought something extremely important to the table. Something the Iranians couldn't provide themselves. Something like a nuclear weapon."

Fox stared down at the photo. "Giving the Iranians a nuke? What would Voronin hope to gain from going that far?"

"Money," Flynn suggested. "And lots of it." He shrugged. "Remember, this guy and his old boss Grishin were willing to sell his own country's stealth bomber to the highest bidder." He paused for a moment. "So what's the going price for a fusion bomb these days?"

"A very large sum, indeed," Ayish said quietly. He frowned. "But I do not believe that even someone like Voronin could gain access to a nuclear weapon. Not without explicit authorization from the very highest levels of the Russian government. Moscow's security protocols for its nuclear arsenal are much too strict to be easily circumvented."

"They are," Fox agreed slowly. Behind his thick glasses, his eyes darkened. "Unfortunately, Gideon, it's only too clear that President Zhdanov himself is Voronin's patron and protector."

Ayish shook his head stubbornly. "You think Zhdanov would approve providing Tehran with such a weapon? The means, I grant you. But the motive? What can Russia hope to gain from so dangerous a move?"

"Plausible deniability," Flynn told him. "If anything goes wrong, the shit hits Iran—and not Russia. By using the Iranians as his front group, Zhdanov can smack one of Moscow's enemies hard and escape retaliation."

"A daring and vicious concept," Ayish agreed carefully. "But while I agree that Piotr Zhdanov is certainly an ambitious and evil man, he is also not a fool. I don't see how Moscow could hope to retain control over a nuclear weapon once it was in Iranian hands. Iran may be an ally of Russia, but it is not a vassal or a puppet state. If the radicals in Tehran change their minds and decide to use their new bomb as they see fit, even against Russia's interests, what are Zhdanov's safeguards?"

"The Raven Syndicate," Flynn said, working it out. "My bet is that's why we keep finding Voronin's men so deeply embedded in this operation. His people are along to make sure that warhead is used for its intended purpose . . . and not for something else—like being taken apart and reverse-engineered to advance Tehran's own nuclear weapons research."

Ayish sighed. "I will not take that bet." He nodded reluctantly. "Very well, Nick, I accept your premise, deeply unsettling though it is. We have to assume that the missile concealed aboard the *Gulf Venture* is now armed with at least one live nuclear warhead." He frowned. "Unfortunately, this knowledge doesn't bring us any closer to understanding where and how our enemies plan to use this weapon."

"No, it doesn't," Flynn agreed. "But one thing's sure: once that tanker sails, it can go anywhere in the world. We can't rule out any target. Not D.C. Not Los Angeles. Not London or Paris."

"Or Tel Aviv or Jerusalem," Ayish added somberly.

Fox nodded. "Indeed." He got up from the table and went to the windows to look out across Dubai's glowing skyline for a long moment. Beyond the brightly lit islands along the coast, a vast band of darkness showed where the Persian Gulf spread across the horizon. Dozens of smaller lights blinked out at sea, signaling the presence of ships ferrying oil, passengers, and other goods down the Gulf. These were some of the busiest waters in the world. With a bleak expression on his face, he turned back to the table. "Okay, if our fears are accurate, we now face a nightmare scenario—a nuclear weapon in the hands of fanatics ready, eager, and willing to use it. Fanatics aided and abetted by one of the world's great powers. The question then is, what we can do to stop these people before it's too late?"

"I don't see that we have much choice," Flynn said forcefully. "Somehow we have to organize a strike force and take that damned ship the moment it crosses into international waters."

The older American shook his head with a slight smile. "I can always count on you for the direct approach, Nick. But in this case, I don't believe Four can put together a team with the sorts of skills and special equipment needed. At least not in the brief time remaining before the *Gulf Venture* is likely to sail." Wearily, Fox pulled off his glasses. With his eyes closed, he rubbed at the bridge of his nose, obviously considering the situation. Then he put his glasses back on and turned to Ayish. "Which leaves your people, I think, Gideon," he said slowly.

The Israeli made a face. "Many of the same problems apply," he said cautiously. "True, in the past, my country has dealt some shrewd blows to Iran's shipping, but staging our forces into this region is always difficult and time-consuming. Unless we already have an operation in progress or planned for the near future, Israel may also lack the ability to act with sufficient speed and power," he warned.

"But you'll still make the case?" Fox pressed.

Ayish nodded gravely. "I will." His gaze fell on Flynn. "But I'll need Nick here at my side when I meet with those who command my nation's special forces. They are likely to ask some very difficult questions that he is best prepared to answer."

One side of Flynn's mouth quirked upward in a quick, sidelong grin. "You sure about that, Professor?" he asked dryly. "I'm not much of a diplomat. Or so I've been told."

"Your reputation for speaking hard truths to those who really *don't* want to hear them precedes you," Ayish admitted with a hint of amusement. "But in this case, with time so short, I believe straight talk may prove far more useful to us than tact."

TWENTY-THREE

ATLIT NAVAL BASE, SOUTH OF HAIFA, ISRAEL

VERY EARLY THE NEXT MORNING

Situated near the ruins of a Crusader castle originally built for the Knights Templar, Atlit was the headquarters for the Israel's elite naval special forces unit, Shayatet 13, the 13th Flotilla. Widely considered to be at least the equal of the U.S. Navy's SEALs, Shayatet 13's force of highly trained frogmen and commandos carried out missions that might range from hostage rescues to the assassination of terrorist leaders to the capture of enemy ships in port or out on the high seas. First organized in 1949, at the very beginning of the modern State of Israel, even the fact of its existence was kept secret for nearly ten years. To this day, most of the details of its daring exploits were still shrouded in mystery and rumor.

Given that history, Flynn had been stunned when he realized where he and Gideon Ayish were being driven after arriving at Ben Gurion Airport aboard a night flight from Dubai. He'd expected Ayish to arrange a discreet briefing for a select few inside Israel's military establishment—perhaps at the offices of his counterterrorism think tank, another Quartet Directorate front, in Jerusalem. Instead, they were met at the airline gate by a uniformed officer of Israel's naval forces and taken straight to this closely guarded base on the coast just south of the port city of Haifa.

They'd been waved through the main gate and into the center of the compound. Steps next to a camouflaged bunker led down into a brightly lit underground command center. Wall screens showed detailed maps of the entire Middle East region, with icons showing the positions of major air, naval, and ground units belonging to different countries. Communications and computer consoles on an upper tier surrounded a central U-shaped conference table in the middle of the room, with seats for unit commanders and their top staff officers.

Several officers from Israel's navy and air force were already seated, waiting for Ayish and Flynn. A middle-aged civilian with short-cropped, ash-gray hair and wire-rim glasses sat at the head of the table. According to the card at his place, his name was Avi Elazar. Although his precise title was never mentioned, it quickly became clear that he was a man to whom everyone else in the command center—including Ayish—very obviously deferred. Flynn bet that indicated this guy Elazar was either someone high up in the Mossad, or, more likely, a high-ranking member of the Israeli prime minister's inner circle.

With a polite nod, Elazar waved them to the two empty chairs left at one end of the conference table. He acknowledged Ayish with a tight, humorless smile. "So, Gideon, I understand you've brought us news of more trouble on the horizon?"

"Not just on the horizon, "Ayish clarified quietly. "This trouble is already nearly at our door."

Flynn hid his astonishment. It was now clear to him that the older man operated with far more freedom of maneuver in his nation's military and political circles than did his American counterparts in the Quartet Directorate. They had to work almost entirely on their own—without the U.S. government's sanction or even knowledge. Which raised another question. How much about Four did these Israeli soldiers and civilians really know? Had Gideon Ayish blown the Quartet Directorate's cover to his own people? Because everything he'd been told in his training indicated secrecy was essential to the group's continued survival and success. Its founders had known from the very beginning that the official intelligence organizations in their home countries would never tolerate the existence of even a friendly private ally.

Elazar turned his curious gaze on Flynn. "And this is your young friend, the one who first reached out to you?"

Ayish nodded. "Mr. Flynn works for a friendly intelligence service," he said carefully. "He is one of their most talented field agents."

"Another of your remarkable web of contacts and confidential sources? Of whom it occasionally seems there is no end, Gideon," the gray-haired civilian commented wryly.

Ayish shrugged with a slight smile. "I talk to people here and there, Avi. Sometimes they confide in me. It's a gift." That drew a murmur of laughter from the officers around the conference table.

Flynn kept a tight rein on his own expression. Ayish's careful circumlocution answered his earlier unspoken question. Somehow, the Israeli professor had kept the details of the Quartet Directorate's existence and real history secret, while still managing to exert far more influence than his nominal role as a think tank academic would suggest. Instead, his countrymen seemed to credit Ayish with cultivating high-level connections to other official Western intelligence organizations, connections that had been very helpful in thwarting past terrorist actions aimed at Israel. And equally plainly, his country's political and military leaders seemed willing to "let Gideon work his miracles" unhindered by inconvenient questions.

That was a remarkably pragmatic and unbureaucratic attitude, Flynn thought with a touch of envy. It was probably one fostered by Israel's past vulnerability in the midst of a sea of potential enemies. The United States—geographically vast, populous, and, for so long, secure behind her twin ocean frontiers—had always been able to survive a degree of sluggishness and inefficiency in its national security machinery. The people of Israel, penned in a country barely ten miles wide at its narrowest point, could not afford the same luxury.

Elazar waited for the quiet amusement to fade. Then he turned toward Flynn. "Very well," he said. "We are at your disposal. Please explain this danger that has Professor Ayish so worried."

Flynn waited while Ayish handed over a USB drive containing the images they'd brought to back up his oral presentation. A junior officer fed the drive into a computer and pulled up the first photo in the series. It was a copy of Arif Khavari's passport picture. "Our first inkling of trouble came in Austria, during a covert rendezvous with this man —" he began.

Over the next thirty minutes, he briefed them on what he and the other members of Four had managed to discover since that first, aborted contact with Khavari. His pictures of the missile convoy taken inside Iran generated intense interest—as did the revelation that Russia's mercenary Raven Syndicate was working hand in glove with the Iranians to carry out the operation they'd code-named MIDNIGHT. Still, watching their reactions while he spoke, he judged his audience's general mood to be focused and highly professional. While they were plainly intrigued by the intelligence he was sharing, it was also clear that none of them were especially worried by anything they'd heard so far. After all, Russian military cooperation with Tehran's radical regime was nothing particularly new—although it was unusual to see the two countries collaborating so directly on a covert operation.

I bet that attitude changes completely in, oh, about thirty seconds, he thought calmly—as he steadily worked through the assumptions underlying the bombshell he was about to drop. *Well, either that, Nick, or they'll just decide you're completely loco*, he realized with an inward grin.

After he finished speaking, a shocked quiet descended on the command center. It lasted for what felt like an hour, but really couldn't have been more than a few moments.

Elazar broke the silence. Carefully, he leaned forward. "Let me be sure that I understand you correctly, Mr. Flynn," he said softly. "You believe this man Voronin has given Iran a nuclear weapon to use in MIDNIGHT? And that he has done so with permission from Piotr Zhdanov himself?"

"Yes, sir," Flynn said firmly. "That's correct."

The other man digested that for several seconds before going on. "Judging by your accent, you are an American, not so?"

Flynn nodded again. "Yes, sir. I am."

"Then may I ask what action your own government plans to take in this matter?" the Israeli civilian asked gently.

"None," Flynn said bluntly, not bothering to hide his own anger and disgust. "Washington doesn't want to rock the diplomatic boat with Tehran right now, especially since much of this is admittedly speculation."

"Speculation which is also logical and quite reasonable, based on the available evidence," Elazar interjected. "And not just some hardliner's wild fantasy."

"Yes, sir, that's how I see it," Flynn agreed. "Then again," he admitted with a self-deprecating smile, "I may be a little biased, since this was basically my idea in the first place."

Next to Elazar, Rafael Alon, the Israeli naval officer who commanded Shayatet 13, raised an eyebrow. Three gold stripes on his shoulder boards showed that he was a *Sgan aluf*, or deputy champion—the equivalent of a commander in the U.S. Navy. "And yet your superiors have approved your sharing this information with us?" he asked skeptically. "Despite their own reluctance to respond?"

"My *immediate* superiors did okay this meeting," Flynn said carefully, sticking to the literal truth. Fox was his boss, after all. That much of what he said was accurate, even if it avoided the fact that neither of them actually served in the official U.S. intelligence community. "But under the circumstances, none of us saw much point in pushing things too far up the political food chain."

Out the corner of his eye, he noticed Ayish manfully maintaining a very straight face at this bit of deliberate misdirection. Again, what

Flynn had just said was also quite literally true. The only thing left out was that the Quartet Directorate avoided contact with U.S politicians under any circumstances—and not just in this special case.

Flynn noticed heads around the table nod in understanding. He hid a smile of his own. He suspected his hosts now viewed him as one of the Gentile equivalents of the *sayanim*, Jewish citizens of other countries who were willing to provide critical aid to Israel in times of need. Throughout its tumultuous history, Israel had good cause to be thankful for their support.

In the silence that followed, Elazar looked around the command center. "All right, since the Americans seem to have tied their own hands, what are *our* options to deal with this Iranian oil tanker and the nuclear missile it now carries?"

"We could sink the ship at anchor with an air strike," one of the Israeli air force officers suggested. "Or out at sea once it sails." He shrugged. "Such a mission would be difficult, especially given the strength of the surface-to-air missile and fighter interceptor units currently deployed around Bandar Abbas. It would certainly require the commitment of a large number of our best planes and pilots. But it *could* be done."

"Unfortunately, sinking the tanker by air or missile attack is now out of the question," Elazar said patiently. "Can you imagine the environmental damage and the resulting international outcry if we send a vessel loaded with hundreds of thousands of barrels of crude oil to the bottom of the sea?" He turned back to the head of Shayatet 13. "Can your commandos plant a limpet mine on the ship, Rafael? Something that would damage its engines and keep it in port without rupturing those oil-storage tanks? That, at least, would buy us additional time to organize a more permanent solution."

Alon frowned. "That oil terminal at Bandar Abbas is a hard target," he said. "Between the IRGC's speedboat patrols and its own frogmen, the odds of carrying out a successful operation there would be very low—while the chances of incurring substantial casualties would be very high."

"And once the *Gulf Venture* sails?" Elazar asked. "What about then?"

"It would be difficult," Alon told him. "Planting a mine on a ship moving at fifteen to twenty knots would require the use of one of our *Dolphin 2*–class submarines carrying a force of divers and high-speed underwater sleds." One of the command center's digital maps zoomed in to show where Israel's three *Dolphin 2*–class subs were currently stationed. They were all in the Mediterranean. "But it'll take us at least five days to transfer the *Drakon*, the *Rahav*, or the *Tanin* through the Suez Canal and around into the Persian Gulf."

"By which time that tanker will have vanished," another officer commented sourly. "The sea is a big place."

Flynn saw what they were driving at. A ship steaming at high speed could cover a couple thousand nautical miles in five days. Finding a needle in a haystack would be easy compared to pinpointing a ship somewhere in the vast expanses of the world's oceans.

"We have a spy satellite in orbit," Elazar pointed out.

The same officer shook his head regretfully. "I'm sorry, Avi," he said. "The orbit of our OFEK-16 imaging satellite is optimized to keep watch on Iran's nuclear facilities and its missile research centers. It's not designed for ocean reconnaissance work."

Flynn kept his mouth shut, listening while the discussion went on. Eventually, it became obvious that Alon and the other Israeli officers saw only one even remotely realistic option: A Shayatet 13–led helicopter boarding operation backed up by a support unit aboard fast boats.

Alon finished conferring with his colleagues and turned back to Elazar. "Given twenty-four hours, we can move two Eurocopter AS565 Panther helicopters and a couple of air-transportable Morena rigid hull, inflatable boats to a staging area in the UAE. Naturally, the helicopters will have to refuel on the way from one of our KC-130 air tankers."

"Under the Abraham Accords, we only have commercial and diplomatic ties with the United Arab Emirates," Elazar objected. "We are not military allies."

Alon offered him a wolflike grin. "Officially, that's true," he agreed. He shrugged his shoulders. "But for years we've worked covertly against Iran with many of the Gulf States. If we're quiet about this, they'll gladly turn a blind eye."

"Two helicopters? And a couple of small boats? With a couple of squads of commandos in the first wave?" another officer commented dryly. "That's not exactly an overwhelming force, Rafael."

Heads nodded throughout the command center. Previous Israeli seizures of Iranian shipping had often involved multiple surface warships, hundreds of soldiers and sailors, and large numbers of combat aircraft flying cover.

"What choice do we have?" Alon retorted. "Wait until the Iranians detonate this nuclear warhead the Russians have given them over Tel Aviv? Or one of our other cities?"

Elazar held up a hand, stifling the heated argument they could all see brewing. "As I see it, this decision comes down to the reliability of the intelligence we've been given by our American friend here. If what he says is true, we do not have any real choice except to gamble." He turned to Flynn with a shrewd, calculating expression on his face. "So then, Mr. Flynn, just how confident are you that your assessment of this situation is correct—and that this Iranian missile is actually armed with a nuclear weapon?"

Aware that all the eyes in the room were fixed on him, Flynn knew he could not afford to hesitate. The slightest show of uncertainty would wreck any chance of stopping MIDNIGHT in time. "Confident enough to volunteer to join your boarding party," he said coolly.

Beside him, Ayish nodded approvingly.

Elazar raised an eyebrow. "That is confidence indeed." He glanced at Alon. "What do you think, Rafael?"

In answer, the Shayatet 13 commander looked hard at Flynn. "How often have you been in action?" he demanded.

"Four times," Flynn replied simply.

"And were you frightened?" the Israeli officer probed.

Flynn smiled back at him with a quick flash of tightly bared teeth. "Afterward? Oh, hell, yeah."

"But during the fighting?" Alon asked bluntly. "Were you scared then?"

Flynn shrugged. "I was too busy to think much about it," he answered truthfully.

The Israeli commando officer matched his devil-may-care grin and turned back to Elazar. "This American's *totach*, a stand-out guy," he said simply. "We'll take him."

The gray-haired civilian nodded. "Excellent." He looked around the conference table. "Very well, I'll recommend to the Prime Minister that we proceed. In the meantime, prepare your forces for movement . . . and outfit Mr. Flynn with the equipment and weapons he'll need."

Later, in private with Ayish, Flynn shook his head in amazement. "I cannot believe that I just talked my way into going along on this raid. So much for the whole Four mantra about the need to keep a low profile." His mouth turned down. "Man, Br'er Fox is not going to be happy about this."

The older man chuckled quietly. "Oh, I doubt that, Nick," he said sincerely. "You see, Fox and I had a wager as to whether you would find some way to join any attack force. And he just won that bet."

TWENTY-FOUR

OVER THE GULF OF OMAN

THE NEXT NIGHT

Two twin-engine AS565 Panther helicopters flew low over the sea at more than one hundred and fifty knots—rapidly closing on the huge black shape of the *Gulf Venture*, which was now less than five miles away. Nick Flynn had one of the fold-down seats inside the lead Panther's crowded troop compartment. He was hemmed in between seven Shayatet 13 commandos. Bulky in their body armor, they were all loaded down with weapons—short-barreled X95 bullpup assault rifles, grenades, fighting knives, and 9mm pistols. As a diplomatic gesture to the need to minimize the Israeli military presence in an Arab state, there were no national markings on either helicopter or on any of their camouflage uniforms.

He glanced down through the open doors on his side of the helicopter. The waning, half sphere of the moon was just rising, casting a pale, silvery glow across the water. Below them, he spotted two small shapes arrowing across the sea at high speed, trailing V-shaped wakes of curling white foam. The two Morena RHIBs carrying the boarding party's small reserve force were approaching on schedule.

Through the Panther's forward cockpit canopy, he could make out the enormous oil tanker that was their target. Satellite photos hadn't done justice to the ship's actual size. The *Gulf Venture* was nearly three football fields in length and as wide as three school buses parked end to end. As massive as one of the U.S. Navy's 100,000-ton *Nimitz*-class supercarriers, its broad bow plowed through the Gulf of Oman at roughly eighteen knots, hurling white-capped waves aside. Now that it was well outside Iran's coastal waters, there were no other vessels in the immediate area.

"*Stand by*," Flynn heard the Panther's pilot say calmly over the intercom. "*We're about sixty seconds out*." To his relief, the language being used for this operation was English, rather than the usual Hebrew. Since Shayatet 13 commandos often cross-trained with American SEALs and operators from the UK's Special Boat Service, they were all perfectly fluent in English.

Flynn noticed the two commandos closest to the doors check the thick, braided lines they would use to fast-rope down onto the ship's deck. His shoulders tightened. This was quite literally an all-or-nothing tactical evolution. When you made an airborne drop from a plane, your static line would pull your parachute, even if you couldn't for some reason. But fast-roping from a helicopter was one hell of a lot more dangerous. The need for speed when assaulting from a hovering helicopter meant there was no such thing as a safety line. If your hands slipped going down the rope, you'd find yourself doing your best Wile E. Coyote impression in midair . . . except that in real life no one walked away from going *splat* onto a metal deck.

Oh, smooth move, he scolded himself mentally. What was the number one rule for anyone with real-world military experience? *Never volunteer for anything*. And what was rule number two? *Never, ever volunteer*. Rules number three through ten were pretty much the same. And yet here he was like some overeager, green-as-grass recruit, getting ready to hurl himself out through the open door of a helicopter perched more than sixty feet above a fast-moving ship.

Swallowing hard, Flynn looked away from the side doors. Instead, he craned his head forward again, trying to get a better look at the tanker they were approaching. Apart from a few lights visible on the *Gulf Venture*'s multi-story-high aft superstructure, the vessel's main deck was completely blacked out.

He frowned. Voronin's Raven Syndicate had to have deployed an armed security force aboard. So the lack of any apparent reaction yet was odd. Both Panthers carrying the Shayatet 13 assault unit had various stealth features—radar-absorbent composite materials in their airframes, enclosed fanlike tail rotors, and reduced thermal signature engine exhausts. But there was no real way to render a military helicopter completely invisible to radars and IR sensors. And even though they were approaching from downwind to reduce their rotor noise, the Panthers were still pretty loud.

Flynn shook his head dubiously. *Someone* aboard that ship should have spotted them by now. They couldn't *all* be asleep or blind and deaf to the attacking force heading their way. "Come into my parlor said the spider to the fly," he muttered. Instinctively, he checked the assault rifle he'd been issued, making sure again that it was loaded and ready.

"You sense danger?" the Israeli commando seated next to him asked, raising his voice to be heard over the din of their helicopter's turboshaft engines and spinning rotors. His teeth flashed white in the darkened interior. "More than we already expect, I mean?"

Flynn grimaced. "Yeah, I do. It could be I'm just turning yellow in my old age, but I've still got a really bad feeling about—"

And then all hell broke loose.

What had appeared to be ordinary shipping containers chained down across the *Gulf Venture*'s deck as some sort of extra storage abruptly fell open—revealing the weapon mounts hidden inside. Besides a number of Samavat twin-barreled 35mm antiaircraft guns, there were several launchers bristling with small Misagh-2 surface-to-air missiles, Iranian-made copies of China's QW-2 Vanguard heat-seekers.

The moment their firing arcs were clear, the antiaircraft guns opened up. Curtains of bright orange tracers rippled through the night sky toward the Israeli helicopters. Seconds later, SAMs started launching—

streaking off the deck in plumes of gray smoke lit from within by their rocket boosters. Reacting immediately, both Panthers veered away, twisting and turning in a series of desperate evasive maneuvers. Dozens of tiny decoy flares tumbled outward behind them, fanning out like a constellation of small meteors falling toward the sea.

Gritting his teeth, Flynn held on tight as the helicopter he was aboard spun wildly through the air. Though the forward canopy and open doors, he could catch only split-second glimpses of what was happening around him. But what he did see was nightmarish.

The *Gulf Venture*, once darkened and seemingly lifeless, was now lit from stem to stern by the strobing flashes of its guns and missiles. A dazzling orange-white explosion suddenly engulfed one of the Iranian antiaircraft guns. Another blast turned a missile mount into smoldering wreckage. The Israeli flight crews were fighting back, he realized, trying hard to knock out the tanker's defenses using their helicopters' pod-mounted 20mm guns. But it was all too clearly a completely unequal fight.

Flashes suddenly peppered the sky near the second Panther. It staggered in midair, obviously hit hard. The badly damaged helicopter dove away at high speed—skimming low over the waves with thick smoke curling away behind it. Frantic voices echoed through Flynn's radio headset. *"Paladin Two breaking off! I've got an engine out and wounded aboard,"* its pilot reported.

"Roger that, Two," he heard his own pilot reply. *"We'll cover you."*

Flynn grabbed hold even tighter as the Panther banked sharply, coming around in another tight turn. Through the door next to him, he saw the sky and sea swing dizzily through a wild arc. The star-flecked blackness outside the helicopter tore apart in a swirling maelstrom of blindingly bright tracer rounds, missiles, and flares.

And then their own luck ran out.

WHAAM. WHAAM. WHAAM. Multiple 35mm shells hammered the Panther's fuselage.

Everything around Flynn seemed to happen in horrifying slow motion. An almost simultaneous series of bone-jarring bangs and jolts nearly threw him out of the helicopter. Jagged splinters punched through the sides and sprayed across the crowded troop compartment. Some were stopped by body armor. Others ripped through unprotected arms and legs. The Israeli commando next to him slumped over, with blood pouring from his wounds. Dazzling showers of sparks erupted wherever the razor-edged fragments struck metal. A thickening haze of smoke filled the torn cabin.

"*Brace for impact!*" one of the Panther's flight crew yelled. "*We're ditching!*"

Flynn threw one arm around the injured commando and wrapped the other around his seat, holding on with all his strength. Through the doors, he saw the wave-topped sea rushing upward at them with terrifying speed as the wrecked helicopter spun down out of the sky. They smashed into the water with an enormous, shattering impact, sending a wave of white-hot agony sleeting through his whole body.

There was a moment of almost unearthly silence, broken only by low moans and the pinging of hot metal contracting in sudden cold as the shell-riddled helicopter settled lower.

Dazed by the crash, Flynn shook his head frantically to clear it. Blood trickled down his chin. He spat to clear a salty taste from his mouth. *Swell*, he thought muzzily. He must have gashed his face on something when they slammed into the sea.

"Everybody out! Now!" he heard the Shayatet 13 detachment commander bark. "Go! Go! Go!"

Yeah, no shit, Flynn realized as everything around him suddenly shifted back into full focus. Seawater was already flooding in through the doors. The Panther was going down fast. He dumped his weapons and other gear with frantic speed. Then, hauling the wounded Israeli commando with him, he struggled to his feet and splashed out into the rising sea.

Sidestroking frantically, he swam away from the sinking helicopter—aware of other heads bobbing all around. When he got far enough away, he started treading water. Still cradling the injured man, he fumbled with the straps holding his body armor—desperately shrugging out of it before the added weight could drag him under.

Moments later, the Panther's mangled fuselage slid out of sight with a sudden spurt of bubbling white foam. Torrents of water were hurled in all directions by its still-spinning rotor blades when they smacked into the sea . . . and then vanished. A few lighter pieces of wreckage bobbed back to the surface, but that was all.

Still treading water, Flynn turned through a full circle, counting off those in the water nearby. Like him, the Israeli commandos who were not seriously wounded were supporting their bleeding, half-conscious comrades. Miraculously, it appeared that everyone else had made it out of the helicopter before it sank. Off in the distance, he could see the two Morena inflatable boats speeding toward them to conduct a rescue.

With a deep sigh, he wheeled back toward the now-distant *Gulf Venture*. The huge black ship hadn't altered its course by so much as a degree. It was still headed away from them, steaming almost due south into the darkness. Small fires guttered in places across the oil tanker's deck, showing where return fire from the two helicopters had knocked out a couple of its antiaircraft guns and missile launchers. But it was obvious that the ship was otherwise completely undamaged—and now free to carry its lethal secret cargo wherever it wished.

Flynn felt a wave of despair wash over him. He'd failed.

MIDNIGHT was fully underway.

TWENTY-FIVE

ABOARD THE *GULF VENTURE*

T MINUS 26 DAYS, A SHORT TIME LATER

Viktor Skoblin took the outside ladder up to the navigation bridge two rungs at a time. He came up onto the starboard wing, nearly one hundred feet above the tanker's main deck. Two bearded IRGC Quds Force commandos were posted at the hatch leading into the bridge itself. Although they wore ordinary ship's coveralls instead of their usual desert tan berets and camouflage battledress, the 9mm submachine guns they carried erased any illusion they were regular civilian sailors. Apart from Skoblin and his ten-man Raven Syndicate security team, all members of the ship's crew were part of the Islamic Revolutionary Guard Corps.

"I need to see the captain," Skoblin growled to the guards. He found it ironic that those in *Gulf Venture*'s mixed Iranian and Russian crew were forced to rely on the language of their most powerful enemy, English, to communicate with each other. But only one of his men spoke any Persian beyond a few simple phrases, and very few of the IRGC soldiers and sailors aboard had any Russian. Then again, he knew that English was the standard tongue employed at sea—just as it was in air traffic control and commercial aviation in general.

Without speaking, one of the stern-faced commandos waved him through the open hatch.

Skoblin entered the dimly lit bridge. He stood off to the side for a moment, waiting quietly while his eyes adjusted. Together with its port and starboard wings, the navigation bridge ran the width of the six-story-high superstructure which occupied most of the tanker's aft end. Large windows lined three sides of the bridge, offering almost un-obstructed views over the deck and out to sea. The only place higher aboard the ship was an open-air platform studded with radar and radio masts located just above the bridge itself.

Down on the main deck, a damage control party had just finished extinguishing the last small fire. The blackened and twisted twin barrels of a Samavat 35mm gun mount were now slathered in foam. Three blanket-covered stretchers next to the wrecked antiaircraft gun held the mangled remains of its crew.

In other places, sailors were busy repositioning the painted wood panels that formed the fake shipping containers used to hide *Gulf Venture*'s newly installed guns and missile launchers until they were needed. By the time the sun rose, all of the oil tanker's weapons would again be camouflaged.

Skoblin nodded approvingly. The Iranians apparently had matters well in hand. The tanker's captain, Reza Heidari, stood near the helms-man's station, listening carefully to a report from his second-in-command, Touraj Dabir. Heidari, lean and hawk-nosed, was a high-ranking officer in the IRGC's naval forces, as was the somewhat younger and bulkier Dabir.

"All fires are now out, Captain," Dabir said calmly. "The ship's propulsion and steering, and the Zuljanah rocket storage and control compartments were not damaged. We have minor leaks in a few of the upper oil-storage bunkers, but those are being plugged rapidly."

Heidari looked pleased. "Very good, Touraj. We certainly don't want to leave a trail of crude oil floating behind us for an enemy to follow." He moved to the front of the bridge and stared down at the deck. "What's the current status of our defensive armament?"

"Two of the guns were knocked out, along with a pair of our Misagh-2 launchers. All other weapons are fully operational."

Heidari nodded. "How much of our ammunition was expended?"

"The battle consumed approximately one-fourth of our stores of 35mm high-explosive and armor-piercing rounds and roughly a third of our surface-to-air missiles," Dabir told him.

The captain frowned. Skoblin understood his irritation. Under attack, the ship's gun and missile crews had fired wildly—hurling hundreds of shells and more than a dozen SAMs at the two enemy helicopters they'd engaged. True, they'd won, downing at least one, and possibly both, of the hostile rotorcraft, but their lack of fire discipline and control had been extremely costly. Without improvements, one or two more such attacks might leave the tanker out of ammunition and missiles, reduced to mere small arms for its own defense.

Still, what else could have been expected, the Russian wondered? The *Gulf Venture* was not a warship equipped with sophisticated, centralized fire-direction gear. In the short time Voronin had allowed, it had already required something of a miracle for the Shahid Darvishi shipyards to fit this ship with its improvised array of armaments. Jury-rigging the advanced fire direction radars and communications systems necessary to exert more control over a battle would have consumed months of dedicated yard time, not just a few days.

"What were our total casualties, Touraj?" Heidari asked after a moment.

Dabir shrugged. "We lost five men killed outright, with another four wounded." He cleared his throat. "I've spoken to the medical staff. Three of the wounded will die unless we transfer them to hospitals with more advanced facilities."

Heidari grimaced. "Arrange a rendezvous with a helicopter to fly them back to Iran? Making it that much easier for someone to find us at sea again?" He shook his head. "Impossible. We are at war now. And our first responsibility is to this ship and its mission. All those who die on this voyage are martyrs."

Reluctantly, Dabir nodded his understanding. "Very well, sir. I'll speak with the sick bay staff. They'll do what is necessary."

Skoblin knew what that meant. Their ship's doctor would euthanize the critically injured men, injecting them with enough pain-killing drugs to kill them quietly. It was harsh, but Heidari was right. Now that the *Gulf Venture* had broken contact with the enemy tracking them, providing them with another opportunity to detect the ship would be foolish.

He waited while Dabir saluted and then left the bridge before approaching the Iranian captain.

Heidari watched him come with a carefully neutral expression on his narrow face. During the frenetic rush to prepare the tanker and its cargo for sea, it had become abundantly clear that the IRGC navy officer was not especially happy to have a group of foreigners aboard who were not explicitly under his direct authority. "What is it, Major?" he asked coldly.

Skoblin smiled thinly. He'd opted to use his former Spetsnaz rank for the remaining duration of MIDNIGHT. He'd done so hoping Heidari would feel more comfortable dealing with the Raven Syndicate team as if they were still fellow professional military men rather than highly paid mercenaries. So far, however, his gambit hadn't made the captain any more welcoming. "I'd like to send a radio message to Moscow, reporting your repulse of the enemy's attempted helicopter raid," he explained. "The news of your success will be very welcome there."

Left unsaid was the fact that Skoblin hoped to bask in the shared glory. After the fiasco in Vienna, he needed to seize every available chance to rehabilitate himself in Voronin's eyes.

Heidari shook his head firmly. "That will not be possible, Major. You heard what I told Dabir with regard to our own wounded." His lips compressed. "My superiors have decreed a total communications blackout for the duration of this mission. I intend to obey their orders to the letter. Therefore, we will not break radio silence for any reason. Is that understood?"

"Of course, Captain," Skoblin assured him smoothly. Exasperating though it was, he wasn't really surprised by this diktat. Before they sailed, Voronin had privately warned him that the Iranians might take such a step. Besides the clear military rationale, the hardline radicals in Iran's revolutionary government undoubtedly wanted to make sure no one else in Tehran could suddenly get cold feet and attempt to order an abort of this high-risk mission. It was equally obvious that these same radicals did not entirely trust their Russian mercenary allies and technical experts. So it made sense for them to sever all communications links between Moscow and the Raven Syndicate team aboard the *Gulf Venture*.

Excusing himself, Skoblin turned and left the bridge. His request had been a formality—a polite nod to the niceties involved in working within an informal alliance. Now he was free to act according to his own orders from Voronin. What Heidari and his fellow Iranians might not completely understand was that their lack of trust was fully reciprocated. For now, Russia's interests and those of its radical Islamic partner coincided. That might not always be the case.

After he reached the Raven Syndicate's own closely guarded section of the tanker's superstructure, he ordered the doors locked and sentries posted in the corridor outside. As a further precaution, all of their compartments aboard the ship were routinely swept for listening devices.

Satisfied that they were safe from Iranian observation and interference, Skoblin turned to Yvgeny Kvyat. "Get your gear ready," he ordered. "I need to talk to the Raven's Nest as soon as possible."

Kvyat swung into action. The short, slightly overweight former GRU intelligence officer had been Skoblin's drone operator in Vienna. Now he was chiefly responsible for the shipboard team's communications and other high-tech equipment. He dragged a large metal case out from under his bunk and opened it, revealing a neatly packed assortment of spare magazines and boxes of extra ammunition for their assault rifles. Pushing two small catches inside the case allowed him to lift out its interior—exposing a smaller compartment hidden underneath. There, securely packed in foam, was a military-grade satellite phone, complete with lengths of cable and a long, flexible black antenna.

Working quickly, Kvyat connected a headset to the phone. When carefully extended through an open porthole, the antenna was virtually invisible at night. He listened closely while the phone hunted for the nearest Russian military communications satellite that could route their rigorously encrypted signals. Within seconds, he heard the soft chime that indicated success. "We're in contact, Viktor," he confirmed.

Skoblin took the phone and headset and dialed the special number he'd been given just before they left Bandar Abbas. After a series of soft clicks, it connected. Their call was answered immediately.

"Go ahead," a voice on the other end said coolly. It was Voronin himself.

Skoblin swallowed hard. "BIRD STRIKE. WELCOME PARTY. FREE RIDE." Those were the pre-set code phrases to let Moscow know that they'd been attacked by hostile helicopters, but the assault had been defeated—and that the Gulf Venture was currently proceeding as planned toward the launch point for MIDNIGHT.

"Understood," Voronin acknowledged. There was a short delay. "Report your current status."

"ECLIPSE. I say again, ECLIPSE," Skoblin replied. That confirmed for the Raven Syndicate's leader that the ship's crew had cut all communications with its home base, as he had anticipated.

"Very well," Voronin said. "Listen carefully, Skoblin. From here on out, you will report your current position, course, and speed to this station once every twenty-four hours. Otherwise, continue as planned. Is that clear?"

"Yes, sir," Skoblin said forcefully. "You can rely on me."

"I'm counting on it," Voronin told him with a hint of frost in his voice. "Don't fail me this time, Viktor. It would make me extremely unhappy. Raven's Nest, out."

The phone went dead.

Slowly, Skoblin unplugged the headset and handed everything back to Kvyat to stow away out of sight. He shivered, despite the warm night air flowing in through the open porthole. Logically, he knew that he was currently far beyond Voronin's immediate reach. And yet, for some strange reason, he still felt as though the cold muzzle of a pistol was pressed firmly against the back of his neck.

One deck below the tanker's bridge, Captain Reza Heidari turned away from the accommodation ladder and strode down a narrow corridor. Several closed doors lined each side of this hallway, which ended in a massive armored hatch. Three more Quds Force commandos stood in front of this sealed entrance. Their leader, a battle-scarred chief warrant officer, stepped forward to stop him with an upraised hand. "Your identity card, please, Captain." The other two covered him with their submachine guns.

Heidari handed it over with a gratified smile on his lean face. These troops were following his own explicit orders. No one was permitted past that hatch without prior permission and a thorough check of his identity.

Carefully, the Quds Force noncom compared the photo on the ID card with his face and then handed it back with a nod. He turned away and entered a quick series of numbers on a keypad below a bulkhead-mounted intercom.

"*LCC*," a voice answered over the loudspeaker. "*Yes?*"

"The captain is here," the chief warrant officer answered. "Status verified."

In reply, the hatch undogged and swung open, revealing a window-less compartment almost as large as the bridge just above it. Computer consoles and display screens filled almost every square meter. Several civilians sat at the consoles, carefully monitoring the data flowing to their stations. Video feeds from cameras mounted at various places around the ship offered their only views of the outside. Heidari stepped through the hatch and waited while the Quds Force sentry on duty closed and sealed it behind him.

A short, stocky scientist with a scruffy white beard looked up from the central console. He smiled pleasantly. "Welcome to the Launch Control Center, Reza," Dr. Hossein Majidi said. "I understand that we've overcome the first hurdle on this long ocean voyage?"

Heidari nodded. "The Israelis attacked us as expected," he said calmly. "And we drove them off. Again, just as we expected."

His little quip drew quick, relieved smiles from the missile technicians on duty. Completely isolated from the rest of the tanker by design, all they could have seen on their screens during the attack were the repeated, pulsing flashes of guns and SAMs firing. He walked over to Majidi's side.

"Come to inspect our cargo?" the scientist asked. Heidari nodded. Majidi flicked a finger at one of his technicians. "Bring up the missile compartment on my display here, Kamshad," he said indulgently.

Instantly, the screens at his console brightened, showing views of a long white rocket with a black nose cone lying on its side, securely cradled inside a metal framework. A web of thick data cables ran to ports located along the flanks of the finned Zuljanah launch vehicle. Since they were unable to physically inspect the rocket currently hidden deep inside the *Gulf Venture*, below storage bunkers containing tens of thousands of barrels of crude oil, Majidi and his technicians were forced to rely on a complex network of remote sensors. These devices provided constant updates of the status of the missile's engines, electronics, and other internal systems—including those of its special nuclear payload.

The scientist indicated the numbers and graphs flowing across other screens at his console. "As you can see," he said to Heidari, who could actually see nothing of the kind, "both solid-fuel stages remain completely stable." He tapped a control on his keyboard. New graphs appeared. "And the volatile hypergolic fuels for the rocket's third stage are safely stored. There are no problems."

"What about the warhead itself?" Heidari asked sharply. "Will it work as planned?"

"Relax, Reza," Majidi said confidently. "All you and your sailors need to do is deliver us safely to the planned launch point." He waved a hand around the compartment. "Once that's accomplished, you can sit back and watch while we finish this mission."

Heidari leaned forward, peering intently at the missile concealed deep in the bowels of his enormous ship. It could only be his imagination he realized, but now the rocket seemed almost to be straining at the data cables and other webbing holding it in place—as though it were a hunting falcon straining at its leash, eager to soar and kill.

TWENTY-SIX

ORLANDO INTERNATIONAL AIRPORT

A COUPLE OF DAYS LATER

Tired and sore, Nick Flynn limped slowly out through the sliding doors of Terminal B. The backpack slung over one shoulder was the only piece of luggage he'd brought on the succession of flights home from Israel. He joined a knot of other arriving travelers, most of them in T-shirts and shorts, who were waiting for taxis or Uber and Lyft drivers to pick them up.

A dark blue late-model Jeep Grand Cherokee pulled up to the curb and flashed its lights four times. "Excuse me, folks. That's my ride," he said politely, as he edged past a couple of parents with three very excited children wearing matching Disney shirts. Carefully, favoring his right leg, he climbed into the back seat of the waiting SUV next to Fox.

The older man greeted him with noncommittal nod and leaned forward. "We'll go straight back to Avalon House," he told the man behind the wheel, Mark Stadler. The tough-looking former Marine was now one of Four's security personnel. "We shouldn't have picked up a tail anywhere, but keep your eyes peeled just in case."

"Yes, sir," Stadler agreed. "I'm on it." After checking his mirrors, he pulled out into the airport's slow-moving traffic.

Fox sat back with a sigh and turned to Flynn. He raised a single, questioning eyebrow. "Well?"

"I'm a little battered and bruised, but I'm not seriously hurt," Flynn assured him. "My Israeli hosts had me checked out at one of their military hospitals during the mission debrief." He pointed to the bandage slanting from one corner of his mouth to the middle of his chin. "Took a couple of stiches here, but the docs say I won't even get much of a scar out of it."

Fox nodded. "Good."

"My pride's taken a hell of beating, though," Flynn admitted. His jaw tightened. Whoever'd said that any crash landing you could walk away from—or in his case, swim away from—was a good one must not have spent much time around those who hadn't been as lucky. "I took those poor Shayatet 13 guys right into a goddamned trap. Some of them may never get out of the hospital."

Fox shook his head. "There's no point in kicking yourself too hard about this, Nick. I've talked to Gideon. No one in the IDF is blaming you. We all knew trying to board that tanker from the air would be extremely difficult and dangerous. What none of us anticipated was the actual strength of those concealed defenses." He frowned. "I saw some of the gun camera footage from the second Panther helicopter. The amount of antiaircraft fire coming your way looked a bit . . . hairy."

"Hairy is an understatement," Flynn said grimly. "That ship is a floating fortress. No boarding party could have made it past that level of firepower." He frowned. "Hell, from what I could make out, it'll take a heavily armed warship to knock out those gun mounts and missile launchers before anyone could hope to make it to the deck alive."

Fox smiled dryly. "Sadly, Four's original organizers neglected to provide us with a navy of our own. Or the resources to acquire one now." Pensively, he looked out his window as they merged onto a highway that would take them north toward Winter Park. "Nor, unfortunately, do I see any hope of persuading our government to take any action in this case."

"Washington's still not taking this threat seriously?" Flynn asked in disbelief. "Even after seeing how heavily the Iranians and Russians have armed the *Gulf Venture*? Those 35mm guns and SAMs sure as hell aren't on that ship just to protect it from Somali or Malay pirates."

"My sources tell me the overall mood in the higher echelons of the CIA and its counterparts is one of smug satisfaction that they've avoided being caught in what's considered the usual crossfire between hardliners in Jerusalem and radical Islamists in Tehran," Fox said quietly.

Flynn gritted his teeth. "Then they're idiots."

"Politicians," Fox corrected him sardonically. "Which I suppose amounts to much the same thing."

"So we're basically screwed," Flynn snapped. "Being able to say 'I told you so' isn't going to be much comfort if a nuke goes off over a city somewhere."

Fox eyed him coldly. "Personally, I have no intention of sitting idly by waiting for that to happen. Do you?"

"No, I don't," Flynn shot back, slightly nettled by the suggestion that he might have been thinking about giving up. Yes, he was incredibly jetlagged and very short on sleep. Truth be told, right now he was essentially running on fumes—a mix of adrenaline and endless cups of crummy airline coffee. To make matters worse, the assortment of bruises and strained muscles he'd collected when his helicopter ditched in the sea made even this SUV's comfortable seats feel akin to a medieval instrument of torture, something like a rack or a spike-lined iron maiden. But he'd be damned if he'd quit that easily.

He offered the older man a rueful smile. "Sorry, Br'er Fox. It's just that I haven't been able to figure out yet how in God's name we're going to put a helicopter- or ship-borne boarding party onto that oil tanker without getting cut to pieces. And I admit that's pissing me off some."

"So I gathered," Fox said with a hint of mild amusement. His expression darkened a bit. "For what it's worth, Nick, I'm drawing a blank there, too. So far, at least." He shrugged. "Which is why I want you and Laura Van Horn and a few others with equally devious and violent minds to begin formulating alternate plans. I know it's a difficult nut to crack, but I have a great deal of confidence in your tactical skills. And in your respective talents for thinking well outside the box." He took off his glasses, stared through them for a moment, and then put them back on with a frown. "In the meantime, however, I'm afraid there are still more challenges we need to address."

Flynn settled back to listen while they continued on toward Avalon House. If nothing else, being asked to focus on different problems would help him ignore his fatigue and aches and pains for a little while longer. At some point soon, he knew, he was going to come crashing down. When the time came, he was going to need some strong painkillers and a lot of sleep, in that order. For now, he'd be happy just to stave off that inevitable collapse until he could get a little more privacy.

First, Fox pointed out somberly, even finding the converted Iranian oil tanker again was going to be enormously tricky. In the days since the failed Shayatet 13 assault, the *Gulf Venture* had disappeared into the enormous expanses of the open ocean. Already, their potential search area had expanded to cover several million square miles of sea. Every new day that passed without anyone picking up the ship's trail would add hundreds of thousands more square miles to that already daunting total.

Flynn saw what the other man meant. Even if the Quartet Directorate could afford to spend huge sums chartering civilian aircraft to patrol the most likely sea routes, it would still take incredible luck to spot the missing ship somewhere in all that vastness. And Four's luck had been in awfully short supply lately. Of course, even assuming they did come up with some way to orchestrate such a massive air search effort, it would be virtually impossible to hide what was going on from the authorities. Or from their enemies.

"So we're playing a game of hide-and-seek, except we've got to do it while stumbling around in the dark with only a tiny pinhole to look through," he commented. "And if we bump into anybody else, even by accident, the game's over."

Fox nodded. "A colorful but reasonably accurate summary of our current situation," he agreed.

"Just terrific," Flynn said wryly. He looked at the older man. "Put simply, we need to find a ship that's armed to the teeth and probably can't be found . . . and then somehow figure out how to capture it. Sounds like a walk in the park." He grinned crookedly. "Do I even want to know what else you think we've got on our plate at the moment?"

"The other issue might seem more abstract," Fox told him quietly. "But I believe it's just as critical. We need to work out what the Iranians—and through them, Voronin and Zhdanov—are really planning."

"It doesn't seem like much of a mystery to me," Flynn said carefully. "Not since we know that tanker is carrying a missile armed with a nuclear warhead. A nuke may not exactly be a subtle or elegant weapon, but it's sure as hell likely to blow the crap out of whatever it hits."

Fox shook his head. "Somehow, somewhere, we're missing something," he insisted. "There's no doubt that this missile being smuggled aboard the *Gulf Venture* can be used to destroy a city. Or to wipe out an important military installation, I guess. But how would that really advance Iran's strategic goals, let alone those of Russia? Hitting a single strategic target, no matter how vital it may be, won't inflict irreversible damage on any of Tehran or Moscow's different enemies. Even Israel, as small as it is, can withstand a single nuclear strike and still be in a position to hit back hard. Our own country is even more resilient—as are our other, larger allies in Europe and Asia."

Flynn saw what he was driving at. While on some grim level the Russians might be satisfied to see an American or European city wiped out, as long as Iran took the heat and bore all the damage from any resulting counterstrike, what could Tehran's own motivation possibly be? Not even the most radical mullah could see any real value in killing a million Americans, if, at the end of the day, the result would be the destruction of their Islamic state—with the United States, the Great Satan, left largely intact. Nor did he really believe Zhdanov and his inner circle would want to take that sort of gamble . . . not without something more to gain. For more than seventy years, the cold, brutal calculus of deterrence had kept ICBMs in their silos, strategic bombers on the ground, and submarine-launched missiles in their tubes. Why would Moscow risk crossing the nuclear threshold for so small a prospective victory? And, after all, what guarantee did the Russians have that the Iranians would stay silent about their involvement once an angry and vengeful America unleashed its fury?

No, Flynn thought darkly, Fox was right. There had to be some key element of their enemies' plans that they did not yet understand. He sat back, wrapped in worried silence through the rest of the short drive to Avalon House. It was becoming increasingly clear that what had already seemed to be an extraordinarily dangerous situation might actually be something even more catastrophic.

This was beginning to resemble a stereotypical nightmare, he realized—the one where you were the only person who saw a great danger and tried desperately to alert everyone around you . . . to no avail. No one in the U.S. government could even acknowledge the existence of the Quartet Directorate—let alone pay any attention to its warnings.

They were entirely on their own. And racing to make sure this particular nightmare didn't come true.

TWENTY-SEVEN

Russian Navy Captain First Rank Mikhail Nakhimov leaned forward over the shoulder of one of his junior officers. Under the control room's blue-tinged lights, the depth gauge still showed them at three hundred and twenty meters. Apart from minor quivers whenever the eighteen-thousand-ton nuclear submarine encountered some new underwater current, the gauge hadn't budged for hundreds of hours—ever since *Podmoskovye* had successfully broken away from the shallower confines of the Barents Sea naval exercise area. For that entire time, they had been creeping onward at ten knots through a world of stygian darkness and near-absolute silence. To escape detection by Western hunter-killer submarines and passive sonar arrays, reducing their acoustic signature—all the noise made by their reactor pumps, propulsion screws, and other machinery—to the bare minimum had been vital.

"Sir!"

Nakhimov turned toward the plot table along one side of the control room. His navigating officer, Senior Lieutenant Pokrovsky, beckoned him over. The younger man had just finished marking off their logged progress using a compass divider and parallel rulers. He indicated a small cross near the end of the line he'd just drawn across the chart. They were far out in the Northern Atlantic, more than eight hundred nautical miles off the French coast. "We're passing through Checkpoint Omega now, Captain."

"And within five minutes of your predicted time," Nakhimov said, after checking the submarine's chronometer. He clapped Pokrovsky on the shoulder. "Good work, Ivan."

Then his smile faded. They'd reached the coordinates where he was instructed to open his sealed orders from Moscow. Now he would learn the real purpose of this top-secret voyage. Unfortunately, this same process also served to remind him yet again that he was no longer the sole master aboard his own vessel. He turned to his executive officer, Captain Second Rank Arshavin, "Invite our guest to my cabin, please."

Arshavin nodded and took a handset from the bulkhead beside him. He punched a button to connect to the aft berthing compartment reserved for their passengers. "Colonel Danilevsky will report to the captain's quarters at once. Repeat, at once." He disconnected without waiting for a reply.

Nakhimov shook his head. "You might have been a bit more . . . polite, Maxim," he commented dryly.

"The fellow's supposed to be a soldier," his executive officer said dourly. "He shouldn't need me to hold his hand."

Podmoskovye's captain bit down on a laugh. Like him, none of his senior officers were happy to be saddled with a complement of hired gunmen from this so-called Raven Syndicate masquerading as genuine naval infantry and Spetsnaz commandos. Their leader, Konstantin Danilevsky, might once have held the rank of colonel in the Spetsnaz, but that didn't change the fact that he was now only a mercenary working for the highest bidder—and no longer solely a loyal servant of the State. Unfortunately, even his preliminary orders from the Kremlin required him to treat Danilevsky as a coequal for the duration of this mission. So far, distasteful and awkward though this unprecedented power-sharing arrangement was, it hadn't caused any real trouble. The ex–Spetsnaz officer had been wise enough not to interfere with day-to-day operations aboard the submarine while it was underway. But now Nakhimov couldn't shake the uncomfortable feeling that might be about to change.

His cabin, little more than a curtained alcove, was just a few steps away from the control room. He wasn't especially surprised to find the Raven Syndicate leader already there waiting for him out in the narrow corridor. Large as it appeared from the outside, most of *Podmoskovye*'s hull space was taken up by her twin nuclear reactors, minisub hangars, torpedoes, and other consumable stores. The living space actually set aside for her 135 officers and ratings, and now, twenty more commandos, was astonishingly small, especially by the standards of those unused to service aboard submarines. Nakhimov's broom closet–sized room gave him more privacy than anyone else in his crew.

The captain swept the curtain aside and coolly nodded Danilevsky in ahead of him. The other man, several inches taller and more powerfully built, perched carefully on the small bunk while Nakhimov sat down at his built-in desk. He waited until the curtain was drawn again before commenting. "I assume that we've reached this Omega point of yours?"

"That's correct, Colonel," Nakhimov confirmed. He opened a small cabinet and entered the combination on his safe. It clicked open, revealing two sealed manila envelopes, one bearing his name and rank, the other that of Danilevsky. Each was marked MOST SECRET. COMMANDING OFFICER'S EYES ONLY.

Frowning, he tore open his own envelope. It contained several pages of closely written text. Slowly, his eyes widened. The document, signed by President Piotr Zhdanov himself, outlined the role his submarine was expected to play in an operation code-named MIDNIGHT, which was already in progress. The plan's combination of intricate deception and treachery—all culminating in the massive application of lethal force—left him shaken to his core. If everything worked as Zhdanov anticipated, Russia would achieve a strategic victory without precedent in world history—and all in less than an hour's time. But if anything significant went wrong, this operation could easily trigger a war Russia could not win . . . a war that *no one* could win. And now the responsibility for making sure MIDNIGHT succeeded rested squarely on his shoulders—and on those of his Raven Syndicate counterpart.

Suddenly finding it surprisingly difficult to breath, Nakhimov carefully put the sheaf of orders down on his desk. He turned to Danilevsky. To his astonishment, he realized that the other man had only casually skimmed the contents of his own envelope before setting it aside. "You knew about all of this? *Before* we sailed?"

The Raven Syndicate mercenary smiled icily. "Of course." His dark eyes held no trace of humor at all. "Do you have a problem with that, Captain?"

Abruptly remembering exactly what Danilevsky and his men were expected to do if the need arose, Nakhimov shook his head stiffly. "No."

For the first time, he fully grasped the horrifying fact that he and his sailors were now confined three hundred meters below the surface of the sea, trapped inside a relatively small steel cylinder with a group of hardened killers. In the past, *Podmoskovye* had carried Spetsnaz soldiers bound on other missions. These men, however, were different. They would kill for financial gain, not because it was their patriotic duty.

Lazily, the other man handed over his copy of their orders and waited while the captain locked them safely away again in his safe. Then he rose. "With your permission, I'll rejoin my troops."

After Danilevsky left, Nakhimov breathed out. Gathering his composure, he headed back to the control room. The safest road now was that of duty. He had his orders and they must be obeyed—no matter how hazardous they appeared, both to himself and to the Motherland.

Faces alight with curiosity turned toward him when he reentered the dimly lit control room. It was an open secret throughout the submarine that their actual mission would only begin once the captain opened his special orders from Moscow. Duty roster or not, all of his senior officers had wanted to be on hand when *Podmoskovye* reached Checkpoint Omega.

Ignoring his subordinates for a moment, Nakhimov took a message pad and rapidly scrawled a status report and request for updated intelligence, as directed by the top-secret orders he'd just read. Finished, he tore the sheet off the pad and held it out to his radio officer, Lieutenant Leonid Volkov. "Encrypt this and send it to Moscow at once. With maximum security."

"Yes, Captain." The younger officer took the message and scanned it quickly. His eyebrows rose. He sat down at his station and rapidly entered the clear text into their encryption machine. A display showed the much shorter sequence of numbers, special characters, and letters now ready for transmission. Then he swiveled toward the senior petty officer manning the communications board. "Launch Relay One."

Throughout the Cold War, communication between nuclear submarines at sea and their fleet headquarters had been extremely difficult. Two-way radio contact was only possible if submarines came to periscope depth—greatly increasing their vulnerability to detection and attack by hostile forces. Absent that, it was only possible for shore stations to transmit one-way, extremely low frequency signals that could be picked up by submarines operating far below the surface. Now, however, the Russian navy, like its American rival, had developed new communications systems to address these problems.

"Launching Relay One," the petty officer confirmed, flicking a series of switches. Lights that had been red turned green.

Far aft of the control room, a small hatch opened on *Podmoskvoye's* starboard flank. Slowly, a small, tethered submersible floated out of the flooded compartment. Connected by fiber-optic cable, it drifted back to trail behind the larger submarine. Steadily, kilometer after kilometer of cable unreeled as the distance between them widened.

"Relay One is in position," the petty officer reported at last. His instruments indicated that the smaller submersible was now being towed ten kilometers behind *Podmoskovye*.

"Release a SATCOM buoy," Volkov ordered.

The petty officer tapped another control on his panel. A signal flashed down the fiber-optic cable, issuing a new command to the submersible's simpleminded computer. In response, it opened one of the several tiny ports on its topside. A much smaller buoy rose through this port and slowly ascended, with another length of cable trailing behind. The moment it bobbed to the surface, an indicator light blinked green aboard *Podmoskovye*. The buoy's antennas had locked on to one of Russia's military communications satellites in orbit.

Immediately, Volkov hit the transmit button on his own display. Compressed into a millisecond-long blip, Nakhimov's message was sent winging on its way to Moscow. Over the next several minutes, a flurry of coded signals passed back and forth between the Kremlin and the submarine. When they were finished, a new command directed the tiny, expendable satellite communications buoy at the surface to scuttle itself. Obeying, it flooded its floatation chambers and detached the length of cable connecting it to the Relay One submersible. Swiftly, the buoy slid beneath the waves, beginning its inexorable plunge down into the vast, unlit depths of the Atlantic. The somewhat larger submersible itself was slowly reeled back into its bay aboard *Podmoskovye*.

While they waited for its safe return, Nakhimov studied the decrypted messages handed to him by Volkov. According to their most recent reports, the *Gulf Venture* was still on the far side of the African continent, almost nine thousand nautical miles away. Based on its last known course and speed, the converted oil tanker must now be somewhere off the northern tip of Madagascar.

He walked over to the plot table and considered the problem for a few minutes. His officers waited in expectant silence.

"Relay One is aboard, Captain," Volkov reported quietly at last. "The hatch is closed and sealed."

Nakhimov looked up. He nodded tightly. "Very well." Making his decision, he leaned over the table and scrawled a tiny cross at an otherwise featureless spot out in the South Atlantic, several hundred miles west of Cape Town, South Africa. He looked up at his navigating officer. "Plot a shortest-time intercept course to this point, Ivan."

Pokrovsky hurried to obey, laying out a course using his parallel rulers and dividers. Finished, he turned to the helmsman. "Helm, come left to one-nine-two degrees."

"Come left to one-nine-two degrees, aye, sir," the helmsman, a grizzled fifteen-year veteran of the submarine service answered. He turned the steering control slightly. "My rudder is right two degrees, coming to course one-nine-two degrees."

Once *Podmoskovye* settled on its new heading, Pokrovsky issued a new command. "Make revolutions for maximum speed!"

"Maximum revolutions, aye," the helmsman affirmed, pushing a throttle control forward.

Aft, in the submarine's Maneuvering Room, duty technicians saw the relayed order and opened valves to reactor-fed steam turbines. Instantly, the propellers began spinning faster and faster. Steadily, the massive Russian nuclear submarine accelerated until it reached its top speed—churning through the depths at more than twenty-four knots. If all went well, it would reach the point selected by Nakhimov in a little more than eleven days.

TWENTY-EIGHT

AVALON HOUSE, WINTER PARK, FLORIDA

A COUPLE OF DAYS LATER

Nick Flynn, Laura Van Horn, and Gwen Park were in the mansion's cluttered upstairs study. Maps, printouts of downloads from different internet sites, reference books, and personnel dossiers littered the small coffee table between them—along with a laptop computer connected to Four's secure local network.

Van Horn finished paging through the draft mission plan Flynn had prepared. She looked up with a tiny frown. "I see where you're going here, Nick, but it's still risky as hell."

Sitting next to her, Park nodded. "That's probably an understatement."

"True enough," Flynn agreed with a shrug. "But it beats every other option we've explored so far. Nothing else gives us the slightest chance of putting an assault team aboard that tanker." He picked up a heavily crossed out sheet of paper. "Using helicopters, for example. We tried that once. Got shot down." He crumpled it up and dropped it the floor. "Let's just say that I'm not exactly eager to repeat the experience."

"Fair point,' Van Horn allowed.

Flynn took out another sheet covered with notes and hand-drawn diagrams. "Then there's the idea of using small fast boats to close and board. Which sounds great until you realize those rapid-fire 35mm guns would blow them to smithereens a mile or two off. Not to mention that any survivors would then have to scale the ship's hull using ropes or ladders while under intense attack from an armed crew."

"The phrase 'sitting ducks' does spring to mind," Park said quietly.

"Yeah, it does. So scratch that." He scrunched up this second sheet and tossed it aside. "Which brings us to the plan of landing the assault force by conventional parachute," he continued. He snorted. "Even setting aside the problem of successfully landing on a moving target . . . at night . . . and probably out in the middle of the ocean . . . something about the whole idea of flying a slow-moving plane into range of those antiaircraft weapons and SAMs seems incredibly stupid, so—"

"What, no piece of notebook paper to mangle for that one?" Van Horn interrupted with a half smile. "I thought that was a nice effect."

Flynn laughed almost unwillingly. "I decided to save Four some money."

"Oh, yeah, saving a few pennies on scratch paper. That'll soothe Br'er Fox's troubled heart," she said with a wider grin. She turned more serious. "So, assuming you're serious about implementing Plan Not-Quite-As-Crazy, what's your next step?"

"I've found a place to train the assault force," he said seriously. "And I think I know where we can pick up most of the specialized gear we'll need. But mostly it's going to come down to whether or not I can pull together the right team." He shrugged. "That might be tricky."

Van Horn raised an eyebrow. "You think?" She slouched back in her worn leather armchair. "Heck, all you need are incredibly competent, physically fit guys with a mix of weapons and demolition skills. Guys who'd also be willing to risk their necks on something like this." She shrugged. "So who've you got in mind?"

"Tad Kossak, Shannon Cooke, and Alain Ricard, for a start."

She nodded. "Yeah, they're nuts enough. Anybody else?"

"I've sounded out Mark Stadler," Flynn said. "He's interested."

Van Horn turned to Park. "Stadler? He's one of your security guys, right, Gwen?" she asked. "The Marine?"

The other woman nodded. "He's also ex–Force Recon."

"Which means he's got shipboard combat experience," Flynn pointed out. He pulled out one of the personnel dossiers. "And Fox has talked to Four's UK station. They suggested one of their new recruits, a former sergeant in the SAS named Tony McGill. He's flying here tomorrow to check me out first."

"Not a dummy, then," Van Horn commented. "You ready to exert all your powers of persuasion?"

"I'll be my usual charming self," he assured her.

"Nick, you'll have to do better than that," she said sternly. "Don't forget that you're actually trying to get this guy McGill to sign on for this stunt. Not to bolt for the nearest exit."

Flynn bowed his head in mock apology. "Yes, ma'am."

"Good. So who else is on your list?"

"Well, that's about it," he admitted. "Turns out that Four's a little short right now on paramilitary daredevil types." He smiled ruefully. "Which probably explains why Fox was so hot to trot to scoop me up last year."

"I could go along on this gig," Van Horn offered. "Assuming you male chauvinist types don't mind fighting with a girl on your side, that is."

Flynn grinned at her. "I don't think anybody's dumb enough or suicidal enough to try to stop you, Laura. But we're going to need your flying skills more. Otherwise, I'm pretty sure this op literally won't ever get off the ground."

She nodded reluctantly. "Probably so." Her eyes were troubled. "Still, counting you, that's only six men, Nick." She picked up his draft mission plan. "And this scheme of yours calls for a minimum assault force of eight—which, considering the odds you're likely to face on board that tanker, is already pushing the envelope. Six shooters isn't going to cut it, not when you're likely to take casualties just getting down onto the deck."

"We don't really have a choice," he said carefully. He shrugged. "It's not like I can place a classified ad to fill the empty slots."

For just a second, a trace of impish glee flickered across Van Horn's worried face. "Well, you could, I guess. But can you imagine the look on Fox's face when he caught sight of a line of pot-bellied, gray-haired guys in hunting camo and Army surplus tactical gear lined up outside Avalon House?"

Flynn's mind goggled at the thought. "That would be something to behold," he agreed slowly. "Not a good thing, mind you."

"I might have another option," Gwen Park said, almost hesitantly. The petite Asian American woman wore a strange expression on her elegant face—an odd mix of embarrassed exasperation coupled with reluctant amusement.

"Oh?" Flynn said.

"About a week ago, two uninvited guests showed up on our doorstep," the Avalon House security chief told him. "And they were asking for you, Mr. Flynn."

"*Me?*"

She nodded. "You."

"Could be process servers, Nick," Van Horn murmured. "If you have to make a run for it, I'll hold them off here."

"Oh, very funny," Flynn said. He turned back to Park. "What's the story on these guys?"

She shrugged. "You were still overseas, so we played dumb. They then threatened to just wait outside for as long as it took us to find you."

"Kind of determined types," Van Horn commented dryly.

"Very determined," Park concurred with that same half-pained expression. "In the end, we compromised. They agreed to go back to their motel and sit tight. And we agreed to contact you on their behalf."

"Which you didn't do," Flynn pointed out.

The security chief smiled thinly. "Of course not. At least not until we'd thoroughly vetted them." She sighed. "We've had them under surveillance ever since. And their story, such as it is, seems to check out."

"And you think they might be able to help Nick with this operation?" Van Horn asked narrowly.

"Possibly," Park allowed. She frowned. "Letting strangers inside Avalon House is against the rules. *My* rules, I mean. But I don't see any other realistic option in this particular case." She held up her smartphone. "I can have them here in minutes. If you're interested?"

Flynn nodded. "Oh, hell, yes."

A short time later, Park knocked briefly on the half-open door to the study and looked in. "Our guests have arrived," she reported. Then she half-turned and crooked a finger down the hall, signaling someone. "In here, gentlemen."

Flynn's eyes widened at the sight of the two men who ambled somewhat sheepishly in behind the security chief. Cole Hynes and Wade Vucovich had been part of the Joint Force security unit he'd briefly commanded on Alaska's frozen north coast. After a risky parachute jump into a winter blizzard, they'd all tangled with a Spetsnaz detachment hunting for Russia's missing stealth bomber—a fight that had ended in victory, but with half of his men dead or wounded. He hadn't seen any of them since he'd been medevacked out to San Antonio for his own injuries. He stood up.

Hynes, short and square-shouldered, nodded to him. "Hey there, Captain," he said uncertainly.

Vucovich, taller and wiry, shyly echoed him, "Hi, sir."

They bobbed their heads at Laura Van Horn. From the appraising looks on their faces, they recognized her as one of the C-130J pilots who'd flown them on that last airborne drop. "Ma'am."

"Cole. Wade. It's . . . well, really good to see you both," Flynn acknowledged, trying less than successfully to conceal his surprise at their appearance here at Avalon House. "But you can drop the 'captain' and 'sir' bit, you know." He indicated his jeans and polo shirt. "I'm not in the Air Force anymore."

"Yes, sir," Hynes said. "We know that. But we've got to call you something . . . and Mr. Flynn doesn't sound right somehow."

Flynn grinned at them. "You *could* try calling me Nick," he suggested.

"Yes, sir," Hynes agreed. "We could." But their stoic faces told him that was a nonstarter.

He studied their own mix of civilian clothes. "So I guess you guys are out of the Army now, too?"

Hynes nodded. "That's right, sir." He shrugged. "The brass wanted me to reenlist when my time ran out. But they offered me Fort Polk," he said in disgust.

"Ouch," Flynn said sympathetically. Fort Polk in Louisiana had a well-deserved reputation as one of U.S. Army's worst duty stations. "That sucks."

"Yeah, Polk. And on a PFC's lousy pay? Forget that," Hynes said. "So I told them to shove it."

Flynn stared at him. "I thought you got your sergeant's stripes back after our brush with the Russians?" Hynes, a superb soldier otherwise, had a pugnacious streak that had cost him his noncom's rank and landed him with Flynn's band of exiles in northern Alaska.

"I did," the shorter man said evenly. "Lost 'em again. Had a disagreement with a dickhead civilian outside a bar in Anchorage a couple of months later."

Flynn hid a grin. He should have figured. Outside of combat, Cole Hynes tended to get bored. And when he got bored, it was all too easy for that temper of his to get the better of him. The veteran infantryman didn't suffer fools gladly. He just decked them.

He turned to Vucovich. "What happened in your case, Wade?"

The other man reddened slightly. "Had a little trouble with the MPs," he admitted. "So my new CO and I came to an agreement that I wouldn't reup when the time came."

"Not another exploding still, Wade?" Flynn asked sympathetically, hearing a muffled snort from Laura Van Horn. Vucovich had tried building a jury-rigged still at the isolated radar station they'd been assigned to guard. The resulting explosion had spewed half-fermented potato slices far and wide across what seemed like half the polar ice cap.

"No, sir," Vucovich replied, sounding hurt. "The next one worked just fine." He shook his head. "But the first sergeant wanted a bigger cut of the proceeds and ratted me out when I turned him down."

"Uh-huh." Flynn looked them over. "So you're both out of the tender mercies of the United States Army, wandering around footloose and fancy-free?"

"That's about the size of it, Captain," Hynes agreed.

"Which leads me to the somewhat more important question of just what you're doing here?" Flynn asked carefully, seeing Gwen Park lean in slightly. This was obviously the same question she wanted answered.

"Well, sir, it's like this," Hynes said. "All of the guys, Sanchez, Pedersen, Kim, and the rest of us, were real curious about what happened to you after that bomber crashed and blew up and they packed you off to some hospital. Since we all got sworn to secrecy by a bunch of spooks about everything that went down, we couldn't ask any questions while we were still in the service. So when Wade and me got out, we decided to go look you up."

"And just how did you plan to do that?" Flynn wondered. "Since I'm pretty sure my personnel records were sealed."

"We visited your folks in Texas," Hynes said patiently. "And since your mom thought you might want to see us, she gave us your address."

"My mother did *what*?" Flynn said in disbelief.

Hynes nodded again. "Sure, Captain. She said she figured you were probably off causing trouble somewhere and that you might be able to use a couple more hands."

Van Horn was red-faced now with suppressed mirth. She swiped away tears of laughter. "Now I *really* have to meet your mother, Nick," she forced out. "She's got you pegged perfectly."

Flynn ignored her. He stared hard at the two former enlisted men. "Even my mother doesn't know where I work. And my address is a post office box," he pointed out quietly.

They nodded matter-of-factly. "Yes, sir," Hynes said. "But it's a P.O. box here in Winter Park. So we just found the post office in town and waited for someone to pick up the mail. Then we followed 'em back here." He looked admiringly around the room. "Heck of a nice place, Captain."

Flynn shook his head in disbelief. They made it sound so easy. And the funny thing was that it really had been that easy. So much for the Quartet Directorate's vaunted aura of secrecy, he thought, fighting down the temptation to burst out laughing himself. Now he knew why Gwen Park looked so embarrassed. Hynes and Vucovich turned out to have slipped straight through a gaping, completely unsuspected hole in the net of secrecy she'd oh-so-carefully thrown around Avalon House. He would *not* want to be the member of her detail who'd been assigned to pick up their mail. Either her security officer had been woefully inattentive, or the two ex-soldiers were a lot better at being sneaky than he would first have imagined.

"And just what sort of work is it that you thought I might be doing now, Cole?" he asked curiously. The brass plaques outside the mansion would have told them it housed offices for the Sobieski Charitable Foundation, the Concannon Language Institute, and Sykes-Fairbairn Strategic Investments.

Hynes shrugged. "Well, Captain, I don't guess you're just working as a translator for some language institute. And I doubt you're handing out charity money. And I sure don't see you as a banker." He grinned. "So I figure all that stuff outside is just bullshit window dressing. And that your mom was right. You're still raising hell. For someone."

"Nick," Van Horn said softly. "What was it that you were saying about Four finding itself short of paramilitary daredevil types?"

He smiled back at her, and then turned to Hynes and Vucovich. "As it happens," he said carefully, "I do have a project in mind. One you guys might be interested in."

Hynes thumped his taller friend in triumph. "Told you so, Wade!" he crowed.

"But it's also extremely hazardous," Flynn warned them. "The chance of getting killed is pretty high."

Vucovich spoke up now. "Yeah," he said simply. "We sort of expected that, sir. You can deal us in."

TWENTY-NINE

IN THE HILL COUNTRY,
NORTHWEST OF AUSTIN, TEXAS

TWO DAYS LATER

Laura Van Horn tweaked her BushCat's centerline control stick gently to the left, banking into a slow, wide orbit a couple of thousand feet over the low, wooded hills of Central Texas. A stretch of mostly open, mostly level ground appeared through the windshield—grazing land for one of the local cattle ranches. She glanced at Fox. "The training area's just down there."

The head of the Quartet Directorate's American station nodded and raised his binoculars to scan the small valley. Bright white chalk lines, like those used on baseball fields, had been laid down across the close-cropped grass. They created a highly visible, mostly rectangular shape with one rounded side that was roughly eight hundred feet long and a little more than a hundred feet across. More chalk lines had been drawn inside this larger outline, suggesting a maze of piping, catwalks, gangways, bollards, and other structures. He lowered his binoculars and turned to Van Horn. "Is that supposed to be a mockup of the *Gulf Venture*, as seen from the air?"

"Yep." She shrugged. "It was the best we could do in the time available." She grinned at him. "We thought about trying to lease a tanker of our own for practice. But that turned out to be way outside our budget. Plus, sailing around in the Gulf of Mexico with a rented ship that size would be a bit too likely to draw attention from the media and the government that we could do without."

"Yes, I'd imagine so," Fox said with a thin smile of his own. He craned his head again to take another look at the chalk-drawn deck plan. He frowned. "So our Mr. Flynn has decided to take his team in by helicopter after all? Despite the tanker's air defenses?"

Van Horn shook her head. "Nope. Nick's got something a little different in mind."

He raised an eyebrow. "Different in what way?"

"You'll see," she said cryptically. She spoke into her radio mike. "Dragon, this is Tiger Cat. We're in position. Standing by."

Through their headsets, they heard Flynn's laconic reply. *"Understood, Tiger Cat. Dragon Team dropping now."*

Van Horn banked again, bringing the little plane around so that they could see another aircraft—this one a larger, twin-engine turboprop—flying several miles away and several thousand feet higher. Its wings winked in the spring sunlight.

Fox raised his binoculars, seeing tiny black specks spilling out of the distant plane. He waited for parachutes to blossom against the clear blue sky. None did. His frown deepened. Something strange was happening out there. Instead of plunging almost vertically toward the ground, the men who'd just hurled themselves out of the aircraft were slanting downward at an angle—gliding straight toward the tanker mockup at high speed. Perplexed, he focused carefully and managed to catch a brief, close-up glimpse of one of the jumpers. The helmeted man was diving headfirst. His arms and legs were spread apart, with layers of nylon fabric connecting them to create an airfoil.

"They're wearing wingsuits," Fox murmured, suddenly realizing what it was that he was seeing.

"Pretty nifty idea, right?" Van Horn said archly.

Starting a couple of decades before, experienced skydiving enthusiasts had begun taking to the air wearing those individual flying suits. Worn in combination with parachutes for the final landing, wingsuits added significant amounts of lift and enabled their users to greatly extend the range and duration of every jump—whether out of airplanes, or off tall buildings, mountains, and cliffs.

One by one, as they arrowed closer to their chalk-outlined target, the jumpers pulled their chutes. Steerable rectangular canopies snapped open, slowing their descents, and they drifted down the last couple of hundred feet. They were clearly aiming for the clear patches of grass and dirt inside the outline—while trying to avoid the white lines that represented pipelines, catwalks, fake shipping containers, and the other obstructions which littered the real oil tanker's deck. In a real combat jump, anyone who slammed into one of those obstacles would almost certainly be seriously injured or killed. Small clouds of dust and chalk puffed up as each man flared his parachute and came down to a soft landing.

Once all eight jumpers were down, Van Horn brought her BushCat around, descended, and landed in the pasture close beside the tanker mockup. By the time Fox climbed out of the light aircraft, Flynn was already on his way over with his wingsuit and parachute bundled under one arm.

"Welcome to the Dragon Exercise Area," Flynn greeted him, coming up with a big grin on his lean, dirt-streaked face. "Otherwise known as the Big Dusty to some of my guys."

Fox stared at the chalk-outlined target area and then shook his head dubiously. The list of things he could imagine going wrong was already depressingly long. He turned back to Flynn. "There's a pretty big difference between hitting your marks on a stationary, one-dimensional target on dry land, and landing safely on a ship steaming at high speed at sea, isn't there?"

Flynn nodded calmly. "Yes, sir, there sure is. And between landing in broad daylight and coming in at night, for that matter." He shrugged.

"Which is why we're going to be running this drill over and over, steadily upping the tempo and difficulty level each time. Once we've mastered the basics of flying these wingsuits and steering our landing chutes, I'll have a contactor come out to the ranch and put up some scaffolding so our mockup's more 3D."

"How long do you plan to train?" Fox asked.

"If possible, practically right up to the moment when you give us the actual target," Flynn told him frankly. "When we do this for real, it's going to be a HALO drop from high altitude. The farther we are from the *Gulf Venture* when we jump, the less likely we are to spook the bad guys until we're right on top of them. It's our best chance to avoid being blown out of the sky by their antiaircraft guns."

Fox narrowed his eyes in thought. The younger man was right. Given the defenses their enemies had fitted to that oil tanker, achieving almost total surprise was their only hope of putting an intact assault team aboard. "How far away do you plan to be when you make your drop?"

"The world wingsuit distance record right now is around twenty miles," Flynn said quietly. "I hope to beat that." He smiled tightly. "We'll manage it for sure—and by a considerable margin—if the experimental high-tech wingsuit gear I've ordered from Germany gets here in time for us to train on it." Then he shrugged. "But since I can't count on that happening, we're training to go using the equipment we have on hand now."

Fox nodded slowly, taking in what he'd been told. The opening phases of this plan might not be quite as crazy as he'd first feared. The tanker's Iranian captain and crew shouldn't automatically assume that an aircraft crossing their course twenty miles or more ahead was launching an attack on them. And that ought to make them hesitate to unmask their concealed weapons—since doing so risked blowing the *Gulf Venture*'s cover as a genuine merchant ship. That was especially true since the Dragon team's transport plane would be flying well outside the effective range of their 35mm guns and surface-to-air missiles.

So at least the aircraft's crew would be safe no matter what happened. Of course, the same thing couldn't be said for Flynn and his men. If the tanker's weapons were manned and ready when they jumped, the gun crews would need less than thirty seconds to drop their camouflage and open fire.

Knowing that revealing his misgivings wouldn't help anyone, Fox did his best to hide his fears. Throughout its long history, the Quartet Directorate's audacious covert operations had helped guard the United States and its allies against their most dangerous enemies. But there was always a terrible price to be paid—a price in brave men's and women's lives. The secret war waged on behalf of the peoples of the free world without their knowledge or gratitude had been costly from its very outset. Sadly, it showed no signs of becoming any less deadly with the passage of time.

Instead, he waved a hand at the tanker mockup and at the group of tough-looking men who were now busy loading their gear aboard the vehicles that would take them back to the local airport for another practice jump. "Has there been any reaction from the locals to all this unusual activity of yours?"

Flynn's grin grew bigger still. "Some, but not a lot. There aren't a lot of people in this part of the state in the first place. And the folks who do live here are mostly the get-along, go-along kind. If it's not obviously illegal, they pretty much reckon it's none of their business." He fished a business card out of his breast pocket. "For when we run into any real nosy parkers, I had these printed up. It usually satisfies them."

Fox took it. Almost unwillingly, his own mouth twitched in a slight smile. The fake business card read: FLYNN'S FLYING CIRCUS— *TEAM AEROBATICS AND STUNTS. AIR SHOWS AND MOVIE SPECTACULARS OUR SPECIALTY.* Then he sighed. If this fun-loving Texas daredevil got himself killed, the world would be a much darker place. Unfortunately, he suspected that was by far the most likely outcome of this hazardous operation.

Later that evening, after the Dragon team had finished the last of its three scheduled practice jumps for that day, Fox briefed Flynn, Van Horn, and the others on the search program the Quartet Directorate had instituted to try to find the converted Iranian oil tanker. They all listened intently. Unless Four could somehow detect and then track the *Gulf Venture* at sea, all of their training and hard work would be in vain.

"Analysis by our top planners confirmed that relying on aircraft for the initial search would be a complete waste of time and resources," he told them bluntly. "So instead, we're using satellites."

"We've got our own fucking satellites?" Hynes blurted out in astonishment. "Seriously?"

Fox stifled a frown. He still wasn't sure that it had been wise to bring the members of Flynn's old unit into the Quartet Directorate secret. They were considerably rougher around the edges than Four's usual recruits. Still, as Gwen Park had pointed out to him—at great length—what other choice did they really have? Killing innocents went against every principle Four held dear. And besides, Hynes and Vucovich, unpolished though they might be, had demonstrated both considerable loyalty to their old commander and a remarkable talent for unconventional operations by tracking him down in the first place. If they lived long enough—doubtful though that seemed at the moment—more training should make them extremely useful agents, especially for missions requiring direct action.

"The satellites aren't ours," he explained patiently. "At least not directly."

Through one of the Quartet Directorate's front groups—ostensibly a science nonprofit focused on climatological research—they were buying time on the European Pléiades constellation. Its twin high-resolution imaging satellites circled the globe in polar orbits, passing over every point on the Earth's surface once every twenty-four hours. These satellites were dual purpose, filling both defense and civilian needs, but most of their users were more interested in pictures taken over the world's land masses. That left an opening for Fox, and he'd seized it with both hands.

Under the contract he'd written, the Pléiades satellites were scanning large swathes of the world's oceans, beginning with zones near the Persian Gulf—and then steadily moving to the east and west and north and south with each new orbit. Depending on weather constraints and their space vehicles' other commitments, the constellation's commercial managers in Toulouse, France, had estimated they should be able to obtain good quality pictures of around 230,000 square miles of ocean per day.

Hynes whistled.

Fox nodded. "Those numbers do sound impressive," he agreed coolly. "Unfortunately, they still represent only a fraction of the sea area we need surveyed." He shrugged. "But without access to our own government's far more capable spy satellites, this is our best option."

The former Army enlisted man frowned. "So you're saying this is still just a crapshoot."

"Not entirely," Fox corrected. "Our search patterns are carefully calculated to maximize the odds of our spotting the *Gulf Venture*. For example, we're focusing most heavily on stretches of the ocean outside the ordinary sea lanes, since we suspect the Iranians and their Russian allies want to avoid even accidental contact with other passing vessels that could report their presence."

Sitting between Hynes and Van Horn, Flynn nodded his understanding. He leaned forward. "One thing, Br'er Fox?"

"Yes?"

"I get why we're renting the Pléiades constellation. But aren't there other imaging civilian satellites that can cover wider areas?"

Fox nodded. "There certainly are, Nick. However, the tradeoff there is that they all produce much lower-resolution imagery. We need high-resolution pictures to have any real hope of positively identifying the *Gulf Venture* from orbit. At lower resolutions and from hundreds of miles up in space, one AFRAMAX-sized oil tanker looks pretty much like another."

"So what's our outside time frame for finding this ship?" Flynn asked quietly.

Fox sighed. "Your guess on that is as good as mine, Nick." He shrugged. "But one thing is all too clear: if we don't spot the *Gulf Venture* before it comes within missile range of whatever target Moscow and Tehran have chosen, it will be far too late."

THIRTY

T MINUS 14, A FEW DAYS LATER

Pavel Voronin waited patiently while his servants handed around glasses of Champagne to his guests—Russia's president, Piotr Zhdanov, and a small group of his closest military and intelligence advisers. They were seated around a table that had been moved into the palatial living room for this special event. A large-screen digital display stood at one end of the table. It was currently blank.

When the servants quietly withdrew, closing the doors behind them, he moved to the head of the table and raised his own glass. "Gentlemen," he said smoothly. "Before we begin, a toast. To our president, a man of courage and vision!"

Voronin noticed one or two of them discreetly rolling their eyes at this bit of gross flattery, but they raised their glasses all the same. Obsequiousness was a survival trait in the highest circles of Russia's current government. "The president," deep voices rumbled in response.

Most of them downed the fine sparkling wine, a Perrier-Jouët worth thousands of American dollars per bottle, as though it were the cheapest vodka—the sort bought purely for its high alcohol content. For all their rank and position, he thought coolly, the majority of Zhdanov's inner circle were still nothing but jumped-up peasants. Where it counted, they were all alike: Kokorin, the elderly minister of defense; Golitsyn and Rogozin, respectively the commanders of the navy and air force; Yumashev, who headed the FSB, Russia's internal security agency; and Veslovsky and Ivashin, the chiefs of the SVR and GRU. They had education, and even technical competence in their own narrow fields, but they had no real grasp of culture. He'd seen their faces when they first saw the extravagant blend of expensive designer furniture and priceless modernist art that filled this room. Looks of baffled incomprehension had been mixed with scorn at what they apparently considered a display of decadence. But underlying it all had been their clear envy of the tremendous wealth he flaunted.

Voronin knew too that these men, almost all of them nearly twice his age, also despised and feared him because of his obvious and growing influence over Zhdanov. His Raven Syndicate was a source of power completely outside their control—one they saw draining the armed forces, the SVR, and the GRU of their best officers. So far, they had failed to stop his rapid rise, watching from the sidelines with barely veiled hostility while he took his place at the president's right hand. Inwardly, he shrugged. Perhaps he should feel sorry for them. They were caught on the wrong side of the one of the oldest equations in human history: Ambition coupled with ruthlessness produced wealth. Wealth, in turn, produced power, and this power, wielded relentlessly, yielded even more wealth. It was a synergistic relationship that few Russians understood. Since the fall of the Soviet Union, the nation's new oligarchs, including his dead mentor, Dmitri Grishin, had shown themselves unable to grasp the fundamental truth that money, in and of itself, was useless unless it was coupled with political and military authority. That left them vulnerable to a hard-edged autocrat like Piotr Zhdanov, who'd begun carving out his own path to the presidency while he was still a young officer in the old KGB.

Voronin had no intention of falling into that same trap. His control over the Raven Syndicate made him the master of highly trained soldiers, spies, and assassins beholden to him—and to no one else. At the same time, his new status as Zhdanov's most trusted counselor gave him nearly unfettered access to the levers of Russia's state power, its fleets, air units, tank armies, and missiles. The day would come when this indirect exercise of power no longer satisfied him, but it would do for the moment.

Now it was time to show these old men the first steps on the road to their nation's renewed greatness. Voronin put his own champagne down largely untasted. He turned to Zhdanov. "Mr. President? With your permission, I'll proceed."

Zhdanov nodded briefly. His eyes were hooded. He'd agreed with the younger man's reasons for keeping MIDNIGHT a closely held secret—even from his other most trusted advisers. Now that the moment had come to brief them on the operation, he was plainly somewhat anxious about how they would react. None of them would be happy to learn just how far they'd all been kept out of the loop.

Voronin ignored the older man's show of nerves. He judged it to be wholly unnecessary. In their hearts, the others Zhdanov had gathered around him were no more than domesticated dogs, not untamed wolves. While they might growl and snap in protest, in the end he knew they would bend to their master's voice and will.

Instead, he ran his own gaze around the table. "The presentation you're about to see has been classified at the very highest level, by the direct order of the president himself. Outside this room, there will be no further discussion of the operation code-named MIDNIGHT, except with his written authorization."

Startled, the senior ministers and military commanders turned as one toward Zhdanov. He nodded slowly, confirming what they'd just been told. They sat back, looking troubled.

Voronin concealed a pleased smile. Now these men knew better who was calling the tune here. And who held the whip. He raised a hand to signal one of his aides. Immediately, the lights dimmed and the large display brightened. "The world is about to change," he told them with grave satisfaction. "And many of the obstacles to Russia's rightful place as the globe's dominant power will be swept away forever."

Video footage of the Zuljanah rocket launch appeared on screen. Steadily, the missile arced high over the Caspian Sea, roaring aloft on a pillar of flickering fire. "What you're witnessing is the final test of a key element in our plan, the space vehicle that will deliver the MIDNIGHT weapon to its intended target."

Yvgeny Rogozin, the lieutenant general in charge of Russia's air force, frowned. "That's not one of our ICBMs."

"Correct, General," Voronin said. "The rocket is an Iranian design."

"The Iranians?" Gennady Kokorian, the defense minister, snapped querulously. "What the devil does Iran have to do with this MID-NIGHT plan of yours?"

"Everything," Voronin said simply. Then he smiled coldly. "And nothing."

Over the next several minutes, he walked his audience through the several stages involved in this high-stakes operation. The more he talked, the longer their faces grew. As he'd suspected from the beginning, they were conditioned by age and inbred caution to focus only on the risks involved—so much so that they could not recognize the enormous re-wards to be reaped. These men are fossils, he thought contemptuously. Much the same, of course, could be said of Zhdanov himself, though at least the aging president still had just enough guts and greed to be useful to him.

When he finished, there was a long moment of horrified silence.

At last, Kokorin shook his bald head. "This plan of yours is insane," he said bluntly. "You would stake everything on a single weapon? A weapon that is no longer even fully in our control?" He grimaced. "Failure would be utterly catastrophic, both for Russia, and for all of us in this room."

"All the more reason to make sure we succeed," Voronin retorted. He shrugged. "Besides, *alea iacta est.*" Seeing their looks of incomprehension at the classic Latin comment from Caesar, spoken as he the crossed to Rubicon to make his bid for power, he smiled thinly. "In other words, the die is cast. The *Gulf Venture* has already sailed and our Iranian allies will not willingly abort the operation now."

They stared at him in shock. Until that instant, none of them had realized MIDNIGHT was already in motion. Voronin resisted the temptation to laugh. Had these tired and timid old men seriously believed they would be consulted first? That they were anything more than the tools Zhdanov would use if it was necessary and discard or ignore if it was not?

"There are risks," he agreed. "But the potential rewards far outweigh them. At the moment, Russia's status as a world power is mostly an illusion—one which rests on a foundation of sand. The longer we sit idle, the more the power conveyed by our military might, especially by our strategic nuclear forces, will be undermined by an aging, shrinking population and shaky economy. If nothing changes, we will only grow weaker as our competitors grow stronger. We must either act decisively now against our chief rival, the United States, or abandon any pretense of being a great nation." He turned his attention to Zhdanov. "And I do not believe our people would react well to learning that all their sacrifices of the past decades were in vain."

The president nodded dourly. He was only too aware that his countrymen would turn against even the strongest leader if they believed he had failed them. Fed a steady diet of propaganda claiming that Russia could still enforce its will on the rest of the world whenever it chose, they would not accept anything less. In essence, his continued hold on power rested on his ability to make reality conform to those lies before the Russian people figured out how badly they'd been duped.

"In any case, MIDNIGHT has been structured deliberately to minimize any significant danger to us," Voronin continued slyly. "Any significant evidence that survives will pin the attack on another of America's long-standing enemies, Iran's radical Islamic regime—and not on us."

Slowly, the men around the table relaxed and muttered their agreement. The younger man's arguments were persuasive, especially since it was clear that his scheme had Zhdanov's total support. Only Kokorin seemed unimpressed. His thin-lipped mouth curled in distaste. "You've certainly spun an elegant web of lies and deceit," the elderly defense minister acknowledged. "So much so that I only wonder what else it conceals." His eyes hardened. "Is your interest in this plan purely patriotic, some burning, selfless desire to see Mother Russia made great again? Or do you hope to achieve more personal gains in all the chaos you're about to unleash?"

Zhdanov leaned forward with a scowl. "Enough, Gennadiy!" he snapped. "Remember, I've personally approved this operation. What I care about is what matters. And what matters to me are competence and boldness, not high-minded slogans that do nothing to advance Russia's strategic interests. So far, MIDNIGHT has been executed flawlessly. That is what counts!"

Voronin bowed his head modestly, acknowledging this praise. Privately, he knew the reason for the president's vehemence was that Kokorin's tart comment had struck close to the bone. Zhdanov, like him, was fully aware that the world's financial markets were about to be turned upside down—and that investments made with that in mind would yield extraordinary gains. Some, he mused, might find it grotesque to expect to profit financially from the probable deaths of a hundred million people. But while Russia's leader undoubtedly intended mainly to pad his own considerable personal wealth, the ill-gotten fruits of years of near-absolute power, he personally had far bigger plans.

The financial rewards he expected to reap were important, but not in themselves. With three billion dollars at his disposal, Voronin had made himself the second most powerful man in Russia. How much more could he achieve with ten or twenty times that amount? His pale eyes narrowed in speculation. It would be quite amusing, he decided, to find out.

THIRTY-ONE

Viktor Skoblin hit the power button on the satellite phone to turn it off.
When the screen went dark, he handed it back to Yvgeny Kvyat. The
former GRU officer got to work stowing its separate components away
out of sight. It was vital to keep their Iranian "allies" unaware that the
Raven Syndicate team had its own line of communication to Russia.

"Well? What's the news from Moscow?" another of his subordinates,
Dmitri Fadeyev, demanded.

Skoblin heard the tension in the other man's voice. It mirrored his
own. During the oil tanker's seemingly endless voyage south through
the Arabian Sea and the Indian Ocean, and now west into the South
Atlantic—day after day without sighting land or any other ships—
frictions had risen steadily between his small unit and the larger Iranian
crew. Apart from their mission, the two sides had nothing in common.
To Captain Heidari and the other Revolutionary Guard sailors and
soldiers, the Russians were "godless mercenaries," not true believers.
The more fanatical among them clearly regarded the very presence of
Skoblin and his men aboard as something that contaminated their ship's
holy purpose. So far, they'd limited themselves to muttered insults and

sullen looks, but the Raven Syndicate's ex-soldiers and spies were now being very careful never to go anywhere aboard the tanker on their own or unarmed.

He looked around the circle of anxious faces. "Mother Wolf is in position," he told them quietly. "She will stay with us all the way to the launch point."

The news that the Russian Navy submarine *Podmoskovye* was now covertly trailing this ship triggered several small, relieved smiles. They were no longer alone in the middle of the ocean.

IN THE HILL COUNTRY, CENTRAL TEXAS

THAT SAME TIME

Nick Flynn stood on the covered porch of the ranch house he'd rented for his Dragon assault team. Together with Laura Van Horn, he was watching a severe spring thunderstorm roll across the Central Texas Hill Country.

Dozens of flashes of lightning slashed down in dazzling, split-second bursts that split the night sky apart. Their eerie ionized glow illuminated towering masses of clouds scudding eastward on the wind. Moments after each separate strike, thunderclaps boomed across the neighboring hills and woods. They were powerful enough to rattle the windows behind them.

Over the noise of the thunder, Flynn heard a loud, rushing roar drawing closer. "Here it comes," he said quietly. Seconds later, a wall of driving rain swept across the ranch house, hammering down on its metal roof with an ear-splitting, near-continuous clatter.

"You know, falling snow's a hell of a lot quieter," Van Horn yelled in his ear. "Maybe Alaska's not so bad after all."

He grinned. "I'll take a little noise, so long as I'm not freezing to death," he shouted back.

Wryly, she pointed out to where torrents of rain were pounding the lightning-lit pasture. "Don't look now, but I think our simulated oil tanker just sank."

Flynn nodded. After the storm passed, the limestone soils here would dry quickly, but they'd definitely need to have a ground crew re-chalk the outline they'd been using for jump practice . . . and repair the scaffolding erected to make the fake obstacles on its deck more realistic. All told, his team would probably lose close to a full day of training time—at a time when every hour was precious. He frowned. "It'd sure be nice if the real *Gulf Venture* was just as easy to put under."

"A category-five hurricane would come in handy right about now," Van Horn agreed. "Too bad that evil SOB Voronin wasn't dumb enough to set his operation in motion during hurricane season."

Suddenly, the lights inside the ranch house went out. A minute later, Shannon Cooke came outside to join them. The ex-Special Forces soldier's face was illuminated by his smartphone's screen. "The electricity's out across the whole area," he reported. "Looks like all this lightning blew a bunch of transformers almost simultaneously. The local cooperative says it'll take several hours to restore power."

"Just swell," Van Horn said. She turned to Flynn with a playful grin on her face. "Well, darn, I guess this'll be an early night after all. And yet here I am still feeling wide awake—"

But Flynn failed to take the bait offered by her not-so-subtle hint. Instead, he stood motionless, gripped by the insights cascading through his mind with all the intensity and speed of the lightning flashes still tearing across the sky above them. Suddenly, everything about what Moscow and Tehran really had planned fell into place with terrifying certainty.

"Son of a bitch," he said at last in stunned realization. "Those bastards aboard the *Gulf Venture* aren't aiming to destroy just *one* city. They're going after dozens." He saw their puzzled looks and said tightly. "We need to see Fox. Pronto."

NEAR AUSTIN-BERGSTROM INTERNATIONAL
AIRPORT

EARLY THE NEXT MORNING

Flynn knocked on the door of Fox's hotel room and waited. The
chief of the Quartet Directorate's American station had come in from
Orlando late the night before aboard a red-eye flight. There was no
sound from inside.

He glanced at Van Horn. "Think he's asleep?"

"Br'er Fox?" she said with some amusement. "I doubt it. Only
humans need sleep." She fought down a yawn. "Like me."

Flynn restrained himself from asking why, if she was that tired
now, she'd seemed so painfully cheerful while flying the BushCat
down to Austin with the sun just poking above the horizon. She had
sharp elbows, and his ribs could only take so much. He raised his
hand to knock again. But before he could even make contact, the door
swung open.

"Nick. Laura. Please come in," Fox said quietly, waving them inside.
He swiped at his chin with a hand towel, removing the last traces of
shaving cream, and then stepped inside the small bathroom to hang it
neatly on the rack. As usual, every motion was controlled and precise
and neat. Only the shadows under his eyes suggested that he was as tired
as they were.

Politely, he ushered them into chairs set around a little round table.
Then he pulled a seat of his own over from the room's tiny desk and

waited while they poured out cups of room service coffee from a carafe. "Very well," he said finally. "You have my full attention."

"We've all been banging our heads trying to figure out what Voronin and his backers in Moscow and Tehran have up their sleeves," Flynn said. "Right?"

Fox nodded. His mouth tightened. "So far, unfortunately, Four's best analysts have all come up empty-handed," he admitted.

"Me, too," Flynn told him. "Until last night." He pulled out his smartphone and brought up an image on the screen. It showed a night-time picture from space of the continental United States. Glowing patches of light showed the presence of major metropolitan areas— New York, Boston, D.C., Miami, Chicago, Houston, Dallas, St. Louis, Salt Lake City, Los Angeles, San Francisco, Seattle, and dozens of others. Bright rings were superimposed on this image, radiating out from a single point over the Midwest marked with a radiation symbol. "It's this."

Fox studied it for a moment in silence. He looked up. "Go on."

"Moscow and Tehran plan to carry out a nuclear EMP, an electromagnetic pulse attack against us," Flynn explained. "A high-altitude nuclear detonation designed to simultaneously knock out electric power grids, cars, trucks, trains, river barges, and aircraft, water purification plants, and computer systems across a huge stretch of the United States."

The image on his smartphone screen showed different areas of effect for an EMP attack, depending on the altitude of the initial nuclear burst. A warhead detonated thirty miles up could fry electronics out to a radius of 480 miles. The damage caused by the same size bomb going off 120 miles over the earth would spread a thousand miles beyond the blast point. The worst-case scenario indicated that a nuclear blast 300 miles above the surface would destroy computers and other electronics up to fifteen hundred miles away—across the entire continental United States, most of Canada, and the northern regions of Mexico.

"A massive EMP pulse would destroy every affected system beyond any possibility of repair," Flynn continued grimly. "Producing replacements and installing them could take months, maybe years in some cases. And in the meantime, deprived of fuel, food, clean water, and electricity, millions of people in our major metro areas will die—either from starvation or disease."

No American city or its surrounding suburbs had more than a few days' worth of fuel, food, and purified water available at any given time. They were entirely dependent on a continuous flow of supplies brought in by road, rail, and river. And without working transportation systems and power grids, there would be no way to ship in the needed goods. Shelves would empty in a matter of hours, followed by looting and the complete breakdown of law and order. The margin between a modern high-tech civilization and Dark Ages barbarism was breathtakingly slim.

Fox frowned when Flynn finished laying out the terrifying scenario he saw developing. "My understanding is that the threat of an EMP attack is somewhat overblown," he said carefully. "Our ICBMs and other nuclear forces are already hardened against electromagnetic pulse effects, so they'd be completely unaffected by any surprise strike. As a result, a major power like Moscow or Beijing has to know that crossing the nuclear threshold like that would automatically trigger massive retaliation—probably leading directly to an all-out and unwinnable war. The same thing goes double for a regional power like Iran, with the exception that we could smash them back to the Stone Age without taking further damage." Tiredly, he took off his glasses and rubbed at his eyes. With a sigh, he put them back on. "And as far the threat of a terrorist-conducted EMP strike goes, that seems even less likely, according to the experts. Developing the specialized warheads needed to pull off an effective attack would be far beyond the capability of any known terrorist group—as would calculating the optimum missile trajectories and detonation points."

Flynn nodded. "All of that is true. Which is precisely why Zhdanov is working through Voronin's Raven Syndicate and the Iranians. It lets him hide Russia's involvement. And without solid evidence that Moscow is directly responsible, would an American president be willing to unleash a nuclear Armageddon that might end all of human civilization?"

"Probably not," Fox agreed slowly. "And even if he was, I'm not sure the rest of the chain of command would go along with him."

"Well, one more thing's for damned sure," Flynn said bluntly. "The Russians definitely have the nuclear weapons technology and expertise needed to build EMP warheads . . . and the supercomputing power required to plan the most destructive attack." He leaned forward, intent on making his point. "Remember how none of us could see what strategic advantage the Russians and the Iranians hoped to gain by destroying a single city? Because the huge risks of sparking a total war never seemed to match up with any possible gain? This is the answer, Br'er Fox," he argued. "A successful EMP attack carried out by hidden intermediaries lets Zhdanov and the nutcases in Tehran cripple us without giving themselves away. With millions dead or dying and our whole civilian economy in ruins, we'd have to turn inward—dedicating every ounce of our remaining resources trying to cope with the avalanche of disaster unfolding here at home." His jaw tightened. "Sure, all our missiles, bombers, warships, tanks, and artillery would be untouched . . . but so what? They'd be rendered effectively useless by the sheer magnitude of the domestic catastrophe we'd be facing. It'd take us decades to recover—decades with the Russians and their allies consolidating power in Europe, the Middle East, Africa, South America . . . hell, wherever they want to."

Finished, he sat back, feeling suddenly exhausted. Even though he didn't have any hard facts to back up his speculation, he was still as sure of this as he'd ever been about anything. And he absolutely needed the higher-ups in the Quartet Directorate to understand the magnitude of the threat they now faced. Four no longer had time to play it safe or to try to conserve scarce resources.

Laura Van Horn broke the uneasy silence. "Nick's right," she said flatly. "His hypothesis is the only one that fits all the data."

Somberly, Fox nodded. "I agree." He sighed. "Which makes our need to seize the *Gulf Venture* and that nuclear-armed missile it's carrying that much more urgent." He spread his hands helplessly. "Unfortunately, none of our leased satellite reconnaissance sweeps of the world's oceans have turned up the tanker yet. We're as much in the dark now as we were when we started looking."

"It has to be heading for either the North Atlantic or the Caribbean," Flynn said abruptly.

Fox stared at him. "Why there, and not the Pacific?"

"Because we have anti-ballistic missile interceptors based in Alaska and California," Flynn explained, feeling more and more certain that he was right about this. "With just one shot in their quiver, the bad guys can't risk watching their warhead blown out of space before it reaches its intended detonation point." His fingers drummed on the table. "They *have* to launch their attack from where we're most vulnerable. And that's off the eastern seaboard."

"The Navy's Second Fleet has destroyers and cruisers armed with SM-3 interceptors," Van Horn pointed out. In combination with powerful AN/SPY-1 Aegis Combat System radars, RIM-161 Standard Missile 3's were designed to shoot down short- and intermediate-range ballistic missiles.

Flynn nodded. "Yep. And if those ships were deployed on a picket line with their radars energized and the crews on alert, they'd have a chance at making an intercept." He shrugged. "But my bet is that most of them are swinging idly at anchor right now at Norfolk, or deployed somewhere else."

"You'd win that bet," Fox told him. "The Russians started a major fleet exercise in the Barents Sea about three weeks ago. The Navy responded by sortieing a large task force of our carriers and other warships into the Norwegian Sea for joint maneuvers with other NATO countries."

"Man, those assholes Voronin and Zhdanov aren't taking any chances, are they?" Flynn said bleakly. "They wave the red cape and off our admirals charge . . . in exactly the wrong direction."

Fox grimaced. "So it appears." He looked across the table at them. "Suggestions?"

"We have to gamble," Van Horn told him. "We need to concentrate all of the Pléiades imaging satellite searches on the approaches to the Atlantic and the Caribbean."

Flynn nodded. "Laura's right. Focusing our satellite passes should roughly double our odds of spotting that oil tanker before it reaches its planned launch point."

"If your guess is wrong, and the *Gulf Venture* is actually steaming toward the West Coast, re-tasking the satellites that way guarantees certain failure," Fox warned.

"That's so, and I wish like hell we had more options," Flynn conceded. "But I've got an itchy feeling at the back of my neck that tells me we're running out of time fast. So we can't hold anything back in reserve," he said forcefully. "We can't split our limited resources trying to cover all the possible bases. Our only choice is to go all in . . . and we have to do that now."

THIRTY-TWO

HEADQUARTERS, 42ND ROCKET DIVISION,
STRATEGIC ROCKET FORCES, OUTSIDE NIZHNY
TAGIL, CENTRAL RUSSIA

T MINUS 6, A FEW DAYS LATER

Pavel Voronin sat beside Piotr Zhdanov in the back of the president's armored black limousine. Other cars carrying plainclothes bodyguards were ahead and behind them. Several more wheeled armored personnel carriers packed with troops brought up the tail end of this convoy.

They turned off the highway and onto a narrow track that ran deeper into the surrounding forest. Studded tires crunched over snow and ice as the column of vehicles drove slowly along the winding trail. A quick thaw across this part of Russia a few days ago had been followed by one last freezing spring storm, leaving the trees sheathed in glistening coats of ice.

Two kilometers off the main road, they came out into a clearing. Razor wire-topped fences stretched in either direction. Patrols of soldiers in white winter parkas accompanied by dogs could be seen along the perimeter. As they approached the main gate of this isolated compound, the leading vehicles turned off the track and parked on the side, clearing the way for Zhdanov's limousine to proceed alone.

The guards manning the gate pulled it open. They waved the big black car through without stopping it. Officially, the Russian president was not here, and so no records of this secret visit would be kept.

At the center of the compound, the limousine pulled up outside what appeared to be a simple forester's hut. Bodyguards riding up front jumped out and opened the rear doors for Zhdanov and Voronin. When they emerged, a major waiting at the open hut door stiffened to attention. "Mr. President, welcome to the Forty-Second Rocket Division," he said briskly. His eyes darted to Voronin and then just as quickly shifted away. Clearly, he'd been briefed against showing too much curiosity about the Russian leader's civilian guest.

"Lead the way, Major," Zhdanov ordered.

Obeying, the young officer ushered them into the hut. It was simply a concrete-floored shell designed to hide an elevator shaft that ran deep underground. Steel doors slid aside, revealing a waiting car. They filed in and waited while the elevator smoothly descended, carrying them nearly two hundred meters below the surface.

At the bottom, the doors rolled back, revealing a short, well-lit corridor. At the far end, another thick armored hatch opened into the missile unit's battle management center. Above the entrance, Voronin noted the emblem of the Strategic Rocket Forces—a wreath-surrounded golden shield backed by two crossed arrows and an upright sword—along with its ominous motto: "*Posle nas—tshina*." "After us—silence." A wry smile twitched at the corner of his mouth. The phrase seemed particularly appropriate, given the role this unit was slated to play in MIDNIGHT.

After he and Zhdanov passed through it, the armored hatch silently swung shut and sealed behind them, leaving their staff escort outside in the corridor. Consoles equipped with computers, displays, and secure communications links lined each of the battle management center's two stepped tiers. In the middle of the lower tier, a single long table faced a theater-sized screen. A small group of senior officers stood there waiting for them. All of the other workstations were empty. Knowledge of the MIDNIGHT targeting plan was restricted to a tiny inner circle of the 42nd Division's leadership.

Voronin noted how Major General Konstantin Rezanov, the rocket division's rail-thin commander, carefully avoided making eye contact with him—instead focusing all his attention on Zhdanov. He concealed his amusement. Rezanov and all the others in this room had already accepted generous compensation from the Raven Syndicate for their part in MIDNIGHT. Pretending not to know their real paymaster wouldn't fool anyone for very long, least of all the president—especially since Voronin had been careful to secure the older man's approval for his bribes to active duty military officers. After all, he had no real need to work behind Zhdanov's back, not for this enterprise anyway.

He took the chair he was offered and studied the large central screen. At the moment, it showed the current locations of the twenty-seven road-mobile RS-24 Yars ICBMs controlled by the 42nd Rocket Division. The huge sixteen-wheeled launchers transporting these missiles were dispersed throughout the surrounding forests. Every RS-24 carried four independently targetable 300-kiloton nuclear warheads, each twenty times more powerful than the atomic bomb dropped on Hiroshima.

Once they were all settled, Zhdanov turned to Rezanov. "Let's not waste more time on meaningless pleasantries, General." He smiled coldly. "This is a war briefing, not a social call. And I want to be back in Moscow before anyone important notices that I'm gone."

"Yes, Mr. President," Rezanov acknowledged. He darted a glance at the most junior officer in the room, a colonel. "Run the targeting program, Mikhail."

The colonel keyed in a sequence of commands at his console. Immediately, a new image appeared on the central screen—a detailed digital map of Iran. Color-coded icons representing important cities, nuclear weapons and missile research sites, Islamic Revolutionary Guard Corps bases, military airfields, and oil production and storage hubs dotted this map. One by one, dozens of these icons blinked red. "New coordinates have been locked into the multiple warheads aboard fourteen of this division's ICBMs," Rezanov confirmed. His voice held no discernible emotion except a cool professionalism.

The screen split, continuing to show the map of Iran on one half, while shifting back to a display of the positions of the fourteen RS-24 missiles on the other. "Upon receipt of your coded order, UNLOCK MIDNIGHT," the general continued, "these fourteen ICBMs will execute a simultaneous launch."

Echoing his words, the symbols representing the selected RS-24 missiles blinked yellow and began moving along arcs which illustrated their planned trajectories—hurtling southward at more than 24,000 kilometers an hour. They vanished off the edge of the digital map of central Russia, and instantly reappeared on the map of Iran. All fourteen ICBM icons divided into four new tracks each, representing the fifty-six separate warheads now fanning out toward their designated targets. One by one, they reached a red-outlined icon and vanished, leaving only a glowing dot. "Approximately seven minutes after launch, our weapons will begin detonating—some in the sky over soft targets like cities, and others, earth penetrators, deep inside heavily protected underground complexes," Rezanov said. "Within ten minutes, our nuclear strike will have completely obliterated Iran's radical Islamic government, military forces, oil industry, and advanced weapons research facilities."

Zhdanov looked pleased. "And your estimate of civilian casualties?" he asked.

Rezanov shrugged. "They will, inevitably, be very high. Our preliminary analysis indicates upward of twenty to forty million Iranians dead or critically injured."

The Russian president raised an eyebrow. "So many?"

"The Iranians have sited a large number of their most critical defense facilities close to population centers," the general explained. He smiled thinly. "Probably as a deterrent to a major attack by the Americans or the Israelis—since they know both countries are reluctant to inflict collateral damage."

"A weakness we do not share," Zhdanov commented dryly.

"No, sir," Rezanov agreed.

Zhdanov turned to Voronin. "Do you have any questions, Pavel?"

He shook his head. "None, Mr. President." He nodded pleasantly at Rezanov and his officers. "The targeting plan these officers have created seems perfectly satisfactory."

In truth, Voronin was delighted. The rain of nuclear fire planned by Rezanov was the final piece in the fiendishly complex and ruthless scheme he'd devised and implemented over the past several months. By wiping Iran off the map shortly after their EMP warhead detonated over the United States, he and Zhdanov would achieve several of their country's long-sought and most crucial strategic objectives.

First, they would eliminate any chance that Iran's radical leaders could betray Russia's involvement in the attack against the United States. And, in fact, Russia's nuclear bombardment could be portrayed as an act of justified retaliation for Tehran's "brutal and unprovoked strike against innocent American civilians." Whether anyone genuinely believed this was immaterial. Having seen the horrific consequences of angering Moscow, no other nation would dare do more than issue weak, pro forma protests.

Second, they would destroy the rising Shia power in the Persian Gulf, one whose very existence threatened all of its Sunni neighbors. That ought to entice a grateful Saudi Arabia and all of the other Arab states to turn to Russia for protection and leadership. The United States, crippled and in ruins, could have nothing to offer them. Left without much choice, even Israel might finally come to realize that its own national interests aligned with those of Moscow.

Finally, the destruction of Iran's oil fields and infrastructure, combined with the havoc wreaked by MIDNIGHT's EMP pulse on U.S. energy production, would create a massive spike in world oil prices. And this, in turn, would vastly increase the value of Russia's own oil production, which was now virtually its only reliable source of economic strength.

Voronin smiled icily. As he had so often promised Iran's fundamentalist leaders during their negotiations, MIDNIGHT would indeed overturn the world's existing balance of power—though not at all in the way they had foolishly imagined.

THIRTY-THREE

IN THE HILL COUNTRY, CENTRAL TEXAS

TWO DAYS LATER

Nick Flynn came drifting down near the aft section of their simulated
oil tanker. He tugged gently on the front risers of his rectangular ram-
air parachute to alter his course a couple of degrees—just enough to
slide past the canvas-covered scaffolding representing one of the catwalks which ran the length of the real ship. A few feet off the ground,
he flared the parachute to slow his descent. His landing was so soft that
it felt more like stepping off a staircase than finishing a wingsuit jump
from twenty thousand feet up and sixteen miles away.

Swiftly, he punched the quick release buckle on his harness to release
his chute and let it flutter away across the ground. For this exercise, speed
was essential. They'd recover the parachutes later. Still moving fast, he
unhooked the mask and oxygen cylinder he'd worn for this high-altitude
practice jump and dropped them to the side. Then he hurriedly unzipped his wingsuit and shrugged out of it, kicking his feet loose from
the bunched nylon fabric. Now freed of all encumbrances, he darted into
the cover offered by the scaffolding "catwalk" and crouched down. Once
there, he rummaged quickly through the largest gear bag attached to his
assault vest, pulling out and readying his primary weapon—a compact

Kel-Tec 7.62mm RFB carbine. He inserted a magazine and pulled back on the charging handle to chamber a round.

"Dragon Lead is down on target portside and ready to move," Flynn reported over their tactical net.

"Dragon Two in position on starboard side," Tadeusz Kossak radioed from the other side of the ship.

"Three is same on port side, at your five o'clock, Lead," Tony McGill called from behind him. Flynn glanced over his shoulder and saw the ever-cheerful ex-SAS sergeant give him a thumbs-up from the corner of one of their mockups of the fake shipping crates positioned along the *Gulf Venture*'s deck. One by one, the other five men in his assault force— Shannon Cooke, Alain Ricard, Mark Stadler, Cole Hynes, and Wade Vucovich—confirmed that they'd landed safely and were ready to move out. All told, it was scarcely more than ninety seconds from the moment his boots first touched dirt.

He stood up with a grin. "Nice job, guys," he told them. "Nobody's in the drink. And nobody bounced into an obstacle. So this one counts as a first phase win." For the first time ever, all eight members of the Dragon team had managed to land on target, without tangling themselves up in the maze of chalk-drawn piping and other structures cluttering the simulated oil tanker's hull. Repeated practice jumps and a grueling training schedule had finally paid off in precision. That meant the first part of his assault plan—getting his troops aboard the ship— wasn't necessarily suicidal.

After that, of course, Flynn reminded himself, all bets were off. At a minimum, they'd be heavily outnumbered by the Iranian crew and any of Voronin's Raven Syndicate security troops aboard. Once they were safely down, he and the others would be counting on surprise, speed, and sheer guts to act as force multipliers for them in their battle to take the ship. He slung his Kel-Tec bullpup carbine and walked over to scoop up his wingsuit. Out in the pasture, the local teens he'd hired as a ground crew were chasing after some of their parachutes using a golf cart.

Alain Ricard and Mark Stadler came over to join him, followed by the rest of the team. Stadler tapped the stock of his own carbine. "Any chance we can get some more range time with these weapons, Nick?"

Ricard nodded in agreement. "Yes, that would be a good thing." The former French Marine Commando officer shrugged expressively. "If we are going to fight using these small rifles, I would very much like to test their characteristics further under close to combat conditions."

Other heads bobbed, indicating most of team felt much the same. They'd chosen the Kel-Tec carbine for its small size—just twenty-six inches from muzzle to butt stock—and the greater hitting and penetration power conferred by the 7.62mm rounds it fired. Compactness was essential, because trying to carry longer firearms outside their wingsuits would screw up their streamlined glide characteristics. But there were downsides as well. While 7.62mm rounds did more damage and could punch through most body armor better than NATO-standard 5.56mm bullets, they were considerably larger and heavier. The Kel-Tec weapon's standard magazines held only twenty rounds, compared to thirty for a similar rifle firing 5.56mm ammunition. That put a premium on accuracy when using it, since "spraying and praying" would just run a shooter out of ammo that much faster.

Flynn considered the situation. They'd built an improvised assault shooting range in the wooded hills above this pastureland—setting up a mix of pop-up targets, obstacles, and trip-wire pyrotechnics. It couldn't replicate all of the challenges they'd face fighting aboard a massive ship with its intricate layout of pipelines, stairs, ladders, hatches, and separate compartments, but it was the best they could do with the time and resources available. And running through the range as often as possible definitely gave his team a chance to keep their combat reflexes and shooting skills sharp, while familiarizing themselves with their new weapons. Although he'd originally scheduled one more practice jump that afternoon, the fact that this last one had gone so well gave him room to switch the training schedule around.

"Yeah, let's do that," he agreed. "Gather up your jump gear and stow it back at the ranch house, and then we'll head over to the range for some running and gunning." He nodded toward Tadeusz Kossak and Tony McGill. "Or in the case of the two terrible T's here, some slithering and shooting."

That sparked grins all around. The Polish sniper and former SAS commando had already demonstrated an uncanny ability to blend with any cover available. McGill gravely claimed that he'd been inspired as a child by reruns of the classic Monty Python skit "How Not to Be Seen."

"Hey, boss! De plane! De plane!" Hynes suddenly yelled in a gravelly falsetto, pointing at the sky over Flynn's shoulder.

Flynn glanced down at his camouflage-pattern battledress and laughed. He wasn't exactly wearing the elegant white suit favored by Ricardo Montalbán in another vintage TV show, *Fantasy Island*. Still shaking his head, he turned around and saw the BushCat coming in for a landing right beside their pretend oil tanker.

The little plane touched down in a puff of dust and taxied closer. It slewed to a stop only fifty yards away. Laura Van Horn scrambled out of her aircraft before its propeller even stopped turning. She loped straight over to him.

"What's up?" Flynn asked quickly.

She pulled a tablet computer out of her shoulder bag and held it out to him. "This morning's Pléiades HR-1A pass spotted the *Gulf Venture*," she said, sounding breathless.

He took the device and studied the digital image it showed. Although it had been taken by a satellite orbiting more than four hundred miles above the earth's surface, the details in the enhanced picture were incredibly clear . . . all the way down to the fake shipping containers that concealed the tanker's antiaircraft guns and SAM launchers. He looked up at her. "Where was the ship when this picture was taken?" he demanded.

In answer, Van Horn reached over and swiped her hand across the tablet's screen to bring up the next image. This one was a map, with a cross indicating the position of the *Gulf Venture* when it was spotted from space.

Flynn whistled softly in relief. He'd guessed right about the ship's probable destination. When the Pléiades satellite made its pass several hours ago, the Iranian tanker had been in the mid-Atlantic, almost exactly halfway between Guyana on South America's northeastern coast and the tiny country of Guinea-Bissau on Africa's western edge.

Then he frowned. The Iranian vessel was currently nearly four thousand miles from the closest point on the U.S. mainland—which put it well out of reach of Four's assault force and its support units. That was especially true considering that his Dragon team was still based here in Central Texas. He studied the map. If they could stage out of Puerto Rico, that would shave off some of the distance, but not enough. He looked up. "Damn it, we still can't hit those bastards."

Van Horn nodded. "Not yet, anyway." She shrugged her shoulders. "But on the other hand, all the missile gurus Fox has consulted peg the likely range of their rocket at somewhere around two thousand miles, assuming they're going for a high-altitude detonation two or three hundred miles up. So, yeah, you can't hit the enemy yet, but by the same token, they're not anywhere close to a possible launch point either. That tanker is going to have to come a lot closer to the U.S. coast. Which should give you and your team time to get into position before the balloon goes up."

"Let's hope so," Flynn said tightly. "But we've got another problem. We were all focused on finding the ship in the first place. But just how in heck are we going to keep tabs on it now?" He waved a hand over the map displayed on her tablet. "We were damned lucky to spot it once. But at best, we'll only get a satellite pass over that part of the ocean once every twenty-four hours. And assuming the *Gulf Venture* is still making eighteen knots, it could steam another five hundred miles in some other direction before the Pléiades comes back around for another look."

"Yeah," Van Horn agreed. "Which is why Br'er Fox and I are working on couple of ways to handle the job." She tapped the digital map. "Anyway, based on its last known position, we think it's a safe bet that the tanker will keep heading northwest for at least another day. If it veers too much in any other direction, it'll end up crossing into busier shipping lanes off South America or Africa—which could blow their cover." She glanced at her watch. "I'm on a flight to Orlando in a couple of hours. I should be out hunting *Gulf Venture* by this time tomorrow or even sooner."

"You can't just send out a scout plane to track that ship," Flynn warned. "The bad guys aren't idiots. They'd be bound to spot a trailer . . . and then my guys and I are boned."

She smiled back at him. "Yeah, copy that. But this isn't my first aerial rodeo, cowboy. Just remember that subtlety is my middle name."

Flynn acted surprised. "Really?" He grinned crookedly. "Man, Laura, you had some weird parents."

Before Van Horn could smack him, his smartphone pinged with a new text message. He scanned it quickly and then looked at her. "I need to bum a ride with you back to Austin, if that's okay."

She nodded. "Can do. What's up?"

"Some good news for a change," Flynn said. "That special hardware I ordered from BMW just came in on an air freight flight. If I pick it up this afternoon, I can get it back here to the ranch by sundown. That should give us enough time for some trial runs with it later tonight and tomorrow morning before we fly out to Florida ourselves."

"Sweet," Van Horn said appreciatively. The tiny laugh lines around her eyes deepened slightly. "So Birdman Flynn and his glide boys are going Iron Man after all? You know, I'm kind of sorry I'll miss seeing the first time you try out these new high-tech gizmos."

He snorted. "Very funny." He shook his head. "We sure can use the extra capability this experimental equipment ought to give us, but figuring out how to use it safely and successfully means more practice jumps . . . right at a time when it seems like the countdown clock is already ticking. Everything we're planning rests on a hell of a lot of different assumptions—about the range of that rocket, about its probable target, the size of the crew aboard, and all the rest. And if we're wrong about just one of those assumptions, we're screwed . . . along with everybody else in the whole U.S."

Van Horn's own expression turned more serious. "I know what you mean, Nick. Basically, we're in a race now, one where the competition is already well out in front . . . and we don't even know where the finish line is."

Flynn straightened his shoulders. "Then I guess we have to dig down deeper and run even harder, right?"

She nodded. "Just as fast and as hard as we can. And if you're the praying type at all, that might not hurt, either."

THIRTY-FOUR

T MINUS 3, THE NEXT DAY

Responding to a summons blared over the ship's intercom system, Viktor Skoblin hurried out onto the navigation's bridge's windswept portside wing. Captain Reza Heidari and his second-in-command, Dabir, were both at the forward railing. Heidari was peering intently through a pair of powerful mounted binoculars at a distant silvery dot high in the blue, nearly cloudless sky ahead of them. White contrails streamed out behind the speeding aircraft as it flew northeastward.

The Revolutionary Guard navy officer turned his head toward the Russian. "Our radar picked up this air contact crossing our course a few minutes ago."

Skoblin frowned. They were well off the normal commercial flight routes between North America and Europe, and still more than two thousand kilometers east of Puerto Rico. That made this sudden appearance of an unknown plane more worrying. "Could this be someone out searching for us?" he asked guardedly. The closer they came to their intended launch coordinates, the more disastrous it would be to be discovered by the Americans.

Heidari stepped back from the binoculars, making room for the Russian to take his place. "See for yourself, Major," he said. He shrugged. "But we're not detecting any surface search radar emissions from that aircraft. Nor has it altered its flight path by even a degree to come any closer to us. I suspect a genuine reconnaissance flight would behave very differently."

Still scowling, Skoblin bent down to look through the binoculars. He focused on the distant plane. It was a twin-engine aircraft, and it looked significantly smaller than most commercial passenger airliners or cargo jets. In and of itself, that meant nothing, since both the American navy and air force maintained fleets of smaller planes, usually used as VIP transports, that might be pressed into service for visual reconnaissance if necessary. But this aircraft wasn't painted military gray, he noted. Instead, it was a mix of bright colors—red, green, and white. He supposed it was possible that the Americans could have repainted one of their transports in those hues as a disguise, but such thoughts verged on paranoia. "That's probably just a business jet," he mused out loud. "Some rich man's private plane ferrying him from a vacation in the Caribbean islands back to Europe. Or perhaps the Arab oil states."

"Yes, that would be my guess as well," Heidari agreed evenly.

Nettled, Skoblin stepped back from the telescope. If the Iranian had been so sure there was no real threat to their mission, why haul him all the way up here on the double? Was it some sort of dominance game—a chess move to remind him of his subordinate status? "Thank you for informing me of this contact, Captain," he said stiffly. "I'm glad this turned out to be nothing to worry about." *Two can play games*, he thought coldly. He waved a hand at the sea and sky around them. "Perhaps in the future you will make sure your lookouts and radar operators are on maximum alert. We can't afford any surprises from here on in."

"Your recommendation is noted, Major," the Iranian naval officer said gravely. "You can be sure that my crew will do its best."

"Until later, then," Skoblin said. He turned on his heel and headed for the ladder leading down toward the compartments reserved for his Raven Syndicate security unit.

Watching the Russian go, Dabir murmured. "That snake will cause us trouble in the end."

Reza Heidari nodded. "Indeed." His own gaze was ice-cold. "But not for long."

Many miles to the north, Laura Van Horn was at the controls of the fast Gulfstream G650 business jet cruising northeast at forty thousand feet. At the moment, she had nothing to do but sit tight, since they were flying on autopilot—behaving just like any genuine luxury private aircraft making a transatlantic crossing. She glanced around the elaborately instrumented cockpit with a pleased smile. This was a heck of a nice ride, night and day from the kit-built BushCat she'd been flitting around Afghanistan, Iran, and Central Texas in. The Quartet Directorate had leased this Gulfstream through one of its front groups.

"How's it going back there? Any luck?" She called over the intercom.

From the aft cabin, Fox replied. "We're almost finished, Laura. And yes, we guessed right. That ship out there is definitely the *Gulf Venture*. There's no doubt at all." Four's American station chief and a couple of vetted contract technicians were manning a long-range tracking camera similar to those used to monitor rocket launches. It allowed them to capture close-up images of the oil tanker more than forty miles away. The clear visibility for this sortie was a plus, but the camera also had an infrared capability, and they also were using it to take detailed readings on the massive vessel's heat signature. The current forecasts predicted worsening weather over the next day or two. If those forecasts were accurate, the IR scans they were getting could prove vital.

Van Horn nodded to herself. As they'd hoped, the Iranian tanker hadn't changed course or speed since their last satellite pass. That strongly suggested the ship was heading directly toward a launch point picked out by planners in Tehran and Moscow. Assuming they planned to launch near the maximum range estimated by Four's experts, that should be a patch of ocean roughly 750 miles due east of Norfolk, Virginia. If so, that would put the enemy a little under four days from being able to fire.

She settled back down to wait as patiently as she could. She couldn't bank the Gulfstream G650 back toward Florida until they were well beyond the *Gulf Venture*'s radar and visual horizon. And she'd have to be sure to stay far to the north on the return leg. One pass by a private jet could be chalked up to coincidence by the crew aboard that ship. But two passes by the same aircraft in a matter of hours would undoubtedly alert them that this was enemy action. This was flying a fine line, she thought, gathering just enough intelligence to give Flynn's assault force a shot at finding the tanker when it steamed into range . . . without putting the Iranians and Russians on board on high alert.

ORLANDO APOPKA AIRPORT, FLORIDA

THE NEXT DAY

The Orlando Apopka Airport was a single runway, privately owned airfield about twenty miles northwest of central Orlando. A highway ran along one side of the airport. The other bordered a large twenty-thousand-acre wildlife area around the shores of Lake Apopka, the fourth largest lake in Florida. More than eighty small hangars housed the small private planes based there.

With the sun hanging low and orange on the western horizon, several vans rolled past a brown stone and dark wood building that contained the little airport's offices and a flight school. At the end of the drive, they turned onto a side road that also served as a taxiway for aircraft. The vans parked on a hard-packed dirt lot next to one of the larger hangars.

Nick Flynn hopped down from of one of the vehicles. He was followed by the rest of his Dragon assault team. A door on the side of the hangar opened, and Fox and Laura Van Horn came out to meet them.

"So, what do you think of your ride?" she asked innocently, pointing behind him.

He turned around and caught sight of a very large four-engine turbo-prop parked at the edge of the runway. This aircraft completely dwarfed the other private planes—mostly a mix of single-engine Cessnas, Beech-craft, and Pipers of various models—scattered around the tarmac and hanger complex. He whistled in surprise. "Holy crap! A C-130J Super Hercules?" He swung back to Van Horn. "What'd you do? Steal a plane from the Alaska Air National Guard like those Stinger missiles you used in Iran? That's pretty bold, even for you."

She grinned. "Nothing quite so piratical this time. This is totally legit." She nodded toward the big turboprop. "That's an LM-100J, the commercial version of the Super Hercules. We're subleasing it from a private aviation company." Her grin widened. "They think we need it to shoot some scenes for a low-budget made-for-streaming action-adventure movie. When they asked what it was called, we told them the working title was something like *Sky Dragons on Spring Break*."

Flynn heard the strangled laughs from the rest of his assault force and matched her expression. "Close enough to the truth, I guess. And at least you know how to fly that thing."

Van Horn's smile disappeared. She shook her head. "It won't be me this time, Nick. I'll be piloting your backup aircraft, which is waiting on the ground in Bermuda for me now. Because the way I see it, that's going to be an even trickier gig than getting you all to the target."

Flynn nodded. He should have figured that would be the case. Coming up with a way to reinforce his team with a qualified crew to sail the tanker if they succeeded—or to rescue any survivors if things went south—had been a difficult problem to solve. As things went, the best idea they'd been able to come up with was still a long shot, one that would require a lot of luck and an incredibly skilled pilot to pull off. "So who's going to be at the controls of that Herky Bird?" he asked. "Because I wouldn't have thought Four had a surplus of qualified multi-engine aircraft pilots just waiting around."

"Oh, ye of little faith," Van Horn said enigmatically. She turned and signaled to the hangar.

Flynn stared at the man who walked out to join them. He'd last seen the newcomer more than a year ago in Alaska and in very differ-ent circumstances. Back then, Major Jack "Ripper" Ingalls had been the commander of the damaged C-130J that had made an emergency landing at his last duty station. Van Horn had been his copilot. He raised an eyebrow. "What's this? An old flight school reunion? Or is everybody in the Air National Guard wearing two hats now, pilot by day, secret agent by night?" Ingalls had the grace to look abashed.

"Actually, sizing up Rip here as a possible Quartet Directorate recruit was my primary mission on that tour of duty. Because as you've noticed, we're kind of short of skilled personnel of all kinds," Van Horn said. "Snagging you for Four was a bonus." She smiled sweetly. "But it does seem like one of my better calls, don't you think?."

Fox spoke up. "As I told you at our first meeting, Nick, having Laura meet and assess you then was pure serendipity."

"So I see," Flynn said dryly. He turned to Van Horn. "Okay, who else have you got stashed in that hangar as a surprise? My mother?"

"Thought about it," she said cheerfully. "But then I decided that might be pushing things a bit too far."

Knowing when he was licked, Flynn just shook his head. He glanced back at his team, ignoring their barely suppressed grins. "Why don't you guys start getting our equipment inside."

Obeying, they split up and began lugging cases from the vans into the hangar. On his way past, Hynes murmured, "You know, sir, having met your mom, signing her up with this outfit might not be such a bad idea. She seemed kind of bad ass to me. Not meaning any disrespect, of course."

Flynn shuddered. "There are some things, Cole," he said sternly, "that are too horrifying to contemplate." He shook his head. "Maybe we're not strictly bound by the laws of war, but I'd still draw the line at inflicting my mother on an enemy force—even on a bunch of terrorists."

Hynes chuckled. "Point taken, sir. One Flynn is a force multiplier. Two Flynns would be a war crime." Still smiling broadly, he moved off to the back of one of the vans.

Flynn followed Van Horn, Fox, and Ingalls into the hangar. It was empty, except for a row of cots, several long, picnic-style tables, folding chairs, and a couple of portable refrigerators plugged in along one wall. Some of the support staff from Avalon House had also rigged up a portable shower area near the back of the hangar. From now on, the Dragon team would be bunking in here. Looking over the facilities, he nodded in satisfaction. He and his men might not exactly be comfortable, but at least they'd be ready and able to fly out practically the moment Fox could give them a solid bearing on the *Gulf Venture*. Over on the far side of the hanger, now that they were safe from prying eyes, Hynes, Kossak, McGill, and the rest of the team started unpacking and checking over their assault gear—their wingsuits, parachutes, weapons, and other special items.

Fox ushered Flynn and the others over to one of the tables where he'd set up an improvised command post. It held an assortment of computers, LED displays, and communications equipment. "I thought you'd like to see our assessment of the current situation," he told them. "It's based on the data we picked up from our second aerial acquisition of the *Gulf Venture*, during the Gulfstream pass we made several hours ago."

Flynn nodded. While he and his men were aboard their commercial flight from Austin to Orlando, they'd been out of secure communication with the reconnaissance group attempting to track the Iranian tanker.

The older man sat down and used a keyboard to bring up a large map of the Atlantic on one of the computer displays. A blinking dot at the end of a long red track showed the projected position of the enemy vessel, based on its last known course and speed. If the estimate was accurate, the ship was now around eighteen hundred miles off the South Florida coast.

Flynn studied the map in silence for a moment. Then he looked over at Ingalls. "What do you think, Rip?"

The former Air National Guard major chewed on his lower lip for a few seconds. "The tanker's within the range of that LM-100J Super Hercules parked outside—at least if it's fully fueled and carrying a very light load." He glanced over at the rest of the Dragon team. "Which you and your people definitely are."

Flynn nodded. A fully loaded C-130J could carry ninety-two fully equipped paratroops or 42,000 pounds of cargo. Compared to that, this four-engine turboprop would be flying almost empty with just the eight of them in its cavernous aft compartment. He turned back to Fox. "We should go tonight," he said forcefully. "If we take off after dark, we can be in the air over that ship in a little more than four and a half hours. And the sooner we hit the bad guys, the better."

The older man shook his head regretfully. "Normally, I'd agree, Nick, but there's another factor to consider."

"Ah, crap, the weather?" Flynn guessed.

"The weather," Van Horn confirmed.

"Show me."

Fox brought up a weather overlay on the map. It showed a band of storms—with thick clouds, strong winds, and high seas—moving to the northwest across that part of the Atlantic. Inset boxes showed the predicted high-altitude wind speeds inside those storm clouds.

Flynn frowned. "Shit," he muttered. Fox was right. Weather was always the controlling factor for any airborne operation. And any jump into those conditions would be suicide. Given those winds and the poor visibility, his team would be scattered across miles of ocean. They'd certainly never be able to touch down safely on the *Gulf Venture*'s deck. Big as that oil tanker was, it was scarcely larger than a grain of sand when compared to the immensity of the sea.

"If there's any consolation in this situation, it's that the same factors apply to any sea-based rocket launch," Fox pointed out. "The same high winds and waves which make it too dangerous for you and your team to drop should also make it too risky for the Iranians and their Raven Syndicate allies to carry out their attack."

Flynn smiled ruefully. "There are a lot of implicit *should*s and *hopefully*s in that analysis, Br'er Fox," he said. "Too many for my comfort."

The older man nodded. "Mine, too," he admitted.

"Any guesses on when this bad weather should clear?"

Fox shrugged. "Right now, the meteorologists say sometime in the next twenty-four to forty-eight hours."

Flynn felt his jaw tighten. Based on the calculations run by Four's missile experts, the *Gulf Venture* was already under forty-five hours' steaming time away from its predicted launch point. This was all coming down to the wire a lot faster than he liked. He took another look at the wall of storms shown on their map and scowled. "There's another danger we have to consider," he said darkly. He traced out the band of bad weather. "The *Gulf Venture* could use the cover provided by this bad weather front to execute a radical course change and vanish again."

"We're aware of the risk," Fox said. "Laura and I have another reconnaissance flight planned for tomorrow around this time. If that tanker isn't where it's supposed to be, we'll still have time to search the area and pinpoint it again."

Van Horn nodded. "We're on this, Nick," she assured him. "From forty thousand feet or more, we'll have a two hundred and forty mile–plus visual horizon. And the long-range tracking camera and telescope rig we're using has IR capability. Storm clouds or not, those bastards won't be able to hide from us. So if they do try to get cute at the last minute, we'll find them for you."

THIRTY-FIVE

OVER THE ATLANTIC OCEAN

THE NEXT EVENING

Flying at fifty thousand feet to stay well above the layers of storm clouds blanketing the ocean below, Four's leased Gulfstream G650 headed steadily southwest. From this high up, the earth's curvature was obvious. A faint orangish glow among the towering cloud masses lining the western horizon marked the position of the swiftly setting sun. For this evening's reconnaissance pass, Laura Van Horn had opted to make a wide loop out to the north from Orlando and then fly well to the east before turning back to cross the *Gulf Venture*'s projected track. Her filed flight plan listed this extravagant, looping course as a "meteorological and climate change data collection" trip on behalf of the same science nonprofit front organization the Quartet Directorate was using for its Pléiades satellite searches.

Most of the seats had been stripped out of the G650's aft cabin, making room for the set of rails that allowed their long-range tracking camera to move from window to window down the length of the aircraft as they flew past a potential target. A motorized pulley system provided the power to make these shifts.

Seated in one of the few chairs left, all placed along the rear bulkhead, Fox felt the twin-engine business jet bounce and rattle as it hit another pocket of turbulence. Grimacing, he tightened his seatbelt slightly.

From the front, one of the two tracking system operators looked back at him with a grin. "Pretty rocking thrill park ride today, sir."

He nodded. "Will all this jolting and shaking give you any trouble?"

"Nope," the other man said confidently from his seat mounted directly behind the telescopic camera. The large device was currently aimed out one of the eight portside cabin windows. "This baby is gyro-stabilized to the nth degree. Heck, we could take it on a real rollercoaster and still get razor-sharp images."

"*Two minutes out*," Laura Van Horn's voice came over the aircraft intercom. "*Tracking crew stand by*."

"Standing by," the second operator replied. He would be responsible for controlling the tracking camera system's movement along the rails as they made their pass. Both men were retired Air Force veterans who did clandestine work for the Quartet Directorate on a part-time contract basis.

"*Thirty seconds*."

Fox tensed. He was following their flight's progress on his laptop. A text box at one side of the map indicated he had a secure communications connection for text messaging with the Dragon team on alert in Florida.

"Target acquisition!" the primary camera operator said rapidly, zooming in on the glowing green thermal image on his monitor. His fingers flew over his controls. "Signature match! That's the *Gulf Venture*, all right." The camera whined slightly, tracking toward the edge of the cabin window. He glanced at his partner. "Shift us aft, Pete."

With a soft *whir* of gears, the tracking camera mount slid down the length of the Gulfstream's cabin until it reached the next large round window. The camera traversed again. "Target reacquisition," the primary operator confirmed. "Good pictures. No observed change to target profile."

"Can you give me a course and speed?" Fox asked.

"Yes, sir, that oil tanker is currently on a heading of three-one-five degrees. I estimate its speed at around eighteen knots."

Fox allowed himself to relax a little. The enemy vessel was still moving on the same course it had been following since it was spotted from space and at the same speed.

"Strike that!" the camera operator said sharply. "Course change observed." He shot a glance at his partner. "Shift us two windows aft this time, Pete. I need a clearer angle."

Fox resisted the urge to unbuckle and move to look at the monitor himself. The Gulfstream was still hitting pockets of significant turbulence and it wouldn't do anyone any good for him to risk being tossed into the ceiling or against a bulkhead.

The tracking camera rolled down the aircraft's cabin, drawing closer to him. It halted smoothly. Again, the camera traversed toward the forward edge of the window it had stopped beside. "Confirm that course change," the operator said. He swung toward Fox with a troubled expression. "Sir, it looks as though the *Gulf Venture* is now engaged in making a series of wide, three-hundred-and-sixty-degree turns."

Fox stared back at him. "The tanker is just steaming in circles?"

"It looks that way," the other man said carefully. "And the ship's speed is coming down to around five knots. Whatever they're doing, it sure doesn't seem like they're in a real hurry anymore."

Frowning in perplexity, Fox studied the map on his open laptop. What were the Iranians and Russians aboard that tanker up to now? Circling in place like this wouldn't bring the ship any closer to the United States—and it was still several hundred miles outside the maximum predicted range for the three-stage rocket hidden inside its hull. Then he froze. "Oh, my God," he muttered. "We've been wrong."

"Mr. Fox?"

He looked up. "We've been wrong about the range of that missile. It's got to be more like twenty-five hundred miles, not two thousand. They're in striking range *now*."

"The weather's still really crappy, though," the camera operator offered. "Even through my IR filter, I can see that ship—big as it is— pitching and rolling pretty significantly."

"Which explains why they're still steaming in circles," Fox realized. "They've reached their pre-set launch coordinates. Now they just have to wait for the weather to clear." He slapped the intercom button on his armrest. "Laura, what's the most recent forecast?" he asked urgently.

"Wait one," she replied from the cockpit. After a moment, she came back on. *"This front's passing faster than first predicted, Br'er Fox. NOAA says its computer models and satellite data now suggest a return to good conditions over this part of the Atlantic sometime in the next four to six hours. They're calling for light winds at just seven to ten knots, with diminishing wave action."*

Fox nodded to himself. While its record of long-range weather prediction was as mixed as that of any other group of meteorologists, the National Oceanic and Atmospheric Administration's short-term forecasts were highly regarded. And they were widely broadcast, which meant the crew of the *Gulf Venture* must now realize they would have an acceptable launch window in just a few hours.

Rapidly, he typed a short text message to Flynn and his assault force standing by in central Florida. Containing the tanker's current latitude and longitude and its observed movements disguised as stock market share prices, it closed with a simple exhortation: EXECUTE BUY-BACK IMMEDIATELY. That was the coded signal for the Dragon team to go . . . and go now.

Fox hit the send button and then keyed the intercom. "We need to set down on Bermuda as soon as possible," he told Van Horn.

"Copy that," she said tersely. *"On this heading, we'll be outside of that ship's radar horizon in thirty minutes. Maybe less. As soon as we're clear, I'll declare a minor in-flight passenger medical emergency and request landing permission from the controllers at L. F. Wade International there. We should be on the ground in less than an hour."* Despite the obvious tension in her voice, there was a tiny undercurrent of humor. *"So one of you guys back there better get busy pretending to be sick. And make it convincing, because I don't want some snotty British bureaucrat making trouble. Not when I have another plane to catch."*

THAT SAME TIME

Viktor Skoblin held on tight to the railings of the bridge ladder while the oil tanker rolled through an arc of more than twenty degrees, slammed broadside on by a large wave. From this high up, he could see that the sea was a vista of white-capped gray rollers all the way out to the close horizon. In the gathering darkness, thick clouds and bands of rain obscured the sky, cutting visibility to less than a nautical mile.

As the big ship rolled back the other direction, he gritted his teeth and pulled himself up the rest of the way and out onto the open starboard wing. They'd been in the grip of this storm for more than a day. But for most of that time, the tanker had been heading northwest on its pre-plotted course—keeping its stern to the oncoming waves and wind. Now, though, for some reason, the *Gulf Venture* was steaming in circles, which greatly worsened the impact of the bad weather on its motion. Instead of simply pitching up and down as the following waves rolled down the length of its hull, the huge vessel was currently pitching, rolling, and yawing almost all at once as it shouldered across an endless succession of foaming, white-capped swells.

For once, the two Quds Force commandos guarding the bridge entrance stepped aside without being asked. Despite their bright yellow foul weather gear, they looked drenched from head to toe. Skoblin hurried past them without making eye contact. Once inside the bridge, he grabbed hold of the edge of the plot table to stay upright as the bow of the tanker smashed through another wave. Spray fountained high into the air before crashing down across the forecastle.

The *Gulf Venture*'s captain, Reza Heidari, and Dr. Hossein Majidi, the missile scientist in charge of the Zuljanah rocket, looked across the plot table at him. "You have a question, Major?" Heidari asked mildly.

"I do," Skoblin said, unable to stop himself from scowling. "Why the devil are we circling in place like this? In the middle of this fucking storm? Why aren't we proceeding directly to the launch point as planned?"

Heidari shrugged. "For the simple reason that there has been a slight change in our plans."

"What sort of change?" Skoblin demanded sharply. His orders from Voronin might counsel patience with their Iranian allies, but there were limits to the amount of nonsense he was willing to put up with. Heidari might command the ship, but he was directly responsible for ensuring that this operation went ahead as intended. If the local sea or weather conditions dictated a need to delay their arrival at the launch point, he should have been briefed first. A flicker of suspicion stirred into flame inside his mind. Were the Iranians in communication with Tehran after all? Despite all their talk about the need for absolute radio silence? And if so, were the ruling theocrats suddenly getting cold feet about going through with MIDNIGHT? It was a contingency Voronin had planned for, which was one of the reasons the nuclear submarine *Podmoskovye* was secretly trailing them now—with additional Raven Syndicate troops aboard.

In answer, Heidari nodded toward a digital countdown clock fixed above the plot table. Its readout showed the estimated time remaining before their intended attack. As Skoblin watched, the numbers it showed abruptly changed—altering from T –26 hours to just T –4 hours.

Caught off guard, he swung back to the two Iranians. "You're launching almost a day early?" he blurted out. "How is that possible?"

Majidi smiled back at him. "Simple," the white-bearded scientist said. "Our Zuljanah rocket has always been able to fly farther than we told your Mr. Voronin and the rest of your people."

Skoblin stared at him. "You lied to us from the beginning?" he growled.

"Naturally," Heidari said flatly. His eyes held no trace of any emotion. He shrugged. "It seemed a simple precaution in the circumstances . . . just in case you had secret orders of your own to alter the conditions of our mutual alliance at the last moment."

"I have no such orders," Skoblin lied.

"That is good to know," Heidari said. He shrugged again. "As I said, this one small deception was only a precaution."

"And are there any other changes of plan I should know about now?" Skoblin demanded angrily.

"Just one," the Iranian Revolutionary Guard naval officer said blandly. He nodded to someone behind the Russian. "Carry on, Rostami."

Skoblin stiffened, hearing the unmistakable sound of a submachine gun bolt cycling. Carefully, he glanced over his shoulder and saw one of the Quds Force commandos at the hatch covering him with his 9mm weapon. He swore inwardly. This act of treachery had been carefully planned. The bearded Iranian commando was too far away for him to reach before being shot down. And both Heidari and Majidi were well out of the line of fire. Slowly, he raised his hands.

"A wise move, Major," Heidari told him. He picked up an internal phone. "Touraj? We're done up here. Carry on with your end of things."

"So what now?" Skoblin asked bitterly. "You kill us?"

The Iranian looked at him quizzically. "Why would we do that, Major? We are allies, are we not?" He nodded toward the commando. "This is only another temporary safeguard. For the time being, I've decided to disarm you and your men. My own soldiers will provide any necessary security until the rocket lifts off. Once that's accomplished, we'll return to the normal state of affairs for the voyage back to Iran."

The phone buzzed sharply. Heidari picked it up and listened intently for a few moments. He nodded abruptly. "Excellent work, Touraj. We'll send Major Skoblin down to join his men shortly." He turned back to the Russian. "I'm sure you'll be glad to know that we've secured and disarmed your Raven Syndicate personnel without any serious injuries—apart from a few bruises, that is. You'll be held securely in one of the ship's storage compartments until after the missile is away." He smiled and gestured to the countdown clock, which now showed T –3 hours and 55 minutes. "I realize your new accommodations may not be very comfortable, but at least you can console yourself with the knowledge that the inconvenience will be of short duration."

THAT SAME TIME

One hundred meters below the surface of the Atlantic, Captain First Rank Mikhail Nakhimov frowned at the circular grease pencil track drawn on the control room's plot table. It showed the *Gulf Venture*'s course according to *Podmoskovye*'s passive sonar systems, which were picking up the noise made by the tanker's enormous screws thrashing through the water. He looked up at Konstantin Danilevsky, his Raven Syndicate coequal for this mission. The ex-Spetsnaz colonel wore a similarly perplexed expression. "Does anything in what you know of operational plan for MIDNIGHT explain this sudden change of course?" Nakhimov asked.

Danilevsky shook his head. "Nothing. That ship is still more than four hundred nautical miles from the projected launch coordinates."

Nakhimov leaned over the table, watching as his navigating officer penciled in another arc, showing that the oil tanker was continuing the series of 360-degree turns it had unexpectedly begun making several minutes before. "And nothing in the covert satellite phone reports from your men on board suggested this was coming?"

"You saw the same communications summaries from Moscow I did," the Raven Syndicate officer replied icily. "So you already know there was nothing."

"I'm also familiar with the concept of special coded messages hidden within otherwise innocuous reports, Colonel," Nakhimov said. "And it occurred to me that you might have seen something that I did not."

Danilevsky allowed himself the hint of a smile. "A reasonable assumption, Captain. But in this case, I've received no such communications." He gestured upward. "Can you come to periscope depth and raise your communications mast? Our team aboard the *Gulf Venture* may be trying to signal us now with some explanation for this change."

Nakhimov shook his head. "That would be far too dangerous. In the current rough sea state, our periscope mast would feather." He saw the bigger man's look of incomprehension and explained. "I mean that our mast would throw up a spray of white foam whenever it hit a wave."

"Which could easily be spotted by lookouts aboard the tanker," Danilevsky realized.

Nakhimov nodded. "Precisely." His mouth turned down. "I don't know just how our Iranian allies would react to learning that they were being trailed by a submarine, but I can't imagine they would be pleased." He made a decision. "We'll drop back a few kilometers so that we're out of sight and contact Moscow using one of our remaining satellite buoys."

"How long will that take?" Danilevsky demanded.

Aware that nothing about this conversation was private in the submarine's crowded control room, Nakhimov turned to his radio officer, Lieutenant Volkov. "What's your estimate, Leonid?"

The younger officer pursed his lips, considering the question. "Between transit time to a safe distance and the time required to launch and recover our Relay One submersible? I would guess somewhere around forty-five minutes, sir."

Danilevsky grunted. "A lot could happen between now and then."

Nakhimov shrugged. "True. But our passive sonar arrays can pick up the propeller noise from that ship out to more than one hundred miles, even in this storm. If anything changes, we'll know soon enough."

THIRTY-SIX

ORLANDO APOPKA AIRPORT, FLORIDA

A SHORT TIME LATER

The Quartet Directorate's leased LM-100J Super Hercules was parked just off Orlando Apopka's single runway. Long shadows cast by the last sliver of sunlight stretched across the thin strip of grass and train tracks separating the runway from a nearby divided road, the Orange Blossom Trail. Lights from some of Orlando's outlying northern suburbs already glowed brightly along the dark eastern horizon.

Nick Flynn waited at the foot of the large aircraft's open rear ramp. Ahead of him, the other seven members of his Dragon assault team struggled up into its cavernous cargo compartment. They were hauling themselves along a rope rigged to the ramp. Between their wingsuits, ram parachute packs, oxygen masks and cylinders, weapons, ammunition, and other special gear, they were carrying significantly more than a hundred and twenty pounds of added weight strapped to their backs, chests, and thighs. He fought down a laugh when Cooke looked back at him and uttered a high-pitched bray, mimicking a heavily loaded pack mule squalling in angry protest.

Two more men in coveralls stood waiting at the top to assist each overburdened member of the assault force into one of the mesh seats that lined one side of the compartment. In flight, they would crew a rail-mounted tracking camera and telescope system—the twin of the one aboard Fox's Gulfstream G650 business jet. If the *Gulf Venture* drastically altered its course before their civilian Super Hercules turbo-prop aircraft reached the target area, that long-range, IR-capable camera would be their only hope of finding the ship.

The big aircraft's four powerful Rolls-Royce engines were slowly spooling up, with their six-bladed propellers starting to spin. Dust and small bits of debris kicked up by the steadily increasing prop blast swirled away into the air.

Flynn saw Gwen Park leave the rented hangar they'd been using as temporary quarters and a base of operations. She hurried over to join him. "What's the word?" he asked loudly, raising his voice to be heard over the rising engine noise.

"NOAA's most recent forecast confirms that weather conditions are improving rapidly over your target zone," Four's chief of security for Avalon House shouted back. "By the time you reach that area, winds near the surface should be minimal. But the high-altitude winds will still be fairly strong."

He nodded. "We've trained for that," he assured her. "Any more news from the Gulfstream?"

"Just that they're headed for Bermuda now," she said. "That, plus a personal message for you from Ms. Van Horn." She leaned closer. "She asked me to tell you again that you are *not*, repeat *not*, to get yourself killed . . . or she will be extremely pissed off."

"Yes, ma'am, I'll do my best on that," Flynn promised solemnly.

Gwen Park nodded. "See that you do." For a brief instant, the trace of a dry smile appeared on her face. "For what it's worth, I've never yet seen Laura get really angry. But I strongly suspect it's an experience I would rather avoid. So spare me that if you can." Then she clapped him gently on the shoulder and stepped back. "Good luck, Nick."

Flynn grabbed hold of the rope and pulled himself slowly up the raised surface of the ramp and into the rear of the Super Hercules. By the time he reached his seat, the ramp was already whirring upward. It closed and latched into position with a sudden vibration that could be felt even over the pulsing throb created by the aircraft's engines, each producing more than 4,500 horsepower.

The LM-100J's pilot, Jack "Ripper" Ingalls, came aft from the cockpit a moment later. He checked to make sure each of his passengers was belted in, making his way steadily down the row of seats toward Flynn.

"No jumpmaster this time?" Flynn asked with a grin.

Ingalls shrugged. "Hell, Nick, I don't even have a copilot on this jaunt." He tapped himself on the chest. "I'm the sole member of this bird's flight crew."

"Isn't that totally illegal?"

Ingalls matched his smile. "Oh, yeah. On the other hand, if we get caught, I'm guessing the act of transporting a bunch of heavily armed private soldiers out to board and capture an Iranian-flagged oil tanker will make the fact that I also tore up a whole bunch of FAA regulations doing it the least of my worries."

Flynn chuckled. "There is that."

"But since I am risking both my personal liberty and pilot's license for you guys, I've got a question I really need answered," Ingalls continued.

"Shoot."

The pilot pointed to the oddest-looking piece of equipment worn by Flynn and all the others on his Dragon team. Each of them had what appeared to be a three-foot-wide streamlined wing with twin engine nacelles attached to a breastplate. "What in God's name is that Rube Goldberg contraption?"

"This, Rip," Flynn said, tapping the aluminum and carbon fiber casing, "is what turns us from being basically falling rocks with a slightly better glide ratio into real live birdmen." He grinned tightly. "Well, at least for a few minutes, anyway."

The experimental assistive propulsion devices were the brainchild of an Austrian stuntman and wingsuit enthusiast named Peter Salzmann.

Together with a team of innovative BMW engineers, he'd pioneered the creation of these miniature flying machines. Each weighed in at only about twenty-six pounds. Their twin nacelles contained tiny carbon fiber impellers capable of spinning at up to 25,000 revolutions per minute. Powered by 50-volt lithium batteries, each unit's electric motors could produce around twenty horsepower for up to five minutes—enabling wingsuit wearers to reach speeds of up to 160 knots in horizontal and even climbing flight, and greatly extending the distance they could glide.

Ingalls whistled loudly when Flynn finished his quick run-through on the technology involved. "And this high-tech gizmo really works?"

"Both times we've tried it," Flynn said.

The aircraft pilot stared at him. "You've flown these things just twice," he said in disbelief. "And now you're going to use them in combat?"

"Yep."

Ingalls breathed out slowly. "Has anyone ever told you that you're batshit crazy, Nick?" he asked carefully.

"Well, I prefer the term sanity-challenged," Flynn replied. "It sounds more official, somehow."

"That is true," Tadeusz Kossak nodded gravely. "Though I prefer the Polish version. We are *Oddział Wariatów*, the Lunatic Squad."

Alain Ricard grinned. "Ah, but Tadeusz, my friend, it sounds better in French, *L'escouade lunatique.*"

Ingalls snorted, unsuccessfully attempting to hide his own sudden grin. "The Lunatic Squad, huh? Catchy name." He bumped fists with Flynn and then went back up the line, doing the same thing with every man in the Dragon team. "All right, I'll go get this plane off the ground. Far be it from me to interfere with crazy people doing their duty."

Just a few minutes later, with everything set, the big LM-100J Super Hercules taxied out onto the beginning of the little airport's short asphalt runway and halted in place. Its engines ran up to full power, thrumming at high volume. When Ingalls released his brakes, the four-engine aircraft shot forward, steadily gathering speed until it lumbered heavily off the ground not far from the end of the short strip. Red, green, and white navigation lights blinking from its wings and tail, the plane climbed steeply into the swiftly darkening sky. It banked sharply to the right and kept climbing, steadily accelerating toward its maximum flying speed of 362 knots as it headed northeast toward the Atlantic Ocean.

ABOARD THE *GULF VENTURE*

TWO HOURS LATER

Captain Reza Heidari studied the repeater screens showing the measurements recorded by various weather instruments—anemometers, barometers, temperature sensors, and others—sited at different places around the hull and superstructure of his ship. They all confirmed the evidence of his own senses. The weather was improving fast, as so helpfully predicted by the Americans themselves. He picked up the intercom phone and connected to the Launch Control Center one deck below the navigation bridge.

Dr. Hossein Majidi answered him on the first ring. "LCC here, Reza."

"What is your evaluation of the meteorological data we're seeing?" Heidari asked.

"I recommend that we proceed with our prelaunch preparations," the scientist said confidently. "Based on current trends, all the necessary conditions—most critically wave motion, wind strength and direction—should be nominal by the time the Zuljanah rocket is in position and ready to lift off."

"Very well, stand by," Heidari acknowledged. He turned to his second-in-command, Touraj Dabir. "Set Launch Preparation Warning Condition One," he ordered.

"Set Warning Condition One, aye, sir," Dabir repeated. He stabbed a button on the control panel in front of him.

Immediately, klaxons blared throughout the massive ship. Bright yellow emergency lights positioned around the hull and superstructure turned on and began rotating. Their quick, strobing pulses of light would alert any sailors working out on the windswept deck or in the noisy turbine and generator rooms to what was happening.

"Warning One set," Dabir reported. He watched a row of lights turn green across his panel. "All departments acknowledge and report they are ready to proceed."

Heidari nodded, pleased by the rapid, efficient response to his orders. During the nearly month-long voyage from Iran to this point deep in the Atlantic, he'd run his crew through repeated drills to simulate the steps required to carry out a successful missile launch. Now all that hard work and practice was paying off. "Begin jettisoning our ballast oil," he instructed.

The younger naval officer pushed a new set of buttons, sending electronic orders to the technicians manning the Pump Control Room, which lay deep inside the hull below the tanker's above-deck superstructure. More lights turned green. "Pump Room acknowledges, Captain."

One after another, the special high-speed pumps installed aboard the *Gulf Venture* during her secret retrofit went into action. A rhythmic vibration, accompanied by a low rumble, steadily built up, until it could be felt in every compartment from the ship's bow to its stern. The cargo pump outlets were located on both the port and starboard sides, roughly halfway down the more than eight-hundred-foot-long hull. Abruptly, black gouts of thick crude oil spewed out—jetting toward the ocean below. The pumps were emptying the tens of thousands of barrels of oil stored in compartments above the concealed Zuljanah ballistic missile.

Heidari watched this operation proceed. He was utterly unmoved by the damage it would do to the ocean and its abundant marine life. He supposed the world's naive environmentalists would have been horrified by this intentional oil spill, but it was necessary. Ridding the ship of the crude oil they'd used as camouflage was the only way to clear the way for their rocket launch. And, as an added bonus, deliberately creating a massive slick would also further dampen any wave motion around the tanker as it steamed in circles through layers of oil slowly spreading across the sea.

He looked at Dabir. "How much longer until all the camouflage compartments are empty?"

The younger man studied his readouts for a moment. "Judging by the observed flow rate, another thirty minutes or so."

Heidari checked the monitors which showed the *Gulf Venture*'s current range of motion. It was already greatly reduced, but there were additional measures available to him. "Deploy all stabilizers," he said quietly.

Dabir obeyed. His hands darted across the control panel, flipping switches. Additional instrumentation lights changed color from red to yellow and then, finally, to green. Large stabilizer fins rigged to the tanker's bow and stern slowly unfolded and locked into position. Like those used by cruise liners, they significantly reduced the ship's roll rate.

Satisfied that matters were well in hand, Heidari settled back to wait for the high-speed pumps to finish their work. Just short of the predicted thirty minutes, the gouts of oil jetting over the side sputtered, slowed, and then stopped. The rumbling vibration rippling through the ship's hull faded away. He glanced at Dabir.

The younger man had his eyes fixed on his control panel. He leaned forward to check a bank of monitors displaying infrared and low-light imagery from inside the ship's upper tier of oil-storage compartments. "All camouflage oil jettisoned," he confirmed.

"Are there signs of excessive sedimentation?" Heidari asked. Over long periods of time, some of the various components of crude oil in storage could settle out, forming a thick, toxic sludge. Given the relatively short duration of this voyage, that should not be a serious problem for them, but there was no point in taking any chances now.

"No, sir," Dabir answered.

"Very well, but purge the tanks anyway," Heidari ordered.

His second-in-command sent more instructions to the technicians manning the pump controls deep inside the hull. Obeying, they opened a series of new valves and then restarted the pumps—flooding the compartments with successive sprays of pure water and then high-pressure steam to wash away any oil residues still clinging to the bulkheads, vertical and horizontal framing, and fittings. Several minutes later, the cleaning process was finished.

Heidari spoke again to Hossein Majidi in the Launch Control Center. "We're ready to proceed with the next phase."

"Understood, Reza," the missile scientist said. "The rocket remains stable. All systems are go for launch pad roof retraction."

Heidari swung toward Dabir. He could feel his pulse beginning to speed up with growing excitement. The months-long process of rebuilding this massive ship to carry out its role in MIDNIGHT and training its specialist crew was now coming very close to fruition. "Set Launch Preparation Warning Condition Two."

The younger man followed his orders. More klaxons blared. And now the rotating emergency lights scattered around the ship glowed red. Again, acknowledgements rippled in from the various departments.

Satisfied that his crew was ready, Heidari issued the final necessary orders. "Retract the launch pad cover." From here on out, Majidi and his technicians would be in charge.

Near the *Gulf Venture*'s midsection, powerful motors activated. In sequence, sections of the deck and inner hull slid apart and folded up—opening bulkheads and frames to reveal the missile storage unit hidden deep inside the ship's hull. Once that was done, the twin doors built into the roof of this secret compartment unlocked and lifted, exposing the Zuljanah rocket for the first time since it had been loaded aboard at Bandar Abbas. Topped by its black nose cone, the twenty-five-meter-tall missile lay on its side, still safely secured to its surrounding framework.

From the sealed control center below Heidari's feet, Majidi reported, "We are beginning the transition to the rocket's vertical launch position."

Slowly, the rocket and its attached gantry elevated, swinging through a 90-degree arc until they pointed skyward through the opening in the oil tanker's deck. Only the upper third of the finned launch vehicle was visible above the hull.

"The gantry is locked in position," Majidi said calmly over the inter-com phone. "And the launch pad's own internal motion compensators and stabilizers are fully engaged. All internal systems remain nominal. We are beginning our final checks of the Zuljanah's first two solid-fueled stages. Once those are complete, we will begin the process of loading the upper stage with its more volatile hypergolic fuel mixture. The clock is now at T minus forty-five minutes and counting."

THAT SAME TIME

Russia's main defense command center occupied a vast complex of Stalinist-era white concrete buildings sprawling across the Moskva River's north bank. Most of its aboveground offices and auditoriums handled the day-to-day routine of managing the military's peacetime functions. The real work of coordinating serious military action around the world was handled by smaller command centers and other facilities safely buried far underground.

Inside one of those secure subterranean conference chambers, President Piotr Zhdanov and Pavel Voronin were seated next to each other at a semicircular table. They had been brought here by the sudden and unexpected flow of flash message traffic from the converted SSBN BS-64 *Podmoskovye* out in the middle of the Atlantic.

Nakhimov's first signals reporting the *Gulf Venture*'s abrupt alteration of course had been worrying enough. The submarine captain's new messages were even more troubling. With the storm diminishing and the coming of night, *Podmoskovye* had been able to creep close enough to the Iranian tanker to use its night vision periscope. The pictures it was taking were being relayed in real-time via communication satellite to Moscow.

Zhdanov glared at the green-tinted images displayed on the large screen in front of them. They showed the Zuljanah rocket now locked into its launch orientation. And none of Voronin's Raven Syndicate security personnel were visible anywhere aboard the huge ship. Instead, several armed Iranian sentries were clearly posted at various points on the tanker's tall aft superstructure. "The fucking bastards in Tehran lied to us," he snarled. "They're launching a day early."

Unconcerned and even a bit amused by this evidence of Iranian duplicity, Voronin shrugged his elegantly tailored shoulders. "Nothing in our own plans is actually affected by this unexpectedly early missile strike, Mr. President," he pointed out. "Our own ICBMs are already on standby, ready to strike as soon as we receive confirmation of a successful EMP attack on the United States. All the Iranians will accomplish by this minor act of treachery is to advance the time of their own destruction by a few hours."

Zhdanov breathed out. "I suppose that is true," he said grudgingly. "But what about the team you had aboard the *Gulf Venture*? Aren't you concerned about them?"

Voronin smiled thinly, a smile that never reached his pale eyes. "If Skoblin and his men are now prisoners aboard the tanker, what of it?" He gestured toward the screen. "They weren't expected to take any action until after that rocket is launched. And with the *Podmoskovye* already lurking below the surface with Colonel Danilevsky's additional commandos, nothing really changes." His smile widened minutely. "Except possibly the personal fate of Skoblin and the others on the *Gulf Venture*. And if they die," he said callously, "they die. Some men are always expendable."

THIRTY-SEVEN

ABOARD THE *GULF VENTURE*

A SHORT TIME LATER

"Captain!" one of the Revolutionary Guard ratings manning the tanker's air search radar console said suddenly. "I have an unidentified large air contact on my screen."

Heidari was at his side in less than a second. "Show me!" he snapped.

The rating tapped a tiny blip blinking into existence every time the radar swept that portion of the sky. "It's right there, sir."

"What's your evaluation?" Heidari asked, closely watching the blip as it moved slowly across the screen. If this was an air attack, he might have only seconds to send his gun and SAM crews to their stations.

The rating frowned. "The contact is currently south of Point Omega, about twenty-two nautical miles out." Point Omega was the featureless spot on the ocean around which the *Gulf Venture* was currently steaming. With the tanker's actual heading constantly changing as it continued turning through complete circles, the coordinates served as a useful reference point. "The bogey is currently on a heading of zero-seven-five degrees. And I estimate its altitude at more than nine thousand meters."

"What is this plane's airspeed?" Heidari demanded.

"Very slow, Captain," the rating told him, scanning his readouts. "Not more than one hundred and fifty knots."

Puzzled, Heidari frowned. This unknown aircraft's flight profile didn't match that of any regular commercial passenger or cargo aircraft that would normally operate this far out in the Atlantic. Could it be one of the U.S. Navy's carrier-based E-2 Hawkeye reconnaissance planes? He swallowed hard, suddenly afraid. The presence of an American carrier task force and its accompanying escorts in this part of the ocean could be catastrophic for MIDNIGHT. During its ascent phase, their Zuljanah rocket would be horribly vulnerable to the SM-3 interceptor missiles carried by some U.S. destroyers and cruisers. Had he and his crew come all this way only to fail ignominiously in what should be their moment of triumph?

Regaining control over his emotions, the Iranian naval officer forced himself to think carefully. This bogey's observed airspeed was far below the normal cruising speed of those American Hawkeye early-warning aircraft. They ordinarily flew at more than 250 knots. He turned to the sailor manning the *Gulf Venture*'s improvised electronic warfare console. "Are you picking up any active radar emissions from that contact?"

"No, sir," the other man assured him. "Not so much as a single pulse."

Heidari's frown deepened. The absence of any surface search or air search radar emissions made it extremely unlikely the unknown aircraft was a military reconnaissance plane out on patrol. And while the weather had greatly improved over the past several hours, there was still a nearly unbroken layer of clouds across the sky at low altitude. No one aboard an aircraft that high up could hope to spot anything on the surface of the sea without using special IR cameras or sensors. So if that distant bogey represented a real threat to his ship and its mission, he couldn't make out what it might be. Nevertheless, he found its sudden appearance, at this critical moment in the rocket's launch sequence, disturbing—especially when he considered it in the light of the several other aircraft they'd spotted over the past few days. At the time, he'd written those contacts off as routine, the sort of chance encounters that might be expected with two to three thousand commercial flights crossing the Atlantic every single day. But what if he'd been wrong?

Should he bring his antiaircraft defenses to full readiness, Heidari wondered? He checked the clock above the plot table. It showed that they were at T –31 minutes and still counting down. He picked up the intercom phone connected to the Launch Control Center.

"Majidi here," the scientist answered tersely. "What is it, Reza?" He and his launch crew were just beginning the delicate task of fueling the rocket's third stage. Short of an ignition failure or the uncontrolled detonation of the first stage's solid propellant on liftoff, this was the most dangerous phase of readying the Zuljanah missile for flight.

Quickly, Heidari ran through the situation and his concerns. Majidi's reaction to his proposal to send their weapons crews to their action stations was immediate and strongly negative. "That would be a terrible mistake," he said urgently. "Many of those out on the deck when we launch would almost certainly be killed or terribly burnt. Even worse, the rocket plume itself could trigger the accidental detonation of exposed ammunition and surface-to-air missiles. And that would be cataclysmic, potentially destroying both the rocket and the ship itself!"

"Very well, we'll hold off for now," Heidari agreed. "But it may be necessary to put the countdown sequence on hold if the situation changes." He hung up and turned toward Touraj Dabir. "Put the weapons crews on full alert. They're to stay safely inside the superstructure for now, but if I sound general quarters, I want them to break every record we've set getting those guns and SAM launchers into action. Is that clear?"

The younger officer nodded. "I'll pass the word, Captain." He cleared his throat nervously. "Perhaps we should release Skoblin and his men, too? If we're attacked somehow, we could use the extra armed manpower."

Rapidly, Heidari considered the idea and just as quickly dismissed it. "No, I don't think that freeing them is worth the risk yet," he said. "Not until the Zuljanah is on its way into space." His eyes narrowed. "But have a team move their weapons and ammunition into position outside the storage compartment where they're confined. Just in case we need help from the Russians after all."

ABOARD THE LM-100J SUPER HERCULES,
OVER THE ATLANTIC

THAT SAME TIME

Breathing carefully through his oxygen mask, Nick Flynn gripped
a bracket mounted through the insulation lining the plane's cargo area.
Ingalls had depressurized the large compartment ten minutes before,
making sure he could safely open the rear ramp the moment they
were within striking range of the *Gulf Venture*. At thirty thousand
feet, the air pressure was barely a third of that at sea level. Without the
oxygen flowing through their masks, all eight members of the Dragon
assault team and the two tracking camera crewmen would have been
unconscious in a minute or less. The others on his team were lined up
behind him, each holding tight to one of the special grips fitted to this
far aft section of the aircraft. Since they would be making a freefall
high-altitude jump, none of them were attached by static or safety lines.
Once the ramp came down, Mark I muscle power would be the only
thing stopping any of them from being bounced out into the open air if
the plane hit turbulence.

"*Dragon team, stand by,*" Ingalls said from the cockpit over their joint
tactical radio circuit. "*Tracking crew give me a read.*"

"*Copy that, Major,*" one of the technicians manning the rail-mounted
tracking camera and telescope system replied. He had his eyes fixed on
the system's monitor, intently studying the green-tinted thermal images
it showed. "*Target sighted!*" he said excitedly. "*Bearing three-two-seven.*"

Range twenty-one point three nautical miles. The ship is still circling at approximately five knots." Rapidly, he rattled off the GPS coordinates that corresponded most closely to the tanker's observed position.

Flynn and the rest of his men automatically checked the personal navigation gear fitted to their helmets, comparing their current readings to those of the ship. Originally designed for hikers, these slim devices contained GPS receivers, electronic compasses, and barometric altimeters. During the early part of their planned drop from high above the thick cloud layer, the data these receivers provided would be crucial. Once they broke through clouds, they should be close enough to the *Gulf Venture* to navigate the rest of the way by sight, using their night vision goggles.

"*Target aspect change!*" the tracking crewman snapped. "*Jesus! I can see the nose cone of what looks like a rocket protruding above the deck at roughly amidships, maybe three hundred feet forward of the aft super-structure.*"

Flynn's jaw tightened. The Russians and Iranians must be in the final phases of preparing their nuclear-armed missile for launch. He'd known from Fox's frantic messages that they were probably running very close to the edge on this mission. But having that assessment confirmed so dramatically wasn't any more welcome. He half-turned to look down the row of solemn faces. "Well, hell, that sure sucks," he said, forcing himself to sound conversational.

Wade Vucovich raised his hand. "*Hey, sir?*" he asked over their tactical circuit. "*What would happen if a stray round hits that rocket?*"

Someone had to ask, Flynn supposed. "Scientifically speaking, it would be bad. Very, very bad." That drew the tension-relieving laugh he'd hoped for. "So I guess y'all better be real careful what you're shooting at once we hit the deck. I'm not real eager to find out what it's like being at ground zero when a rocket blows up."

His wry caution drew tight, answering grins from his men. Triggering an uncontrolled detonation of the Iranian missile's solid and liquid fuel propellants would certainly eliminate the EMP attack threatened against the United States, but none of them wanted to commit suicide in the process. They were acting as soldiers on this mission, not kamikazes. On the plus side, he suddenly realized, their enemies should be equally hampered by the need to avoid accidentally destroying their own missile and ship. That wasn't much comfort, he supposed, but right now he'd take anything he could get.

"Your guys set, Nick?" Ingalls asked from the cockpit. *"We're approximately thirty seconds out from the drop point you calculated."*

Flynn took a deep breath. Time had seemed to pass with leaden slowness during the hours-long, uncomfortable flight out from Florida across the ocean. Now everything felt much faster, as though seconds were flashing by in the blink of an eye. "Dragon is ready to go, Rip!" he radioed back and turned to face the rear ramp.

"Okay, I'm opening the rear ramp now!" Ingalls warned.

A moment later, the tail section of the LM-100J opened. Its top half lifted higher, while the wide rear ramp rotated down and ratcheted into position. As it lowered, the metal ramp took on an eerie silvery glow, touched by the light of the nearly full moon almost directly overhead.

Even before the whole twenty-second-long opening process was complete, the deafening roar from the Super Hercules's four huge turboprop engines drowned every other sound. Temperatures inside the cargo compartment plunged instantly. Thirty thousand feet above the surface of the ocean, the thin outside air was far below freezing, more than fifty degrees Fahrenheit below zero.

Here goes . . . everything, Flynn thought, suddenly fighting down a wave of fear—not so much for himself, but of the horrible consequences to the United States and hundreds of millions of innocent civilians if they failed. The jump light above the ramp flashed green. He let go of the bracket he'd been holding, raised his clenched fist up high, and then yanked it down as a signal. "Go! Go! Go!" he yelled.

Without waiting any longer, Flynn sprinted down the ramp and dove headfirst out into the moonlit night sky.

THIRTY-EIGHT

OVER THE ATLANTIC OCEAN

THAT SAME TIME

Caught by the aircraft's prop blast, Flynn whirled away through the brutally cold air. The tremendous force generated by four large six-bladed propellers, each revolving hundreds of times per minute, sent him tumbling head over heels. For a split-second, he fought down a growing sense of alarm. This churning maelstrom was far worse than anything he'd experienced during their dozens of practice jumps—all of which had been made from much smaller civilian aircraft. If these howling winds ripped his wingsuit or tore off the BMW electric impeller strapped to his chest, he'd fall far short of the *Gulf Venture* . . . and then drown in the icy waters of the Atlantic.

And then he fell out of the turbulent wake curling off the LM-100J's wings. Instantly, the subzero, roiling currents around him smoothed out. The wind's shrieking madness faded away, replaced by the low rumble and hiss of air rushing past the nylon fabric of his wingsuit as he plunged toward the ocean at more than 140 knots. But he was still tumbling out of control.

Carefully, Flynn spread his arms and legs into tapered V shapes—creating a wider surface to bite into the air rushing past him—and then just as quickly curled his arms back toward his chest whenever he felt himself again starting to lose control. The effect was much the same as that created when a space capsule rolling too fast rhythmically pulsed its thrusters in opposite directions to counteract the spin and slow its rate of rotation. Gradually, he regained complete control over the wingsuit and was at last able to turn himself over to face downward and extend its fabric fully to create a stable airfoil. His speed had decreased to a little over 120 knots. The glowing figures on his navigation display showed that he was now descending through 26,000 feet above sea level. "Dragon Lead proceeding to target as planned," he said into his throat mike.

"Dragon Two is same," Tadeusz Kossak replied over the circuit. *"I have your helmet IR beacon in sight, Lead."* One by one, the rest of his team checked in, reporting that they too had made it safely through the vortex created by the Super Hercules and were following him down.

As his fear of plummeting out of control faded, Flynn felt a surge of elation. Despite the incredible danger involved, the sensation of wing-suit flying was intensely exhilarating. It was the closest thing possible to achieving the sensation of free, unencumbered flight so long dreamed of by humans. For these minutes, as he glided onward toward the still-distant *Gulf Venture*, he would be almost a true master of the air—mimicking the birds, and the gods of myth and legend.

He looked ahead along his glide path. Those towering masses of cloud below, etched in silver and gray by the moonlight, were now much closer. He checked his heading and lowered his right shoulder slightly, banking a few degrees to bring himself back on the most direct course toward the oil tanker's predicted position. Under the overall sense of euphoria provoked by this near-silent flight through the darkness, he was conscious of a gnawing worry. How close were their enemies to launching their missile? If he and his men were too late after all, the first warning would be a brightening glow through those same clouds—a diffuse glow that would quickly resolve into a blinding plume of fire as the Iranian-made rocket and its Russian-produced nuclear warhead soared onward toward space, completely untouchable and unstoppable.

Still gliding toward the ocean's surface at about 120 knots, Flynn arrowed into the clouds. Instantly, the sky around him disappeared. He was surrounded by a sea of impenetrable gray. Ice pellets hammered at his arms, legs, and chest. And then, as he descended into warmer air, the ice impacts stopped, replaced by rivulets of rain that blurred across his clear polycarbonate face shield and streamed away to either side. Without any visual reference points, he had only the faint sensation of falling through endless nothing. Time seemed to slow again. Only the steadily decreasing numbers on his altimeter and GPS readouts provided any sense of movement. Resolutely, he held to his current course. While slashing through this mass of cloud with near-zero visibility, the risk of a fatal collision with one of the other Dragon team wingsuiters was high. Several close calls during training had shown that the only way to minimize the danger was to stay on a rigidly defined flight path—and make any needed corrections only once you were free of the cloud layer.

Sooner than he'd expected, Flynn broke back out into the open. With the moon obscured by the solid overcast, the sea below and the surrounding sky were nearly pitch-black. But there, still thousands of feet below and some miles ahead, he could make out a tiny, brightly lit point against the unrelieved darkness of the ocean. As he continued his descent, it steadily grew larger and clearer. "Target in sight," he reported.

Confirmations of the sighting from the rest of his assault force echoed through his headset. They were all now about six thousand feet up and a little more than six nautical miles out from the *Gulf Venture*, trailing behind him in a ragged line across the sky. This was another danger point for Flynn and his men. At their present speed and rate of descent, they were still approximately three minutes out from the tanker. And if a sharp-eyed lookout using IR binoculars spotted them on the way in, that was more than enough time for the enemy weapons crews to man their guns and blow them out of the sky. So it was time to make use of the tactical edge offered by their BMW assistive propulsion gear, Flynn decided. "Follow me!" he ordered. "And stand by on your impellers!"

He sharpened his dive angle, plunging ever faster toward the surface of the Atlantic. Swiftly, his altitude decreased, flickering from six thousand to four thousand to a thousand feet in less than a minute. Moments later, scarcely a hundred feet above the rolling wave tops, he flared his wingsuit slightly, shedding velocity to pull out of this steep dive and into near-level flight. In the same motion, the gloved fingers of his right hand curled inward and pushed buttons on a controller strapped to his wrist. "Impellers on!"

With a high-pitched whine, the BMW electric propulsion unit activated. Inside its twin engine nacelles, the tiny carbon fiber impellers spun up to 25,000 RPM, pulling him through the air like the conventional propellers used on larger aircraft. Flynn accelerated instantly. As his speed jumped, he adjusted his angle of flight carefully so that he was now flying straight and level—racing across the surface of the sea with only feet to spare. Ahead, he could see the massive bow of the *Gulf Venture* swinging toward him as the huge ship continued maneuvering in a series of repeated 360-degree turns. One corner of his mind noted that a huge patch of the ocean around the vessel seemed oddly flat, as though it were being held down by weights.

Through his headset, he heard sudden loud whoops of glee from Hynes and several of the others. A wild grin flashed across his intent face. He figured that overexcitement at this breathtaking flight just above the waves was better than screams of sheer terror.

The oil tanker grew rapidly in Flynn's sights. They were drawing together with a combined velocity of almost 170 knots—closing the remaining gap between them nearly three hundred feet with every passing second. His eyes narrowed as he rapidly judged distances. There wasn't any more time to rely on instruments. Things were happening too fast. Everything was going to come down to instinct honed by training and practice.

With only about three hundred yards to go, the *Gulf Venture*'s tall, rounded bow loomed out of the darkness, rising high above him as it shouldered through the slowly heaving sea. Flynn's shoulders tensed. Ready . . . set . . . now! "Go for pop-up!" he yelled. He threw his shoulders back and arched his back to zoom skyward, going vertical to bleed off forward velocity and gain altitude in the same maneuver. In less than a second, he'd climbed three hundred feet above the deck of the oncoming ship.

"Dump impellers and deploy your chutes!" Flynn radioed. His gloved fingers pressed another control. Electronic latches on his breast-plate opened. Cut loose, the winged BMW propulsion unit tumbled away into the darkness, throwing up a white-foamed splash when it hit the surface of the ocean. In that same moment, his ram parachute streamed out behind him and snapped open with a tooth-rattling jolt. Tugging on the front risers to control his heading, he slid downwind along the length of the enormous oil tanker, aiming for a comparatively clear patch of deck a couple of hundred feet forward of the ship's tow-ering aft superstructure. A quick glance over his shoulder showed him seven more camouflaged rectangular parachutes floating down out of the sky behind him. The Quartet Directorate's Dragon assault force was coming in right on target.

"Enemy in sight!" A lookout screamed suddenly. "Directly over the ship!"

Startled, Captain Reza Heidari jolted upright from his seat at the navigation plot table. With the countdown clock now at T –21 minutes and proceeding smoothly, he'd been busy calculating the series of turns needed to bring the tanker directly through the selected launch coordinates at precisely the right moment. He stared out the bridge window, stunned by the horrifying sight of parachutes unexpectedly blossoming just above his ship's hull. This was impossible, one part of his mind screamed. The unknown aircraft his radar had been tracking had never approached closer than twenty-two nautical miles. That was well outside the range of any feasible conventional airborne assault.

With an effort, he closed his open mouth and regained a measure of control. Theoretically impossible or not, it was happening. A hostile landing force was touching down on his deck—right in front of his bewildered eyes. All that mattered now was to destroy this group of enemy paratroopers before they wrecked MIDNIGHT beyond repair.

Heidari whirled round on his second-in-command. Like him, the younger officer stood rigid at his station, gaping up at the descending parachutes with utter amazement. "Dabir!" he snapped. "Sound general quarters! Order our Quds Force commandos to attack immediately! I want that deck cleared!"

A swift counterattack to hit the enemy airborne troops while they were still struggling out of their parachutes was the only sound tactical move. Allowing them time to get their bearings and seize the initiative would be disastrous.

"But the rocket!" Dabir protested. "Stray bullets from a gun battle could set it off!"

"Fuck the rocket!" Heidari growled. Then he forced himself to think clearly. "Belay that. I still want our commandos to attack. But they are to engage the enemy only at close range! And using precise, aimed fire. Make that clear to them!"

"Yes, sir!" the younger officer nodded rapidly. He hit a button at his station. Klaxons blared out across the whole ship, deafeningly loud. Then he grabbed an intercom phone and started yelling into it, relaying the captain's orders to the senior warrant officer in charge of the two reinforced squads of Quds Force soldiers aboard. He stopped in mid-sentence and looked back at Heidari. "What about the guards posted outside Launch Control?"

"Send them all!" Heidari snarled. This was no time to plan a cautious, defensive fight. Allowing the enemy free reign over the *Gulf Venture*'s deck was tantamount to accepting ignominious death and defeat. For all he knew, they had orders to plant explosives to destroy the Zuljanah rocket and his ship together. This far from land, such a move would probably be suicidal, but not all infidels were cowards afraid to sacrifice their own lives when needed. "In fact, pass the word to the antiaircraft gun and missile crews. I want them out on deck in combat, too!"

For a moment, Dabir only stared at him. "But, Captain," he protested. "Our sailors don't carry personal weapons! They'll be cut to pieces by trained enemy troops."

"The crews can fight with fire axes and other tools," Heidari said grimly. "Or using their bare hands, if necessary!" He saw the younger man's horrified expression. "Don't you understand, Touraj?" he said through gritted teeth. "Lives mean nothing now. Not theirs. Not yours.

Not mine." Shaken, Dabir nodded hurriedly and bent back to the phone to pass on his orders.

Heidari swung around toward one of his petty officers, a reliable veteran of years of service aboard the Revolutionary Guard's fast-attack combatants. "You!" he said curtly.

"Sir?" the middle-aged sailor answered, stiffening to attention.

The captain fumbled in his pocket, pulled out a set of keys, and tossed them over. "Get down to the storage locker where we confined those Russians and let them out. Tell that idiot Skoblin to throw his men into this battle before we lose everything!" The petty officer nodded once and hurried off, rushing toward the nearest ladder.

Thinking furiously, Heidari turned back to the windows. Outside, on the deck, the first enemy paratrooper had just landed. He swallowed hard, seeing the digital clock over the plot table still counting down. Somehow, he and his men had to either drive this hostile force into the sea . . . or hold the launch control center until Majidi and his technicians were finally ready to send their missile soaring aloft toward the United States.

THIRTY-NINE

DRAGON ASSAULT FORCE, ON DECK

THAT SAME TIME

The moment his boots touched the tanker's steel deck, Nick Flynn punched out of his parachute harness and yanked off his oxygen mask and cylinder. The pungent stench of raw crude oil stung his eyes and nose. *These sons of bitches have been dumping their oil overboard*, he realized. That odd coating he'd noticed spreading over the sea was a thick oil slick which must already be more than a mile or two across. He shouldn't be surprised. Even deliberately causing a major environmental disaster was petty vandalism compared to the vicious act of mass murder the Russians and their Iranian partners intended to carry out against the United States.

The alarm sirens blaring across the ship suddenly cut out. In the comparative silence, he heard shouts from the six-story-high superstructure looming above him. Feet rang on metal as armed men rushed down the companionways and ladders leading to the deck. Whoever was in charge up there obviously wanted to hit the Quartet Directorate force while it was most vulnerable.

Flynn sighed. He hated it when the enemy reacted intelligently. But it figured that Iran and Russia's mercenary Raven Syndicate would have entrusted this high-risk operation to some of their best officers and men. He tore at the zippers sealing his wingsuit and kicked out of the bunched nylon fabric as quickly as possible. Then he dropped prone and rolled into cover behind a ladder to the steel catwalk running above this section of the hull. While readying his Kel-Tec carbine, he kept an eye on the deck ahead. There, not more than a couple of hundred feet away, hunched shapes were already moving toward him, darting from cover to cover as they drew steadily closer.

"Dragon Lead in position portside, near frame thirty. Hostiles on the move," he warned over the team's tactical net. From his personal perspective, facing aft, he was on the *Gulf Venture*'s righthand side, but the relative directions of port and starboard on a ship were always set from its bow, not its stern.

"Dragon Two ready, too," Tadeuz Kossak answered coolly from the other side of the massive vessel. *"Another group is advancing up the starboard side."*

Voices crackled through Flynn's headset as McGill, Cooke, Hynes, and the rest of his men confirmed that they were safely down on the deck and moving aft to join up. As the first two out of the Super Hercules, he and Kossak had landed the closest to the tanker's superstructure. And that now put them directly in the path of this oncoming enemy counterattack. They would have to hold long enough for the others to make their way along several hundred feet of hull crowded with a maze of piping, machinery, and shipping containers concealing the ship's heavy weapons.

He risked a quick glance over his left shoulder and saw the dark nose cone of the Iranian rocket just visible above a collection of the large cylindrical oil pipelines that ran the length of the ship's upper hull. It was positioned along the ship's centerline, about halfway toward the distant bow. Which meant anyone shooting toward him risked hitting their own highly explosive rocket by accident. Given the tangled assortment of ladders, catwalks, crossovers, pipelines, and other machinery in the way, the odds of that happening were fairly low—but it was still something for the bad guys to worry about, unless they were willing to take a chance on blowing themselves up. They would be reluctant to fire without a clear target. He and Kossak, on the other hand, had relatively clear fields of fire against the attackers. *Advantage, Flynn and company*, he thought calmly—sighting through the optic fitted to the short barrel of his carbine. "Lead to Two," he radioed the Pole. "Engage when ready."

"*Copy that, Lead*," Kossak said.

Flynn saw a bearded man appear in his sights, not more than a hundred feet and fifty away. That was practically point-blank range. The Iranian attacker wore standard-issue sailor's coveralls, but he moved like a trained soldier and carried a submachine gun held ready to fire when he jumped out from behind a mooring bollard and sprinted forward.

Flynn squeezed off two quick shots, holding the carbine's stock tight against his shoulder as it recoiled slightly. There was no real visible muzzle flash, thanks to the suppressor threaded onto the end of the barrel. Both spent 7.62mm cases were ejected forward out through a port and rolled away.

Hit twice, the Iranian folded over and collapsed in a heap. Blood, black in the dim light, pooled across the deck. There were cries of alarm as his companions dove back into cover. A sharp, piercing *crack-crack* echoed from the other side of the ship as Kossak opened fire, too.

Jaw tight, Flynn shifted his aim. A quick blur of movement at his one o'clock had caught his eye. He saw another enemy crewman rearing up from behind a pump housing with a grenade in his hand. *Shit*. These bastards were both evilly smart and experienced. Even if a random fragment from a grenade blast somehow flew all the way to the launch pad a couple of hundred feet behind him, it would have lost so much energy on the way that it probably wouldn't even penetrate the rocket's relatively thin skin. Despite his ballistic helmet and body armor, Nick wasn't likely to come off as well.

He fired three times in rapid succession. Flashes sparked off the pump casing from two near misses. But one bullet tore through the Iranian's chest and exploded out his back in a spray of blood and shattered bone and tissue. With a muffled groan, the man fell backward. The grenade dropped out of his hand, rolled onto the deck in front of him, and went off with a blinding flash.

WHAANNGG.

Flynn buried his face against the steel deck as razor-sharp fragments sleeted past overhead, pinging and clanging off the catwalk and piping above him. He heard agonized screams from the area around the pump casing. Some of the other attackers must have been caught in the blast.

Taking advantage of the sudden chaos, he rolled out from behind the ladder to go prone again behind the corner of one of the big fake shipping containers the Iranians used to hide their gun mounts and SAM launchers. Staying in any one place too long against enemies of this caliber would be a lethal error.

He was just in time.

Submachine guns crackled, firing short bursts aimed at his first position. 9mm rounds tore at the ladder rungs and deck plating and went howling away in coruscating clouds of pulverized steel. Flynn steadied his weapon, waiting.

And sure enough, just as the flashes faded, two more bearded Iranians charged forward, shouting as they came. He squeezed the trigger several more times, holding the Kel-Tec carbine on target as it kicked back a little against his shoulder with every separate shot.

One of the attackers stumbled and went down. The other dropped to one knee, swung his submachine gun toward Flynn, and opened fire. Rounds whip-cracked low over his head, punching holes in the metal-sided container.

Sharp splinters exploded outward. Most were stopped by his armor. One tiny, burning piece of steel tore across the side of his right leg, tracing a line of white-hot fire across his skin. Teeth clenched on a hiss of pain, he shot back, firing again and again and again. Hit repeatedly, the second Iranian crumpled to the deck and lay still.

Flynn pulled back behind the container and rolled over to check his wound. It was minor, just a thin, bloody slice along the outside edge of his calf. Not even worth slapping on a bandage, he thought with relief. Then his eyes widened in shock as a new shape loomed up from around the other side of the container—the side facing the ocean. While his comrades had drawn Flynn's fire at the price of their lives, another Iranian had somehow squeezed through the narrow gap between the container and the railing to outflank him. Desperately, Flynn whipped his carbine around, already sure that it was far too late. Adrenaline rushed through his body, slowing time until every second seemed an eternity. But all that did was give him more time to realize just how badly he'd screwed up.

Suddenly, gunfire erupted close by, shatteringly loud. The Iranian lurched away in a torrent of ripped cloth and flesh. Screaming, he pitched backward over the railing and toppled into the ocean far below.

"Sorry I cut that one a bit close, Nick," Flynn heard a voice say through his ringing ears. He looked around and saw Tony McGill lower his own carbine. The ex–SAS sergeant had just skidded to a stop a few yards away. His bright white teeth gleamed against the backdrop of his camouflage-painted face, rather like those of the Cheshire Cat from *Alice in Wonderland* just before it disappeared.

He breathed out. "Close was good enough, Tony," he said gratefully. Behind McGill, Cole Hynes and Mark Stadler took up their own firing positions, going prone behind whatever cover they could find.

"Geez, sir," Hynes called over to him, sounding aggrieved. "Couldn't you have waited a little for the rest of us to get here?"

Flynn risked a quick look around the corner of the bullet-riddled container. Bodies littered the deck in front of him. For the moment, there was no further sign of any movement ahead. "Sorry about that," he told Hynes wryly. "I meant to ask the bad guys to wait until you were in position, but in all the excitement, I clean forgot."

"All hostiles are down on the starboard side," Tadeuz Kossak reported over the radio. *"Cooke, Ricard, Vucovich, and I are set to advance."*

Flynn nodded. "Same situation here on the port side, Dragon Two," he replied. "We've smashed their counterattack." He climbed back to his feet. So far all they'd accomplished was to stave off immediate defeat. The only way to win this was to break into the tanker's massive superstructure to find and then destroy the enemy's launch control center. And a nagging itch at the back of his mind suggested they were fast running out of time to get that done.

"Holy shit!" Hynes yelled suddenly. "Here come more sons of bitches! A whole shitload of them!"

Flynn looked ahead to see another wave of attackers erupt out of the shadows around the tanker's superstructure. He bit down on a startled oath. There must be at least twenty charging across the deck toward his little group of four men. And unlike their predecessors, these sailors made no effort to take cover. Instead, they ran straight toward him, shouting and yelling wild battle cries, and waving fire axes, crowbars, and heavy wrenches. He stared in shock for a split-second. *Holy Christ*, he thought in utter astonishment, this was a human wave attack like something out of the Middle Ages—or a ship-to-ship boarding action in the Napoleonic Wars. Tools and axes against rifles? What kind of crazy bullshit was this?

Then he recovered. An axe or crowbar swung hard enough could kill you just as dead as a 7.62mm bullet. "Open fire!" he shouted, sighting on the charging mob and starting to squeeze off shots.

Hynes and the others followed suit.

Iranian sailors started dropping, knocked to the deck by the impact of rounds moving at more than twenty-five-hundred feet per second. But there were a hell of a lot of them, and they only had a couple hundred feet of relatively open deck to cover, Flynn realized. His first magazine ran dry and he quickly dropped it out and slammed in a fresh one with twenty more rounds. But by the time he had his weapon back up and ready to fire again, the mob's survivors were on top of them.

At close quarters, everything came down to reflexes and instinct. Flynn ducked the wild swing of an axe, slammed the muzzle of his carbine against the attacker's ribs, and pulled the trigger. *Crack*. Blood spattered across his face. The dying axman dropped to his knees, still feebly trying to grapple him. He kneed the Iranian hard in the face, feeling bones and teeth shatter . . . and then whirled away as a long wrench flashed right past his shoulder.

This was bad, he thought desperately, sidestepping to dodge another sailor charging at him, this one wielding a crowbar. Really, really bad—

ON THE SUPERSTRUCTURE

THAT SAME TIME

Out on an open catwalk three levels above the tanker's main deck, Viktor Skoblin took the folding-stock assault rifle offered to him by Yvgeny Kvyat. He automatically checked to make sure it was fully loaded. His eyes narrowed. The Iranians might have returned their weapons, but the fools had neglected to include their body armor—and now there was no time left to retrieve that valuable protective gear. He glared back at the Iranian petty officer who'd come to let them out of their improvised prison. "What did Heidari say?" he demanded.

"He wants you to join our counterattack," the other man repeated. "And destroy what remains of the enemy paratroops at close range!"

Skoblin risked a glance over the edge of the catwalk. The scene below was one of unrelieved madness. Corpses by the dozen sprawled across the deck. Forward of the superstructure, on the both the port and starboard sides of the ship, he could see tiny knots of men fighting hand-to-hand. A horrific cacophony of gunshots, shrieks, and yells rose above the conflict. He looked back at the petty officer and shook his head. "I won't waste my troops like that," he snapped. "Your captain can shove those stupid orders up his tight ass."

Almost unbidden, the Revolutionary Guardsman's right hand dropped to the pistol holstered at his waist. "Are you refusing a legal command, Major Skoblin?" His tone was dangerously calm.

At once, Skoblin offered him an apologetic smile. "Naturally, I meant no disrespect," he assured the other man. The fingers of his left hand twitched in a private signal to Dmitri Fadeyev.

The former GRU assassin nodded minutely. Then, without warning, he hacked at the Iranian's right wrist, paralyzing the nerves there. Stunned by the sudden onslaught, the petty officer's mouth opened wide to yell a warning that might be heard by those on the bridge above them. But before he could make a sound, Fadeyev's clenched fist smashed into his throat, crushing his larynx. Gasping, straining for breath that would not come, the dying man sank to his knees.

Skoblin studied him dispassionately for a second and then turned to two more of his men. "See if this asshole can fly," he ordered.

Nodding grimly, they grabbed the choking petty officer under his arms and hurled him over the edge of the catwalk to plunge fifty feet straight down onto the steel deck.

Nervously, Kvyat licked his full lips. "What do we do now?" he asked softly.

Skoblin stabbed a finger at the pudgy ex-GRU intelligence officer. "You take four men and hold this catwalk against any attack from the deck," he said. He nodded to Fadeyev, Yuri Linnik, Kirill Zaitsev, and two more members of his Raven Syndicate security team. "The rest of us will head up two decks and guard the approaches to the Launch Control Center." He hefted his assault rifle. "That's the key point. If we hold that, nothing else matters."

"Captain Heidari won't be happy that we've disobeyed his orders," Kvyat pointed out carefully.

Skoblin shrugged his massive shoulders. "I don't give a shit, one way or the other." He nodded toward the deck below. "If any of the enemy make it alive out of that bloody mess, we'll stop them cold."

"And if the Iranians win?"

Skoblin considered the possibility dispassionately. "Even if they do, there won't be many of them left in one piece," he said coolly. "Which will leave us with all the power aboard this damned ship. And then, once that rocket is away, we can carry out the rest of the orders Voronin gave us . . . and finish off that pig Heidari and all of his remaining fanatical madmen."

His men nodded eagerly. After the indignity of so easily being taken captive by the Iranians, they were looking forward to turning the tables on their supposed allies. Then, while Kvyat and his four men settled somewhat uncertainly into firing positions along the catwalk, Fadeyev, Linnik, and the rest followed Skoblin as he loped toward the nearest accommodation ladder up to the higher reaches of the *Gulf Venture*'s superstructure.

FORTY

THAT SAME TIME

Frantically, Flynn backpedaled away from a desperate crewman wildly swinging a wrench and fired directly into the man's open-mouthed face. Killed instantly, the Iranian crumpled. Silence fell across this part of the deck. Panting, he turned rapidly through an arc, looking for any remaining threats.

There weren't any. All of the sailors who'd rushed them were dead or obviously dying. The only ones still on their feet were his own men. But not all of them, he realized with sorrow.

Surrounded by the Iranians he'd taken down with him, Mark Stadler lay facedown on the deck. He had an axe head buried deep in his back. Obviously swung with tremendous force, it had smashed right through his armor. Cole Hynes, with blood dripping from a long gash across his cheek, knelt down, and quickly checked the former Marine over. He looked up, grim-faced, and shook his head. "Mark's gone, sir."

Flynn winced. He'd known the odds were against all of them making out of this mission alive, but somehow he'd hoped to beat those odds. As it was, he knew, they were extraordinarily lucky to have lost only one man so far. From what he could see, the others, like him, were bruised and shaken, but not otherwise seriously injured. The combination of firepower superiority and the protection offered by their helmets and body armor had given them just enough of an edge to survive that swirling, brutal melee.

"What's next, Nick?" Alain Ricard asked somberly. After destroying their own wave of enemies in close combat, the former French Marine Commando officer, Kossak, Cooke, and Vucovich, had crossed over to this side of the oil tanker.

Flynn pointed toward the aft superstructure looming above them. "We take the key areas of the rest of this ship, especially whatever compartment they're using as a control center. And we do it before that goddamned rocket lifts off."

Ricard studied the stretch of open deck between their current position and the metal staircases and ladders climbing up the outside of the hundred-foot-high superstructure. Corpses were strewn everywhere. "Unless we've just eliminated the whole crew, getting there may not be easy," he warned. "That clear section is a perfect killing zone."

"As we just proved," Flynn agreed. "So we'll do this the smart way." He saw Hynes open his mouth to make a crack at that and shrugged. "Yeah, Cole, I know," he sighed. "The smart way would have been not to be here at all, right?"

"Something like that, sir," the shorter man said with a crooked grin.

Quickly, Flynn indicated Ricard, Hynes, and Kossak. They were his best long-range marksmen. "You three take up positions here. You're our base of fire, while the rest of us maneuver. Once we've cleared those catwalks, I'll call you forward. Got it?"

They nodded, and swiftly dispersed to find good cover around this part of the deck. Flynn looked at the rest of his assault team. Cooke, Vucovich, and McGill returned his serious gaze. "Okay, listen up," he said quietly. "The only way to do this at all is to do it fast. If someone gets hit, leave them. Don't stop to return fire. Keep moving and fire on the move only if you have a target. If we get bogged down out there or on those stairs and ladders, we're dead."

McGill nodded. "Speed is life," he commented.

"Thus endeth the lesson," Cooke agreed.

Wade Vucovich only nodded.

"Right, then let's ammo up and do this," Flynn said. He checked the magazine of his carbine and saw that it was only half full. He dropped it out and slid it into a reserve pouch on his assault vest before slapping in a fresh magazine. The others did the same with their own weapons. "Dragon Two, are you and your guys ready?" he radioed.

"*We're set, Lead,*" Kossak confirmed.

Flynn took a deep breath. "Follow me!" he snapped. Cradling his weapon, he leaped out from cover and sprinted forward. McGill and the others were at his heels, spreading out as they ran to make it harder for any single burst of fire to hit them all. They'd only covered a few yards when a near continuous crackle of assault rifle shots erupted from one of the catwalks halfway up the superstructure.

5.45mm rounds hammered down across the deck at a steep angle, ripping through the thin plating at supersonic speeds. Gouts of glowing, half-molten steel splashed away from each oblique impact point. Ignoring the danger, Flynn lowered his head, lengthened his stride, and ran even harder—racing all-out toward the shelter offered by a low overhang near the first flight of stairs heading up.

Kneeling behind a bulbous mooring bollard seventy yards from the superstructure, Tadeusz Kossak sighted in on one of the hostile gunmen leaning over the catwalk to fire down at Flynn and the others. His scope's crosshairs settled on the figure and he stroked the Kel-Tec carbine's trigger twice. *Crack-crack.*

He saw the gunman fling his arms wide and fall backward.

The Pole's lips creased in a satisfied smile. *One down*, he thought. From their own positions, he could hear Hynes and Ricard firing, too. He tracked along the railing and spotted another of the enemy riflemen folded lifelessly over it, hanging limp with his head and arms dangling in the air. The others stationed there seemed to have gone to ground, driven back into deeper cover by the sudden deaths of two of their comrades.

Ahead, he saw Flynn reach the overhang and then lunge up the stairs, with McGill and Cooke close behind him. Wade Vucovich had stumbled and gone down about three quarters of the way across the deck. His left leg was a mangled mess, ripped wide open by a bullet slanting down from above. Kossak could see the American fumbling desperately through one of his equipment pouches for a combat tourniquet to stop the bright arterial blood spurting from his wound.

"Cover me!" Hynes yelled. He darted out from behind a big oil pump and sped toward his injured friend. When he reached Vucovich, he grabbed hold of the back of his assault vest and dragged him onward toward the overhang.

Suddenly, Kossak spotted movement on the catwalk high above them. One of the enemy soldiers stationed there had just reappeared. Assault rifle at the ready, the man was leaning far out over the railing, obviously lining up to butcher the two helpless Americans. "*Gówno*. Shit," the Pole snarled, furious with himself. Awed by Hynes's heroic and foolish gesture, he'd lost track of the tactical situation at exactly the wrong moment.

Two more gunshots rang out.

Hit in the head by Alain Ricard's carefully aimed fire, the hostile gunman whirled around and toppled behind the railing. "My bird, I think," the Frenchman called out cheerfully.

Kossak breathed out in relief and grimly sighted down the short barrel of his own carbine, sweeping it back and forth across the superstructure—scanning closely for the slightest sign of any movement. He'd made one bad mistake already in this battle, one that might easily have cost the lives of friends and comrades. He didn't plan to make another.

ABOARD BS-64 *PODMOSKOVYE*

THAT SAME TIME

His mouth set in a frown, Captain First Rank Mikhail Nakhimov looked across the crowded control room toward his diving officer, Senior Lieutenant Anatoly Yalinsky. "Surface the boat!" he ordered.

The realization that an enemy airborne commando force was attacking the *Gulf Venture* had triggered an immediate reaction from the Raven Syndicate's Colonel Danilevsky. His instructions from Moscow were clear: the huge tanker and its missile must not be allowed to fall into enemy hands. That imperative, plus the obvious need to swiftly reinforce the ship's defenders, overrode any further interest in keeping their presence here a secret.

"Surfacing the boat, aye, sir," Yalinsky replied. His fingers danced across the control board in front of him. With a faint hiss, compressed air replaced some of the water in the eighteen-thousand-ton nuclear submarine's forward ballast tanks. As *Podmoskovye*'s bow rose a few degrees, the deck took on a perceptible slant. Around the control room, officers and ratings held on tight.

"Passing through ten meters," the diving officer reported, watching his instruments closely. Abruptly, the submarine's broad, rounded bow broke through the oil-coated surface, followed by its tall sail. The bow climbed several meters into the open air before splashing back down in a rolling wave of dirty brown foam. "Surfaced!" Yalinsky snapped. He leapt into action to open valves across his board. More water flooded into different ballast tanks along *Podmoskovye*'s long hull to make sure it rode evenly, gliding across the ocean at five knots—matching the slow speed of the oil tanker they were tracking.

For several seconds, Yalinsky studied his various gauges and dials. Then he whipped around to Nakhimov. "The boat is stable, Captain!" he reported. There was no longer any serious danger of losing control over the submarine's buoyancy and plunging back underwater.

"Very well," Nakhimov acknowledged. He darted a finger at the two sailors in foul-weather gear clustered at the base of a ladder to a hatch on the ceiling of the control room. It opened into a chamber at the base of the sail. From there, another ladder led up to the observation platform at the top. "Lookouts to your posts!"

They swarmed upward and through the hatch. Donning his own jacket, Nakhimov followed them up. The raw, acrid smell of oil greeted him as soon as he scrambled through the final hatch and came out into the narrow navigating station at the top of *Podmoskovye*'s sail.

He raised his binoculars, focusing on the huge oil tanker a couple of thousand yards off the submarine's starboard bow. Repeated flashes lit the night at different points on the ship's aft superstructure, accompanied by the distinct *pop-pop-pop* of distant gunfire. He lowered his binoculars. The battle was still in progress. He swiveled around and leaned over the coaming to peer toward the stern.

Danilevsky and the other Raven Syndicate mercenaries were already out on the hull there. Bulky in their body armor and life jackets, they were busy wrestling equipment and weapons out through a large hatch. Held by lines, three inflatable, high-speed boats bobbed alongside, buffeted by low waves curling off the submarine's glistening flank. Even as he watched, Danilevsky and his troops slithered carefully down into the three crowded boats. One by one, the three rubber-sided craft cast off and motored away toward the *Gulf Venture*—cutting V-shaped wakes through the thick layer of crude oil covering the sea.

FORTY-ONE

ON THE *GULF VENTURE'S* SUPERSTRUCTURE

THAT SAME TIME

Flynn took the metal steps two at a time, with his carbine raised and ready at his shoulder. Staying on the right half of the accommodation ladder, he swiveled from side to side, looking for the faintest hint of any movement . . . or even a shadow in the wrong place. Shannon Cooke followed him, a few feet behind and on his left. Tony McGill brought up the rear, guarding against any sudden ambush that might erupt from behind them. On their way up these external staircases and their adjoining catwalks, they'd already passed two solid, weathertight doors into the superstructure. Both had seemed bolted shut from the inside. For now, Flynn was content to bypass those entrances into the lower levels of this massive ship. With severely limited time and only a handful of men available, the Dragon assault force couldn't afford to get caught up in a prolonged fight to clear a labyrinth of unimportant corridors and compartments.

Both logic and their examination of "before" and "after" photos of the *Gulf Venture* indicated that the mission-critical locations—the launch control center and the bridge—were on the two highest sections of the superstructure. The bridge itself was obvious, with its array of large windows and two open side wings. Flynn's bet was that the rocket's control center was on the level immediately below it. Before the tanker's refit, that part of the ship had portholes like all the other inhabited areas. Those glassed-in openings were gone now, replaced by a layer of what appeared to be solid steel. That design change only made sense if you wanted to create a highly secure compartment for vital equipment and personnel—like the computers, technicians, scientists, and engineers required to launch a powerful rocket.

"Contact left high!" Cooke blurted. He fired twice in rapid succession and then kept firing as quickly as he could pull the trigger, aiming at the rectangular opening to the next catwalk up. The gunman who had popped upright there to jump them shot back just as frantically.

Without thinking, Flynn exploded into action, charging straight up the stairs, firing on the move. Caught exposed and without any possible cover, attacking into the ambush was his only option. Rounds slashed past and caromed off rungs and risers in a glittering spray of sparks and white-hot splinters. One 5.45mm bullet clipped the edge of his body armor, ripping through cloth and cracking one of his composite ceramic ballistic plates. Sudden pain flared red along his ribs.

Hit by somebody's fire, the enemy gunman fell backward, with his hands clutching futilely at the red-rimmed holes torn through his chest. The assault rifle he'd dropped slid down the stairs and came to rest at Cooke's feet.

Flynn reached the top of the stairs and threw himself down, rolling onto his side to keep his carbine pointed down the length of the catwalk. More corpses were sprawled there—one draped over the railing and two others curled up on the deck. He caught a glimpse of movement and saw a pudgy-faced man, pale with terror, fumbling with a Russian-made assault rifle. He'd been lying prone behind one of the dead men and was now hurriedly trying to bring his weapon on target.

Flynn shot him. The gunman slumped forward—with the top of his head blown off.

———

Two levels up, outside the sealed Launch Control Center, Viktor Skoblin heard the sudden burst of gunfire die away. He was crouched inside one of the small compartments that lined the narrow corridor leading directly to the center's armored hatch. He'd left the compartment door open just far enough to let him aim down the corridor. There, at the far end, another sealed weathertight hatch barred the way out onto a wide covered platform just below the starboard bridge wing.

"Do you think Kvyat and the others have stopped the enemy?" Fadeyev hissed from his concealed position in another compartment just across the corridor.

Skoblin shook his head dismissively. "Not likely," he growled. He shrugged. "If we're lucky, they got one or two before dying themselves." All along, he'd never had any illusions that Kvyat's small force would accomplish anything more than delay the attackers fighting their way up the tanker's superstructure. Like the ex-GRU intelligence officer, the four other Raven Syndicate operatives he'd assigned to hold the lower catwalk were more experienced at surveillance work and other nonlethal dirty tasks. He'd deliberately held back his most skilled and ruthless killers—Fadeyev, Linnik, and the rest—to hold this position.

Grimly, he sighted down the barrel of his rifle. It wouldn't be long now.

Flynn watched Tony McGill mold tiny pieces of plastic explosive over the hinges of the latched weathertight door blocking their way into the *Gulf Venture*'s superstructure. During his service with the SAS, the former sergeant had mastered the art of opening locked doors by blasting them open. "Not exactly a transferrable skill to civvie street," he'd commented wryly during their planning sessions for this mission. "Unless I went in for aiding and abetting bank heists, that is."

With his charges in place, McGill finished off by tamping in non-electric blasting caps attached to short sections of detonator cord, which were, in turn, tied into a length of thin, flexible shock tube with an igniter at the other end. Only a millimeter wide on the inside, the shock tube contained tiny particles of HMX/aluminum explosive powder. Once it was set off, the resulting shockwave would travel down the tube at more than 6,500 feet per second toward the sections of det cord and their connected blasting caps. "That should do it," he told Flynn.

Unreeling the shock tube as they went, they backed away from the door and down the nearest accommodation ladder. Setting off a breaching charge without seeking good cover might look cool in movies. In real life, it was a ticket to traumatic brain injury and even death.

Cooke, who was now providing rear security for three of them, suddenly stopped dead, staring out across the catwalk's low railing. "Jesus Christ, Nick. These bastards have a goddamned submarine with them."

Flynn saw what he meant. There, about a mile away across the sea he could see the tall, sharklike fin and humpbacked bow of a huge submarine silently gliding along. It was keeping pace with the oil tanker.

"Bloody hell," McGill said in awe. "That's a Russian *Delta IV*–class SSBN."

"It's worse than that," Flynn said abruptly, pointing at the trio of inflatable boats headed their way. They were crammed full of heavily armed soldiers. "My bet is that's the *Podmoskovye*. I heard Moscow outfitted it as a special operations sub a few years back."

Cooke stared at them. "So those boats are probably full of Spetsnaz commandos?"

Flynn nodded. "That or Raven Syndicate thugs. Which amounts to the same thing."

"Well, heck," the ex–Army Special Forces operator said reflectively, his southern Virginia accent thicker suddenly. "I suppose it's too late to resign from this mission?"

Flynn grinned back at him. "Sorry, but, yeah, it is. Way too late." He went back on their radio circuit. "Dragon Two, this is Lead."

"Two here," Tadeusz Kossak replied immediately. *"Alain and I are moving up the accommodation ladders toward your position now, Dragon Lead. Hynes will join us as soon as he finishes putting a tourniquet on Vucovich."*

"Scratch that, Tadeusz," Flynn said tersely. "Check the view out to portside."

After a brief moment of stunned silence, Kossak murmured, *"Święta Matko Boża. Holy Mother of God."*

"You said it," Flynn agreed. "These guys are playing for keeps."

"What are our orders?" Kossak asked.

Flynn thought quickly. There was only one alternative that made sense in the tactical circumstances they now faced. If those Russian reinforcements made it onto the *Gulf Venture*'s deck, he and his men were as good as dead. There was no way they could take on that many highly trained and well-equipped opponents and win. "Repel boarders," he said simply. "Keep them off our backs while we finish the job up here."

"Understood," the Pole told him calmly. *"We will stop the Russians cold. Or die trying. Dragon Two, out."*

Damn, I wish I could tell them not to push it that far, Flynn thought bleakly. He was getting very tired of seeing good friends killed and wounded following his orders. But he knew there was no choice. Tad Kossak, Alain Ricard, and Cole Hynes represented the only armed force he had left to block this enemy move. Assuming, of course, that you could really call just three men an "armed force" when they were outnumbered so heavily.

"We'd best get a move on, then," McGill said softly, still holding the length of flexible shock tube with its attached igniter. "If we can still take out that rocket, at least all this will have mattered."

Flynn nodded sharply. The other man was right. "Let it rip," he ordered.

They all moved back out of the direct line of the stairs and hunkered down. "Fire in the hole!" McGill called out. He yanked the igniter ring. A puff of gray smoke eddied away.

Wha-WHUMMP.

The catwalk they were sheltering on flexed slightly, absorbing the shock wave flashing outward from the detonating plastic explosives. Barely a second later, a dense cloud of smoke and burnt fragments of paint swirled down through the opening from above.

With Flynn in the lead, they all jumped to their feet and raced back up the stairs. When they burst out of the smoke, they found that the watertight door, scorched and blackened, had been blown inward and now leaned drunkenly to the side, still partially held upright by one twisted and torn pair of hinges at the bottom. The other fastenings had all vanished. Through the smoke still curling away from the blast, they could make out a ten-yard-long hallway with doors opening to either side, and a solid-looking armored hatch at the far end. But before they could plunge through that narrow gap, the defenders hiding inside opened up with rapid three-round bursts. The warped door rattled and clanged, torn by bullets that punched through from end to end, tearing off strips of wood and steel and paint. Sparks danced around the deck-level coaming.

"Son of a bitch!" Flynn dove to the right out of the line of fire and hit the deck.

McGill did the same to the left.

Hit by ricochets that shattered his left arm, Cooke stumbled away and went down next to Flynn. "Ah, crap," the Army veteran muttered. White-faced with pain, he grabbed the carbine he'd dropped when he fell and tried to aim the weapon toward the door one-handed. Through gritted teeth, he forced out, "Only one way anyone's getting down that damn corridor, Nick. And alive ain't it. Those guys have too much fire-power."

"Grenades?" Flynn wondered. Each of them carried a couple of different makes.

"Might get one or two of them, if we were lucky, and they were dumb," Cooke allowed. Then he shook his head. "But you saw all those hidey-holes in there. Odds are they can just ride out the blasts and then blow us to hell the moment we show our faces in that doorway."

From his own position flat against the deck, McGill nodded tightly. "And even if we could winkle those bastards out, that hatch up ahead looks like a bloody bank vault. Like something out of your Fort Knox, say. I'm not sure that I could blow it open with the limited demolitions gear we've got."

Frustrated, Flynn slammed his fist into the deck and then immediately regretted the childish gesture. The Quartet Directorate had signed him on to accomplish missions, not to bitch and moan about how difficult they were. *So, think, Nick,* he told himself sternly. That was his job as a leader. He stared at the blown-open door. The enemy soldiers inside had stopped shooting, obviously preferring to conserve their ammunition to repel the next real attack.

His eyes narrowed in contemplation. Cooke and McGill were right. A hey-diddle-diddle, straight-up-the-middle charge would only be suicide. So what other approach did that leave? Instinctively, his eyes rose to the last remaining deck above them on the tanker's superstructure. The navigation bridge there must be directly over whatever compartment was behind that armored hatch. And then he saw a possible answer. It was time to make this battle a three-dimensional fight. He fought down a grin. And after all, he had been a captain in the U.S. Air Force, hadn't he? So maybe he'd been intelligence puke and not a real balls-to-the-wall fighter jock, but tactics were tactics, right?

Quickly, Flynn looked around and saw a ladder that led straight up toward the open bridge wing above them. He turned back to McGill and motioned to him. "Toss me your demolition charges, Tony."

The other man unslung the satchel from around his neck and lobbed it across to him. "What've you got in mind?" he asked.

Flynn told him.

McGill smiled narrowly. "Nice," he said appreciatively. "It might even work."

"I sure hope so," Flynn said simply, as he looped the satchel over his own shoulder. "Because otherwise, our only option is to shoot the hell out of that doggone rocket and hope we can blow it up on the pad— along with this whole ship and all of us with it."

Cooke winced. "I vote for your first plan." He swallowed hard, clearly fighting down a wave of agony shooting up his broken arm. "What do you want Tony and me to do?"

"Keep those assholes down that corridor busy," Flynn told him. "Don't give them a chance to wonder what else is going on out here."

"Can do, Nick," Cooke said. Awkwardly, he braced his carbine against his remaining good shoulder and started squeezing off rounds toward the doorway. McGill followed his example. The odds were very much against either man scoring any hits on the enemy troops forted up inside the ship's superstructure, but pouring a volume of fire down that corridor ought to keep their heads down and persuade them their opponents were still trying to break in . . . instead of making an end run.

Flynn scooted away until he was sure he was out of sight and then scrambled toward the ladder heading up. On the way, he slid another fresh magazine, his last full one, into his carbine. Given their time constraints and the enemy forces assembling against them, this was basically their last throw of the dice, he realized, feeling cold. So he'd better not crap out.

FORTY-TWO

ON THE *GULF VENTURE'S* BRIDGE

THAT SAME TIME

Seemingly surrounded by danger on every side, Captain Reza Heidari struggled to remain calm and centered on his primary mission. The unexpected sight of the huge Russian submarine surfacing off his port bow was only the latest shock he'd experienced. From this vantage point high above the tanker's hull, he could see bodies carpeting the deck. His counterattacks had failed utterly. And now, from the staccato rattle of rifle shots drawing ever closer, the enemy's commando force was steadily fighting its way up through the superstructure toward the bridge—coming closer with every passing minute. "Hold your course," he directed the helmsman. "Maintain five knots."

"Steady on one-five-zero degrees at five knots, aye, sir," the helmsman said. The young sailor sounded frightened, but still determined to do his duty.

Heidari nodded encouragingly at him. "Keep up the good work, Seaman Vaziri. Soon we will strike the Americans a blow from which they can never recover." The countdown clock now showed less than five minutes remaining before launch, so he'd brought the *Gulf Venture* out of its seemingly endless succession of 360-degree turns onto a straight course. They were now heading directly for the point picked out by the experts in Tehran and Moscow as the ideal set of coordinates to fire the Zuljanah rocket toward its planned detonation point high over the American Midwest.

The intercom phone connected to Launch Control buzzed. He snatched it up. "Yes? Heidari here."

"We're under attack down here, Reza!" Hossein Majidi blurted out. "There's a pitched battle going on just outside the hatch! We can hear bullets striking the armor!"

Heidari bit down on an oath. "The whole ship is under attack, Doctor," he said with forced patience. "You and your technicians are safer in there than anyone else aboard this vessel. You certainly have nothing to fear from mere small-arms fire." He checked the digital readout. It was still counting down. "What is the status of the rocket?"

With an audible effort, Majidi pulled himself together. "We've almost finished fueling the third stage. Once that's complete, we'll run the last sequence of checks to verify the final readiness of the Zuljanah's engines, staging systems, navigation, and the EMP warhead itself. As soon as those are done, we will be go for launch."

"Very good," Heidari said. He put iron in his voice. "Focus on your task, Hossein. Let nothing distract you. Everything now depends on the missile in your charge. Is that understood?"

"Yes, Reza," the scientist assured him. "The Zuljanah will strike home and destroy America. I swear it."

Heidari nodded. "As God wills. Bridge out." He hung up.

From across the bridge, his second-in-command, Touraj Dabir spoke up, the tension plain in his voice. "Those boatloads of soldiers the Russian submarine is sending across have nearly reached our hull, Captain."

"I saw them," Heidari replied.

"Then if we can hold long enough, this battle is won," the younger officer said hopefully. "Isn't it?"

Heidari eyed him. "You think so?" He shrugged. "I am not so sure."

"But the Russians are our allies!" Dabir protested.

"If so, they have a curious way of showing it," Heidari said dryly. The petty officer he'd sent to release Skoblin and his men had never returned to the bridge. Nor had the Raven Syndicate mercenaries obeyed his orders to clear the lower deck. That, plus the realization that they'd been secretly trailed—probably for days at least—by this Russian submarine was a clear sign that Moscow was now only following its own interests, without any regard for those of its one-time ally.

Dabir looked even more worried now. "Then perhaps we should—"

Before he could finish, the sailor posted as a guard at the open hatch to the port wing shouted a sudden warning while drawing his pistol. "Look out! The enemy is—" He spun around, caught by a burst of point-blank gunfire, and went down hard. Before the dying sailor had even stopped moving, a man in unfamiliar camouflage leaped through the opening with a short, stubby rifle at the ready.

Heidari fumbled for his own sidearm, cursing himself for his slowness—furiously aware that he was already far too late.

Flynn caught the sign of movement over near a table piled high with charts and some sort of digital readout. He fired twice and saw the hawk-nosed naval officer he'd shot fold over and go down. Then, still moving to the side, he swung his carbine through a wide arc—squeezing off shots every time his sights settled on a new figure. Caught by surprise by his rapid, unrelenting attack, most of the Iranian sailors stationed on the bridge died before they could pull their own weapons and shoot back.

Only one man, a taller and heavier-set officer, was able to duck behind a console. Shouting loudly, he came back up with a pistol in his hand and opened fire.

Flynn felt a crushing impact across his chest. Pain exploded across his sternum. It knocked the breath out of him and rocked him back on his heels. He'd been hit by a 9mm pistol round. *Hell, that hurt,* he thought fuzzily, seeing the bridge around him go weirdly red. Reacting instinctively, he shot back—and hit the other man twice, in the stomach and in the chest. The Iranian groaned and collapsed to lie unmoving on the blood-spattered deck.

Panting, straining for air, Flynn scanned the rest of the bridge, ready to open fire again at the least sign of movement. But it was empty, populated only by the bodies of those he'd just killed. Only then did he risk looking down at himself. A blackened ring with the faint gleam of brass at its center showed where the pistol bullet had embedded itself in the middle layer of his body armor. He relaxed a little. He'd be bruised and battered as hell for days from the impact, but that was a lot better than fighting a punctured lung.

Recovering a bit, he automatically replaced his carbine's nearly empty magazine with one that still held around ten 7.62mm rounds. If this battle went on much longer, he thought tiredly, he was going to be reduced to waging it with his own pistol and combat knife.

The digital readout over that chart table ticked down again. Now it showed T –3 minutes and 10 seconds. Oh, crap, Flynn realized. That must be the time remaining until the crew launched their rocket. This battle was just about over, after all. Ignoring the pain spreading across his chest, he kneeled down in the middle of the bridge, swung McGill's demolitions satchel off his shoulder, unzipped it, and started quickly laying out the gear he would need.

ALONGSIDE THE *GULF VENTURE*

THAT SAME TIME

Colonel Konstantin Danilevsky crouched near the prow of the second inflatable, watching closely as the Raven Syndicate operatives aboard the first rubber boat reached the tanker and hooked on to the metal ladder at its side. The men aboard his own boat tied up to the side of the first, with the last inflatable doing the same thing on the other side. All three small craft rocked in the low wake curling off the massive hull towering high above them. Wavelets coated with a thick scum of drifting oil sloshed over their low sides.

"Any change in orders?" the leader of the first boat asked. His eyes shone bright against the rivulets of black crude oil staining his face. Motoring through the widening slick surrounding the *Gulf Venture* had doused them all with splashes of the foul-smelling gunk.

Danilevsky shook his head. "None! Clear the aft deck and superstructure. Kill everyone you encounter. Then, once that missile is away, we'll scuttle this damned tanker and shoot anyone trying to escape from belowdecks." He nodded vigorously. "Now get moving!"

Loaded down with weapons and equipment, one by one, the first boatload of former Spetsnaz soldiers leaped for the ladder and started swarming upward. Men from the second and third inflatables crowded in behind them, ready to begin their own laborious ascent to the ship's deck as soon as the way ahead was clear.

Tadeusz Kossak and Alain Ricard swung over the edge of the first catwalk, lowered themselves by their arms, and then let go—dropping heavily onto the deck several feet below. Jumping up, they unslung their carbines and sprinted aft along the edge of the hull toward the stern.

There in the darkness ahead, they could see a man clambering up and over the ship's outer railing. More men crowded the ladder behind him.

The two Four agents opened fire on the move, peppering the area around the ladder with 7.62mm rounds. With a muffled cry, the first Russian aboard fell sprawling. Another, caught by a bullet just as he threw a leg over the railing, screamed shrilly, and tumbled backward into the sea. Kossak and Ricard charged on, still shooting.

Around the edge of the superstructure, Cole Hynes heard the sudden burst of firing. His head reared up and his eyes widened. The Russians were already coming aboard.

Weakly, Wade Vucovich put his hands on the combat tourniquet his friend had been frantically applying. "I got this, Cole," he said, gripping the tourniquet rod and starting to twist it to stop the blood pulsing from his bullet-torn leg. "You go."

Hynes nodded once. "Don't screw this up, Wade," he warned, scrambling to his feet and grabbing his weapon. "Make sure that sucker is tighter than an off-base loan shark."

Vucovich tried to grin back at him. "Count on it."

But Hynes was already gone, racing toward the sound of the gunfire.

Ricard and Kossak skidded to a stop beside the railing and leaned over to open fire. More Raven Syndicate troops fell screaming from the ladder to plunge into the ocean. They were dragged under instantly by the weight of their weapons and equipment. Instead of panicking at this sudden threat, the Russians still crowded aboard the boats started shooting back, aiming for the two dimly seen shapes high above them.

Kossak drew a line across the closest boat, firing rapid, aimed shots that knocked down two men in as many seconds. Suddenly, he heard a startled gasp from beside him. He turned his head in surprise. "Alain?"

Hit in the head and killed instantly, Ricard slumped forward and slowly crumpled to the deck.

"Damn it," Kossak murmured. Somberly, he swung back toward the boats below, determined to pile up more dead Russians to avenge his comrade of many years. But then two hammer blows hurled him back from the railing. He spun around and slid down to his knees. Distantly, he realized that he was very badly wounded—perhaps fatally so, if help could not arrive in time. Already, the world around him seemed to be growing even darker and colder.

No, the Pole thought angrily, summoning all his willpower to push back against the darkness. Doggedly, he pawed through one of the pouches on his assault vest. He would not yield to death or unconsciousness. Not yet. He would not lose this fight. He would not make another mistake. At last, his hand closed on the cylindrical shape he'd been hunting and pulled it out. Desperately, he strained to stand back up.

And then Cole Hynes leaned over him. Almost gently, he took the grenade from Kossak's trembling hand. "I got this, Tad," he said quietly.

Kossak looked up with a smile. *"Wyślij ich do piekła.* Send them to hell," he said in Polish, not caring that the American would not understand his words. Letting go at last, he slid gratefully into darkness.

Hynes stepped toward the railing, already twisting the grenade's pull ring and then yanking it out to release the pin. With one smooth motion, he lobbed the AN-M14 TH3 incendiary grenade into the nearest Raven Syndicate boat and ducked back down. With a snakelike hiss, it ignited—spewing a glowing ball of blinding white flame burning at more than 4,000 degrees Fahrenheit. Instantly, it set the oil-coated sea ablaze.

THAT SAME TIME

Flynn finished wiring the last of the several demolition charges he'd fixed to the bridge's steel deck. Lines of det cord now snaked across the floor in different directions, all connected to another length of flexible shock tube. Sweating, he sat back on his heels and checked the time shown on the readout over the enemy's chart table. He now had less than two minutes left before the countdown reached zero and that rocket roared aloft on its way toward the United States. But one detail remained to make sure his hastily rigged charges would work as planned.

He grabbed a water-filled IV bag out of McGill's satchel and duct-taped it down across the lump of plastic explosives he'd just set. Then he hurried over to the others and did the same thing. This was a field expedient pioneered by the U.S. Marine Corps to create shaped charges out of ordinary C4. The liquid in those IV bags should compress the explosions when they went off—directing much of their force downward through the deck.

The countdown clock now showed just over a minute remaining.

Unreeling the shock tube as carefully as he could while still hurrying, Flynn backed out through the hatch and onto the bridge's port wing. He moved all the way to the far end, about thirty feet from the open hatch. This was still way too close, he knew, but he was now completely out of both time and sensible, safe options. "Fire in the hole!" he yelled over the Dragon Team's tactical radio net as a warning to Cooke, McGill, and the others. Then he laid down with his head aimed toward the bridge to present his helmet to the oncoming blast, pressed his face hard against the deck, and yanked the igniter ring.

FORTY-THREE

THAT SAME TIME

From the small navigating station atop the submarine's tall sail, Nakhimov stared through his binoculars—transfixed in horror by the gruesome sight of Danilevsky and all of his Raven Syndicate soldiers abruptly transformed into blazing human torches. Writhing and screaming in eerie, high-pitched agony that could be heard across the water even that far away, they flailed wildly at each other before toppling into the oil fires that were now roaring skyward all around the *Gulf Venture*.

He lowered his binoculars, feeling nauseated.

At that instant, a powerful explosion ripped through the very top of the tanker's aft superstructure, lighting up the night sky for miles around. First, a blinding flash silhouetted the large bridge windows from within and then they all blew out simultaneously. A huge cloud of smoke and shards of shattered glass and burning debris billowed outward, cascading down across the tanker's weather deck and into the sea.

"*Sukin syn,*" Nakhimov murmured, scarcely able to believe what he was seeing. "Son of a bitch." But then he leaned forward and punched the intercom to the control room. "Helm, this is the captain. Full left rudder. Come left to zero-nine-zero degrees and increase speed to ten knots."

"*Full left rudder. Coming left to zero-nine-zero degrees. Making revo-lutions for ten knots, aye, sir,*" the helmsman repeated from below.

Nakhimov felt his submarine heeling sharply as it began executing the rapid turn he'd just ordered. He wanted out of this damned oil slick before they too were engulfed by the flames he could now see rippling outward across the ocean. He raised his binoculars again, tracking back toward the tanker.

A plume of gray-white smoke curled away from the ruined bridge. The open-air platform just above it was now a tangle of fallen radio and radar masts. He frowned. Moscow's orders in this situation were explicit. Whether or not the Iranian missile launch was successful, there must be no survivors left alive for anyone to interrogate. And now that Danilevsky and his Raven Syndicate mercenaries had failed so miserably, that task fell to him.

"Control Room, this is the captain," Nakhimov snapped. "Get me Captain Second Rank Arshavin."

"*Arshavin here,*" his executive officer replied.

"Listen closely, Maxim," Nakhimov said. "I want you to plot an immediate torpedo attack against that tanker, using two of our UGST wire-guided torpedoes."

For one brief moment, there was only silence. But then Arshavin came back on the intercom. "*Understood, Captain. I'll report when our torpedoes are ready.*"

ABOARD THE *GULF VENTURE*

THAT SAME TIME

Groggy, with his ears ringing from the enormous blast, Nick Flynn pushed himself back up—first to his knees, and then, with a renewed effort, all the way onto his feet. He stood there swaying for several seconds. Then he shook his head to try to clear it and peered through the roiling smoke at what was left of the tanker's bridge. Small tongues of flame guttered red and orange through openings that had once been windows. He limped forward toward the hatch. The watertight door was just . . . gone, blown off its hinges by the blast and hurled out to sea. One of the ship's radio masts had fallen across the port wing and now partially blocked the opening with a bent and twisted metal pole and a snarl of broken wiring.

Awkwardly, he climbed over the obstruction and entered the ruined bridge. Consoles, tables, and other furnishings had been converted to mounds of crumpled metal and splintered, charred wood. He averted his eyes from the explosion-pulped remains of those he'd gunned down earlier.

Swallowing against the sour taste of bile, Flynn edged his way carefully around the worst of the wreckage until he came right to the edge of the jagged hole his demolition charges had blown through the deck. He looked down—and saw a scene of carnage and destruction. The mangled bodies of white-coated technicians who'd been ripped apart by flying steel splinters or crushed by the blast were heaped across smoldering equipment consoles. A couple of monitors flickered eerily in the red-tinged darkness, somehow seemingly left intact by the massive shockwave that had smashed down across the compartment.

Flynn let his breath out. No one would be firing that rocket now, he thought coldly. Not from a shambles like that. MIDNIGHT was dead, as dead as all those charged with launching the genocidal attack on the United States from this ship.

He straightened up. His job now was to get the survivors of his Dragon team off this vessel. He switched the frequency on his tactical radio. "Lariat One, this is Dragon Lead. Requesting evac soonest. Over."

In reply, he heard only a hash of fuzzy, indistinct static, perhaps broken by what might have been blurred words or, more likely, simply the meaningless pops made by random radio waves as they sleeted through the ionosphere.

Flynn repeated his call. There was still nothing distinguishable coming through his headset. He frowned. Either his radio was on the fritz, knocked out by the blast he'd just set off, or all the metal debris heaped across the ruined bridge was interfering with his signal. Or just possibly his hearing was still damaged from that shattering explosion, he thought. Turning, he carefully made his way back outside onto the open wing.

ABOARD BS-64 *PODMOSKOVYE*

THAT SAME TIME

"Arshavin here, sir," Nakhimov heard his executive officer report over the intercom. *"The Torpedo Room reports ready to fire."*

"Stand by, Maxim," he replied, again raising his binoculars and focusing them on the *Gulf Venture*. His submarine was now roughly three thousand meters off the big tanker's port side. Surrounded by a widening ring of burning oil, the Iranian vessel was still steaming . straight ahead at barely five knots. He nodded to himself. That was as close to a sitting duck as anything moving at sea could ever be. He leaned over the intercom. "Torpedo Room, this is the captain. Shoot!"

"One fired!"

Nakhimov hadn't even felt the weapon go. That wasn't really surprising, he supposed. Compared to the *Podmoskovye*'s eighteen thousand ton mass, the energy involved in launching a two-ton, wire-guided torpedo was like an elephant flicking a fly away with its tail. He waited another several seconds before ordering the next launch to avoid the risk of either torpedo interfering with the other. "Shoot!"

"Two fired!"

Tensely, Nakhimov counted in his head. Both torpedoes were now slashing through the water at sixty knots. At a range of roughly three thousand meters, their run should take about ninety seconds. Which meant the first weapon should reach the tanker and detonate under its keel just about . . . *now*.

A huge plume of water and foam erupted around the forward section of the *Gulf Venture*. The blast was powerful enough to shake the massive tanker from stem to stern. Only seconds later, the second torpedo exploded, this one almost directly below its aft engineering spaces. Propelled upward by the enormous shockwave generated by the underwater detonation, the stern of the Iranian ship visibly rose out of water before crashing back down. Within moments, the tanker lay dead in the water with its back obviously broken. Fires now raged across its foredeck, fed by oil gushing out of torn storage tanks.

That vessel was doomed now, Nakhimov knew. No ship, no matter how large, could take so much damage and stay afloat for long.

OUTSIDE THE LAUNCH CONTROL CENTER

THAT SAME TIME

With a groan, Viktor Skoblin rolled over and sat up. He mopped at his face, trying to clear his vision. His hand came away stained red with blood. The rapid succession of three massive explosions had tossed him around the inside of this small metal compartment like a dried pea rattling around inside a tin can. He had a hazy memory of striking the walls, door, and even the ceiling before ending up splayed across a far corner. His assault rifle lay across his legs, apparently undamaged. He scooped it up.

What the hell just happened, he wondered? Was all that noise and confusion produced by the Iranian rocket as it roared aloft? Or had it blown up on the pad? The deck tilted beneath him, settling suddenly toward the stern.

Skoblin's eyes widened in terror as he realized the truth. The tanker was sinking! He had to get out. And get out now. Swearing, he scrambled upright and struggled across the sloping compartment toward the door into the corridor.

Fadeyev, Zaitsev, and Linnik were already there. All were injured in some way, but they still carried their weapons.

"Where are the others?" Skoblin demanded. His voice sounded far off in his numbed ears.

Fadeyev shook his head. "Dead," he mouthed. "Their necks were broken."

Skoblin nodded grimly. The same thing could have happened to any of them. He gripped his rifle tighter and hobbled along the corridor. Beyond the blast-scorched doorway ahead, the night sky glowed with reddish-orange light. There were fires raging somewhere outside. "Come on," he snapped. "We're getting off this damned ship before it sinks under us. Shoot anyone who gets in our way."

Growling their agreement, the three survivors of his Raven Syndicate team swung in behind him. They didn't see the two grenades rolling across the deck toward them until it was far too late.

Tony McGill saw the twin flashes as his grenades detonated and smiled thinly. "Too bad, so sad, chums," he muttered. With the ship obviously going down, he'd figured the bastards holding out near that missile control center would finally make a break for it.

"Nice work," Shannon Cooke said tightly through pain-clenched teeth. He gripped the forearm of his broken left arm with his right hand. When those explosions rocked the tanker, they'd both been bounced across the deck, ending up being slammed against the nearest railing, and unfortunately his already-injured arm had taken the brunt of the impact. "So now what do we do?"

"We're leaving, and pronto," they both heard Flynn say wearily. He'd just slid down the ladder from the bridge wing above them. "This tub is going down fast. And I don't plan on letting any of our guys who're still alive go down with it. So come on."

McGill and Cooke levered themselves off the deck and followed him down the stairs to the next catwalk, holding on tight as they stumbled down the steeply inclined steps. The *Gulf Venture* was listing to port now as more and more seawater poured into her ruptured storage tanks. Ahead, the ocean was on fire. Oil-fed flames danced across the surface. A thickening cloud of greasy black smoke hung low above the inferno.

INSIDE THE LAUNCH CONTROL CENTER

THAT SAME TIME

Biting down hard to avoid screaming, Hossein Majidi painfully pulled himself along the slanting deck. He left a spreading trail of blood behind him. He knew he was dying, but the faint glow of a working computer console—the only one left intact in the bomb-ravaged control center—drew him like a moth to a flame.

Gasping aloud, he slid the horrifically mangled body of one of his technicians aside a few inches, just far enough so that he could see the display and reach the console's keyboard. The dead man must have shielded this equipment from the worst of the blast. All the steel shards that would otherwise have ripped through the computer had instead shredded his corpse.

Through a fog of almost unendurable agony, Majidi studied the readouts currently displayed on the screen. Most indicators glowed red. A small inset on the display showed images captured by the single surviving external camera mounted on the *Gulf Venture*'s superstructure. In it, he could make out the ring of fire surrounding the sinking tanker, along with the shark fin–like sail of the Russian nuclear submarine slicing through the water not far off.

Carefully, focusing all of his remaining energies, he tapped a control on the keyboard, opening a new menu. It was labeled SPECIAL WEAPON PARAMETERS. With the shattered halves of the ship flooding fast, successfully launching the Zuljanah rocket was no longer possible. That left him with only one remaining choice. He coughed once and then found he could not stop coughing. Blood dripped down his chin and spattered across the console. His life was fading, along with his vision. Knowing he had only seconds remaining, Majidi very deliberately altered several key parameters governing the nuclear warhead's operation. He hung on just long enough to see several of the readouts on his screen turn green and fell back, dead.

FORTY-FOUR

Carrying Tadeusz Kossak between them, Flynn and Hynes struggled up a steeply inclined accommodation ladder and fought their way along a tilting exterior catwalk to a landing perched in the middle of the tanker superstructure's second level. Bandages, already reddening, swathed the Pole's chest, but he was still breathing—if only just barely. McGill and Cooke were there ahead of them, standing guard over the badly wounded Wade Vucovich.

Below this landing, a bright orange enclosed lifeboat hung down at an angle. It was perched along twin slide tracks that stretched outward from the ship—aimed toward the sea. Like all modern oil tankers, the *Gulf Venture* was equipped with gravity-launched, fire-resistant lifeboats.

"Let's go!" Flynn shouted, stumbling to a stop as the ship lurched over another few degrees. Sweat glistened on his face. With the vessel listing ever faster, the fires raging across the water below were suddenly that much closer. "Cast loose and get that damned hatch open!"

McGill leaped to obey. Swiftly, the former SAS sergeant released the secondary lashing lines securing the lifeboat to the davit. Then he yanked the rear hatch wide open. Working feverishly, he and Hynes loaded first Vucovich and then Kossak aboard.

Flynn was the last one in. He banged the hatch shut and latched it tight. Emergency lights glowed faintly, revealing a fully enclosed cabin. Rows of airplane-style seats faced the steeply raised stern of the lifeboat. The others were already strapping the injured men and themselves into chairs.

Perched on a raised platform above the passenger compartment, a single seat faced forward, offering a view through narrow slit windows. This was the lifeboat's control station. Straining, Flynn pulled himself up and dropped into the seat. He quickly snapped his safety harness closed to avoid falling face-first into the panel ahead of him. With the *Gulf Venture*'s rapidly increasing list, they were hanging almost straight down off the side of the massive ship.

Rapidly, he scanned the rudimentary steering, engine, and davit release controls. Fortunately, they matched those in the manuals and training videos he'd studied while preparing for this mission. Using these lifeboats had always been one of their best options for evacuating the tanker in an emergency.

Flynn glanced over the side of his seat. Kossak and Vucovich lolled unconscious in their chairs, only held upright by their harnesses. McGill and the others flashed him thumbs-up signals. "Hey, remember, ladies and gentlemen, that no smoking is allowed for the duration of this flight," Hynes reminded them all with a twisted grin. "Which oughta be about one second."

No one laughed.

"Gee, tough crowd tonight," Hynes said with a shrug.

McGill grinned at him. "Comedy is hard," he remarked thoughtfully. "Soldiering is easy. Stick to what you do best, Cole."

"Jesus," Flynn muttered to himself, feeling the tanker roll even farther over. Through the windows ahead of him, the oil-fed fires licked higher. All the technical mumbo-jumbo boasting about "fire-resistance" in those manuals had better be accurate, he thought. Or this would be the shortest, most lethal thrill ride in history. Swallowing hard, he turned the key to start the lifeboat's engine. It roared into life smoothly.

One hurdle down. Then he reached down and removed the pin securing the release lever. A quick twist closed the lifeboat's bypass valve.

"Here goes," he said loudly. "Hang on tight." Then he pumped the lever several times in rapid succession. Outside, the two metal clamps still holding the lifeboat in place opened wide. Suddenly freed, it slid straight down the rails, picking up speed as it went, reached the end of the track, and plunged almost straight down toward the ocean.

Flynn slammed forward hard against his harness as they splashed into the sea with tremendous force—hurling a column of burning, oil-coated water high into the air. He bit down hard on his lip as the jolt sent a wave of pain flaring out from the bruised areas of his chest and ribs. The stern fell backward with another splash and they settled on an even keel. Flames roared higher on all sides, accompanied by drifting smoke that reduced visibility to only a few yards. The temperature inside the lifeboat spiked rapidly. Without waiting any longer, he shoved the engine throttle all the way forward, took hold of the wheel, and began steering the little craft away from the dying oil tanker's side.

"See if you can raise Lariat One, Tony," Flynn called down to McGill. Squinting against the hellish, flickering glare, he stared ahead through the smoke, trying to find the quickest path through this sea of fire. "Tell 'em that we could sure use a lift. And ASAP."

They all knew escaping aboard this lifeboat was only a means of staving off the inevitable for a little while longer. With that Russian submarine lurking nearby, they were doomed.

Through his headset, Flynn heard the other man start calling over the radio, enunciating clearly in a calm, measured tone. *"Dragon Team calling Lariat One. Dragon Team calling Lariat One. Do you read me? Over—"*

A SHORT TIME LATER

"Sir! Small surface contact! Off the starboard bow! Range four thousand meters!" one of the two sailors posted as lookouts yelled.

Nakhimov looked in that direction. There, barely visible in all the drifting smoke and dazzling flame, he caught a brief glimpse of a small orange boat crossing behind the stern of the sinking *Gulf Venture*. One of the lifeboats from the tanker, he realized immediately. So there were a few survivors after all. He focused his binoculars on the distant craft, only to see it vanish again—hidden from view by the much larger burning, listing ship. He leaned over the intercom. "Sonar! Do you have the new contact?"

"*Negative, Captain,*" he heard his sonar officer say apologetically. "*The breaking-up noises from that tanker are drowning out anything else in the immediate area.*"

No great surprise, there, Nakhimov realized. His passive sonars were deafened by the horrific din created by huge pieces of machinery inside the *Gulf Venture*'s hull tearing loose and the pounding roar made by millions of gallons of seawater flooding into its ruptured compartments.

Then he shrugged. The lifeboat couldn't get far. Not up against *Podmoskovye*'s greatly superior speed, even with the submarine still riding on the surface. He bent down and snapped out the necessary helm orders. They would circle around the sinking ship. Once they were on the other side, they'd have a clear line of fire and be able to get a sonar fix to guide on. And even a single torpedo ought to suffice to reduce that tiny lifeboat to a few torn shards of orange plastic floating on the sea.

A few minutes later, Nakhimov heard one of his lookouts exclaim, "There the tanker goes!"

He turned his gaze toward the *Gulf Venture* in time to see its two broken halves sliding fast into a boiling cauldron of froth and foam. The Zuljanah rocket, still securely clamped to its launch gantry, vanished from sight. In moments, nothing remained to be seen but a blazing ring of oil-fueled fires and drifting pieces of debris.

"Air contact dead ahead!" the other lookout suddenly screamed. "It's crossing our bows only a few thousand meters off!"

Nakhimov whipped around in shock. There, roaring in low over the surface of the ocean, he saw a large twin-engine aircraft. The floats fixed to the ends of its high wing showed that it was amphibious, a seaplane capable of landing on and taking off from the water. It was flying straight toward the tiny lifeboat—already descending even lower as it came in to make a landing. "Sonar, this is the captain! Can you get a fix on that small surface contact yet?" he growled.

"*Negative, sir,*" his sonar officer admitted. "*The noises made by the sinking tanker still obscure everything else.*"

Nakhimov swore under his breath. Zhdanov would never forgive him, he realized, feeling an ice-cold shiver of fear run down his spine. His only chance of escaping the wreckage of the Russian president's cherished Operation MIDNIGHT had been to ensure that no one escaped to report what Moscow and Iran had been planning. And now he'd failed, even at that.

Numbly, he watched the float plane touch down and taxi over to the wallowing lifeboat.

LARIAT ONE

A SHORT TIME LATER

Laura Van Horn glanced back from the cockpit of the Viking Aircraft CL-415. Originally designed as a firefighting aircraft, the Canadian-made seaplane had a narrow aft compartment. It was crowded now with the Dragon Team's survivors and a small cadre of qualified merchant marine officers, more of the Quartet Directorate's part-timers. They were on this flight out from Bermuda in case Flynn and his men had been able to take the *Gulf Venture* intact. Her eyes widened slightly at the sight of the two severely wounded men being laid carefully across the seaplane's deck. A former combat medic who'd signed on with Four was already hard at work on Tadeusz Kossak. "Everybody on board?"

"We're all here," Flynn replied. He sounded exhausted. "Alain and Mark didn't make it."

She nodded tightly, holding her own regret under wraps for the moment. "Then strap in," she ordered. "This takeoff might be a little rough."

"Compared to being shot at, hacked by axes, blown up, torpedoed, and diving head-on into a bunch of flames?" Hynes said carefully. He shrugged. "I'll take it."

"We *were* inside a lifeboat when we dove into that fire," Flynn reminded him, with a weary grin. "So it's not quite as bad as you're making it sound."

Inside, her heart beat a little faster. So Nick was still himself where it counted, she thought warmly, despite how battered, tired, and sad he looked right now. Hiding her own smile, Van Horn swung back to her controls and pushed her engine throttles forward. Slowly, the big seaplane picked up speed, bouncing across shallow waves as it roared ahead. Twin plumes of white foam and spray lengthened behind her floats. At last, she pulled back strongly on the yoke.

With a final sharp jolt, the CL-415 broke free of the ocean and climbed away—gaining altitude fast. She banked sharply back to the west and flew high over the Russian submarine, which had turned after her in vain pursuit during her takeoff run.

Hundreds of feet below the surface, the environmental sensors inside the Zuljanah rocket's warhead obeyed Hossein Majidi's last commands. As the torn remains of the Gulf Venture plunged into the ink-black Atlantic depths, they detected rapid changes in pressure and temperature. Milliseconds later, critical relays inside the sinking weapon closed . . . and the five-hundred-kiloton bomb detonated.

Several miles behind the speeding twin-engine seaplane, a huge flash as bright as the noonday sun suddenly erupted beneath the surface of the sea. Seconds later, an enormous column of water— hundreds of yards across—erupted like a volcano, soaring thousands of feet into the air before slowly collapsing back in on itself. At the same time, a massive, tsunami-like wave roared outward from the center of the blast, racing across the ocean at hundreds of miles an hour.

Caught broadside by a shockwave with pressures far beyond human comprehension, the *Podmoskovye* was crushed flat in the blink of an eye, along with its entire 135-man crew. And when the blast-created tsunami arrived, the submarine's twisted wreckage was casually tossed aside like a crumpled beer can caught in the surf. Carried along for some miles, it finally sank below the surface, spiraling around and around as it plummeted into the abyss.

As it rippled outward from the detonation point, the shockwave's power fell off rapidly, but even miles from the center, it was still strong enough to hurl the seaplane into a left-hand spin. Thrown suddenly out of control, the CL-415 corkscrewed down out of the sky.

Watching the ocean and sky whirling across her cockpit canopy with dizzying speed, Van Horn reacted instantly. One hand slammed both engine throttles back to idle. The only way out of this spin was to get her plane's nose down and fly out it. Powering up would only make things worse, since it would tend to raise the aircraft's nose. Next, she brought her ailerons to their neutral position, and applied right rudder to reduce the CL-415's rolling and yawing movement as it twisted down out toward the sea.

Her final move was the most counterintuitive of all. Even though it felt as though they were falling straight out of the sky, she shoved her yoke forward—deliberately lowering the seaplane's nose to reduce its angle of attack. For long seconds as they kept spinning, she was afraid her various measures weren't going to work, at least not in time to stop them from crashing into the Atlantic.

But then the spin slowed and finally stopped. With her aircraft back under control, Van Horn quickly zeroed out her rudder, pulled back gently on the yoke, and carefully added power to level out the heavy twin-engine seaplane only a few feet above the white, foaming sea. Breathing heavily, she regained altitude and flew on.

At a thousand feet, she risked a glance over her shoulder into the cramped passenger cabin behind the cockpit. "Everybody okay?" she called out cheerfully.

Shaken, Flynn and the others slowly disentangled themselves from where they'd been thrown. Hynes looked at her reproachfully. "You know, ma'am, when you said that takeoff would be a little rough, I figured you were just exaggerating."

"Mea culpa," she said with a crooked grin. "But that little joyride wasn't entirely my fault." She banked the CL-415 around so that they could all see the vast seething cauldron below. "When you guys set out to sink a ship, you sure don't screw around."

Flynn whistled softly, staring at the foaming turmoil below. He shook his head in astonishment. "I guess not." He looked back at her. "Are you thinking what I'm thinking?"

"That we just saw that Russian warhead go off?" Van Horn said. "Uh-huh, that's what I'm thinking." Her expression turned serious. "And, Nick?"

"Yeah," he said absently, still watching the ocean boil below them.

"I'm damned glad it went off out here. And not over the United States," she said softly. "You and your guys did good today. Really good. No one died in vain."

Having made her point, Van Horn turned back to the west and advanced her throttles to full power. The thundering roar of the two big Pratt & Whitney turboprops grew louder. She'd seen the grave look on the medic's face while he kept working on the seriously wounded Tadeusz Kossak. The sooner she got them all back on the ground, the happier she would be. She'd lost two of her Quartet Directorate comrades that day. She wouldn't lose any more. Not if she could possibly help it.

EPILOGUE

A SHORT TIME LATER

Nervously, President Piotr Zhdanov lit another cigarette. He took a single deep drag and then, viciously, ground the cigarette to ash on the polished table in front of him. For a time, he stared down at his hands before looking up again to glower at the group of senior military officers and government officials arrayed around the conference table. "Well?" he grated out. "What the devil is going on?"

Now there *was a foolish question*, Pavel Voronin thought with carefully concealed contempt from his place beside the older man. Zhdanov knew full well that no one in this subterranean room had any more information than he did at this instant. Fragmentary signals from the *Podmoskovye* had indicated that something had gone badly wrong in the final stages of MIDNIGHT. But for long minutes now, there had been only silence from the submarine. And so far, all efforts to reestablish contact with Nakhimov and his crew through Russia's network of military communications satellites had failed.

A secure phone buzzed sharply next to Gennadiy Kokorin, the elderly minister of defense. He picked up. "Yes?" Slowly, his face turned pale. "I see," he said at last. "I'll relay the news to the president." He hung up and looked at Zhdanov. "Piotr, our EKS missile warning satellites have just detected an underwater nuclear detonation in the Atlantic Ocean."

"Show me!" Zhdanov snapped.

Kokorin murmured to one of his aides. The younger officer input commands on his computer. In response, an icon appeared on the large digital map displayed on the wall screen. It matched the last known location of both their strangely silent nuclear submarine and the *Gulf Venture*.

For a long, almost unbearable moment there was absolute silence in the room as Zhdanov and Voronin absorbed the catastrophic news. Somehow, their carefully laid and intricate plan to cripple the United States and permanently alter the balance of power in both the Middle East and the world itself had been wrecked.

At last, the president turned his baleful gaze toward Kokorin. "Signal the Forty-Second Rocket Division to stand its missiles down," he snarled. "There will be no 'retaliatory' nuclear attack against Iran."

Kokorin nodded gravely. "Yes, Piotr." He cleared his throat. "Do you have any other orders for us tonight?"

Zhdanov turned pale with barely suppressed rage. "Only one." He gestured curtly toward the exit. "Get out. All of you. Now." He swung his head to Voronin. "Except you, Pavel. *You* will stay."

Ah, Voronin thought calmly. The moment of maximum risk. The moment of truth. He kept his countenance while all the rest of them filed out the room.

When they were alone, Zhdanov stared icily at him. "Well?" he demanded. "What now?"

Aware that he was now on very dangerous ground, Voronin projected an air of complete confidence. "True, the destruction of the *Podmoskovye* is a blow, but our navy has more such submarines in its arsenal, does it not? And wars, after all, cannot be fought and won without casualties." He looked straight at the older man. "Today, we may have lost a hand," he continued coolly. "However, the great game goes on. Our enemies were lucky this time. But *they* have to be lucky every time. *We* do not."

Slowly, Zhdanov nodded. MIDNIGHT was not the only aggressive scheme Voronin had proposed. In the undeclared shadow war that he and the younger man's Raven Syndicate were now waging against the United States and its allies, the side on offense had the edge. Sooner or later, one of their deadly covert operations was bound to penetrate the West's defenses. His mood shift was apparent.

Privately, though, despite his outwardly calm demeanor, Voronin felt a wave of cold rage welling up deep inside. The failure of MIDNIGHT had cost him dearly—in money, in the loss of many of his most experienced and best trained agents, and, most bitterly of all, in prestige. His enemies in Zhdanov's inner circle would undoubtedly try to use this setback in a bid to discredit him. For now, he was confident of his ability to retain the president's trust, but he knew only too well that Russia's ruler had limited patience with those whose promises went unfulfilled. Before that day came, it was vital that he hunt down whoever was responsible for inflicting this unexpected defeat on him. He would hunt them down, he vowed . . . and then he would destroy them utterly.

AVALON HOUSE, WINTER PARK, FLORIDA

A FEW DAYS LATER

Close beside the Spanish-style mansion used as a headquarters for the Quartet Directorate's American station, a simple stone column rose at the center of an elegant, carefully maintained garden. Loosely modeled on those put up after the Second World War by veterans of the British Special Operations Executive to honor their fallen comrades, the pillar bore only an inscription— "They Gave Their Lives So That Others Might Live"—and a list of names. Two new ones had been engraved: Alain Ricard and Mark Stadler.

Now Nick Flynn, Laura Van Horn, and Gwen Park stood in a solemn line, facing Fox. They each held a glass of whiskey.

"We fight our battles in secret," Fox said quietly to them. "Without acclaim. Without cheers. Without parades. And without public honors." He looked somber. "What we accomplish is known to us alone. As are the losses we bear, painful though they are. This is our burden. And a heavy burden it is."

Flynn nodded and saw the others doing the same.

"But we bear it nonetheless," the older man continued gently. "Because the inscription this pillar carries is the truth. We risk our lives—and sometimes lose them—not for money or medals, but for the freedoms and lives of others, others we may never even know. We do it, because it must be done." He raised his glass. "To fallen friends and comrades!"

"To fallen friends and comrades!" Flynn said firmly, echoed by Van Horn and Park.

With one quick motion, they all drained their glasses, to the very bottom, and then hurled them against the base of the pillar, where they shattered. The glittering fragments of other such final toasts, made over the course of many years and decades, gleamed in the sunlight there.

Later, sitting with Flynn and Van Horn on the tiled veranda that ran the length of Avalon House's lakeside, Fox briefed them on the fallout thus far from their daring raid against the *Gulf Venture.* "To date," he said dispassionately, "the news of an underwater nuclear blast in the middle of the Atlantic has been kept from the public and the press."

Flynn nodded. That wasn't surprising, in a way. Their battle occurred far outside the normal shipping and air traffic routes, so there were no witnesses to the massive explosion. "What about the sub the Russians lost?"

"Moscow has reported the apparent sinking of its converted ballistic missile submarine, the *Podmoskovye,*" Fox told him. He shrugged his narrow shoulders. "But they're blaming the loss on a probable torpedo accident during the Northern Fleet's most recent peacetime naval exercise." He smiled thinly. "As part of the cover-up, Zhdanov has ordered a massive search and rescue operation in the Arctic waters off Russia's northern coast . . . to 'find Captain Nakhimov and his gallant sailors.' Naturally, of course, their efforts haven't succeeded in turning up any trace of the missing submarine."

"Naturally," Van Horn said with disgust.

Flynn leaned forward. "What about our own government?" he asked curiously. "They must know that a warhead went off."

Fox nodded seriously. "They do. And the entire intelligence community and the whole of the defense and political establishments have been scrambling to try to figure out what just happened. Without any success . . . as yet."

"Do they have any theories?" Flynn asked.

"A few," Fox said with a wry smile. "The CIA's upper echelons are apparently convinced that something must have gone wrong aboard the *Gulf Venture*—resulting in the premature detonation of the missile the Iranians were smuggling." He steepled his hands. "In fact, my understanding is that Langley has decided to toot its own horn in administration circles by slyly suggesting one of its own covert operations was actually responsible for thwarting a major terrorist nuclear threat against the United States."

Flynn and Van Horn stared at him in disbelief. "You're kidding me," Flynn growled. "We took all the risks. We suffered all the losses. So that the CIA's pencil pushers and ass-kissers can claim all the credit? For preventing an attack they ignored from the very beginning?"

Fox nodded. "I told you the truth a few moments ago, when we honored Alain and Mark," he reminded them quietly. "This is the darker side of our secret war. And it is one we must accept. Four can only be effective—and, in fact, only survive—so long as we operate entirely in the shadows, outside the public square and beyond the control of risk-averse government bureaucrats."

With a sigh, Flynn pushed away his disgust and anger. For the moment, anyway. One of his mother's favorite sayings was that life wasn't fair. That obviously went triple for anything in the world of covert operations. He sighed. "Well, if we're skipping the medal ceremony for this mission, I guess I'll take some leave instead."

"In the civilian world, we call it vacation," Laura Van Horn reminded him dryly.

He grinned back at her. "Leave. Vacation. Time off. I don't care what it's called as long as it involves lots of doing nothing much. Preferably on a sunny beach . . . with tall, iced, strongly alcoholic drinks."

She raised an eyebrow. "Got anywhere in particular in mind right now?"

"Somewhere in the Caribbean," Flynn told her. "Probably Aruba. I had a hell of a lot of fun there a few years back, when I was a just a kid. I bet it's even more fun as an adult."

"An excellent choice," Van Horn agreed. She looked speculative. "I've been meaning to take a break myself. Care for some company?"

Flynn's grin widened. "I think I could be persuaded."

Sitting across from them, Fox, they suddenly noticed, had a thoughtful look on his face. "You know, Aruba is only a few miles off the coast of Venezuela," he commented, almost idly. "And lately, we've been hearing some very disturbing rumors coming out of Caracas. Rumors we should probably investigate. So perhaps you could handle that for—?"

"No," Flynn told him bluntly.

With a smile, Fox turned to Van Horn. "Well, then, how about you, Laura?"

She smiled sweetly at him. "Nick here is a man of very few words, Br'er Fox," she said. "Personally, I prefer to be a little more eloquent."

"And?" Fox asked, curious.

"Hell, no," Van Horn replied.